... ttre de la main du Capitaine Dan...
... erlin, au major de Schwartzkoppen
... du major Mueller ... ...
chef du service des renseignements au Grand État major.

Grand État major
Section III B.
J. N° 1455.

(de la main de Schwartzkoppen, repondu le ... 92)

Monsieur le major

Le Major Muella m'a chargé d'avoir l'honneur de vous faire
connaître, qu'aucune réponse n'est encore arrivée à la dernière lettre
dont copie avoit été envoyée à la maison Eijenbrodt (Orange). S
On considère par suite la chose comme définitivement rompue.
Je suis en outre chargé de vous demander si vous ne désireriez pas une
avance plus considérable, par exemple 5 à 6 000 frs sur vos ...
L'argent est disponible ici. On pourroit, avec des moyens plus sérieux
renouer les anciennes relations avec le fournisseur des plans directs
attendu que tous les désiderata que l'on a ici relativement à ces
plans, n'ont pas encore été remplis.
Le major Mueller regrette bien, empêché qu'il est par ses
nombreuses occupations de service, de ne pouvoir vous écrire
lui-même.

Avec mes salutations respectueuses
De

XXX

Jeudi 16 ...

Cher ange,
J'avais écrit ce
petit billet hier soir
et je voulais te l'expédier
ce matin lorsque ...
est venu me dire qu'il
désirait aller à l'Expos...
de l'Épatant avec ...

9/19/14

Also by Robert Harris

FICTION
The Fear Index
Conspirata
The Ghost Writer
Imperium
Pompeii
Archangel
Enigma
Fatherland

NONFICTION
A Higher Form of Killing
(with Jeremy Paxman)
Selling Hitler

An OFFICER
and
A SPY

An OFFICER

and

A SPY

Robert Harris

Alfred A. Knopf · New York · 2014

THIS IS A BORZOI BOOK
PUBLISHED BY ALFRED A. KNOPF

www.aaknopf.com

Knopf, Borzoi Books, and the colophon are registered trademarks of
Random House LLC.

ISBN 978-0-385-34958-1 (hardcover)
ISBN 978-0-385-34959-8 (eBook)
LCCN 2013044985

Jacket images: View of Paris, The Granger Collection, NYC; (seal) Jon
Shireman / Getty images; (ribbon) Michael M. Schwab / Getty Images
Jacket design by Evan Gaffney Design

Manufactured in the United States of America
First United States Edition

To Gill

Author's Note

This book aims to use the techniques of a novel to retell the true story of the Dreyfus affair, perhaps the greatest political scandal and miscarriage of justice in history, which in the 1890s came to obsess France and ultimately the entire world. It occurred only twenty-five years after the Germans had crushed the French in the war of 1870 and occupied the territories of Alsace and Lorraine—the seismic shock to the European balance of power that was the precursor of the First and Second World Wars.

None of the characters in the pages that follow, not even the most minor, is wholly fictional, and almost all of what occurs, at least in some form, actually happened in real life.

Naturally, however, in order to turn history into a novel, I have been obliged to simplify, to cut out some figures entirely, to dramatise, and to invent many personal details. In particular, Georges Picquart never wrote a secret account of the Dreyfus affair; nor did he place it in a bank vault in Geneva with instructions that it should remain sealed until a century after his death.

But a novelist can imagine otherwise.

—Robert Harris
Bastille Day 2013

Dramatis Personae

THE DREYFUS FAMILY

Alfred Dreyfus

Lucie Dreyfus, *wife*

Mathieu Dreyfus, *brother*

Pierre and Jeanne Dreyfus, *children*

THE ARMY

General Auguste Mercier,
Minister of War, 1893–5

General Jean-Baptiste Billot,
Minister of War, 1896–8

General Raoul le Mouton de Boisdeffre,
Chief of the General Staff

General Charles Arthur Gonse,
Chief of the Second Department (Intelligence)

General Georges Gabriel de Pellieux,
Military Commander, Département of the Seine

Colonel Armand du Paty de Clam

Colonel Foucault,
military attaché in Berlin

Major Charles Ferdinand Walsin Esterhazy,
74th Infantry Regiment

THE STATISTICAL SECTION

Colonel Jean Sandherr, *Chief, 1887–95*

Colonel Georges Picquart, *Chief, 1895–7*

Major Hubert Joseph Henry

Captain Jules-Maximillien Lauth

Captain Junck

Captain Valdant

Felix Gribelin, *archivist*

Madam Marie Bastian, *agent*

THE SÛRETÉ (DETECTIVE POLICE)

François Guénée

Jean-Alfred Desvernine

Louis Tomps

HANDWRITING EXPERT

Alphonse Bertillon

THE LAWYERS

Louis Leblois, *Picquart's friend and attorney*

Ferdinand Labori, *attorney to Zola,
Picquart and Alfred Dreyfus*

Edgar Demange, *attorney to Alfred Dreyfus*

Paul Bertulus, *examining magistrate*

GEORGES PICQUART'S CIRCLE

Pauline Monnier

Blanche de Comminges and family

Louis and Martha Leblois, *friends from Alsace*

Edmond and Jeanne Gast, *cousins*

Anna and Jules Gay, *sister and brother-in-law*

Germain Ducasse, *friend and protégé*

Major Albert Curé, *old army comrade*

THE DIPLOMATS

Colonel Maximilian von Schwartzkoppen,
German military attaché

Major Alessandro Panizzardi,
Italian military attaché

THE "DREYFUSARDS"

Émile Zola

Georges Clemenceau,
politician and newspaper editor

Albert Clemenceau, *lawyer*

Auguste Scheurer-Kestner,
Vice President, French Senate

Jean Jaurès, *leader of the French socialists*

Joseph Reinach, *politician and writer*

Arthur Ranc, *politician*

Bernard Lazare, *writer*

Part One

I

————

M ajor Picquart to see the Minister of War . . ."
        The sentry on the rue Saint-Dominique steps out of his
box to open the gate and I run through a whirl of snow across the
windy courtyard into the warm lobby of the hôtel de Brienne, where
a sleek young captain of the Republican Guard rises to salute me.
I repeat, with greater urgency: "*Major Picquart to see the Minister of
War . . . !*"

We march in step, the captain leading, over the black-and-white
marble of the minister's official residence, up the curving staircase,
past suits of silver armour from the time of Louis the Sun King, past
that atrocious piece of Imperial kitsch, David's *Napoleon Crossing
the Alps at the Col du Grand-Saint-Bernard,* until we reach the first
floor, where we halt beside a window overlooking the grounds and
the captain goes off to announce my arrival, leaving me alone for a
few moments to contemplate something rare and beautiful: a garden made silent by snow in the centre of a city on a winter's morning. Even the yellow electric lights in the War Ministry, shimmering
through the gauzy trees, have a quality of magic.

"General Mercier is waiting for you, Major."

The minister's office is huge and ornately panelled in duck-egg
blue, with a double balcony over the whitened lawn. Two elderly
men in black uniforms, the most senior officers in the Ministry of
War, stand warming the backs of their legs against the open fire.
One is General Raoul le Mouton de Boisdeffre, Chief of the General
Staff, expert in all things Russian, architect of our burgeoning alliance with the new tsar, who has spent so much time with the Imperial court he has begun to look like a stiff-whiskered Russian count.

The other, slightly older at sixty, is his superior: the Minister of War himself, General Auguste Mercier.

I march to the middle of the carpet and salute.

Mercier has an oddly creased and immobile face, like a leather mask. Occasionally I have the odd illusion that another man is watching me through its narrow eye-slits. He says in his quiet voice, "Well, Major Picquart, that didn't take long. What time did it finish?"

"Half an hour ago, General."

"So it really is all over?"

I nod. "It's over."

And so it begins.

"Come and sit down by the fire," orders the minister. He speaks very quietly, as he always does. He indicates a gilt chair. "Pull it up. Take off your coat. Tell us everything that happened."

He sits poised in expectation on the edge of his seat: his body bent forwards, his hands clasped, his forearms resting on his knees. Protocol has prevented him from attending the morning's spectacle in person. He is in the position of an impresario who has missed his own show. He hungers for details: insights, observations, colour.

"What was the mood on the streets first thing?"

"I would say the mood was . . . expectant."

I describe how I left my apartment in the predawn darkness to walk to the École Militaire, and how the streets, to begin with at least, were unusually quiet, it being a Saturday—"The Jewish Sabbath," Mercier interrupts me, with a faint smile—and also freezing cold. In fact, although I do not mention this, as I passed along the gloomy pavements of the rue Boissière and the avenue du Trocadéro, I began to wonder if the minister's great production might turn out to be a flop. But then I reached the pont de l'Alma and saw the shadowy crowd pouring across the dark waters of the Seine, and that was when I realised what Mercier must have known all along: that the human impulse to watch another's humiliation will always prove sufficient insulation against even the bitterest cold.

I joined the multitude as they streamed southwards, over the river and down the avenue Bosquet—such a density of humanity that they spilled off the wooden pavements and into the street. They reminded me of a racecourse crowd—there was the same sense of shared anticipation, of the common pursuit of a classless pleasure. Newspaper vendors threaded back and forth selling the morning's editions. An aroma of roasting chestnuts rose from the braziers on the roadside.

At the bottom of the avenue I broke away and crossed over to the École Militaire, where until a year before I had served as professor of topography. The crowd streamed on past me towards the official assembly point in the place de Fontenoy. It was beginning to get light. The École rang with the sound of drums and bugles, hooves and curses, shouted orders, the tramp of boots. Each of the nine infantry regiments quartered in Paris had been ordered to send two companies to witness the ceremony, one composed of experienced men, the other of new recruits whose moral fibre, Mercier felt, would benefit by this example. As I passed through the grand salons and entered the cour Morland, they were already mustering in their thousands on the frozen mud.

I have never attended a public execution, have never tasted that particular atmosphere, but I imagine it must feel something like the École did that morning. The vastness of the cour Morland provided an appropriate stage for a grand spectacle. In the distance, beyond the railings, in the semicircle of the place de Fontenoy, a great murmuring sea of pink faces stirred behind a line of black-uniformed gendarmes. Every centimetre of space was filled. People were standing on benches and on the tops of carriages and omnibuses; they were sitting in the branches of the trees; one man had even managed to scale the pinnacle of the 1870 war memorial.

Mercier, drinking all this up, asks me, "So how many were present, would you estimate?"

"The Préfecture of Police assured me twenty thousand."

"Really?" The minister looks less impressed than I had expected. "You know that I originally wanted to hold the ceremony at Longchamps? The racetrack has a capacity of *fifty* thousand."

Boisdeffre says flatteringly, "And you would have filled it, Minister, by the sound of it."

"Of course we would have filled it! But the Ministry of the Interior maintained there was risk of public disorder. Whereas I say: the greater the crowd, the stronger the lesson."

Still, twenty thousand seemed plenty to me. The noise of the crowd was subdued but ominous, like the breathing of some powerful animal, temporarily quiescent but which could turn dangerous in an instant. Just before eight, an escort of cavalry appeared, trotting along the front of the crowd, and suddenly the beast began to stir, for between the riders could be glimpsed a black prison wagon drawn by four horses. A wave of jeers swelled and rolled over it. The cortège slowed, a gate was opened, and the vehicle and its guard clattered over the cobbles into the École.

As I watched it disappear into an inner courtyard, a man standing near to me said, "Observe, Major Picquart: the Romans fed Christians to the lions; we feed them Jews. That is progress, I suppose."

He was swaddled in a greatcoat with the collar turned up, a grey muffler around his throat, his cap pulled low over his eyes. I recognised him by his voice at first, and then by the way his body shook uncontrollably.

I saluted. "Colonel Sandherr."

Sandherr said, "Where will you stand to watch the show?"

"I haven't thought about it."

"You're welcome to come and join me and my men."

"That would be an honour. But first I have to check that everything is proceeding in accordance with the minister's instructions."

"We will be over there when you have finished your duties." He pointed across the cour Morland with a trembling hand. "You will have a good view."

My duties! I wonder, looking back, if he wasn't being sarcastic. I walked over to the garrison office, where the prisoner was in the custody of Captain Lebrun-Renault of the Republican Guard. I had no desire to see the condemned man again. Only two years earlier he had been a student of mine in this very building. Now I had nothing to say to him; I felt nothing for him; I wished he had never been born and I wanted him gone—from Paris, from France, from Europe.

A trooper went and fetched Lebrun-Renault for me. He turned out to be a big, red-faced, horsey young man, rather like a policeman. He came out and reported: "The traitor is nervous but calm. I don't think he will kick up any trouble. The threads of his clothing have been loosened and his sword has been scored half through to ensure it breaks easily. Nothing has been left to chance. If he tries to make a speech, General Darras will give a signal and the band will strike up a tune to drown him out."

Mercier muses, "What kind of tune does one play to drown a man out, I wonder?"

Boisdeffre suggests, "A sea shanty, Minister?"

"That's good," says Mercier judiciously. But he doesn't smile; he rarely smiles. He turns to me again. "So you watched the proceedings with Sandherr and his men. What do you make of them?"

Unsure how to answer—Sandherr is a colonel, after all—I say cautiously, "A dedicated group of patriots, doing invaluable work and receiving little or no recognition."

It is a good answer. So good that perhaps my entire life—and with it the story I am about to tell—may have turned upon it. At any rate, Mercier, or the man behind the mask that is Mercier, gives me a searching look as if to check that I really mean what I say, and then nods in approval. "You're right there, Picquart. France owes them a lot."

All six of these paragons were present that morning to witness the culmination of their work: the euphemistically named "Statistical Section" of the General Staff. I sought them out after I had finished talking with Lebrun-Renault. They stood slightly apart from everyone else in the southwest corner of the parade ground, in the lee of one of the low surrounding buildings. Sandherr had his hands in his pockets and his head down, and seemed entirely remote—

"Do you remember," interrupts the Minister of War, turning to Boisdeffre, "that they used to call Jean Sandherr 'the handsomest man in the French Army'?"

"I do remember that, Minister," confirms the Chief of the General Staff. "It's hard to believe it now, poor fellow."

On one side of Sandherr stood his deputy, a plump alcoholic with a face the colour of brick, taking regular nips from a gunmetal hip flask; on the other was the only member of his staff I knew by sight— the massive figure of Joseph Henry, who clapped me on the shoulder and boomed that he hoped I'd be mentioning him in my report to the minister. The two junior officers of the section, both captains, seemed colourless by comparison. There was also a civilian, a bony clerk who looked as if he seldom saw fresh air, holding a pair of opera glasses. They shifted along to make room for me and the alcoholic offered me a swig of his filthy cognac. Presently we were joined by a couple of other outsiders: a smart official from the Foreign Ministry, and that disturbing booby Colonel du Paty de Clam of the General Staff, his monocle flashing like an empty eye socket in the morning light.

By now the time was drawing close and one could feel the tension tightening under that sinister pale sky. Nearly four thousand soldiers had been drawn up on parade, yet not a sound escaped them. Even the crowd was hushed. The only movement came from the edges of the cour Morland, where a few invited guests were still being shown to their places, hurrying apologetically like latecomers at a funeral. A tiny slim woman in a white fur hat and muff, carrying a frilly blue umbrella and being escorted by a tall lieutenant of the dragoons, was recognised by some of the spectators nearest the railings, and a light patter of applause, punctuated by cries of "Hurrah!" and "Bravo!," drifted over the mud.

Sandherr, looking up, grunted, "Who the devil is that?"

One of the captains took the opera glasses from the clerk and trained them on the lady in furs, who was now nodding and twirling her umbrella in gracious acknowledgement to the crowd.

"Well I'll be damned if it isn't the Divine Sarah!" He adjusted the binoculars slightly. "And that's Rochebouet of the Twenty-eighth looking after her, the lucky devil!"

Mercier sits back and caresses his white moustache. Sarah Bernhardt, appearing in his production! This is the stuff he wants from me: the artistic touch, the society gossip. Still, he pretends to be displeased. "I can't think who would have invited *an actress* . . ."

At ten minutes to nine, the commander of the parade, General Darras, rode out along the cobbled path into the centre of the parade ground. The general's mount snorted and dipped her head as he pulled her up; she shuffled round in a circle, eyeing the vast multitude, pawed the hard ground once, and then stood still.

At nine, the clock began to strike and a command rang out: "Companies! Attention!" In thunderous unison the boots of four thousand men crashed together. At the same instant, from the far corner of the parade ground a group of five figures appeared and advanced towards the general. As they came closer, the tiny indistinct shapes resolved themselves into an escort of four gunners, surrounding the condemned man. They came on at a smart pace, marching with such perfect timing that their right feet hit the stroke of the chime exactly on every fifth step; only once did the prisoner stumble, but quickly he corrected himself. As the echo of the last strike died away, they halted and saluted. Then the gunners about-turned and marched away, leaving the convict to face the general alone.

Drums rolled. A bugle sounded. An official stepped forward, holding a sheet of paper up high in front of his face, like a herald in a play. The proclamation flapped in the icy wind, but his voice was surprisingly powerful for so small a man.

"In the name of the people of France," he intoned, "the first permanent court-martial of the military government of Paris, having met in camera, delivered its verdict in public session as follows. The following single question was put to the members of the court: Is Alfred Dreyfus, captain of the Fourteenth Artillery Regiment, a certified General Staff officer and probationer of the army's General Staff, guilty of delivering to a foreign power or to its agents in Paris in 1894 a certain number of secret or confidential documents concerning national defence?

"The court declared unanimously: 'Yes, the accused is guilty.'

"The court unanimously sentences Alfred Dreyfus to the penalty of deportation to a fortified enclosure for life, pronounces the discharge of Captain Alfred Dreyfus, and orders that his military degradation should take place before the first military parade of the Paris garrison."

He stepped back. General Darras rose in his stirrups and drew his sword. The condemned man had to crane his neck to look up at him. His pince-nez had been taken from him. He wore a pair of rimless spectacles.

"Alfred Dreyfus, you are not worthy to bear arms. In the name of the French people, we degrade you!"

"And it was at this point," I tell Mercier, "that the prisoner spoke for the first time."

Mercier jerks back in surprise. *"He spoke?"*

"Yes." I pull my notebook from my trouser pocket. "He raised both his arms above his head, and shouted . . ." And here I check to make sure I have it exactly right: "'Soldiers, they are degrading an innocent man . . . Soldiers, they are dishonouring an innocent man . . . Long live France . . . Long live the army . . .'" I read it plainly, without emotion, which is appropriate, because that is how it was delivered. The only difference is that Dreyfus, as a Mulhouse Jew, flavoured the words with a slight German accent.

The minister frowns. "How was this allowed to happen? I thought you said they planned to play a march if the prisoner made a speech?"

"General Darras took the view that a few shouts of protest did not constitute a speech, and that music would disturb the gravity of the occasion."

"And was there any reaction from the crowd?"

"Yes." I check my notes again. "They began to chant: 'Death . . . death . . . death . . .'"

When the chanting started, we looked towards the railings. Sandherr said: "They need to get a move on, or this could get out of hand."

I asked to borrow the opera glasses. I raised them to my eyes, adjusted the focus, and saw a giant of a man, a sergeant major of the Republican Guard, lay his hands on Dreyfus. In a series of powerful movements he yanked the epaulettes from Dreyfus's shoulders, wrenched all the buttons from his tunic and the gold braid from his sleeves, knelt and ripped the red stripes from his trousers. I focused on Dreyfus's expression. It was blank. He stared ahead as he was tugged this way and that, submitting to these indignities as a child might to having its clothes adjusted by an irritable adult. Finally, the sergeant major drew Dreyfus's sword from its scabbard, planted the tip in the mud, and snapped the blade with a thrust of his boot. He threw the two halves on to the little heap of haberdashery at Dreyfus's feet, took two sharp paces backwards, turned his head towards the general and saluted, while Dreyfus gazed down at the torn symbols of his honour.

Sandherr said impatiently: "Come on, Picquart—you're the one with the glasses. Tell us what he looks like."

"He looks," I replied, handing the binoculars back to the clerk, "like a Jewish tailor counting the cost of all that gold braid going to waste. If he had a tape measure around his neck, he might be in a cutting room on the rue Auber."

"That's good," said Sandherr. "I like that."

"Very good," echoes Mercier, closing his eyes. "I can picture him exactly."

Dreyfus shouted out again: "Long live France! I swear I am innocent!"

Then he began a long march, under escort, around all four sides of the cour Morland, parading in his torn uniform in front of every detachment, so that the soldiers could remember for ever how the army deals with traitors. Every so often he would call out, "I am innocent!" which would draw jeers and cries of "Judas!" and "Jewish traitor!" from the watching crowd. The whole thing seemed to drag on endlessly, though by my watch it lasted no more than seven minutes.

When Dreyfus started to walk towards our position, the man from the Foreign Ministry, who was taking his turn with the binoculars, said in his languid voice: "I don't understand how the fellow can allow himself to be subjected to such humiliation and still maintain he's innocent. Surely if he really was innocent he would put up a struggle, rather than allow himself to be led around so tamely? Or is this a Jewish trait, do you suppose?"

"Of course it's a Jewish trait!" retorted Sandherr. "This is a race entirely without patriotism, or honour, or pride. They have done nothing but betray the people they live among for centuries, starting with Jesus Christ."

When Dreyfus passed where we were standing, Sandherr turned

his back to demonstrate his contempt. But I could not take my eyes from him. Whether because of the past three months in prison or the bitter cold of that morning, his face was greyish-white and puffy: the colour of a maggot. His buttonless black tunic was hanging open, revealing his white shirt. His sparse hair was sticking up in tufts; something gleamed in it. He did not break step as he marched by with his guards. He glanced in our direction and briefly his gaze locked on to mine and I saw straight into his soul, glimpsed the animal fear, the desperate mental struggle to keep himself together. As I watched him go, I realised the gleam in his hair was saliva. He must have wondered what part I had played in his ruin.

Only one stage of his Calvary remained: for him the worst part of it, I am sure, when he had to pass along the railings in front of the crowd. The police had linked arms to try to keep the public at a distance. But when the spectators saw the prisoner approaching, they surged forwards. The police line bulged, tautened and then burst apart, releasing a flood of protesters, who poured across the pavement and spread along the railings. Dreyfus stopped, turned and faced them, raised his arms and said something. But he had his back to me and I couldn't hear his words, only the familiar taunts of "Judas!," "Traitor!" and "Death to the Jew!" that were thrown back in his face.

Finally, his escort pulled him away and steered him towards the prison wagon, waiting just ahead with its mounted outriders. The condemned man's hands were cuffed behind his back. He stepped up into the wagon. The doors were closed and locked, the horses whipped, and the cortège jolted forwards, out of the gate and into the place de Fontenoy. For a moment I doubted if it would escape the surrounding crowd, stretching out their hands to strike the sides of the wagon. But the cavalry officers used the flats of their swords to drive them back. I heard the whip crack twice. The driver shouted a command. The wagon accelerated free of the mob, turned left and disappeared.

An instant later the order was given for the parade to march past. The stamp of boots seemed to shake the ground. Bugles were blown. Drums beat time. As the band struck up "Sambre-et-Meuse" it started to snow. I felt a great sense of release. I believe we all did.

Spontaneously we turned to one another and shook hands. It was as if a healthy body had purged itself of something foul and pestilential, and now life could begin anew.

I finish my report. The minister's room falls silent, apart from the crackle of the fire.

"The only pity," Mercier says eventually, "is that the traitor will continue to remain alive. I say this more for his sake than anyone else's. What kind of life is left to him? It would have been kinder to finish him off. That's why I wanted the Chamber of Deputies to restore the death penalty for treason."

Boisdeffre nods ingratiatingly. "You did your best, Minister."

With a creak of knee joints, Mercier stands. He walks over to a large globe, which stands in a mount beside his desk, and beckons me to join him. He puts on a pair of spectacles and peers down at the Earth, like a short-sighted deity.

"I need to put him in a place where it's impossible for him to talk to anyone. I don't want him smuggling out any more treasonous messages. And just as important, I don't want anyone communicating with *him*."

The minister places a surprisingly delicate hand on the northern hemisphere and gently turns the world. The Atlantic slides past. He halts the sphere and points to a spot on the coast of South America, seven thousand kilometres from Paris. He looks at me and raises an eyebrow, inviting me to guess.

I say, "The penal colony at Cayenne?"

"Close, but more secure than that." He leans in and taps the globe. "Devil's Island: fifteen kilometres off the coast. The sea around it is infested with sharks. The immense waves and strong currents make it hard even to land a boat."

"I thought that place had been closed down years ago."

"It was. The last inhabitants were a colony of convict lepers. I will need to seek approval in the Chamber, but this time I will get it. The island will be reopened especially for Dreyfus. Well, what do you think?"

My immediate reaction is surprise. Mercier, married to an Englishwoman, is considered a republican and a free-thinker—he refuses to attend Mass, for example—qualities I admire. And yet, for all that, there lingers about him something of the Jesuit fanatic. *Devil's Island?* I think. *We're supposed to be on the brink of the twentieth century, not the eighteenth . . .*

"Well?" he repeats. "What's your view?"

"Isn't it a trifle . . ." I choose the word carefully, wishing to be tactful, *"Dumas?"*

"Dumas? What do you mean, Dumas?"

"Only that it sounds like a punishment from historical fiction. I feel an echo of *The Man in the Iron Mask.* Won't Dreyfus become known as 'The Man on Devil's Island'? It will make him the most famous prisoner in the world . . ."

"Exactly!" cries Mercier, and slaps his thigh in a rare display of feeling. "That's *exactly* what I like about it. The public's imagination will be captured."

I bow to his superior political judgement. At the same time I wonder what the public has to do with it. Only when I am collecting my coat and about to leave does he offer a clue.

"This may be the last time that you will see me in this office."

"I'm sorry to hear that, General."

"You understand I take little interest in politics—I am a professional soldier, not a politician. But I gather there is great dissatisfaction among the parties, and the government may only last another week or two. There may even be a new president." He shrugs. "Anyway, there it is. We soldiers serve where we are ordered." He shakes my hand. "I have been impressed by the intelligence you have shown during this wretched affair, Major Picquart. It will not be forgotten, will it, Chief?"

"No, Minister." Boisdeffre also rises to shake my hand. "Thank you, Picquart. Most illuminating. One might almost have been there oneself. How are your Russian studies, by the way?"

"I doubt I'll ever be able to speak the language, General, but I can read Tolstoy now—with a dictionary, of course."

"Excellent. There are great things happening between France and Russia. A good knowledge of Russian will be very useful to a rising officer."

I am at the door and about to open it, feeling suitably warmed by all this flattery, when Mercier suddenly asks: "Tell me, was my name mentioned at all?"

"I'm sorry?" I'm not sure what he means. "Mentioned in what sense?"

"During the ceremony this morning."

"I don't think so . . ."

"It doesn't matter at all." Mercier makes a dismissive gesture. "I just wondered if there was any kind of demonstration in the crowd . . ."

"No, none that I saw."

"Good. I didn't expect there would be."

I close the door softly behind me.

Stepping back out into the windy canyon of the rue Saint-Dominique, I clutch my cap to my head and walk the one hundred metres to the War Ministry next door. There is nobody about. Clearly my brother officers have better things to do on a Saturday than attend to the bureaucracy of the French army. Sensible fellows! I shall write up my official report, clear my desk, and try to put Dreyfus out of my mind. I trot up the stairs and along the corridor to my office.

Since Napoleon's time, the War Ministry has been divided into four departments. The First deals with administration; the Second, intelligence; the Third, operations and training; and the Fourth, transport. I work in the Third, under the command of Colonel Boucher, who—also being a sensible fellow—is nowhere to be seen this winter's morning. As his deputy, I have a small office to myself, a monk's bare cell, with a window looking out on to a dreary court-yard. Two chairs, a desk and a filing cabinet are the extent of my furniture. The heating is not working. The air is so cold I can see my breath. I sit, still wearing my overcoat, and contemplate the drift of paperwork that has accumulated over the past few days. With a groan, I reach for one of the dossiers.

It must be a couple of hours later, early in the afternoon, when I hear heavy footsteps approaching along the deserted corridor. Who-ever it is walks past my office, stops, and then comes back and stands outside my door. The wood is thin enough for me to hear their heavy breathing. I stand, cross quietly to the door, listen, and then fling it open to discover the Chief of the Second Department—that is, the head of all military intelligence—staring me in the face. I am not sure which of us is the more flustered.

"General Gonse," I say, saluting. "I had no idea it was you."

Gonse is famous for his fourteen-hour days. I might have guessed that if anyone else was likely to be in the building, it would be him. His enemies say it is the only way he can keep on top of his job.

"That's quite all right, Major Picquart. This place is a warren. May I?" He waddles into my office on his short legs, puffing on a cigarette. "Sorry to interrupt you, but I just had a message from Colonel Guérin at the place Vendôme. He says that Dreyfus confessed at the parade this morning. Did you know that?"

I gape at him like a fool. "No, General, I did not."

"Apparently, in the half-hour before the ceremony this morning, he told the captain who was guarding him that he *did* pass documents to the Germans." Gonse shrugs. "I thought you ought to know, as you were supposed to be keeping an eye on it all for the minister."

"But I've already given him my report . . ." I am aghast. This is the sort of incompetence that can wreck a man's career. Ever since October, despite the overwhelming evidence against him, Dreyfus has refused to admit his guilt. And now I'm being told that finally he has confessed, practically under my nose, and I missed it! "I had better go and get to the bottom of this."

"I suggest you do. And when you have, come back and report to me."

Once again I hurry out into the chilly grey half-light. I take a cab from the rank on the corner of the boulevard Saint-Germain, and when we reach the École Militaire I ask the driver to wait while I run inside. The silence of the vast empty parade ground mocks me. The only sign of life is the workmen clearing the litter from the place de Fontenoy. I return to the cab and ask to be driven as fast as possible to the headquarters of the military governor of Paris in the place Vendôme, where I wait in the lobby of that gloomy and dilapidated building for Colonel Guérin. He takes his time, and when he does appear he has the air of a man who has been interrupted in the middle of a good lunch to which he is anxious to return.

"I've already explained all this to General Gonse."

"I'm sorry, Colonel. Would you mind explaining it to me?"

He sighs. "Captain Lebrun-Renault was detailed to keep an eye on Dreyfus in the guardroom until the ceremony started. He handed him over to the escort, and just as the degradation started he came over to where a group of us were standing and said something like 'Well I'll be damned, the scum just admitted everything.'"

I take out my notebook. "What did the captain say Dreyfus had told him?"

"I don't recall his actual words. The essence of it was that he'd handed over secrets to the Germans, but they weren't very important, that the minister knew all about them, and that in a few years' time the whole story would come out. Something like that. You need to talk to Lebrun-Renault."

"I do. Where can I find him?"

"I've no idea. He's off duty."

"Is he still in Paris?"

"My dear Major, how would I know that?"

"I don't quite understand," I say. "Why would Dreyfus suddenly admit his guilt to a total stranger, at such a moment and with nothing to gain by it, after denying everything for three months?"

"I can't help you there." The colonel looks over his shoulder in the direction of his lunch.

"And if he'd just confessed to Captain Lebrun-Renault, why did he then go out and repeatedly shout his innocence into a hostile crowd of tens of thousands?"

The colonel squares his shoulders. "Are you calling one of my officers a liar?"

"Thank you, Colonel." I put away my notebook.

When I get back to the ministry, I go straight to Gonse's office. He is labouring over a stack of files. He swings his boots up onto the desk and tilts back in his chair as he listens to my report. He says, "So you don't think there's anything in it?"

"No, I do not. Not now I've heard the details. It's much more likely this dim captain of the Guard got the wrong end of the stick. Either that or he embellished a tale to make himself look important to his comrades. Of course I am assuming," I add, "that Dreyfus wasn't a double agent planted on the Germans."

Gonse laughs and lights another cigarette. "If only!"

"What would you like me to do, General?"

"I don't see there's anything much you can do."

I hesitate. "There is one way of getting a definite answer, of course."

"What's that?"

"We could ask Dreyfus."

Gonse shakes his head. "Absolutely not. He's now beyond communication. Besides, he'll soon be shipped out of Paris." He lifts his feet from the desk and sets them on the floor. He pulls the stack of files towards him. Cigarette ash spills down the front of his tunic. "Just leave it with me. I'll go and explain everything to the Chief of Staff and the minister." He opens a dossier and starts to scan it. He doesn't look up. "Thank you, Major Picquart. You are dismissed."

2

That evening, in civilian clothes, I travel out to Versailles to see my mother. The draughty train sways through Paris suburbs weirdly etched by snow and gaslight. The journey takes the best part of an hour; I have the carriage to myself. I try to read a novel, *The Adolescent* by Dostoyevsky, but every time we cross a set of points the lights cut out and I lose my place. In the blue glow of the emergency illumination I stare out of the window and imagine Dreyfus in his cell in La Santé prison. Convicts are transported by rail in converted cattle trucks. I presume he will be sent west, to an Atlantic port, to await deportation. In this weather the journey will be a bitter hell. I close my eyes and try to doze.

My mother has a small apartment in a modern street near the Versailles railway station. She is seventy-seven and lives alone, a widow for almost thirty years. I take it in turns with my sister to spend time with her. Anna is older than I, and has children, which I do not: my watch always falls on a Saturday night, the only time I can be sure of getting away from the ministry.

It is well past dark by the time I arrive; the temperature must be minus ten. My mother shouts from behind the locked door: "Who's there?"

"It's Georges, Maman."

"Who?"

"Georges. Your son."

It takes me a minute to persuade her to let me in. Sometimes she mistakes me for my older brother, Paul, who died five years ago; sometimes—and this is oddly worse—for my father, who died when I was eleven. (Another sister died before I was born, a brother when

he was eleven days old; there is one thing to be said for senility—
since her mind has gone, she does not lack for company.)

The bread and milk are frozen solid; the pipes are canisters of
ice. I spend the first half-hour lighting fires to try to thaw the place
out, the second on my back fixing a leak. We eat boeuf bourguignon,
which the maid who comes in once a day has bought at the local
traiteur. Maman rallies; she even seems to remember who I am. I tell
her what I've been doing but I don't mention Dreyfus or the degradation: she would struggle to understand what I am talking about.
Later we sit at the piano, which occupies most of her tiny sitting
room, and play a duet, the Chopin rondo. Her playing is faultless;
the musical part of her brain remains quite intact; it will be the last
thing to go. After she has put herself to bed, I sit on the stool and
examine the photographs on top of the piano: the solemn family
groups in Strasbourg, the garden of the house in Geudertheim, a
miniature of my mother as a music student, a picnic in the woods of
Neudorf—artefacts from a vanished world, the Atlantis we lost in
the war.[*]

I was sixteen when the Germans shelled Strasbourg, thus kindly
enabling me to witness at first hand an event that we teach at the
École Supérieure de Guerre as "the first full-scale use of modern
long-range artillery specifically to reduce a civilian population." I
watched the city's art gallery and library burn to the ground, saw
neighbourhoods blown to pieces, knelt beside friends as they died,
helped dig strangers out of the rubble. After nine weeks the garrison surrendered. We were offered a choice between staying put and
becoming German or giving up everything and moving to France.
We arrived in Paris destitute and shorn of all illusions about the
security of our civilised life.

Before the humiliation of 1870 I might have become a professor of music or a surgeon; after it, any career other than the army
seemed frivolous. The Ministry of War paid for my education; the

---

[*] The war of 1870 between France and Germany resulted in a crushing defeat
for the French army, which suffered over 140,000 casualties. Under the terms
of the armistice, the eastern territories of Alsace and Lorraine became part of
Germany.

army became my father, and no son ever strove harder to please a demanding papa. I compensated for a somewhat dreamy and artistic nature by ferocious discipline. Out of a class of 304 cadets at the military school at Saint-Cyr, I emerged fifth. I can speak German, Italian, English and Spanish. I have fought in the Aurès Mountains in North Africa and won the Colonial Medal, on the Red River in Indochina and won the Star for bravery. I am a Chevalier of the Legion of Honour. And today, after twenty-four years in uniform, I have been singled out for commendation by both the Minister of War and the Chief of the General Staff. As I lie in my mother's spare bedroom in Versailles, and the fifth of January 1895 turns into the sixth, the voice in my head is not that of Alfred Dreyfus proclaiming his innocence, but Auguste Mercier's hinting at my promotion: *I have been impressed by the intelligence you have shown . . . It will not be forgotten . . .*

The following morning, to the sound of bells, I take my mother's fragile arm and escort her to the top of the icy road and around the corner to the cathedral of Saint-Louis—a particularly bombastic monument to state superstition, I always think; why couldn't the Germans have blown up *this*? The worshippers are a monochrome congregation, black and white, nuns and widows. I withdraw my arm from hers at the door. "I'll meet you here after Mass."

"Aren't you coming in?"

"I never come in, Maman. We have this conversation every week."

She peers at me with moist grey eyes. Her voice quivers. "But what shall I tell God?"

"Tell Him I'll be in the Café du Commerce in the square over there."

I leave her in the care of a young priest and walk towards the café. On the way I stop to buy a couple of newspapers, *Le Figaro* and *Le Petit Journal*. I take a seat at a table in the window, order coffee, light a cigarette. Both papers have the degradation on their front pages—the *Journal*, indeed, has almost nothing else. Its report is illustrated by a series of crude sketches: of Dreyfus being marched into the parade ground, of the plump little official in his cape reading out the judgment, of the insignia being ripped from Dreyfus's uniform, and of Dreyfus himself looking like a white-haired old man at thirty-five. The headline is "The Expiation": "We demanded for the traitor Dreyfus the supreme penalty. We continue to believe that the only appropriate punishment is death . . ." It is as if all the loathing and recrimination bottled up since the defeat of 1870 has found an outlet in a single individual.

I sip my coffee and my gaze skims over the *Journal*'s sensational description of the ceremony until suddenly it hits this: "Dreyfus turned towards his escort and said: 'If I did hand over documents, it was only to receive others of greater importance. In three years the truth will come out and the minister himself will reopen my case.' This half-confession is the first that the traitor has made since his arrest . . ."

Without taking my eyes from the newsprint, I slowly put down my cup and read the passage again. Then I pick up *Le Figaro*. No mention of any confession, half or otherwise, on the front page: a relief. But on the second is a late news item—"Here now is the account of a witness, received in the last hour . . ."—and I find myself reading another version of the same story, only this time Lebrun-Renault is identified as the source by name, and this time there is no mistaking the authentic voice of Dreyfus. I can hear his desperation in every line, frantic to convince anyone, even the officer guarding him:

"Look, Captain; listen. A letter was discovered in a cupboard in an embassy; it was a covering note for four other documents. This letter was shown to handwriting experts. Three said I had written it; two said I hadn't. And it's solely on the basis of this that I've been condemned! When I was eighteen, I entered the École Polytechnique. I had a brilliant military career ahead of me, a fortune of five hundred thousand francs and the prospect of an annual income of fifty thousand a year. I've never chased girls. I've never touched a playing card in my life. Therefore I had no need of money. So why would I commit treason? For money? No. So why?"

None of these details is supposed to be made public, and my first response is to curse Lebrun-Renault beneath my breath as a bloody young fool. Shooting one's mouth off in front of journalists is unpardonable for an officer at any time—but on a matter as sensitive as this? He must have been drunk! It crosses my mind that I should return to Paris immediately and go straight to the War Ministry. But then I consider my mother, no doubt even at this moment down on her knees praying for my immortal soul, and decide that I am probably better off out of it.

And so I allow the day to proceed as planned. I retrieve my mother from the clutches of a pair of nuns, we walk back to the house, and at noon my cousin, Edmond Gast, sends his carriage to collect us for lunch at his home in the nearby village of Ville-d'Avray. It is a pleasant, easy gathering of family and friends: the sort of friends who have been around long enough to feel like family. Edmond, a couple of years my junior, is already the mayor of Ville-d'Avray, one of those lucky individuals with a gift for life. He farms, paints, hunts, makes money easily, spends it well, and loves his wife—and who can be surprised, since Jeanne is still as pretty as a girl by Renoir? I envy no man, but if I did it would be Edmond. Next to Jeanne in the dining room sits Louis Leblois, who was at school with me; beside me is his wife, Martha; opposite me is Pauline Romazzotti, who, despite her Italian surname, grew up with us near Strasbourg, and who is now married to an official at the Foreign Ministry, Philippe Monnier, a man eight or ten years older than the rest of us. She is wearing a plain grey dress trimmed with white which she knows I like because it reminds me of one she wore when she was eighteen.

Everyone around the table apart from Monnier is an exile from Alsace and nobody has a good word to say for our fellow Alsatian, Dreyfus, not even Edmond, whose politics are radical republican. We all have tales of Jews, especially from Mulhouse, whose loyalties, when it came to the crunch and they were offered their choice of citizenship after the war, turned out to be German rather than French.

"They shift with the wind, according to who has power," pronounces Monnier, waving his wineglass back and forth. "That is how their race has survived for two thousand years. You can't blame them, really."

Only Leblois ventures a scintilla of doubt. "Mind you, speaking as a lawyer, I'm against secret trials in principle, and I must admit I wonder if a Christian officer would have been denied the normal judicial process in the same way—especially as according to Le Figaro the evidence against him sounds so thin."

I say coldly, "He was 'denied the normal judicial process,' as you put it, Louis, because the case involved matters of national security that simply couldn't have been aired in open court, whoever was the defendant. And there was plenty of evidence against him: I can give you my absolute assurance of that!"

Pauline frowns at me and I realise I have raised my voice. There is a silence. Louis adjusts his napkin but says nothing more. He doesn't want to spoil the meal, and Pauline, ever the diplomat's wife, seizes the chance to move the conversation on to a more congenial topic.

"Did I tell you that Philippe and I have discovered the most wonderful new Alsatian restaurant on the rue Marbeuf . . ."

It is five by the time I arrive home. My apartment is in the sixteenth arrondissement, close to the place Victor Hugo. The address makes me sound much smarter than I am. In truth, I have just two small rooms on the fourth floor, and I struggle to afford even these on a major's pay. I am no Dreyfus, with a private income ten times my salary. But it has always been my temperament to prefer a tiny amount of the excellent to a plenitude of the mediocre; I get by, just about.

I let myself in from the street and have barely taken a couple of paces towards the stairs when I hear the concierge's voice behind me—"Major Picquart!"—and turn to discover Madame Guerault brandishing a visiting card. "An officer came to call on you," she announces, advancing towards me. "A general!"

I take the card: "General Charles-Arthur Gonse, Ministry of War." On the reverse he has written his home address.

His place is close to the avenue du Bois de Boulogne; I can walk to it easily. Within five minutes I am ringing his bell. The door is opened by a very different figure from the relaxed fellow I left on Saturday afternoon. He is unshaven; the pouches beneath his eyes are dark and heavy with exhaustion. His tunic is open to the waist, revealing a slightly grubby undershirt. He holds a glass of cognac.

"Picquart. Good of you to come."

"My apologies that I'm not in uniform, General."

"No matter. It's a Sunday, after all."

I follow him through the darkened apartment—"My wife is in the country," he explains over his shoulder—and into what seems to be his study. Above the window is a pair of crossed spears—mementos of his service in North Africa, I assume—and on the chimneypiece a photograph of him taken a quarter of a century ago, as a junior staff officer in the 13th Army Corps. He refreshes his drink from a decanter and pours one for me, then flops down on to the couch with a groan and lights a cigarette.

"This damned Dreyfus affair," he says. "It will be the death of us all."

I make some light reply—"Really? I would have preferred mine to be slightly more heroic!"—but Gonse fixes me with a look of great seriousness.

"My dear Picquart, you don't seem to realise: we have just come very close to war. I have been up since one o'clock this morning, and all because of that damned fool Lebrun-Renault!"

"My God!" Taken aback, I set down my untasted glass of cognac.

"I know it's hard to believe," he says, "that such a catastrophe might have resulted from one idiot's gossip, but it's true."

He tells me how, an hour after midnight, he was woken by a messenger from the Minister of War. Summoned to the hôtel de Brienne, he found Mercier in his dressing gown with a private secretary from the Élysée Palace who had with him copies of the first editions of the Paris newspapers. The private secretary then repeated to Gonse what he had just told Mercier: that the President was appalled—appalled! scandalised!—by what he had just read. How could it be that an officer of the Republican Guard could spread such stories—in particular, that a document had been stolen by the French government from the German Embassy, and that the whole episode was some kind of espionage trap for the Germans? Was the Minister of War aware that the German ambassador was coming to the Élysée that very afternoon to present a formal note of protest from Berlin? That the German emperor was threatening to withdraw his ambassador from Paris unless the French government stated once and for all that it accepted the German government's assurances that it had never had any dealings with Captain Alfred Dreyfus? Find him, the President demanded! Find this Captain Lebrun-Renault *and shut him up!*

And so General Arthur Gonse, the Chief of French Military Intelligence, at the age of fifty-six, found himself in the humiliating position of taking a carriage and going from door to door—to regimental headquarters, to Lebrun-Renault's lodgings, to the fleshpots of Pigalle—until finally, just before dawn, he had run his quarry to earth in the Moulin Rouge, where the young captain was still holding forth to an audience of reporters and prostitutes!

At this point I have to press my forefinger across my lips to hide a smile, for the monologue is not without its comic elements—all the greater when delivered in Gonse's hoarse and outraged tones. I can only imagine what it must have been like for Lebrun-Renault to turn around and see Gonse bearing down upon him, or his frantic attempts to sober up before explaining his actions, first to the Minister of War, and then, in what must have been an exquisitely embarrassing interview, to President Casimir-Perier himself.

"There is nothing at all funny about this, Major!" Gonse has detected my amusement. "We are in no condition to fight a war against Germany! If they were to decide to use this as a pretext to attack us, then God help France!"

"Of course, General." Gonse is part of that generation—Mercier and Boisdeffre are of it too—who were scarred as young officers by the rout of 1870 and have been frightened of the Germans' shadow ever since. "Three-to-two" is their mantra of pessimism: there are three Germans to every two Frenchmen; they spend three francs on armaments to every two that we can afford. I rather despise them for their defeatism. "How has Berlin reacted?"

"Some form of words is being negotiated in the Foreign Ministry to the effect that the Germans are no more responsible for the documents that get sent to them than we are for the ones that come to us."

"They have a nerve!"

"Not really. They're just providing cover for their agent. We'd do the same. But it's been touch and go all day, I can tell you."

The more I think of it, the more amazing it seems. "They'd really break off diplomatic relations and risk a war just to protect one spy?"

"Well, of course, they're embarrassed at being caught out. It's humiliating for them. Typical damned Prussian overreaction . . ."

His hand is shaking. He lights a fresh cigarette from his old one and drops the stub into the sawn-off cap of a shell case which serves as his ashtray. He picks a few shreds of tobacco from his tongue then settles back in his couch and regards me through the cloud of smoke. "You haven't touched your drink, I see."

"I prefer to keep a clear head when talk turns to war."

"Ah! That's exactly when I find I need one!" He drains his glass and toys with it. He smiles at me. I can tell he's desperate for another by the way he glances over at the decanter, but he doesn't want to look like a drunk in front of me. He clears his throat and says: "The minister has been impressed by you, Picquart; by your conduct throughout this whole affair. So has the Chief of Staff. You've obviously gained valuable experience of secret intelligence over the past three months. So we have it in mind to recommend you for promotion. We're thinking of offering you command of the Statistical Section."

I try to hide my dismay. Espionage is grubby work. Everything I have seen of the Dreyfus case has reinforced that view. It isn't what I joined the army to do. "But surely," I object, "the section already has a very able commander in Colonel Sandherr?"

"He *is* able. But Sandherr is a sick man, and between you and me he isn't likely to recover. Also, he's been in the post ten years; he needs a rest. Now, Picquart, forgive me, but I have to ask you this, given the nature of the secret information you'd be handling—there isn't anything in your past or private life that could leave you open to blackmail, is there?"

With gathering dismay I realise my fate has already been decided, perhaps the previous afternoon when Gonse met Mercier and Bois-deffre. "No," I say, "not that I'm aware of."

"You're not married, I believe?"

"No."

"Any particular reason for that?"

"I like my own company. And I can't afford a wife."

"That's all?"

"That's all."

"Any money worries?"

"No money." I shrug. "No worries."

"Good." Gonse looks relieved. "Then it's settled."

But still I struggle against my destiny. "You realise the existing staff won't like an outsider coming in—what about Colonel Sand-herr's deputy?"

"He's retiring."

"Or Major Henry?"

"Oh, Henry's a good soldier. He'll soon knuckle down and do what's best for the section."

"Doesn't he want the job himself?"

"He does, but he lacks the education, and the social polish for such a senior position. His wife's father keeps an inn, I believe."

"But I know nothing about spying—"

"Come now, my dear Picquart!" Gonse is starting to become irri-tated. "You have exactly the qualities for the post. Where's the prob-lem? It's true the unit doesn't exist officially. There'll be no parades or stories in the newspapers. You won't be able to tell anyone what you're up to. But everyone who's important will know exactly what you're doing. You'll have daily access to the minister. And of course you'll be promoted to colonel." He gives me a shrewd look. "How old are you?"

"Forty."

"Forty! There's no one else in the entire army of that rank at your age. Think of it: you should make general long before you're fifty! And after that . . . You could be Chief one day."

Gonse knows exactly how to play me. I am ambitious, though not consumed by it, I hope: I appreciate there are other things in life besides the army—still, I would like to ride my talents as far as they will take me. I calculate: a couple of years in a job I don't much like, and at the end of them my prospects will be golden. My resistance falters. I surrender.

"When might this happen?"

"Not immediately. In a few months. I'd be grateful if you didn't mention it to anyone."

I nod. "Of course, I shall do whatever the army wants me to do. I'm grateful for your faith in me. I'll try to prove worthy of it."

"Good man! I'm sure you will. Now I insist you have that drink that's still sitting next to you . . ."

And so it is settled. We toast my future. We toast the army. And then Gonse shows me out. At the door, he puts his hand on my arm and squeezes it paternally. His breath is sweet with cognac and cigarette smoke. "I know you think spying isn't proper soldiering, Georges, but it is. In the modern age, this is the front line. We have to fight the Germans every day. They're stronger than we are in men and matériel—'three-to-two,' remember!—so we have to be sharper in intelligence." His grip on my arm tightens. "Exposing a traitor like Dreyfus is as vital to France as winning a battle in the field."

Outside it is starting to snow again. All along the avenue Victor Hugo countless thousands of snowflakes are caught in the glow of the gas lamps. A white carpet is being laid across the road. It's odd. I am about to become the youngest colonel in the French army but I feel no sense of exhilaration.

In my apartment Pauline waits. She has kept on the same plain grey dress she wore at lunch so that I may have the pleasure of taking it off her. She turns to allow me to unfasten it at the back, lifting her hair in both hands so that I can reach the top hook. I kiss the nape of her neck and murmur into her skin: "How long do we have?"

"An hour. He thinks I'm at church. Your lips are cold. Where have you been?"

I am about to tell her, but then remember Gouse's instruction. "Nowhere," I say.

3

Six months pass. June arrives. The air warms up and very soon Paris starts to reek of shit. The stench rises out of the sewers and settles over the city like a putrid gas. People venture out of doors wearing linen masks or with handkerchiefs pressed to their noses, but it doesn't make much difference. In the newspapers the experts are unanimous that it isn't as bad as the original "great stink" of 1880—I can't speak to that: I was in Algeria at the time—but certainly it ruins the early days of summer. "It is impossible to stand on one's balcony," complains *Le Figaro*, "impossible to sit on the terrace of one of the busy, joyful cafés that are the pride of our boulevards, without thinking that one must be downwind from some uncouth, invisible giant." The smell infiltrates one's hair and clothes and settles in one's nostrils, even on one's tongue, so that everything tastes of corruption. Such is the atmosphere on the day I take charge of the Statistical Section.

Major Henry, when he comes to collect me at the Ministry of War, makes light of it: "This is nothing. You should have grown up on a farm! Folks' shit, pigs' shit: where's the difference?" His face in the heat is as smooth and fat as a large pink baby's. A smirk trembles constantly on his lips. He addresses me with a slight overemphasis on my rank—"*Colonel* Picquart!"—that somehow combines respect, congratulations and mockery in a single word. I take no offence. Henry is to be my deputy, a consolation for being passed over for the chief's job. From now on we are locked in roles as ancient as warfare. He is the experienced old soldier who has come up through the ranks, the sergeant major who makes things work; I the younger commissioned officer, theoretically in charge, who must somehow be prevented from doing too much damage. If each of us doesn't push the other too far, I think we should get along fine.

Henry stands. "So then, *Colonel*: shall we go?"

I have never before set foot in the Statistical Section—not surprising, as few even know of its existence—and so I have requested that Henry show me round. I expect to be led to some discreet corner of the ministry. Instead he conducts me out of the back gate and a short walk up the road to an ancient, grimy house on the corner of the rue de l'Université which I have often passed and always assumed to be derelict. The darkened windows are heavily shuttered. There is no nameplate beside the door. Inside, the gloomy lobby is pervaded by the same cloying smell of raw sewage as the rest of Paris, but with an added spice of musty dampness.

Henry smears his thumb through a patch of black spores growing on the wall. "A few years ago they wanted to pull this place down," he says, "but Colonel Sandherr stopped them. Nobody disturbs us here."

"I am sure they don't."

"This is Bachir." Henry indicates an elderly Arab doorman, in the blue tunic and pantaloons of a native Algerian regiment, who sits in the corner on a stool. "He knows all our secrets, don't you, Bachir?"

"Yes, Major!"

"Bachir, this is *Colonel* Picquart . . ."

We step into the dimly lit interior and Henry throws open a door to reveal four or five seedy-looking characters smoking pipes and playing cards. They turn to stare at me, and I just have time to take the measure of the drab sofa and chairs and the scaly carpet before Henry says, "Excuse us, gentlemen," and quickly closes the door again.

"Who are they?" I ask.

"Just people who do work for us."

"What sort of work?"

"Police agents. Informers. Men with useful skills. Colonel Sandherr takes the view that it's better to keep them out of mischief here rather than let them hang around on the streets."

We climb the creaking staircase to what Henry calls "the inner sanctum." Because all the doors are closed, there is almost no natural light along the first-floor passage. Electricity has been installed, but crudely, with no attempt to redecorate where the cables have been buried. A piece of the plaster ceiling has come down and been propped against the wall.

I am introduced to the unit one by one. Each man has his own room and keeps his door closed while he works. There is Major Cordier, the alcoholic who will be retiring shortly, sitting in his shirtsleeves, reading the anti-Semitic press, *La Libre Parole* and *L'Intransigeant*, whether for work or pleasure I do not ask. There is the new man, Captain Junck, whom I know slightly from my lectures at the École Supérieure de Guerre—a tall and muscular young man with an immense moustache, who now is wearing an apron and a pair of thin gloves. He is opening a pile of intercepted letters, using a kind of kettle, heated over a jet of gas flame, to steam the glue on the envelope: this is known as a "wet opening," Henry explains.

In the next-door room, another captain, Valdant, is using the "dry" method, scraping at the gummed seals with a scalpel: I watch for a couple of minutes as he makes a small opening on either side of the envelope flap, slides in a long, thin pair of forceps, twists them around a dozen times to roll the letter into a cylinder, and extracts it deftly through the aperture without leaving a mark. Upstairs, M. Gribelin, the spidery archivist who had the binoculars at Dreyfus's degradation, sits in the centre of a large room filled with locked cabinets, and instinctively hides what he is reading the moment I appear. Captain Matton's room is empty: Henry explains that he is leaving—the work is not to his taste. Finally I am introduced to Captain Lauth, whom I also remember from the degradation ceremony: another handsome, blond cavalryman from Alsace, in his thirties, who speaks German and ought to be charging around the countryside on horseback. Yet here he is instead, also wearing an apron, hunched over his desk with a strong electric light directed onto a small pile of torn-up notepaper, moving the pieces around with a pair of tweezers. I look to Henry for an explanation. "We should talk about that," he says.

We go back downstairs to the first-floor landing. "That's my office," he says, pointing to a door without opening it, "and there is where Colonel Sandherr works"—he looks suddenly pained—"or used to work, I should say. I suppose that will be yours now."

"Well, I'll need to work somewhere."

To reach it, we pass through a vestibule with a couple of chairs and a hatstand. The office beyond is unexpectedly small and dark. The curtains are drawn. I turn on the light. To my right is a large table, to my left a big steel filing cupboard with a stout lock. Facing me is a desk; to one side of it a second door leads back out to the corridor; behind it is a tall window. I cross to the window and pull back the dusty curtains to disclose an unexpected view over a large formal garden. Topography is my speciality—an awareness of where things lie in relation to one another; precision about streets, distances, terrain—nevertheless, it takes me a moment to realise that I am looking at the rear elevation of the hôtel de Brienne, the minister's garden. It is odd to see it from this angle.

"My God," I say, "if I had a telescope, I could practically see into the minister's office!"

"Do you want me to get you one?"

"No." I look at Henry. I can't make out whether he's joking. I turn back to the window and try to open it. I hit the catch a couple of times with the heel of my hand, but it has rusted shut. Already I am starting to loathe this place. "All right," I say, wiping the rust off my hand, "I'm clearly going to rely on you a great deal, Major, certainly for the first few months. This is all very new to me."

"Naturally, Colonel. First, permit me to give you your keys." He holds out five, on an iron ring attached to a light chain, which I could clip to my belt. "This is to the front door. This is to your office door. This is your safe. This: your desk."

"And this?"

"That lets you into the garden of the hôtel de Brienne. When you need to see the minister, that's the way you go. General Mercier presented the key to Colonel Sandherr."

"What's wrong with the front door?"

"This way's quicker. And more private."

"Do we have a telephone?"

"Yes, it's outside Captain Valdant's room."

"What about a secretary?"

"Colonel Sandherr didn't trust them. If you need a file, ask Gribelin. If you need help copying, you can use one of the captains. Valdant can type."

I feel as if I have wandered into some strange religious sect, with obscure private rituals. The Ministry of War is built on the site of an old nunnery, and the officers of the General Staff on the rue Saint-Dominique are nicknamed "the Dominicians" because of their secret ways. But already I can see they have nothing on the Statistical Section.

"You were going to tell me what Captain Lauth was working on just now."

"We have an agent inside the German Embassy. The agent supplies us regularly with documents that have been thrown away and are supposed to go to the embassy furnace to be burned with the trash. Instead they come to us. Mostly they've been torn up, so we have to piece them together. It's a skilled job. Lauth is good at it."

"This was how you first got onto Dreyfus?"

"It was."

"By sticking together a torn-up letter?"

"Exactly."

"My God, from such small beginnings . . . ! Who is this agent?"

"We always use the code name 'Auguste.' The product is referred to as 'the usual route.'"

I smile. "All right, let me put it another way: who is 'Auguste'?" Henry is reluctant to reply, but I am determined to press him: if I am ever to get a grip on this job, I must know how the service functions from top to bottom, and the sooner the better. "Come now, Major Henry, I am the head of this section. You will have to tell me."

Reluctantly he says, "A woman called Marie Bastian; one of the embassy cleaners. In particular she cleans the office of the German military attaché."

"How long has she been working for us?"

"Five years. I'm her handler. I pay her two hundred francs a month." He cannot resist adding boastfully, "It's the greatest bargain in Europe!"

"How does she get the material to us?"

"I meet her in a church near here, sometimes every week, sometimes two—in the evenings, when it's quiet. Nobody sees us. I take the stuff straight home."

"You take it home?" I can't conceal my surprise. "Is that safe?"

"Absolutely. There's only my wife and me, and our baby lad. I sort through it there, take a quick look at whatever's in French—I can't understand German: Lauth handles the German stuff here."

"I see. Good." Although I nod in approval, this procedure strikes me as amateurish in the extreme. But I am not going to pick a fight on my first day. "I have a feeling we are going to get along very well, Major Henry."

"I do hope so, Colonel."

I look at my watch. "If you'll excuse me, I shall have to go out soon to see the Chief of Staff."

"Would you like me to come with you?"

"No." Again I am not sure if he is being serious. "That won't be necessary. He's taking me to lunch."

"Splendid. I'll be in my office if you need me." Our exchange is as formal as a *pas de deux*.

Henry salutes and leaves. I close the door and look around me. My skin crawls slightly; I feel as if I am wearing the outfit of a dead man. There are shadows on the walls where Sandherr's pictures hung, burns on the desk from his cigarettes, ring marks on the table from his drinks. A worn track in the carpet shows where he used to push back his chair. His presence oppresses me. I find the correct key and unlock the safe. Inside are several dozen letters, unopened, addressed to various places around the city, to four or five different names—aliases presumably. These, I guess, must be reports from Sandherr's agents that have been forwarded since he left. I open one—*Unusual activity is reported in the garrison at Metz . . .*—then close it again. Espionage work: how I loathe it. I should never have taken this posting. It seems impossible to imagine that I will ever feel at home.

Beneath the letters is a thin manila envelope containing a large photograph, twenty-five centimetres by twenty. I recognise it immediately from Dreyfus's court-martial—a copy of the covering note, the famous *bordereau*, that accompanied the documents he passed to the Germans. It was the central evidence against him produced in court. Until this morning I had no idea how the Statistical Section had got its hands on it. And no wonder. I have to admire Lauth's handiwork. Nobody looking at it could tell it had once been ripped into pieces: all the tear marks have been carefully touched out, so that it seems like a whole document.

I sit at the desk and unlock it. Despite the slow progressive nature of his illness, Sandherr seems to have ended up vacating the premises in a hurry. A few odds and ends have been left behind. They roll about when I pull open the drawers. Pieces of chalk. A ball of sealing wax. Some foreign coins. Four bullets. And various tins and bottles of medicine: mercury, extract of guaiacum, potassium iodine.

General de Boisdeffre gives me lunch at the Jockey Club to celebrate my appointment, which is decent of him. The windows are all closed, the doors are shut, bowls of freesias and sweet peas have been placed on every table. But nothing can entirely dispel the sweetly sour odour of human excrement. Boisdeffre affects not to notice. He orders a good white burgundy and drinks most of it, his high cheeks gradually flushing the colour of a Virginia creeper in autumn. I drink sparingly and keep a tiny notebook open beside my plate like a good staff officer.

The president of the club, Sosthènes de La Rochefoucauld, duc de Doudeauville, is at the neighbouring table. He comes across to greet the general. Boisdeffre introduces me. The duc's nose and cheekbones look as delicately ridged and fragile as meringues; his handshake is a brush of papery skin against my fingers.

Over potted trout the general talks about the new tsar, Nicholas II. Boisdeffre is anxious to be informed of any Russian anarchist cells that may be active in Paris. "I want you to keep your ears open wide for that one; anything we can pass on to Moscow will be valuable in negotiations." He swallows a morsel of fish and goes on: "An alliance with Russia will solve our inferiority vis-à-vis the Germans with one diplomatic stroke. It is worth a hundred thousand men, at least. That is why half my time is devoted to foreign affairs. At the highest level, the border between the military and the political ceases to exist. But we must never forget the army must always be above mere party politics."

This prompts him to reminisce about Mercier, no longer Minister of War but now seeing out the years before his retirement as commander of the 4th Army Corps at Le Mans. "He was right to foresee that the President might fall, wrong to believe that he stood any chance of replacing him."

I am so surprised I stop eating, my fork poised midway to my mouth. "General Mercier thought that he might become president?"

"Indeed, he entertained that delusion. This is one of the problems with a republic—at least under a monarchy no one seriously imagines he can become king. When Monsieur Casimir-Perier resigned in January, and the Senate and the Chamber of Deputies convened at Versailles to elect his successor, General Mercier's 'friends'—as it would be delicate to call them—had a flyer circulated, calling on them to elect the man who had just delivered the traitor Dreyfus to the court-martial. He received precisely three votes out of eight hundred."

"I didn't know that."

"I believe it was what our English friends call 'a long shot.'" Boisdeffre smiles. "But now of course the politicians will never forgive him." He dabs at his moustache with his napkin. "You'll have to think a little more politically from now on, Colonel, if you're going to fulfil the great hopes we all have of you." I bow my head slightly, as if the Chief of Staff is hanging a decoration round my neck. He says, "Tell me, what do you make of the Dreyfus business?"

"Distasteful," I reply. "Squalid. Distracting. I'm glad it's over."

"Ah, but is it, though? I am thinking politically here, rather than militarily. The Jews are a most persistent race. For them, Dreyfus sitting on his rock is like an aching tooth. It obsesses them. They won't leave it alone."

"He's an emblem of their shame. But what can they do?"

"I'm not sure. But they'll do something, we may count on that." Boisdeffre stares over the traffic in the rue Rabelais and falls silent for a few moments. His profile in the odiferous sunlight is immensely distinguished, carved in flesh by centuries of breeding. I am reminded of the effigy of a long-suffering Norman knight, kneeling in some Bayeux chapel. He says thoughtfully, "What Dreyfus said to that young captain, about not having a motive for treason—I think we ought to be ready with an answer to that. I'd like you to keep the case active. Investigate the family—'feed the file,' as your predecessor used to say. See if you can find a little more evidence about motives that we can hold in reserve in case we need it."

"Yes, of course, General." I add it to the list in my notebook, just beneath "Russian anarchists": "Dreyfus: motive?"

The *rillettes de canard* arrive and the conversation moves on to the current German naval review at Kiel.

That afternoon I extract the agents' letters from the safe in my new office, stuff them into my briefcase and set off to visit Colonel Sandherr. His address, given to me by Gribelin, is only a ten-minute walk away, across the river in the rue Léonce Reynaud. His wife answers the door. When I tell her I'm her husband's successor, she draws back her head like a snake about to strike: "You have his position, monsieur, what more do you want from him?"

"If it's inconvenient, madame, I can come back another time."

"Oh, can you? How kind! But why would it be convenient for him to see you at *any* time?"

"It's all right, my dear." From somewhere behind her comes Sandherr's weary voice. "Picquart is an Alsace man. Let him in."

"You," she mutters bitterly, still staring at me although she is addressing her husband, "you're too good to these people!" Nevertheless, she stands aside to let me pass.

Sandherr calls out, "I'm in the bedroom, Picquart, come through," and I follow the direction of his voice into a heavily shaded room that smells of disinfectant. He is propped up in bed in a nightshirt.

He switches on a lamp. As he turns his unshaven face towards me, I see it is covered in sores, some still raw and weeping, others pitted and dry. I had heard there had been a sharp deterioration in his condition; I had no idea it was as bad as this. He warns: "I'd stay there if I were you."

"Excuse me for this intrusion, Colonel," I say, trying not to allow my distaste to show, "but I rather need your help." I hoist the briefcase to show him.

"I thought you might." He points a wavering finger at my case. "It's all in there, is it? Let me see."

I take out the letters and approach the bed. "I assume they're from agents." I place them on his blanket, just within his reach, and step back. "But I don't know who they are, or who to trust."

"My watchword is: don't trust anyone, then you won't be disappointed." He turns to stretch for his spectacles on the nightstand and I see how the sores that swirl under the stubble of his jaw and throat run in a livid track across the side of his neck. He puts on the glasses and squints at one of the letters. "Sit down. Pull up that chair. Do you have a pencil? You will need to write this down."

For the next two hours, with barely a pause for breath, Sandherr takes me on a guided tour through his secret world: this man works in a laundry supplying the German garrison in Metz; that man has a position in the railway company on the eastern frontier; she is the mistress of a German officer in Mulhouse; he is a petty criminal in Lorraine who will burgle houses to order; he is a drunk; he is a homosexual; she is a patriot who keeps house for the military governor and who lost her nephew in '70; trust this one and that one; take no notice of him or her; he needs three hundred francs immediately; he should be dispensed with altogether . . . I take it down at dictation speed until we have worked through all the letters. He gives me a list of other agents and their code names from memory, and tells me to ask Gribelin for their addresses. He starts to tire.

"Would you like me to leave?" I ask.

"In a minute." He gestures feebly. "In the chiffonier over there are a couple of things you ought to have." He watches as I kneel to open it. I take out a metal cash box, very heavy, and also a large envelope. "Open them," he says. The cash box is unlocked. Inside is a small fortune in gold coins and banknotes: mostly French francs, but also German marks and English pounds. He says, "There should be about forty-eight thousand francs' worth. When you run short, speak to Boisdeffre. Monsieur Paléologue of the Foreign Ministry is also under instructions to contribute. Use it for agents, special payments. Be sure to keep plenty by you. Put the box in your bag."

I do as he tells me, and then I open the envelope. It contains about a hundred sheets of paper: lists of names and addresses, neatly handwritten, arranged by *département*.

Sandherr says, "It needs to be kept updated."

"What is it?"

"My life's work." He emits a dry laugh, which degenerates into a cough.

I turn the pages. There must be two or three thousand people listed. "Who are they all?"

"Suspected traitors, to be arrested immediately in the event of war. The regional police are only allowed to know the names in their respective areas. There is one other master copy apart from that one, which the minister keeps. There's also a longer list that Gribelin has."

"Longer?"

"It contains one hundred thousand names."

"What a list!" I exclaim. "It must be as thick as a Bible! Who are they?"

"Aliens, to be interned if hostilities break out. And that doesn't include the Jews."

"You think if there's a war the Jews should be interned?"

"At the very least they should be obliged to register, and placed under curfew and travel restrictions." Shakily, Sandherr removes his spectacles and places them on the nightstand. He lies back on the pillow and closes his eyes. "My wife is very loyal to me, as you saw—more loyal than most wives would be in these circumstances. She thinks it's a disgrace I've been placed on the retired list. But I tell her I'm happy to fade into the background. When I look around Paris and see the number of foreigners everywhere, and consider the

degeneracy of every moral and artistic standard, I realise I no longer know my own city. This is why we lost in '70—the nation is no
longer pure."

I begin gathering up the letters and packing them into my briefcase. This sort of talk always bores me: old men complaining that
the world is going to the dogs. It's so banal. I am anxious to get away
from this oppressive presence. But there is one other thing I need
to ask. "You mention the Jews," I say. "General Boisdeffre is worried
about a potential revival of interest in the Dreyfus case."

"General Boisdeffre," says Sandherr, as if stating a scientific fact,
"is an old woman."

"He's concerned at the lack of an obvious motive . . ."

"Motive?" mutters Sandherr. His head starts shaking on the pillow, whether in disbelief or from the effects of his condition I cannot
tell. "What is he prattling on about? Motive? Dreyfus is a Jew, more
German than French! Most of his family live in Germany! All his
income was derived from Germany. How much more motive does
the general require?"

"Nevertheless, he'd like me to 'feed the file.' Those were his
words."

"The Dreyfus file is fat enough. Seven judges saw it and unanimously declared him guilty. Talk to Henry about it if you have any
trouble."

And with that Sandherr draws the blankets around his shoulders
and rolls onto his side with his back to me. I wait for a minute or so.
Eventually I thank him for his help and say goodbye. But if he hears
me, he makes no answer.

I stand on the pavement outside Sandherr's apartment, mometarily
dazzled by the daylight after the gloom of his sickroom. My briefcase
stuffed with money and the names of traitors and spies feels heavy
in my hand. As I cross the avenue du Trocadéro in search of a cab,
I glance to my left to make sure I am not about to be run over, at
which point I vaguely register an elegant apartment block with a
double door, and the number 6 on a blue tile beside it. At first I

think nothing of it, but then I come to a dead stop and look at it again: *no. 6 avenue du Trocadéro*. I recognise this address. I have seen it written down many times. This is where Dreyfus was living at the time of his arrest.

I glance back to the rue Léonce Reynaud. It is, of course, a coincidence, but still a singular one: that Dreyfus should have lived so close to his nemesis they could practically have seen each other from their respective front doors; at the very least they must have passed in the street often, walking to and from the War Ministry at the same times every day. I step to the edge of the pavement, tilt my head back and shield my eyes to examine the grand apartment building. Each tall window has a wrought-iron balcony, wide enough to sit on, looking out across the Seine—a much more opulent property than the Sandherrs', tucked away in its narrow cobbled street.

My eye is caught by something at a first-floor window: the pale face of a young boy, like an invalid confined indoors, looking down at me; an adult comes to join him—a young woman with a face as white as his, framed by dark curls—his mother, perhaps. She stands behind him with her hands on his arms, and together they stare at me—a uniformed colonel watching them from the street—until she whispers in his ear and gently pulls him away, and they disappear.

4

The following morning I describe the strange apparition to Major
Henry. He frowns.

"The first-floor window of number six? That must have been
Dreyfus's wife, and his little boy—what is he called?—Pierre, that's
it. And there's a girl, Jeanne. Madame Dreyfus keeps the kids at
home all day, so they don't pick up stories about their father. She's
told them he's on a special mission abroad."

"And they believe her?"

"Why wouldn't they? They're only tiny."

"How do you know all this?"

"Oh, we still keep an eye on them, don't worry."

"How close an eye?"

"We have an agent on their domestic staff. We follow them. We
intercept their mail."

"Even six months after Dreyfus was convicted?"

"Colonel Sandherr had a theory that Dreyfus might turn out to
be part of a spying syndicate. He thought that if we watched the
family we might uncover leads to other traitors."

"But we haven't?"

"Not yet."

I lounge back in my chair and study Henry. He is friendly-looking,
apparently out of condition but still, I would guess, underneath the
layer of fat, physically strong: the sort of fellow who would be stood
a lot of drinks in a bar, and would know how to tell a good story
when he was in the mood. We are about as dissimilar as it is possible
for two men to be. "Did you know," I ask, "that Colonel Sandherr's
apartment is only about a hundred metres from the Dreyfus place?"

From time to time a sly look can come into Henry's eyes. It is the only crack in his armour of bonhomie. He says, in an off-handed way, "Is it as close as that? I hadn't realised."

"Yes. In fact it seems to me, looking at the location, they're bound to have met occasionally, even if only casually in the street."

"That may well be. I do know the colonel tried to avoid him. He didn't like him—thought he was always asking too many questions."

I bet he didn't like him, I think. *The Jew with the vast apartment and a view of the river* . . . I imagine Sandherr striding briskly towards the rue Saint-Dominique at nine o'clock one morning and the young captain attempting to fall in beside him and engage him in conversation. Dreyfus always seemed to me, when I dealt with him, to have something missing from his brain: some vital piece of social equipment which should have told him when he was boring people or that they didn't wish to speak to him. But he was incapable of recognising his effect on others, while Sandherr, who could see a conspiracy in a pair of butterflies alighting on the same bloom, would have become increasingly suspicious of his inquisitive Jewish neighbour.

I open my desk drawer and take out the various medicines I discovered the previous day: a couple of tins and two small dark blue bottles. I show them to Henry. "Colonel Sandherr left these behind."

"That was an oversight. May I?" Henry takes them from me with fumbling hands. In his clumsiness he almost drops one of the bottles. "I'll see they get returned to him."

I can't resist saying, "Mercury, extract of guaiacum and potassium iodine . . . You do know what these are normally used to treat, don't you?"

"No. I'm not a doctor . . ."

I decide not to pursue it. "I want a full report of what the Dreyfus family are up to—who they're seeing, whatever they might be doing to help the prisoner. I also want to read all of Dreyfus's correspondence, to and from Devil's Island. I assume it's being censored, and we have copies?"

"Naturally. I'll tell Gribelin to arrange it." He hesitates. "Might I ask, Colonel: why all this interest in Dreyfus?"

"General Boisdeffre thinks it might turn into a political issue. He wants us to be prepared."

"I understand. I'll get on to it at once."

He leaves, cradling Sandherr's medicines. Of course he knows exactly what they're prescribed for: we've both hauled enough men out of unregistered brothels in our time to know the standard treatment. And so I am left to ponder the implications of inheriting a secret intelligence service from a predecessor who is apparently suffering from tertiary syphilis, more commonly known as general paralysis of the insane.

That afternoon I write my first secret intelligence report for the General Staff—a *blanc*, as they are known in the rue Saint-Dominique. I cobble it together from the local German newspapers and from one of the agents' letters that Sandherr has elucidated for me: *A correspondent from Metz reports that, for the past few days, there has been great activity among the troops in the Metz garrison. There is no noise and alarm in the city, but the military authorities are pushing the troops intensively* . . .

I read it over when I've finished and ask myself: is this important? Is it even true? Frankly, I have not the faintest idea. I know only that I am expected to submit a *blanc* at least once a week, and that this is the best I can do for my first attempt. I send it over the road to the Chief of Staff's office, bracing myself for a rebuke for crediting such worthless gossip. Instead, Boisdeffre acknowledges receipt, thanks me, forwards a copy to the head of the infantry (I can imagine the conversation in the officers' club: *I hear on the grapevine that the Germans are up to something in Metz* . . .), and fifty thousand troops in the eastern frontier region have their lives made slightly more miserable by several days of additional drills and forced marches.

It is my first lesson in the cabalistic power of "secret intelligence": two words that can make otherwise sane men abandon their reason and cavort like idiots.

A day or two later, Henry brings an agent to my office to brief me about Dreyfus. He introduces him as François Guénée, of the Sûreté.* He is in his forties, yellow-skinned with the effects of nicotine or alcohol or both, with that manner, at once bullying and obsequious, typical of a certain type of policeman. As we shake hands I recognise him from my first morning: he was one of those who were sitting around smoking their pipes and playing cards downstairs. Henry says, "Guénée has been running the surveillance operation on the Dreyfus family. I thought you'd want to hear how things stand."

"Please." I gesture and we take our places around the table in the corner of my office. Guénée has a file with him; so has Henry.

Guénée begins. "In accordance with Colonel Sandherr's instructions, I concentrated my inquiries on the traitor's older brother, Mathieu Dreyfus." From the file he extracts a studio photograph and slides it across the table. Mathieu is handsome, even dashing: he is the one who ought to have been the army captain, I think, rather than Alfred, who looks like a bank manager. Guénée continues, "The subject is thirty-seven years old, and has moved from the family home in Mulhouse to Paris with the sole purpose of organising the campaign on behalf of his brother."

"So there is a campaign?"

"Yes, Colonel: he writes letters to prominent people, and has let it be known he is willing to pay good money for information."

"You know they're very rich," puts in Henry, "the wife of Dreyfus even more so. Her family are the Hadamards—diamond merchants."

"And is the brother getting anywhere?"

"There's a medical man from Le Havre, a Dr. Gibert, who is an old friend of the President of the Republic. Right at the start he offered to intercede on the family's behalf with President Fauré."

"Has he done so?"

Guénée consults his file. "The doctor met the President for breakfast at the Élysée on February twenty-first. Afterwards Gibert went straight to the hôtel de l'Athénée, where Mathieu Drey-

---

* The French detective police force.

fus was waiting—one of our men had followed him there from his apartment."

He gives me the agent's report. *Subjects were seated in lobby and appeared greatly animated. Positioned myself at adjoining table and heard B remark to A the following: "I'm telling you what the President said—it was secret evidence given to judges that secured conviction, not evidence in court." Same point repeated with emphasis several times . . . After departure of B, A remained seated in state of obvious emotion. A paid bill (see copy attached) and left hotel at 9:25.*

I look at Henry. "The *President* has revealed that the judges were shown secret evidence?"

Henry shrugs. "People talk. It was bound to come out one day."

"Yes, but the *President* . . . ? You're not concerned?"

"No. Why? It's just a bit of legal procedure. It doesn't alter a thing."

I brood on this; I'm not so sure. I think of how my lawyer friend Leblois might react if he heard about it. "I agree it doesn't alter Dreyfus's guilt. But if it were to become widely known that he was convicted on the basis of secret evidence that he and his lawyer never even saw, then some will certainly argue he didn't get a fair trial." Now I start to understand why Boisdeffre scents political trouble. "How are the family planning to use this information, do we know?"

Henry glances at Guénée, who shakes his head. "They were all very excited about it at first. There was a family conference in Basel. They brought in a journalist, a Jew called Lazare. He moves in anarchist circles. But that was four months ago; since then, they've done nothing."

"Well, they have done *one* thing," says Henry, with a wink. "Tell the colonel about Madame Léonie—that'll cheer him up!"

"Oh yes, Madame Léonie!" Guénée laughs and rummages through his report. "She's another friend of Dr. Gibert." He hands me a second photograph, of a plain-faced woman of about fifty, staring straight at the camera, wearing a Norman bonnet.

"And who is Madame Léonie?"

"She's a somnambulist."

"Are you serious?"

"Absolutely! She goes into a clairvoyant sleep and tells Mathieu facts about his brother's case which she claims to get from the spirit world. He met her in Le Havre and was so impressed he brought her to Paris. He's given her a room in his apartment."

"Can you believe it?" Henry roars with laughter. "They are literally stumbling around in the dark! Really, Colonel, we have nothing to worry about from these people."

I lay the photographs of Mathieu Dreyfus and Madame Léonie side by side and I feel my uneasiness begin to lift. Table-tapping, fortune-telling, communing with the dead: these are all the fashion in Paris at the moment; sometimes one despairs of one's fellow men. "You're right, Henry. It shows they're getting nowhere. Even if they have discovered there was a secret file of evidence, they obviously realise that on its own it means nothing. We just need to make sure it stays like that." I turn to Guénée. "How are you handling the surveillance?"

"We have them very tightly surrounded, Colonel. Madame Dreyfus's nanny reports to us weekly. The concierge in Mathieu Dreyfus's apartment building in the rue de Châteaudun is our informant. We have another who works as his wife's maid. His cook and her fiancé keep an eye out for us. We follow him wherever he goes. All the family's communications are diverted here by the postal authorities, and we make copies."

"And this is the correspondence of Dreyfus himself." Henry holds up the file he has brought with him and hands it over to me. "They need it back tomorrow."

It is tied with black ribbon and stamped with the official seal of the Colonial Ministry. I unfasten it and flick open the cover. Some of the letters are originals—the ones the censor has decided not to let through and which therefore have been retained in the ministry—others are copies of the correspondence that was cleared. *My dear Lucie, I ask myself in truth how I can go on living* . . . I put the letter back and take out another. *My poor Fred darling, what anguish I felt as I parted from you* . . . It jolts me. It's hard to think of that stiff, awkward, chilly figure as "Fred."

I say, "From now on, I'd like to be copied in to all their correspondence as soon as it arrives at the Colonial Ministry."

"Yes, Colonel."

"In the meantime, Monsieur Guénée, you should continue the surveillance of the family. As long as their agitation is confined to the level of clairvoyance, there is nothing to concern us. However, if it starts to go beyond that, we may have to think again. And at all times be on the lookout for something that might suggest an additional motive for Dreyfus's treason."

"Yes, Colonel."

And with that, the briefing ends.

At the end of the afternoon, I put the file of correspondence into my briefcase and take it home.

It is a still, warm, golden time of day. My apartment is high enough above the street to muffle most of the city's noise; the rest is deadened by the book-lined walls. The floor space is dominated by a grand piano—an Erard—miraculously salvaged from the rubble of Strasbourg and given to me by my mother. I sit in my armchair and tug off my boots. Then I light a cigarette and gaze across at the briefcase sitting on the piano stool. I am supposed to change and go straight out again. I should leave it until I return. But my curiosity is too strong.

I sit at the tiny escritoire between the two windows and take out the file. The first item is a letter sent from the military prison of Cherche-Midi dated 5 December 1894, more than seven weeks after Dreyfus's arrest. It has been neatly copied out by the censor on lined paper:

My dear Lucie,

At last I am able to write you a word. I have just been informed that my trial takes place on the 19th of this month. I am not allowed to see you.

I will not describe to you all that I have suffered; there are no terms in the world strong enough in which to do so.

Do you remember when I used to say to you how happy we were? All life smiled upon us. Then suddenly came a terrible thunderclap, from which my brain is still reeling. I, accused of the most

*monstrous crime that a soldier could commit! Even now I think I
am the victim of a terrible nightmare . . .*

I turn the page and scan the lines rapidly to the end: *I embrace
you a thousand times, for I love you, I adore you. A thousand kisses to
the children. I dare not speak more to you of them. Alfred.*

The next letter, again a copy, is written from his cell a fortnight
later, the day after his conviction: *My bitterness is so great, my heart
so envenomed, that I should already have rid myself of this sad life if the
thought of you had not stayed me, if the fear of increasing your grief still
more had not withheld my hand.*

And then a copy of the reply from Lucie on Christmas Day: *Live
for me, I entreat you my dear friend; gather up your strength, and strive —
we will strive together until the guilty man is found. What will become of
me without you? I shall have nothing to link me with the world . . .*

I feel grubby reading all this. It is like hearing a couple making
love in the next-door room. But at the same time I cannot stop
myself reading on. I leaf through the file until I come to Dreyfus's
description of the degradation ceremony. When he writes of *the
glances of scorn cast upon me* by his former comrades, I wonder if he
has me in mind: *It is easy to understand their feelings; in their place, I
could not have restrained my contempt for an officer who, I was assured,
was a traitor. But alas! that is the pity of it; there is a traitor, but I am not
the man . . .*

I stop and light another cigarette. Do I believe these protesta-
tions of innocence? Not for an instant. I have never met a scoundrel
in my life who hasn't insisted, with exactly this degree of sincerity,
that he is the victim of a miscarriage of justice. It seems to be a
necessary part of the criminal mentality: to survive captivity, one
must somehow convince oneself one is not guilty. Madame Dreyfus,
on the other hand, I do feel sorry for. It is obvious she trusts in him
entirely—no, more than that, she venerates him, as if he is some
kind of holy martyr: *The dignity of your demeanour made a deep impression upon many hearts; and when the hour of rehabilitation comes, as it
will come, the remembrance of the sufferings that you endured on that
terrible day will be graven in the memory of mankind . . .*

———

With some reluctance I have to break off here. I lock the file inside the escritoire, shave, change into a clean dress uniform, and set off to the home of my friends the comte and comtesse de Comminges.

I have known Aimery de Comminges, baron de Saint-Lary, since we were stationed in Tonkin together more than a decade ago. I was a young junior staff officer; he an even younger and more junior lieutenant. For two years we fought the Vietnamese in the Red River delta and knocked around Saigon and Hanoi, and when we returned to France our friendship prospered. He introduced me to his parents and to his younger sisters, Daisy, Blanche and Isabelle. All three women were musical, single, high-spirited, and gradually a salon arose, consisting of them and their friends and those army comrades of Aimery's who took—or, for the sake of meeting the sisters, pretended to take—an interest in music.

Six years on the salon persists, and it is to one of these musical soirées that I am bidden tonight. As usual, for purposes of fitness as much as economy, I walk to the party rather than take a cab—and walk briskly at that, for I am in danger of being late. The de Comminges' family *hôtel* stands, ancient and massive, on the boulevard Saint-Germain. I can tell it from a distance by the carriages and cabs drawn up to drop off guests. Inside I am greeted with a friendly salute and a warm double handshake by Aimery, now a captain on the staff of the Minister of War, and then I kiss his wife, Mathilde, whose family, the Waldner von Freundsteins, is one of the oldest in Alsace. Mathilde is the mistress of this house now, and has been for a year, ever since the old comte died.

"Go on up," she whispers, her hand on my arm. "We'll be starting in a few minutes." Her method of playing the charming hostess—and it is not a bad one—is to make even the most commonplace remark sound like an intimate secret. "And you'll stay to dinner, won't you, my dear Georges?"

"I would love to, thank you." In truth, I had been hoping to get away early, but I submit without demur. Bachelors of forty are society's stray cats. We are taken in by households and fed and made a fuss of; in return we are expected to provide amusement, submit with good grace to occasionally intrusive affection ("So when are you going to get married, eh, Georges?"), and always agree to make up the numbers at dinner, however short the notice.

As I move on into the house, Aimery shouts after me, "Blanche is looking for you!" and almost at the same moment I see his sister dodging through the crowded hall towards me. Her gown, with matching headdress, contains a great number of feathers dyed dark green, crimson and gold.

"Blanche," I say, as she kisses me, "you look like a particularly succulent pheasant."

"Now I hope you are going to be a Good God this evening," she replies chirpily, "and not a Horrid God, because I have prepared a nice surprise for you," and she takes my arm and leads me towards the garden, in the opposite direction to everyone else.

I offer token resistance. "I think Mathilde wants us all to go upstairs . . ."

"Don't be silly! It's barely seven!" She lowers her voice. "Is this a *German* thing, do you suppose?"

She marches me towards the glass doors that open onto the tiny strip of garden, separated from its neighbours by a high wall strung with unlit Chinese lanterns. Waiters are collecting discarded glasses of orangeade and liqueurs. The drinkers have all left to go upstairs. Only one woman stands alone, with her back to me, and when she turns I see it is Pauline. She smiles.

"There," says Blanche, with a strange edge to her voice, "you see? A surprise."

It is always Blanche who arranges the concerts. Tonight she presents her latest discovery, a young Catalan prodigy, Monsieur Casals, only eighteen, whom she found playing second cello in the theatre orchestra of the Folies-Marigny. He begins with the Saint-Saëns cello sonata, and from the opening chords it is clear he is a marvel. Normally I would sit rapt, but tonight my attention wanders. I glance around the audience, arranged against the walls of the grand salon, facing the players in the centre. Out of sixty or so spectators, I count a dozen uniforms, mostly cavalrymen like Aimery, half of whom I know for a fact are attached to the General Staff. And after a while it seems to me that I am attracting some sidelong looks myself: the youngest colonel in the army, unmarried, sitting beside the attractive wife of a senior official of the Foreign Ministry, and no sign anywhere of her husband. For a colonel in a position such as mine, to be caught in an adulterous affair would be a scandal that could ruin a career. I try to put it out of my mind and concentrate on the music, but I am uneasy.

In the interval Pauline and I return to the garden, Blanche walking between us, clasping each of us by the arm. A couple of officers, old friends of mine, come over to congratulate me on my promotion, and I introduce them to Pauline. "This is Major Albert Curé—we were in Tonkin together with Aimery. This is Madame Monnier. And this is Captain William Lallemand de Marais—"

"Also known as the Demigod," interrupts Blanche.

Pauline smiles. "Why?"

"In honour of Loge in *Das Rheingold,* of course—the demigod of fire. You must see the resemblance, my dear? Look at that passion! Captain Lallemand is the Demigod, and Georges is the Good God."

"I don't know very much Wagner, I'm afraid."

Lallemand, the keenest student of music in our circle, affects shocked disbelief. "Don't know very much Wagner! Colonel Picquart, you must take Madame Monnier to Bayreuth!"

Curé asks, a little too pointedly for my liking, "And does Monsieur Monnier enjoy the opera?"

"Unfortunately my husband dislikes all forms of music."

After they have moved off, Pauline says quietly, "Do you want me to leave?"

"No, why would I want that?" We are drinking orangeade. The great stink has lifted in the last day or so; the breezes of the faubourg Saint-Germain are warm and blossomy with the scent of a summer evening.

"Only you seem very uncomfortable, my darling."

"No, it's just I wasn't aware that you and Blanche were acquainted, that's all."

"Isabelle took me to tea with Alix Tocnaye a month ago, and she was there."

"And where is Philippe?"

"He's out of Paris tonight. He doesn't get back until tomorrow."

The implication, the offer, hangs unspoken in the air.

"What about the girls?" Pauline's daughters are ten and seven. "Do you have to get back to them?"

"They're staying with Philippe's sister."

"Ah, so now I know what Blanche meant by my 'surprise'!" I am not sure whether to be amused or annoyed. "Why did you decide to confide in her?"

"I didn't. I thought you had."

"Not I!"

"But the way she spoke—she led me to believe you had. That's why I let her arrange this evening." We stare at each other. And then, by a process of intuition or deduction too rapid for me to follow, she says, "Blanche is in love with you."

I laugh in alarm. "She is not!"

"At least you must have had an affair with her?"

I lie. What else should a gentleman do on these occasions? "My darling Pauline, she's fifteen years younger than I am. I'm like an older brother to her."

"But she watches you all the time. She's obsessed with you and now she's guessed about us."

"If Blanche was in love with me," I say quietly, "she'd hardly arrange for me to spend the night with you."

Pauline smiles and shakes her head. "That's exactly what she would do. If she can't have you, she'll have the satisfaction of controlling whoever does."

Instinctively we both check to see we are unobserved. A footman is doing the rounds, whispering to the guests that the concert is about to resume. The garden is beginning to empty. A captain in the dragoons stops on the threshold and turns to look at us.

Pauline says suddenly, "Let's just go now, before the second part. Let's miss the dinner."

"And leave two empty places for everyone to notice? We might as well put an announcement in *Le Figaro*."

No, there is nothing for it but to endure the evening—the string quartet in the second half, the two encores, the champagne afterwards, the lingering goodbyes of those who have not been invited to dinner but hope for a last-minute reprieve. Throughout all this Pauline and I carefully avoid each other, which is of course the surest sign of a couple who are having an affair.

It is after ten by the time we sit down to eat. We are a table of sixteen. I am between Aimery's widowed mother, the dowager comtesse—all black ruffled silk and dead white skin, like the ghost in *Don Giovanni*—and Blanche's sister, Isabelle, recently married into an immensely wealthy banking family, proprietors of one of the five great vineyards of Bordeaux. She speaks expertly of appellations and grand crus, but she might as well be talking Polynesian for all I am taking in. I have an odd, almost dizzying sense of disconnection— the sophisticated talk is just a babble of phonemes, the music mere scrapes and twangs of gut and wire. I look down to the far end of the table, to where Pauline is listening to Isabelle's banker husband, a young man whose pedigree breeding has given him an appearance so refined that it is almost foetus-like, as if it were an error of taste even to emerge from the womb. I catch Blanche's eye in the candlelight, glittering out at me from within her game-bird plumage, the woman scorned, and I look away. We finally rise at midnight.

I am careful to leave the house before Pauline, to preserve appearances. "You," I say to Blanche at the door, wagging my finger, "are a wicked woman."

"Good night, Georges," she says sadly.

I walk up the boulevard searching for the white light of a cab heading home to its depot at the Arc de Triomphe. Plenty of blues and reds and yellows bob past until eventually a white appears, and by the time I have stepped out into the street to hail it, and it has clattered to a halt, Pauline is already coming along the pavement to join me. I take her arm and help her up. I tell the driver, "Rue Yvon-Villarceau, the corner of the rue Copernic," and then I haul myself in after her. She lets me kiss her briefly then pushes me away.

"No, I need to know what all that was about."

"Surely not? Do you really?"

"Yes."

I sigh and take her hand. "Poor Blanche is simply very unhappy in her love affairs. Whichever man in the room is the most unsuitable or unobtainable, you may be sure that he is the one whom Blanche will fall for. There was quite a scandal a couple of years ago, all hushed up, but it caused a lot of embarrassment for the family, especially to Aimery."

"Why especially to Aimery?"

"Because the man involved was an officer on the General Staff—a superior officer, recently widowed, a lot older than Blanche—and it was Aimery who brought him into the house and introduced them."

"What happened?"

I take out my cigarette case and offer one to Pauline. She refuses. I light up. I feel uncomfortable talking about the whole business, but I guess Pauline has a right to know, and I trust her not to spread the tale.

"She and this officer had an affair. It went on for some time, a year perhaps. Then Blanche met someone else, a young aristocrat her own age and much more suitable. This young man proposed. The family were delighted. Blanche tried to break off her relationship with the officer. But he refused to accept it. Then Aimery's father, the old comte, began receiving messages from a blackmailer, threatening to expose the affair. The comte ended up going to the Préfecture of the Paris police."

"My God, it's like a story out of Balzac!"

"It gets better than that. At one stage the comte paid five hundred francs for the return of a particularly compromising letter Blanche had written to her widowed lover, which was allegedly in the hands of a mysterious woman. The woman was supposed to have turned up in a park wearing a veil in order to return it. The police investigated the matter and the blackmailer proved to be the widowed officer himself."

"No? I don't believe it! What happened to him?"

"Nothing. He's very well connected. He was allowed to continue with his career. He's still on the General Staff—a colonel, in fact."

"And what did Blanche's fiancé make of it?"

"He refused to have anything more to do with her."

Pauline sits back in her seat, considering all this. "Then I feel sorry for her."

"She is silly on occasions. But curiously good-hearted. And gifted in her way."

"What is the name of this colonel, so I can slap his face if I ever meet him?"

"You won't forget his name once you've heard it—Armand du Paty de Clam. He always wears a monocle." I am on the point of adding the curious detail that he was the officer in charge of the investigation into Captain Dreyfus, but in the end I don't. That information is classified, and besides, Pauline has started nuzzling her cheek against my shoulder and suddenly I have other things on my mind.

My bed is narrow, a soldier's cot. To prevent ourselves slipping to the floor, we lie entwined in each other's arms, naked to the warm night air. At three in the morning, Pauline's breathing is slow and regular, rising from some deep soft seabed of sleep. I am wide awake. I stare over her shoulder at the open window and try to imagine us married. If we were, would we ever experience a night like this? Isn't an awareness of their transience what gives these moments their exquisite edge? And I have such a horror of constant company.

I extract my arm carefully from beneath hers, feel for the rug with my feet, and pull myself away from the bed.

In the sitting room the night sky sheds enough light for me to find my way around. I pull on a robe and light the gas lamp on the escritoire. I unlock a drawer and take out the file of Dreyfus's correspondence, and while my lover sleeps I resume reading from where I left off.

5

The story of the four months after the degradation is easy to follow in the file, which has been arranged by some bureaucrat
in strict chronological order. It was twelve days later, in the middle
of the night, that Dreyfus was taken from his prison cell in Paris,
locked in a convict wagon in the gare d'Orleans and dispatched on
a ten-hour rail journey through the snowbound countryside to the
Atlantic coast. In the station at La Rochelle, a crowd was waiting.
All afternoon they hammered on the sides of the train and shouted
threats and insults: "Death to the Jew!" "Judas!" "Death to the traitor!" It wasn't until nightfall that his guards decided to risk moving
him. Dreyfus ran the gauntlet.

Île de Ré prison
21 January 1895

My darling Lucie,

*The other day, when I was insulted at La Rochelle, I wanted
to escape from my warders, to present my naked breast to those
to whom I was a just object of indignation, and say to them: "Do
not insult me; my soul, which you cannot know, is free from all
stain; but if you think I am guilty, come, take my body, I give it
up to you without regret." Then, perhaps, when under the stinging
bite of physical pain I had cried "Vive la France!" they might have
believed in my innocence!*

*But what am I asking for night and day? Justice! Justice! Is this
the nineteenth century, or have we gone back some hundred years?
Is it possible that innocence is not recognised in an age of enlight-
enment and truth? Let them search. I ask no favour, but I ask the*

justice that is the right of every human being. Let them continue to search; let those who possess powerful means of investigation use them towards this object; it is for them a sacred duty of humanity and justice . . .

I reread the final paragraph. There is something odd about it. I see what he is doing. Ostensibly he is writing to his wife. But knowing his words are bound to pass through many hands along the way, he is also sending a message to the arbiters of his fate in Paris; to me, in fact, although he would never have guessed that I would be sitting at Sandherr's desk. *Let those who possess powerful means of investigation . . .* It does not alter my belief in his guilt, but it is a clever tactic; it gives me pause for thought: he certainly does not give up, this fellow.

Paris
January 1895

Fred, my dearest,
Very fortunately I had not read the newspapers yesterday morning; my people had tried to conceal from me the knowledge of the ignoble scene at La Rochelle, otherwise I should have gone mad with despair . . .

Next in the file is a letter from Lucie to the minister, requesting permission to visit her husband on the Île de Ré to say goodbye. The request is granted for 13 February, subject to stringent restrictions, which are also listed. The prisoner is to remain standing between two guards at one end of the room; Madame Dreyfus is to remain seated at the other end, accompanied by a third guard; the prison governor will stand between them; they are not to discuss anything connected with the trial; there is to be no physical contact. A letter from Lucie offering to have her hands tied behind her back if she can approach a little closer is stamped "refused."

Fred to Lucie: *The few moments I passed with you were full of joy to me, though it was impossible to tell you all that was in my heart* (14 February). Lucie to Fred: *What emotion, what a fearful shock we both felt at seeing each other again, especially you, my poor beloved husband* (16 February). Fred to Lucie: *I wanted to tell you all the admiration I feel for your noble character, for your admirable devotion* (21 February). Hours later, Dreyfus was on a warship, the *Saint-Nazaire*, steaming out into the Atlantic.

Up to now, most of the letters in the file have been copies, presumably because the originals were delivered to the addressee. But from this point on the majority of the pages I turn are in Dreyfus's own hand. His descriptions of the voyage—in an unheated cell on an upper deck, open to the elements, through violent winter storms, watched night and day by warders with revolvers who refuse to speak to him—have been retained by the censors in the Colonial Ministry. On the eighth day the weather began to grow warmer. Still Dreyfus did not know his destination and no one was allowed to tell him; his guess was Cayenne. On the fifteenth day of the voyage he wrote to Lucie that the warship had at last anchored, off *three small humps of rock and vegetation in the middle of the ocean's wastes:* Royal Island, St. Joseph's Island and (tiniest of all) Devil's Island. To his astonishment, he discovered that the latter was intended for him alone.

Dearest Lucie . . . My darling Lucie . . . Lucie, dearest . . . Darling wife . . . I love you . . . I yearn for you . . . I think of you . . . I send you the echo of my deep affection . . . So much emotion and time and energy expended in the hope of some connection, only for it to end up in the darkness of this file! But maybe it is better, I think, as I skim the increasingly desperate complaints, that Lucie doesn't read all of this: isn't aware that after the *Saint-Nazaire* dropped anchor in the tropics, her husband had to spend four days locked in his steel box under the ferocious sun without once being allowed on deck, or that when eventually he was landed on Royal Island—while the old leper colony on Devil's Island was demolished and his new quarters prepared—he was locked in a cell with closed shutters and was not allowed out for a month.

My dear,

At last, after thirty days of close confinement, they came to remove me to Devil's Island. By day I am able to walk about in a space a few hundred metres square, followed at every step by warders with rifles; at nightfall (six o'clock) I am locked in my hut, four metres square, closed by an iron grille, before which relays of warders watch me all night long. My rations are half a loaf of bread a day, one third of a kilo of meat three times a week and on other days tinned bacon. To drink I have water. I must gather wood, light a fire, cook my own food, clean my clothes and try to dry them in this humid climate.

It is impossible for me to sleep. This cage, before which the guard walks up and down like a phantom in my dreams, the torment of the vermin that infest me, and the agony in my heart all conspire to make rest impossible.

There was a deluge of rain this morning. When there was an interval I made the round of the small portion of the little island which is reserved to me. It is a barren place; there are a few banana trees and cocoa palms, and dry soil from which basaltic rock emerges everywhere, and that restless ocean which is always howling and muttering at my feet!

I have been thinking much of you, my dear wife, and of our children. I wonder whether my letters reach you. What a sad and terrible martyrdom is this for both of us, for all of us! The guards are forbidden to speak to me. Days pass without a word. My isolation is so complete that it often seems to me that I have been buried alive.

The conditions under which Lucie is allowed to write are strict. She is not allowed to mention the case, or any events relating to it. She is instructed to deposit all letters at the Colonial Ministry by the twenty-fifth of each month. These are then carefully copied and read by the relevant officials in that ministry and in the Ministry of War. Copies are also passed to Major Étienne Bazeries, chief of the cipher bureau in the Foreign Ministry, who checks to see if they may contain encoded messages. (Major Bazeries also scrutinises Dreyfus's letters to Lucie.) I see from the file that the first batch of her letters reached Cayenne at the end of March, but was returned to Paris to be checked again. Only on 12 June, after a four-month silence, did Dreyfus finally receive word from home:

My darling Fred,

I cannot tell you the sadness and the grief I feel while you are going further and further away. My days pass in anxious thoughts, my nights in frightful dreams. Only the children, with their pretty ways and the pure innocence of their souls, succeed in reminding me of the one compelling duty I must fulfil, and that I have no right to give way. So then I gather strength and put my whole heart into bringing them up as you always desired, following your good counsels, and endeavouring to make them noble in heart, so that when you come back you will find your children worthy of their father, and as you would have moulded them.

With my love always, my dearest husband,
Your devoted
Lucie

The file ends here. I put down the last page and light a cigarette. I have been so absorbed, I haven't registered that dawn has come. Behind me in the bedroom I can hear Pauline moving around. I go into my tiny kitchen to make coffee and by the time I emerge carrying two cups she is already dressed and looking around for something.

"I won't," she says distractedly, noticing the coffee, "thank you. I have to go but I'm missing a stocking. Ah!"

She sees it and swoops to retrieve it. She rests her instep on a chair and unrolls the white silk over her toes and heel and strokes it up her calf.

I watch her. "You look like a Manet: *Nana in the Morning.*"

"Isn't Nana a whore?"

"Only in the eyes of bourgeois morality."

"Yes, well I am bourgeois. And so are you. And so, more to the point, are most of your neighbours." She pulls on her shoe and smooths down her dress. "If I leave now, they may not see me."

I pick up her jacket and help her on with it. "At least wait while I put on some clothes, and I'll take you home."

"That would rather defeat the purpose, wouldn't it?" She picks up her bag. Her brightness is terrible. "Goodbye, my darling," she says. "Write to me soon," and with the briefest of kisses she is out of the door and gone.

———

I arrive at the office so early that I expect to have the building to myself. But Bachir, who is dozing in his chair, wakes when I shake him and says that Major Henry is already in his room. I walk upstairs, along the passage, knock briefly on his door and go straight in. My second-in-command is bent over his desk with a magnifying glass and a pair of tweezers; various documents are strewn in front of him. He looks up in surprise. The spectacles perched on the end of his snub nose make him look unexpectedly old and vulnerable. He seems to feel the same; at any rate he quickly takes them off as he gets to his feet.

"Good morning, Colonel. You're in bright and early."

"So are you, Major. I'm starting to think you live here! This needs to go back to the Colonial Ministry." I hand him the Dreyfus correspondence file. "I've finished with it."

"Thanks. What did you make of it?"

"The degree of censorship is extraordinary. I'm not sure there's any need to restrict their correspondence quite so drastically."

"Ah!" Henry gives one of his smirks. "Perhaps you have a more tender heart than the rest of us, Colonel."

I refuse the bait. "Actually, it's not that. If we were to allow Madame Dreyfus to tell her husband what she's doing, it would save us the trouble of having to find out. And if he were permitted to say more about his case, he might make a mistake and reveal something we don't know. In any case, if we're going to eavesdrop, let's at least encourage them to say something."

"I'll pass that along."

"Do." I glance down at the desk. "What's all this?"

"Agent Auguste has made a fresh delivery."

"When did you pick it up?"

"Two nights ago."

I examine a couple of the torn-up notes. "Anything interesting?"

"Not bad."

The letters have been ripped into fragments the size of a fingernail: the German military attaché, Colonel Maximilian von Schwartzkoppen, is obviously careful to shred his communications into unusually tiny pieces. But it is stupid of him not to realise that the only secure way to dispose of paper is to burn it. Henry and Lauth are adept at piecing the scraps back together using tiny strips of transparent adhesive paper to repair the tears. The extra layer imparts to the documents a mysterious texture and stiffness. I turn them over. These are in French rather than German, and filled with romantic touches: *mon cher ami adoré . . . mon adorable lieutenant . . . mon pioupiou . . . mon Maxi . . . je suis à toi . . . toujours à toi . . . toute à toi, mille et mille tendresses . . . à toi toujours.*

"I take it these aren't from the Kaiser. Or maybe they are."

Henry grins. "Our adorable 'Colonel Maxi' is having an affair with a married woman, which is a very foolish thing for a man in his position to do."

For an instant I wonder if this is a barb aimed at me, but when I glance at Henry, he is not looking in my direction but at the letter, with an expression of lascivious satisfaction.

I say, "I thought that Schwartzkoppen was homosexual?"

"Wives or husbands, apparently it's all the same to him."

"Who is she?"

"She signs herself Madame Cornet, which is a false name. She uses her sister's address as a poste restante. But we've followed Schwartzkoppen five times now to their little assignations and we've identified her as the wife of the councillor of the Dutch legation. She's called Hermance de Weede."

"A pretty name."

"For a pretty girl. Thirty-two. Three young kids. He certainly spreads his favours, the gallant colonel."

"How long has this been going on?"

"Since January. We've observed them having lunch in a booth at La Tour d'Argent—they took a room in the hotel upstairs afterwards. We've also followed them strolling around the Champs de Mars. He's careless."

"And why is it of such interest to us that we expend our resources following a man and a woman who are having an affair?"

Henry regards me as if I am a halfwit. "Because it leaves him open to blackmail."

"By whom?"

"By us. By anyone. It's hardly something he'd want known, is it?"

The notion that we might try to blackmail the German military attaché for an adulterous liaison with the wife of a senior Dutch diplomat strikes me as far-fetched, but I keep my counsel.

"And you say this batch came in two nights ago?"

"Yes, I worked on it at home."

There is a pause while I weigh what I need to say. "My dear Henry," I begin carefully, "I don't want you to take this the wrong way, but I really think that material as sensitive as this should come straight into the office the moment it's collected. Imagine if the Germans found out what we're doing!"

"It never left my sight, Colonel, I assure you."

"That's not the point. It's sloppy procedure. In future I want all of the Auguste material to come direct to me. I'll keep it in my safe, and I'll decide what leads are followed and who handles it."

Henry's face flushes. Astonishingly for such a big and hearty fellow, he seems to be close to tears. "Colonel Sandherr had no complaint about my methods."

"Colonel Sandherr isn't here anymore."

"With respect, Colonel, you're new to this game—"

I hold up my hand. "That is enough, Major." I know I have to stop him there. I can't back down. If I don't take control now, I never shall. "I have to remind you that this is a military unit and that your job is to obey my orders."

He jumps to attention like a wind-up toy soldier. "Yes, Colonel."

As in a cavalry charge, I make use of my momentum. "There are several other changes I'd like to make while we're on the subject. I don't want informers and other dubious characters hanging around downstairs. They should come in when we summon them, and leave immediately afterwards. We need to introduce a system of passes, and only authorised persons should be allowed upstairs. And Bachir is hopeless."

"You want to get rid of Bachir?" A tone of disbelief.

"No, not until we've found him some other billet. I believe in looking after old comrades. But let's get an electric bell system fitted that will ring each time the front door is opened, so that if he's asleep, as he was when I arrived, at least we'll know someone's entered the building."

"Yes, Colonel. Is that all?"

"That's all for now. Gather up the Auguste material and bring it to my office."

I turn on my heel and leave, without closing the door. That's another thing I'd like to change, I think, as I march down the passage to my office: this damned culture of furtiveness, with every man skulking in his own room. I try to fling open the doors on either side of me, but they are locked. When I reach my desk I take out a sheet of paper, and write a stern memorandum, for circulation to all my officers, setting out the new rules. I also compose a note to General Gonse requesting that the Statistical Section be given a new set of offices within the main ministry building, or, at the very least, that the existing premises be redecorated. After I have finished, I feel better. It seems to me that finally I have assumed command.

Later that morning, Henry comes to see me as requested, bringing the most recent delivery from Auguste. I am braced for further trouble and resolved not to give way. Despite the fact that his experience is vital to the smooth running of the section, if it comes to it I am even willing to have him transferred to another unit. But to my surprise he is as meek as the shorn lamb. He shows me how much he has already reconstructed and what remains to be done, and politely offers to teach me how the pieces are glued together. To humour him I have a try, but the work is too fiddly and time-consuming for me: besides, although Auguste may be our most important agent, I have the entire section to run. I repeat my position: all I want is to be the first to take a preliminary look at the material; the rest I am content to leave to him and Lauth.

He thanks me for my frankness and in the months that follow there is peace between us. He is cheerful, wise, friendly and dedicated—at least to my face. Occasionally I step out from my office into the corridor and catch him with Lauth and Junck speaking quietly together; there is something about the speed with which they disperse that tells me they have been talking about me. One time I pause outside the door to Gribelin's archive to rearrange some papers in a file I am returning, and I hear Henry's voice distinctly from within: "It's the way he thinks he's so much cleverer than the rest of us that I can't stand!" But I don't know for certain that he's referring to me—and even if he is, I am willing to ignore it. What chief of any organisation is not complained about behind his back, especially if he is trying to run it with some discipline and efficiency?

Throughout the remainder of that summer and into the autumn and winter of 1895, I make it my business to get the measure of my job. I learn that whenever Agent Auguste has a consignment to drop off, she signals it by placing, first thing in the morning, a particular flowerpot on the balcony of her apartment in the rue Surcouf. This means that she will be at the basilica of Sainte-Clotilde at nine o'clock that evening. I see an opportunity to extend my experience. "I'd like to make the collection tonight," I announce to Henry one day in October. "Just to get a sense of how the process works."

I watch him literally swallow his objections. "Good idea," he says.

In the evening I change into civilian clothes, pick up my brief-case and walk to the nearby basilica—that vast twin-spired mock-Gothic factory of superstition. I know it well from the days when César Franck was the organist and I used to attend his recitals. I arrive in plenty of time and follow Henry's instructions. I go into the deserted side chapel, walk to the third row of chairs from the front, edge along it three places to the left of the aisle, kneel, take out the prayer book positioned there and insert between its pages two hundred francs. Then I retreat to the back row and wait. No one is around to see me, but if there was I would just look like a troubled civil servant on his way home from the office, stopping off to seek advice from his Maker.

Yet although there is absolutely no danger in what I am doing, my heart pounds. Ridiculous! Perhaps it is the flickering candlelight and the smell of incense, or the echo of footsteps and whispered voices from the immense nave. Whatever it is, and even though I have long since lost my faith, I feel there is something sacrilegious about this whole transaction taking place on hallowed ground. I keep checking my watch: ten to nine, nine o'clock, five past nine, twenty past nine . . . Perhaps she isn't coming? I can imagine Henry's polite commiserations if I have to tell him tomorrow that she didn't show up.

But then, just before half past, the silence is broken by a clang as the door behind me opens. A squat female figure in a black skirt and shawl walks past. Halfway up the aisle she stops, makes the sign of the cross, curtseys to the altar, and then heads straight to the designated seat. I see her kneel. Less than a minute later she rises and strides back down the aisle towards me. I keep my eyes fixed on her, curious to see what she is like, this Madame Bastian, a commonplace cleaning woman, yet perhaps the most valuable secret agent in France, in Europe. She gives me a long, hard look as she passes—surprised, I suppose, not to see Major Henry in my place— and I note there is absolutely nothing commonplace in her fierce, almost masculine features, and the challenge of her stare. She is a bold one, maybe even reckless; but then she would have to be, to have smuggled secret documents out of the German Embassy for five years under the noses of the guards.

The moment she has gone, I stand and walk to the place where I left the money. Henry impressed on me not to waste any time. Tucked beneath the chair is a cone-shaped paper sack. It rustles alarmingly as I tug it out and stuff it into my briefcase. I leave the basilica in a hurry, through the doors and down the steps, striding along the dark and empty streets that surround the ministry. Ten minutes after collecting the sack, euphoric with success, I am tipping the contents over the desk in my office.

There is more than I expected: a cornucopia of trash—paper torn and crumpled and dusted with cigarette ash, paper white and grey, cream and blue, tissue and card, tiny pieces and large fragments, handwritten in pencil and ink, typewritten and printed, words in French and German and Italian, train tickets and theatre stubs, envelopes, invitations, restaurant bills and receipts from tailors and taxi cabs and bootmakers . . . I run my hands through it all, scoop it up and let it trickle through my fingers—mostly it will be rubbish,

I know, but somewhere within it there may be gold. I experience a prospector's thrill.

I am beginning to enjoy this job.

I write to Pauline twice, but guardedly, in case Philippe opens her letters. She does not reply and I don't try to seek her out to dis-cover if anything is wrong, principally because I don't have the time. I have to devote my Saturday nights and Sundays to my mother, whose memory is worsening, and most evenings I am required to stay at the office late. There are so many things to keep an eye on. The Germans are laying telephone cables along the eastern fron-tier. There is a suspected spy at our embassy in Moscow. An English agent is said to be offering to sell a copy of our mobilisation plans to the highest bidder . . . I have to write my regular *blancs*. I am fully absorbed.

I still go to the de Commingeses' salons, but "your sweet Madame Monnier," as Blanche likes to call her, is never there, even though Blanche insists she always makes a point of inviting her. After one concert I take Blanche out to dinner, to the Tour d'Argent, where we are given a table overlooking the river. Why do I choose this particular restaurant? For one thing it's a convenient walk from the de Commingeses' house. But I am also curious to see where Colo-nel von Schwartzkoppen entertains his mistress. I look around the dining room; it is almost entirely filled with couples. The candlelit booths are made for intimacy—*je suis à toi, toujours à toi, toute à toi* . . . The latest police agent's report describes Hermance as "early thirties, blonde, petite, in cream-coloured skirt and jacket trimmed in black." "At times their hands were not visible above the table."

Blanche says, "What are you smiling at?"

"I know a colonel who brings his mistress here. They take a room upstairs."

She stares at me, and in that instant the thing is settled. I have a word with the maître d'hôtel, who says, "My dear Colonel, of course there is a room available," and after we have eaten our dinner we are shown upstairs by an unsmiling young man who takes a large tip without acknowledgement.

Later, Blanche asks, "Is it better to make love before dinner or after it, do you think?"

"There's a case for either. I think probably before." I kiss her and get out of bed.

"I agree. Let's do it before next time."

She is twenty-five. Whereas Pauline at forty undresses in the darkness and drapes herself languorously with a sheet or a towel, Blanche stretches naked on her back under the electric light, smoking a cigarette, her left knee raised, her right foot resting on it, examining her wriggling toes. She flings out her arm and flicks ash in the vague direction of the ashtray.

"Surely," she says, "the correct answer is both."

"It can't be both, my darling," I correct her, ever the tutor, "because that would be illogical." I am standing at the window with the curtain wrapped around me like a toga, looking across the embankment to the Île Saint-Louis. A boat glides past, ploughing a glossy furrow in the black river, its deck lit up as if for a party but deserted. I am trying to concentrate on this moment, to file it away in my memory, so that if anyone ever asks me, "When were you content?" I can answer, "There was an evening with a girl at the Tour d'Argent . . ."

"Is it true," asks Blanche suddenly from the bed behind me, "that Armand du Paty had some kind of hand in the Dreyfus business?"

The moment freezes, vanishes. I don't need to turn round. I can see her reflection in the window. Her right foot is still describing its ceaseless circle. "Where did you hear that?"

"Oh, just something Aimery said tonight." She rolls over quickly and stabs out her cigarette. "In which case, it means of course that the poor Jew is bound to turn out to be innocent."

This is the first time anyone has suggested to me that Dreyfus might not be guilty. Her flippancy shocks me. "It's not a subject to joke about, Blanche."

"Darling, I'm not! I'm absolutely serious!" She thumps the pillow into shape and lies back with her hands clasped behind her head. "I thought it was odd at the time, the way he had his insignia torn off publicly and was marooned on a desert island—all a little too much, no? I should have guessed Armand du Paty was behind it! He may dress like an army officer, but beneath that tunic beats the heart of a romantic lady novelist."

I laugh. "Well, I must bow to your superior knowledge of what goes on beneath his tunic, my dear. But I happen to know more than you about the Dreyfus case, and believe me, there were many other officers involved in that inquiry apart from your former lover!"

She pouts at me in the glass; she doesn't like being reminded of the lapse of taste that was her affair with du Paty. "Georges, you look exactly like Jove standing there. Be a Good God and come back to bed . . ."

The exchange with Blanche unsettles me very slightly. The tiniest speck of—no, I shall not call it *doubt*, exactly—let us say *curiosity* lodges in my mind, and not so much about Dreyfus's guilt as his punishment. Why, I ask myself, do we persist in this absurd and expensive rigmarole of imprisonment, which requires four or five guards to be stranded with him in silence on his tiny island? What is our policy? How many hours of bureaucratic time—including mine—are to be tied up in the endless administration, surveillance and censorship his punishment entails?

I keep these thoughts to myself as the weeks and months pass. I continue to receive reports from Guénée on the monitoring of Lucie and Mathieu Dreyfus; it yields nothing. I read their letters to the prisoner (*My good dear husband, What endless hours, what painful days we have experienced since this disaster struck its stunning blow . . .*) and his replies, which are mostly not delivered (*Nothing is so depressing, nothing so exhausts the energy of heart and mind as these long agonising silences, never hearing human speech, seeing no friendly face, nor even one that shows sympathy . . .*). I am also copied into the regular dispatches from the Colonial Ministry's officials in Cayenne, monitoring the convict's health and morale:

*The prisoner was asked how he was. "I am well for the moment,"
he replied. "It is my heart that is sick. Nothing . . ." and here he
broke down and wept for a quarter of an hour. (2 July 1895)*

*The prisoner said: "Colonel du Paty de Clam promised me, before
I left France, to make inquiries into the matter; I should not have
thought that they could take so long. I hope that they will soon come
to a head." (15 August 1895)*

*On receiving no letter from his family, the prisoner wept and said,
"For ten months now I have been suffering horrors." (31 August
1895)*

*The prisoner was taken with a sudden burst of sobbing, and said,
"It cannot last long; my heart will end by breaking." The prisoner
always weeps when he receives his letters. (2 September 1895)*

*The prisoner sat for long hours today not moving. In the evening
he complained of violent heart spasms, with frequent paroxysms of
suffocation. He requested a medicine chest in order to make an end
of his life when he could stand it no longer. (13 December 1895)*

Gradually over the winter I discern that we do in fact have a
policy with regard to Dreyfus, it has simply never been explained to
me in so many words, either verbally or on paper. We are waiting for
him to die.

6

The first anniversary of Dreyfus's degradation comes and goes on 5 January 1896 with little comment in the press. There are no letters or petitions, no demonstrations for him or against. He seems to have been forgotten on his rock. Come the spring, I have been in charge of the Statistical Section for eight months, and all is calm.

And then, one morning in March, Major Henry asks to see me in my office. His eyes are pink and swollen.

"My dear Henry," I say, laying aside the file I have been reading. "Are you all right? What is the matter?"

He stands in front of my desk. "I'm afraid I need to ask for some urgent leave, Colonel. I have a family crisis."

I tell him to close the door and take a seat. "Is there anything I can do?"

"There isn't anything that can be done, Colonel, I'm afraid." He blows his nose on a large white handkerchief. "My mother is dying."

"Well, I'm extremely grieved to hear that. Is anyone with her? Where does she live?"

"In the Marne. A little village called Pogny."

"You must go to her at once, and take as much leave as you need. Get Lauth or Junck to cover for your work. That's an order. Each of us only has one mother, you know."

"You're very kind, Colonel." He stands and salutes. We shake hands warmly; I ask him to pay my respects to his mother. After he has gone, I wonder briefly what she must be like, this pig farmer's wife on the flatlands of the Marne, with her noisy soldier-son. It can't have been an easy life, I imagine.

I don't see my deputy again for about a week. But then late one afternoon there is a knock at my door and Henry enters carrying one of the bulging brown paper cones that signifies a delivery from Agent Auguste. "I'm sorry to disturb you, Colonel. I'm in a rush between trains. I just wanted to drop this off."

I can feel at once from the weight of it that there is more than usual. Henry notices my surprise. "I'm afraid because of Mother I missed the last meeting," he confesses, "so I arranged for Auguste to make the drop today, during daylight hours for a change. That's where I've just come from. I've got to get back to the Marne."

It is on the tip of my tongue to issue a reprimand. I ordered him to hand his duties over to Lauth or Junck: surely someone else could have made the pickup, and done it in the darkness as usual, when there would have been less risk of our agent being seen? Besides, isn't it a golden rule of intelligence—as he has often impressed upon me—that the faster information is processed, the more useful it is likely to prove? But Henry looks so haggard, having barely slept for a week, that I make no comment. I simply wish him bon voyage and lock the cone away in my safe, where it remains overnight until Captain Lauth comes in the next morning.

My relations with Lauth have not moved on from the first day we met: professional but cool. He is only a couple of years younger than I, clever enough, a German-speaker from Alsace: we ought to get on better than we do. But there is something Prussian about his blond good looks and stiffly upright figure that stops me warming to him. However, he is an efficient officer, and the speed with which he reconstructs these torn-up documents is phenomenal, so when I take the cone to his office I am polite as usual: "Would you mind attending to this now?"

"Of course, Colonel."

He dons his apron, and while he fetches his box of equipment from his cupboard, I empty the paper sack over his desk. Immediately my eye is caught by a sprinkling among the white and grey of several dozen pale blue fragments, like patches of sky on a cloudy day. I poke a couple with my forefinger. They are slightly thicker than normal paper. Lauth picks one up with his tweezers and examines it, turning it back and forth in the beam of his powerful electric lamp.

"A *petit bleu*," he murmurs, using the slang expression for a pneumatic telegram card. He looks at me and frowns. "The pieces are torn up smaller than usual."

"See what you can do."

It must be four or five hours later that Lauth comes to my office. He is carrying a thin manila folder. He winces with distress as he offers it to me. His whole manner is anxious, uneasy. "I think you ought to look at this," he says.

I open it. Inside lies the *petit bleu*. He has done a craftsman's job of sticking it back together. The texture reminds me of something that might have been reconstructed by an archaeologist: a fragment of broken glassware, perhaps, or a blue marble tile. It is jagged on the right-hand side, where some of the pieces are missing, and the lines of the tears give it a veined appearance. But the message in French is clear enough:

Monsieur,

Above all, I await a more detailed explanation than the one you gave me the other day of the matter in hand. I ask that you supply it to me in writing so that I may decide whether or not to continue my association with the house of R.

C

Puzzled, I glance up at Lauth. His manner when he came in suggested something sensational; this doesn't seem to warrant his agitation. "'C' being Schwartzkoppen?"

He nods. "Yes. It's his preferred code name. Now turn it over."

On the reverse side is the web-work of tiny strips of transparent adhesive paper that holds the postcard together. But again the writing is perfectly legible. Beneath the printed word "TELE-GRAMME," and above the word "PARIS," in the space left for the address, is written:

Major Esterhazy
27, rue de la Bienfaisance

I don't recognise the name. Even so I feel as shocked as if I had just seen an old friend listed in a deaths column. I tell Lauth, "Go and talk to Gribelin. Ask him to check if there's a Major Esterhazy in the French army." There's just a chance, I think, a slim hope that given the surname he might be Austro-Hungarian.

"I already have," says Lauth. "Major Charles Ferdinand Walsin Esterhazy is listed with the Seventy-fourth Infantry."

"The Seven-four?" I'm still trying to take it in. "I have a friend in that regiment. They're garrisoned in Rouen."

"Rouen? 'The house of R'?" Lauth stares at me, his pale blue eyes widening with alarm, for it all now points in only one direction, and his voice drops to a whisper. "Does this mean there's another traitor?"

I don't know how to answer him. I reexamine the seven lines of the message. After eight months of reading Schwartzkoppen's notes and drafts I am familiar with his handwriting, and this regular and formal script is quite unlike it. In fact it's too regular and for-mal to be anyone's *normal* hand. This is the kind of lettering one sees on an official invitation; this writing has been disguised. And naturally so, I think: if one was an officer of a foreign power com-municating with an agent through the open mail of a host country, one would take the minimal precaution of concealing one's hand. The tone of the message is irritated, peremptory, urgent: it suggests a crisis in relations. The pneumatic tube network follows the Paris sewers and can deliver a telegram so quickly Esterhazy would have it in his hands within an hour or two. But still it's a risk, which perhaps is why Schwartzkoppen, having laboriously copied out his communication—and wasted a prepaid fifty-centimes telegram card on it—in the end decided not to send it, but shredded it into the tiniest pieces he could manage and dropped it into his waste-paper basket.

I say to Lauth, "It's obviously important. So if he didn't send this, what did he send?"

"Another card?" suggests Lauth. "A letter?"

"Have you checked the rest of the material?"

"Not yet. I concentrated on the *bleu*."

"Very well. Go through it now and see if there's another draft of something else."

"And what shall we do about the pneumatic telegram?"

"Leave it with me. Don't mention it to anyone else. Is that clear?"

"Yes, Colonel." Lauth salutes.

As he leaves, I call after him, "Good work, by the way."

After Lauth has gone I stand at my window and look across the garden to the minister's residence. I can see the light burning in his office. It would be an easy matter to walk over and alert him to what we have discovered. Or at least I could go and see General Gonse, who is supposed to be my immediate superior. But I know that if I do that I will have lost control of the investigation before it has even started: I shall not be able to make a move without clearing it with them first. And then there is the risk of a leak. Our suspect may be a humble major with an unfashionable regiment in a garrison town, but Esterhazy is a grand name in central Europe: perhaps someone on the General Staff might feel it his duty to alert the family. I decide that for now it would be wiser to play this one close to my chest.

I replace the *petit bleu* in its folder and lock it in my safe.

The next day, Lauth comes to see me again. He has worked late into the night and pieced together another draft letter. Unfortunately, as often happens, Auguste has not managed to retrieve every scrap of paper: words, maybe even half-sentences, are missing. Lauth watches me as I read.

To be delivered by the concierge

Sir,

I regret not speaking personally . . . about a matter which . . . My father has just the . . . funds necessary to continue . . . in the conditions which were stipulated . . . I will explain to you his reasons, but I must begin by telling you straight away . . . your conditions too harsh for me and . . . the results that . . . of the trip. He proposes to me . . . tour concerning which we might . . . the relations I have . . . for him up until now out of proportion . . . I have spent on the trips. The point is . . . to speak to you as soon as possible.

I am returning to you with this the sketches you gave me the other day; they are not the last.

C

I reread the document several times. Even with its gaps, the sense is clear. Esterhazy has been handing over information to the Germans, including sketches, for which he has been paid by Schwartzkoppen; now the German attaché's "father," presumably a euphemism for some general in Berlin, is objecting that the price is too high for the value of the intelligence they are getting.

Lauth says, "It could be a trap, of course."

"Yes." I have already thought of this. "If Schwartzkoppen has discovered we're reading his rubbish, he might well decide to use that knowledge against us. He could easily plant material in his own waste basket to send us off on a false trail."

I close my eyes and try to put myself in his shoes. It seems unlikely somehow that a man so reckless in his love affairs, so slapdash in his handling of documents, would suddenly become that devious.

"Does it really make sense for him to go to those lengths," I muse aloud, "if one recalls how violently the Germans reacted when we exposed them employing Dreyfus? Why would Schwartzkoppen want to risk another embarrassing espionage scandal?"

"Of course, none of this is evidence, Colonel," says Lauth. "We could never use this document or the *petit bleu* as a pretext to arrest Esterhazy, because neither was ever sent to him."

"That's true." I open the safe and take out the manila folder. I put the draft letter inside, along with the *petit bleu*. On the file I write "Esterhazy." Here, I reflect, is the paradox of the spy's world. These are significant documents only if one knows where they come from. And as the very fact of where they come from can never be revealed, because that would blow our agent's cover, legally they are worthless. I am reluctant to show them even to the Minister of War or the Chief of the General Staff in case one of their junior officers should see them and start gossiping: they are so obviously reconstructed rubbish. "Is there any way," I ask Lauth, taking out the *petit bleu* again, "that you could photograph this and somehow cover up the tear marks so that it looks as if we just intercepted it in the mail, as you did with the Dreyfus document?"

"Perhaps," he says doubtfully. "But that was only in six pieces, whereas this is in about forty. And even if I could, the side with the address, which is the most vital part of the evidence, isn't franked, so anyone examining it for half a minute would know it had never been delivered."

"Maybe we could get it franked?" I suggest.

"I don't know about that." Lauth looks even more dubious.

I decide not to press it. "All right," I say. "Let's just keep these documents between ourselves for the present. In the meantime, we should investigate Esterhazy and try to discover what other evidence there may be against him."

I can tell that Lauth is still unhappy about something. He frowns; he chews his lip; he seems on the point of making a remark but then changes his mind. He sighs. "I wish Major Henry were here, and not on leave."

"Don't worry," I reassure him. "Henry will be back soon enough. Until then, you and I can deal with this."

I send a telegram to my old comrade from Tonkin, Albert Curé, a major with the 74th Infantry Regiment in Rouen, telling him I'll be in the area the next day, and asking if I can drop by and see him. I receive a one-word reply: "Delighted."

The following morning I eat an early lunch in the buffet of the gare Saint-Lazare and catch the Normandy train. Despite the gravity of my mission, as we leave the suburbs and head into open country I feel a surge of exhilaration. I am away from my desk for the first time in weeks. It is a spring day. I am on the move. My briefcase sits unopened beside me while the rural scenes slide past my window in a pastoral diorama—the brown and white cows like shiny lead toys in their lush green meadows, the squat grey Norman churches and red-roofed villages, the brightly coloured barges on the placid canal, the sandy lanes and the high hedges just coming into leaf. It is the France for which I fight—if only by piecing together the garbage of a priapic Prussian colonel.

Just under two hours later we are pulling into Rouen, chugging at walking pace alongside the Seine towards the great cathedral. Seagulls swoop and cry over the wide river; I always forget how close the Norman capital is to the English Channel. I set off on foot from the station towards the Pélissier barracks, through a typical garrison district with its dreary chandleries and bootmakers and that certain kind of grim-looking bar, invariably owned by an ex-soldier, in which local civilians are not encouraged to drink. The 74th occupies three large triple-storeyed buildings of alternating stripes of red brick and grey stone peeping over the top of a high wall. It could be a factory or a lunatic asylum or a prison for all one can tell from the outside. At the gate I show my credentials and an orderly leads me between the two dormitory blocks, across the parade ground with its flagpole and tricolour, its plane trees and water troughs, towards the administration building on the far side.

I climb the nail-studded stairs to the second floor. Curé is away from his office. His sergeant tells me he has just started a kit inspection. He invites me to wait. The room is bare apart from a desk and a couple of chairs. The high, small-paned window is slightly ajar, letting in the spring breeze and the sounds of the garrison. I hear the ring of horses' hooves on the cobbles of the stable block, the rhythmic tramp of a company marching in from the road, and farther in the distance a band rehearsing. I might be at Saint-Cyr again, or back as a captain at divisional HQ in Toulouse. Even the smells are the same—horse dung, leather, canteen food and male sweat. My sophisticated friends in Paris express amazement that I can stand it year after year. I never try to explain the truth: that it's rather the unchanging sameness that attracts me.

Curé bustles in full of apologies. First he salutes me, then we shake hands, and finally, awkwardly—on my initiative—we embrace. I haven't seen him since the de Commingeses' concert last summer, when I got the impression something was needling him. Curé is an ambitious man, a year or two older than I. It would only be human for him to feel a little envy of my new rank.

"Well," he says, standing back and looking at me, "Colonel!"

"It does take some getting used to, I agree."

"How long are you in town?"

"Only a couple of hours. I'll get the evening train back to Paris."

"This calls for a drink." He opens a drawer in his desk and takes out a bottle of cognac and a pair of tumblers. He fills them to the brim. We toast the army. He fills them again and we toast my promotion. But I sense that somewhere, deep beneath the congratulations, the narrowest of gaps has opened between us. Not that anyone walking in would have guessed it. Curé pours a third round. We unbutton our tunics and loll back in our chairs, smoking, our feet on his desk. We talk of old comrades and old times. We laugh. A brief silence falls and then he says, "So what exactly is it you're doing in Paris these days?"

I hesitate; I am not supposed to mention it.

"I have Sandherr's job, running secret intelligence."

"Do you, by God?" He frowns at his empty glass; this time he doesn't suggest another toast. "So you're up here snooping?"

"Something like that."

A flicker of his former mirth returns. "Not into me, I hope!"

"Not this time." I smile and put down my glass. "There's a major with the Seven-four called Esterhazy."

Curé turns to me. His expression is unreadable. "There is indeed."

"What is he like?"

"What has he done?"

"I can't tell you."

Curé nods slowly. "I thought you'd say that." He pulls himself to his feet and starts buttoning his tunic. "I don't know about you, but I need to clear my head."

Outside the wind is bracing, edged sharp by the sea. We stroll around the perimeter of the parade ground. After a while Curé says, "I understand you can't tell me what this is about, but if I could give you a piece of advice, you want to be careful how you approach Esterhazy. He's dangerous."

"What, you mean physically dangerous?"

"In every way. How much do you know about him?"

"Nothing. You're the first person I've come to."

"Just bear in mind he's well connected. His father was a general.

He calls himself 'Count Esterhazy,' but I think that's merely an affectation. Be that as it may, his wife is the daughter of the marquis de Nettancourt, so he knows a lot of people."

"How old is he?"

"Oh, he must be nearly fifty, I should think."

"Fifty?" I glance around the barracks. It's the end of the afternoon. Soldiers, pasty-faced and with grey shaven heads, are leaning out of their dormitory windows, like prison inmates.

Curé follows my gaze. "I know what you're thinking."

"Do you?"

"Why, if he's fifty and the son-in-law of a marquis, is he stuck in a dump like this? Certainly it's the first thing I'd want to know."

"Well then, since you bring it up, why is he?"

"Because he has no money."

"Even with all these connections?"

"He gambles it away. Not just at the table, either. On the race-track and the stock market."

"Surely his wife must have some capital?"

"Ah, but she's got wise to him. I heard him complain that she's even put the country house in her name, to protect herself from his creditors. She won't let him have a sou."

"He also has an apartment in Paris."

"You may be sure that's hers as well."

We walk on in silence. I'm remembering Schwartzkoppen's letter. That was all about money. *Your conditions too harsh for me . . .* "Tell me," I say, "what kind of an officer is he?"

"The worst."

"He neglects his duties?"

"Entirely. The colonel's stopped giving him anything to do."

"So he's never here?"

"On the contrary, he's always here."

"Doing what?"

"Getting in the way! He likes to hang around and ask a lot of damn fool questions about things that have nothing to do with him."

"Questions about what?"

"Everything."

"Gunnery, for example?"

"Definitely."

"What does he ask about gunnery?"

"What doesn't he ask! He's been on at least three artillery exercises, to my certain knowledge. The last one the colonel absolutely refused to assign him to, so he ended up paying for the trip himself."

"I thought you said he didn't have any money?"

"True, that's a point." Curé halts in his tracks. "Now I think about it, I happen to know he also paid a corporal in his battalion to copy the firing manuals—you know we're not allowed to keep them for more than a day or two."

"Did he give a reason?"

"He said he was thinking of suggesting some improvements . . ."

We resume walking. The sun has dipped behind one of the dormitory blocks, casting the parade ground into shadow. The air is suddenly chilly. I say, "You mentioned earlier that he was dangerous."

"It's not easy to describe. There's a kind of . . . wildness about him, and also cunning. And yet he can be quite charming. Put it this way: despite the way he acts, nobody wants to cross him. He also has a quite extraordinary appearance. You'd need to see him to understand what I mean."

"I'd like to. The trouble is, I can't risk letting him see me. Is there a place I might get a glimpse of him, without him realising it?"

"There's a bar near here he goes to most nights. It's not certain, but you could probably spot him there."

"Could you take me?"

"I thought you were getting out on the evening train?"

"I can stay until the morning. One night won't hurt. Come on, my friend! It will be like old times."

But Curé seems to have had enough of the "old times" routine. His glance is hard, appraising. "Now I know it must be serious, Georges, if you're willing to give up a night in Paris for it."

Curé presses me to come back to his quarters and wait with him for nightfall, but I prefer not to linger within the confines of the barracks in case I'm recognised. There is a small hotel for commercial travellers close to the station which I remember passing; I walk back and pay for a room. It is a stale-smelling, dingy place, without electricity; the mattress is hard and thin; whenever a train passes, the walls shake. But it will do for a night. I stretch out on the bed: it's short; my feet hang over the edge. I smoke and contemplate the mysterious Esterhazy, a man who appears to possess in abundance the very thing that Dreyfus so singularly lacked: motive.

The day fades in the window. At seven, the bells of Our Lady of Rouen begin to peal—heavy and sonorous, the noise rolls across the river like a barrage, and when it stops, the sudden silence seems to hang in the air like smoke.

It is dark by the time I rouse myself to go downstairs. Curé is already waiting for me. He suggests I wrap my cape tight around my shoulders to hide the insignia of my rank.

We walk for five or ten minutes through the shuttered back streets, past a couple of quiet bars, until we reach a cul-de-sac filled with the shadows of people, soldiers mostly, and a few young women. They are talking quietly, laughing, hanging around a long, low building with no windows that looks like a converted warehouse. A painted sign proclaims: "Folies Bergère." The hopelessness of this provincial aspiration is almost touching.

Curé says, "Wait here. I'll see if he's in yet."

He moves off. A door opens, briefly silhouetting his figure against a purplish oblong gleam; I hear a snatch of noise and music and then he is swallowed up by darkness. A woman baring a large expanse of cleavage, white as gooseflesh in the cold, comes up to me holding an unlit cigarette and asks for a light. Without bothering to think I strike a match. In the yellow flare she is young and pretty. She peers at me short-sightedly. "Do I know you, my darling?"

I realise my mistake. "I'm sorry. I'm waiting for someone." I blow out the flame and walk away.

She calls after me, laughing: "Don't be like that, sweetheart!"

Another woman says: "Who is he, anyway?"

And then a man yells drunkenly: "He's just a stuck-up cunt!"

A couple of soldiers turn to stare.

Curé appears in the doorway. He nods and beckons. I walk over to him. "I ought to leave," I say.

"One quick look, then go." He takes my arm and steers me ahead of him, along a short passage, down a few steps, through a heavy black velvet curtain and into a long room, misty with tobacco smoke, packed with people sitting at small round tables. At the far end a band is playing, while on stage half a dozen girls in corsets and crotchless knickers hoist their skirts and kick their legs listlessly at the clientele. Their feet thump against the bare boards. The place smells of absinthe.

"That's him."

He nods to a table less than twenty paces away, where two couples share a bottle of champagne. One of the women, a redhead, has her back to me; the other, a brunette, is twisted round in her seat looking towards the stage. The men face each other, talking in a desultory way. There is no need for Curé to tell me which it is he has brought me to see. Major Esterhazy reclines with his chair pushed well back from the table, his tunic unbuttoned, his pelvis thrust forward, his arms hanging down either side almost to the floor; in his right hand he holds casually at an angle, as if it is barely worth considering, a glass of champagne. His head in profile is flattish and tapers like a vulture's to a great beak of a nose. His moustache is large and swept back. He seems to be drunk. His companion notices us standing by the door. He says something, and Esterhazy slowly turns his head in our direction. His eyes are round and protuberant: not natural, but crazy, like glass balls pressed into the skull of a skeleton in a medical school. The overall effect, as Curé warned, is unsettling. *My God,* I think, *he could burn this entire place down and everyone in it, and not care a damn.* His glance settles on us briefly, and for a second I detect a hint of curiosity in the tilt of his head and the narrowing of his gaze. Fortunately, he is befuddled by drink, and when one of the women says something his attention wanders vaguely back to her.

Curé touches my elbow. "We should go." He pulls aside the curtain and ushers me away.

7

I arrive back in Paris just before noon the following day, a Saturday, and decide against going into the office. It is therefore not until Monday, four days after my last conversation with Lauth, that I return to the section. Even as I am climbing the stairs I can hear Major Henry's voice, and when I reach the landing I see him along the corridor, just emerging from Lauth's room. He is wearing a black armband.

"Colonel Picquart," he says, coming up to me and saluting. "I am reporting for duty."

"It's good to have you back, Major," I reply, returning his salute, "although naturally I am very sorry for the circumstances. I do hope your mother's passing was as peaceful as possible."

"There aren't many easy ways out of this life, Colonel. To be frank, by the end, I was praying for it to be over. From now on I intend to keep hold of my service revolver. I want a good clean bullet when my own time comes."

"That's my intention, too."

"The only problem is whether one will still have the strength to pull the trigger."

"Oh, I expect there will be plenty around who will be only too happy to oblige us."

Henry laughs. "You're not wrong there, Colonel!"

I unlock my door and invite him in. The office has the cold, stale feel of a room that has not been used for several days. He takes a seat. The spindly wooden legs creak under his weight.

"So," he says, lighting a cigarette, "I hear you've been busy while I've been away."

"You've spoken to Lauth?" Of course, I might have guessed Lauth would have told him: those two are very thick together.

"Yes, he's filled me in. May I see the new material?"

I feel a certain irritation as I unlock my safe and hand him the file. I say, conscious of sounding petty, "I had assumed I would be the one to brief you first."

"Does it matter?"

"Only to the extent that I asked Lauth not to mention it to anyone."

Henry, with his cigarette clamped between his lips, puts on his spectacles, and holds up the two documents. He squints at them through the smoke. "Well," he mutters, "perhaps he doesn't regard me as just 'anyone.'" The cigarette wobbles as he speaks, showering ash into his lap.

"Nobody is suggesting you are."

"Have you done anything about this yet?"

"I haven't told anyone in the rue Saint-Dominique, if that's what you mean."

"That's probably wise. They will only start flapping."

"I agree. I want us to make our own inquiries first. I've already been to Rouen—"

He peers at me over the top of his spectacles. "You've been to Rouen?"

"Yes, there's a major in the Seven-four—Esterhazy's regiment—who's an old friend of mine. He was able to give me some personal information."

Henry resumes reading. "And might I ask what this old friend told you?"

"He said that Esterhazy is in the habit of asking a lot of suspicious questions. That he's even paid for himself to go on artillery exercises, and had the firing manuals copied afterwards. Also that he's desperate for money and isn't a man of good character."

"Really?" Henry turns the *petit bleu* over to examine the address. "He seemed fine when he worked here."

I have to give him credit for the aplomb with which he delivers this bombshell. For a moment or two I simply stare at him. "Lauth never mentioned that Esterhazy was employed here."

"That's because he didn't know." Henry sets the documents down on my desk and takes off his spectacles. "It was long before Lauth's time. I'd only just been posted here myself."

"When was this?"

"Must be fifteen years ago."

"So you know Esterhazy?"

"I did once, yes—slightly. He wasn't here long—he worked as a German translator. But I haven't seen him for years."

I sit back in my chair. "This raises the matter to a whole new level."

"Does it?" Henry shrugs. "I'm not sure I follow. Why?"

"You seem to be taking this very calmly, Major!" There is something mocking about Henry's studied indifference; I can feel my anger rising. "Obviously it's more serious if Esterhazy has received some training in our intelligence techniques."

Henry smiles and shakes his head. "If I may offer you some advice, Colonel, I wouldn't get too dramatic about it. It doesn't matter how many gunnery courses he's been on. I don't see how Esterhazy can have had access to anything important, stuck out in Rouen. And in fact that letter from Schwartzkoppen tells us plainly that he didn't, because the Germans are threatening to break off relations with him. They wouldn't do that if they thought they had a valuable spy."

"It's always an easy mistake to make," continues Henry, "if you're new to this game, to think that the first dodgy fellow you come across is a master spy. It's seldom the case. In fact you can end up doing a lot more damage by overreacting than the so-called traitor has caused in the first place."

"You are not suggesting, I hope," I reply stiffly, "that we just leave him to carry on supplying information to a foreign power, even if it may be of little value?"

"Not at all! I agree absolutely we should keep an eye on him. I just think we should keep it in proportion. Why don't I ask Guénée to start sniffing around, see what he can find out?"

"No, I don't want Guénée handling this." Guénée is another member of Henry's gang. "I want to use someone else for a change."

"As you wish," says Henry. "Tell me who you'd like and I'll assign him."

"No, actually, thank you for the offer, but *I'll* assign him." I smile at Henry. "The extra experience will do me good. Please . . ." I indicate the door. "And again: welcome back. Would you mind telling Gribelin to come down and see me?"

What is particularly galling about Henry's pious little sermon is that I can see the truth in it. He's right: I have allowed my imagination to build Esterhazy up into a traitor on the scale of Dreyfus, whereas in fact, as Henry says, all the evidence indicates that he hasn't done anything very much. Still, I am not going to give him the satisfaction of letting him take over the operation. I shall keep this one to myself. Thus when Gribelin comes to see me, I tell him I want a list of all the police agents the section has used recently, together with their addresses and a brief service history. He goes away and comes back half an hour later with a dozen names.

Gribelin is an enigma to me: the epitome of the servile bureaucrat; an animated corpse. He could be any age between forty and sixty and is as thin as a wraith of black smoke, the only colour he wears. Mostly he closets himself alone upstairs in his archive; on the rare occasions he does appear he creeps along close to the wall, dark and silent as a shadow. I could imagine him slipping around the edge of a closed door, or sliding beneath it. The only sound he emits occasionally is the clinking of the bunch of keys that is attached to his waist by a chain. He stands now with perfect stillness in front of my desk while I scan the list. I ask him which of the agents he would recommend. He refuses to be drawn: "They are all good men." He doesn't ask me why I need an agent: Gribelin is as discreet as a papal confessor.

In the end I select a young officer with the Sûreté, Jean-Alfred Desvernine, attached to the police division at the gare Saint-Lazare. He's a former lieutenant of the dragoons from the Médoc, risen through the ranks, obliged to resign his commission because of gambling debts, but who has made an honest fist of his life since: if anyone has a chance of prising open the secrets of Esterhazy's addiction, I reckon it will be him.

After Gribelin has slunk away, I write Desvernine a message

asking him to meet me the day after tomorrow. Rather than inviting him to the office, where Henry and Lauth will be able to see
him, I propose a meeting at nine in the morning outside the Louvre
museum, in the place du Carrousel. I tell him I shall be in civilian
dress, with a frock coat and a bowler hat, and with a red carnation in
my buttonhole and a copy of *Le Figaro* under my arm. As I seal the
envelope, I reflect how easily I am slipping into the clichés of the
spying world. It alarms me. Already I trust no one. How long before
I am raving like Sandherr about degenerates and foreigners? It is a
déformation professionnelle: all spymasters must go mad in the end.

On Wednesday morning, suitably accoutred, I present myself
outside the Louvre. From the lines of tourists suddenly emerges a
keen-looking, fresh-faced man with a salt-and-pepper moustache,
who I take to be Desvernine. We exchange nods. I realise he must
have been watching me for several minutes.

"You're not being followed, Colonel," he says quietly, "at least
not as far as I can tell. However, I suggest we take a walk into the
museum, if that's agreeable, where it will look more natural if I need
to make notes."

"Whatever you advise: this sort of thing is not my line."

"Quite right too, Colonel—leave it to the likes of me."

He has a sportsman's open shoulders and rolling walk. I follow
him towards the nearest pavilion. It is early in the day, and therefore not yet crowded. In the vestibule there is a cloakroom by the
entrance, stairs straight ahead, and galleries to our left and right.
When Desvernine turns right, I make a protest: "Do we have to go
in there? That's the most awful rubbish."

"Really? It all looks the same to me."

"You handle the police work, Desvernine; leave the culture to
me. We'll go in here."

I buy a guidebook and in the Galerie Denon, which has the smell
of a schoolroom, we stand together and contemplate a bronze of
Commodus as Hercules—a Renaissance copy from the Vatican. The
gallery is almost deserted.

I say, "This must remain between the two of us, understood? If
your superiors try to discover what you're doing, refer them to me."

"I understand." Desvernine takes out his notebook and pencil.

"I want you to find out everything you can about an army major by the name of Charles Ferdinand Walsin Esterhazy." My voice echoes even when I whisper. "He sometimes calls himself Count Esterhazy. He's forty-eight years old, serving with the Seventy-fourth Infantry Regiment in Rouen. He's married to the daughter of the marquis de Nettancourt. He gambles, plays the stock market, generally leads a dissolute life—you'll know where to look for such a character better than I."

Desvernine flushes slightly. "When do you need this done?"

"As quickly as possible. Would it be possible to have a preliminary report next week?"

"I'll try."

"One other thing: I'm interested in how often Esterhazy goes to the German Embassy."

If Desvernine finds this last request surprising, he is too professional to show it. We must make an odd couple: I in my bowler and frock coat, apparently reading the guidebook and holding forth; he in a shabby brown suit, taking down my dictation. But nobody is looking at us. We move along to the next exhibit. The guidebook lists it as *Boy Extracting a Thorn from His Foot.*

Desvernine says, "We should meet somewhere different next time, just as a precaution."

"What about the restaurant at the gare Saint-Lazare?" I suggest, remembering my trip to Rouen. "That's on your patch."

"I know it well."

"Next Thursday, at seven in the evening?"

"Agreed." He writes it down then puts away his notebook and stares at the bronze sculpture. He scratches his head. "You really think this stuff is good, Colonel?"

"No, I didn't say that. As so often in life, it's just better than the alternative."

Not all my time is devoted to investigating Esterhazy. I have other things to worry about—not least, the treasonable activity of homing pigeons.

Gribelin brings me the file. It has been sent over from the rue

Saint-Dominique, and as he hands it to me I detect at last a faint gleam of malicious pleasure in those dull eyes. It seems that pigeon-fanciers in England are in the habit of transporting their birds to Cherbourg and releasing them to fly back across the Channel. Some nine thousand are set loose each year: a harmless if unappealing pastime which Colonel Sandherr, in the final phase of his illness, decided might pose a threat to national security and should be banned, for what if the birds were used to carry secret messages? This piece of madness has been grinding its way through the Ministry of the Interior for the best part of a year, and a law has been prepared. Now General Boisdeffre insists that I, as chief of the Statistical Section, must prepare the Ministry of War's opinion on the draft legislation.

Needless to say, I have no opinion. After Gribelin has gone I sit at my desk, reviewing the file. It might as well be written in Sanskrit for all the sense I can make of it, and it occurs to me that what I need is a lawyer. It further occurs to me that the best lawyer I know is my oldest friend, Louis Leblois, who by a curious coincidence lives along the rue de l'Université. I send him a *bleu* asking if he could call round to see me on his way home to discuss a matter of business, and at the end of the afternoon I hear the electric bell ring to signal that someone has entered. I am halfway down the staircase when I meet Bachir coming up, carrying Louis's card.

"It's all right, Bachir. He's known to me. He can come to my office."

Two minutes later, I am standing at my window with Louis, showing him the minister's garden.

"Georges," he says, "this is a most remarkable building. I've often passed it and wondered who it belonged to. You do appreciate what it used to be, don't you?"

"No."

"Before the revolution it was the hôtel d'Aiguillon, where the old duchess, Anne-Charlotte de Crussol Florensac, used to have her literary salon. Montesquieu and Voltaire probably sat in this very room!" He wafts his hand back and forth in front of his nose. "Are their corpses in the cellar, by any chance? What on earth do you do here all day?"

"I can't tell you that, although it might have amused Voltaire. However, I can put some work your way, if you're interested." I thrust the carrier pigeon file into his hands. "Tell me if you can make head or tail of this."

"You want me to look at it now?"

"If you wouldn't mind: it can't leave the building, I'm afraid."

"Why? Is it secret?"

"No, otherwise I wouldn't be showing it to you. But I have to keep it here." Louis hesitates. "I'll pay you," I add, "whatever it is you would normally charge."

"Well, if I'm actually going to extract some money from you for once in my life," he laughs, "then naturally I'll do it," and he sits at my table, opens his briefcase, takes out a sheaf of paper and starts reading the file while I return to my desk. "Neat" is the word for Louis: a dapper figure, exactly my age, with neatly trimmed beard and neat little hands that move rapidly across the page as he sets down his neatly ordered thoughts. I watch him fondly. He works with utter absorption, exactly as he did when we were classmates together at the lycée in Strasbourg. We had both lost a parent at the age of eleven, I my father and he his mother, and that made us a club of two, even though what bound us was never spoken of, then or now.

I take out my own pen and begin composing a report. For an hour we work in companionable silence until there is a knock at my door. I shout, "Come!" and Henry enters, carrying a folder. His expression on seeing Louis could not have been more startled if he had caught me naked with one of the street girls of Rouen.

"Major Henry," I say, "this is a good friend of mine, Maître Louis Leblois." Louis, deep in concentration, merely raises his left hand and continues writing, while Henry looks from me to him and back again. "Maître Leblois," I explain, "is writing us a legal opinion on this absurd carrier pigeon business."

For a few moments Henry seems too choked with emotion to speak. "May I have a word outside a moment, Colonel?" he asks eventually, and when I join him in the corridor, he says coldly: "Colonel, I must protest. It is not our practice to allow outsiders access to our offices."

"Guénée comes in all the time."

"Monsieur Guénée is an officer of the police!"

"Well, Maître Leblois is an officer of the courts." My tone is more amused than angry. "I have known him for thirty years. I can vouch for his integrity absolutely. Besides, he is only looking at a file on carrier pigeons. They are hardly classified."

"But there are other files in your office which are highly secret."

"Yes, and they are locked up out of sight."

"Even so, I wish to register my strong objection—"

"Oh really, Major Henry," I interrupt him, "don't be so pompous, please! I am the chief of this section and I shall see whoever I like!"

I turn on my heel and return to my office, closing the door behind me. Louis, who must have heard every word, says, "Am I causing you a problem?"

"Not at all. But these people—honestly!" I drop into my chair and sigh and shake my head.

"Well, this is finished in any case." Louis stands and gives me the file. On top of it are several pages of notes in his meticulous hand. "It's very straightforward. Here are the points you need to make." He looks down at me with concern. "Your glittering career is all very well, Georges, but you know, none of us ever sees you anymore. One needs to keep one's friendships in good repair. Come home with me now and have some supper."

"Thank you, but I can't."

"Why not?"

I want to say: "Because I can't begin to tell you what's on my mind, or what I do all day, and when there's no longer a possibility of unguarded intimacy, social life becomes a fraud and a strain." Instead I merely remark blandly, "I fear I am poor company these days."

"We'll be the judge of that. Come. Please."

He's so good and honest that I have no option except to surrender. "Well, I would like that very much," I say, "but only if you're sure Martha won't mind."

"My dear Georges, she will be absolutely delighted!"

Their apartment could scarcely be closer, literally just across the boulevard Saint-Germain, and Martha does indeed seem pleased to see me, throwing her arms around me the moment I enter their apartment. She is twenty-seven, fourteen years our junior. I was the best man at their wedding. She goes everywhere with Louis, I presume because they have no children. But if that is a source of sadness, they do not let it show; neither do they demand to know when I am going to get married, which is also a great relief. I pass three happy hours in their company, talking about the past and politics—Louis is deputy mayor of the local arrondissement, the seventh, and takes a radical view on most issues—and the evening ends with my playing their piano while they sing. As he shows me out, Louis says, "We should do this every week. It might just keep you sane. And remember, whenever you're working late, you know you can always come back here to sleep."

"You're a generous friend, dear Lou. You always have been." I kiss him on the cheeks and lurch off into the night, humming the tune I have just been playing, slightly the worse for drink but much the better for company.

The following Thursday evening, at seven precisely, I sit in a corner of the cavernous yellow gloom of the platform café of the gare Saint-Lazare, sipping an Alsace beer. The place is packed; the double-hinged door swings back and forth with a squeak of springs. The roar of chat and movement inside and the whistles and shouts and percussive bursts of steam from the locomotives outside make it a perfect place not to be overheard. I have managed to save a table with two seats that gives me a clear view of the entrance. Once again, however, Desvernine surprises me by appearing at my back. He is carrying a bottle of mineral water, refuses my offer of a beer, and is pulling out his little black notebook even as he sinks into his place on the crimson banquette.

"He's quite a character, your Major Esterhazy, Colonel. Big debts all over Rouen and Paris: I have a list here for you."

"What does he spend the money on?"

"Mostly gambling. There's a place he goes to in the boulevard Poissonnière. It's a sickness that's hard to cure, as I know to my cost." He passes the list across the table. "He also has a mistress, a Mademoiselle Marguerite Pays, aged twenty-six, a registered prostitute in the Pigalle district, who goes by the name of 'Four-Fingered Marguerite.'"

I can't help laughing. "You're not serious?"

Desvernine, the earnest former noncommissioned officer turned policeman, does not see the humour. "She's from the Rouen area originally, daughter of a Calvados distiller, started work in a spinning factory when she was a kid, lost a finger in an accident and her job with it, moved to Paris, became an *horizontale* in the rue Victor-Masse, met Esterhazy last year either on the Paris–Rouen train or at the Moulin Rouge—there are different versions depending on which of the girls you speak to."

"So this affair is common knowledge?"

"Absolutely. He's even set her up in an apartment: 49, rue de Douai, near Montmartre. Visits her every evening when he's in town. She's furnished it, but the lease is in his name. The girls at the Moulin Rouge call him 'the Benefactor.'"

"That kind of life can't come cheap."

"He's working every racket he can think of to keep it going. He's even trying to join the board of a British company in London—which is a rum thing for a French officer to do, when you think about it."

"And where is his wife during all this?"

"Either on her estate at Dommartin-la-Planchette in the Ardennes or at the apartment in Paris. He goes back to her after he's finished with Marguerite."

"He seems to be a man to whom betrayal is second nature."

"I'd say so."

"What about the Germans? Any links there?"

"I haven't got anywhere on that yet."

"I wonder—perhaps we could follow him?"

"We could," says Desvernine doubtfully, "but he's a wary bird from what I've seen. He'd soon get wise to us."

"In that case, we can't risk it. The last thing I need is to have a well-connected major complaining to the ministry that he's being harassed."

"Our best bet would be to put a watch on the German Embassy, see if we can catch him there."

"I'd never get authorisation for that."

"Why not?"

"It would be too obvious. The ambassador would complain."

"Actually, I think I know a way we can do it without them discovering." He produces his pocket book and passes me a tiny square of carefully snipped-out newsprint. It is an advertisement for an apartment to rent in the rue de Lille, the same street as the hôtel de Beauharnais, which houses the German Embassy. "It's on the first floor, almost directly opposite the Germans. We could set up an observation post, and monitor everyone entering and leaving." He looks at me, proud of his initiative, willing me to approve. "And here's the best part: the apartment underneath is already being rented by the embassy. They use it as a kind of officers' club."

The idea attracts me at once. I admire the audacity of it, but not only that: it would be an operation independent of Henry.

"We'd need a tenant with a plausible cover story," I say, thinking it over, "to avoid arousing suspicion—someone who might have reason to be inside all day."

"I wondered about a night-shift worker," suggests Desvernine. "He could arrive home every morning at seven, and not leave for work until six in the evening."

"How much is the rent on this apartment?"

"Two hundred a month."

I shake my head. "No night-shift worker could afford such an amount. It's a fashionable street. A more likely tenant, surely, would be some wealthy young layabout with a private income—out all hours of the night and sleeping it off inside during the day."

"I'm not sure I move in those circles, Colonel."

"No. But I do."

I send a *bleu* to a young man of my acquaintance and arrange to meet him late on Sunday afternoon in a café on the Champs-Élysées. I watch him eat hungrily, as if he hasn't seen food for a day or two, and afterwards we go for a stroll in the Tuileries Garden.

Germain Ducasse is a sensitive, cultured, gentle soul in his thirties, with dark curly hair and soft brown eyes, popular with elderly bachelors and with married ladies who need a knowledgeable escort to the opera of whom their husbands will have no cause for jealousy. I have known him for more than a decade, ever since he completed his military service under my command in the 126th Line Regiment at Pamiers, in Ariège. I encouraged him to study modern languages at the Sorbonne, and from time to time I take him along to soirées at the de Commingeses'. Nowadays he scratches a shabby-genteel living as a translator and secretary, and when I mention that I may be able to put some work his way, his gratitude is almost painful.

"I say, Georges, that's awfully handsome of you. Look at this." He holds my arm and lifts his foot to show me a hole in his shoe. "You see? It's shaming, isn't it?" His hand stays on my arm.

"That must be a bore for you." Gently, I disengage his grip. "I should say right away that the job I have in mind is unorthodox and boring. It's also full-time, and I shall need your assurance before I go any further that you won't mention it to anyone."

"How mysterious! Naturally you have my word. What is it?"

I don't answer until I have found a bench for us to sit on, away from the Sunday afternoon crowds.

"I want you to go tomorrow morning and rent this apartment." I give him the newspaper advertisement. "You'll offer the agents three months' money in advance. If they ask for references, use the de Commingeses—I'll clear it with Aimery. Say you want the place immediately: that afternoon if possible. The day after you move in, a man will come to visit you. He'll introduce himself as Robert Houdin. He works for me and he'll tell you what you have to do. Basically it involves watching the building opposite all day. The evenings will be your own."

Ducasse studies the advertisement. "I must say, this sounds very thrilling. Am I becoming a spy?"

"Here is six hundred francs for the deposit on the apartment," I continue, counting out the banknotes I have withdrawn from the special fund in my safe the previous evening, "and here is another four hundred for you. That's two weeks' pay in advance. Yes, you are becoming a spy, but you are never to mention it to a living soul. From now on, we mustn't be seen together. And for heaven's sake, my dear Germain, before you go to the property agency, buy yourself some decent shoes: you're supposed to look like a man who can afford to live in the rue de Lille."

I open an active case file. I decide to call it Operation Benefactor, "Benefactor" being our code name for Esterhazy, borrowed from the girls of Pigalle. Ducasse rents the apartment without difficulty and moves in with a few personal belongings; the following afternoon Desvernine, posing as Houdin, visits him to explain the nature of his work. A delivery van unloads sealed packing cases containing optical and photographic equipment and the chemicals required for a darkroom; the men in leather aprons who carry them upstairs are from the technical department of the Sûreté. A few days later, I arrange to make an inspection for myself.

It is a late afternoon on a balmy day in April, the trees in blossom, the birds singing in the minister's garden: it seems to me that Nature mocks my occupation. I am in civilian dress with the brim of my hat tilted slightly downwards to obscure the upper part of my face. The German Embassy is barely two hundred metres from our front door—all I have to do is turn left out of our office, turn right and immediately I am walking down the narrow rue de Lille: I can see the hôtel de Beauharnais directly ahead on the left, at number 78. A high wall separates it from the road but the big wooden doors are wide open, giving access to a paved courtyard with a couple of parked motorcars. On the far side of the courtyard is an imposing five-storey mansion with a pillared portico. Red-carpeted steps lead up to the entrance; the German Imperial Eagle droops from the flagstaff.

The apartment we have taken is opposite, in number 101. I let myself in and walk towards the stairs. I can hear guttural male German voices from behind the closed door of the ground-floor flat; one says something in a tone of rising hilarity and abruptly they all burst out laughing together. The masculine roar pursues me up the stairs to the first floor. I knock four times; Ducasse opens the door a crack, sees it is me and opens it wider so I can enter.

Inside the apartment the air is stuffy. The windows are all shuttered, the electric lights are lit. The sound of the Germans below is still audible, but more muffled. Ducasse, who is in his stockinged feet, puts his finger to his lips and beckons me through to the drawing room. The carpet has been rolled up against the wall. Desvernine lies flat on his stomach on the bare floorboards, shoeless, with his head in the fireplace. I start to say something but he holds up a warning hand for silence. Suddenly he withdraws his head and scrambles to his feet.

"I think they're finished," he whispers. "It's damnably frustrating, Colonel! They're sitting right by the hearth and I can almost make out what they're saying, but not quite. Would you mind taking off your shoes?"

I sit on the edge of a chair to tug off my boots and glance around, admiring the thoroughness with which he has set up this hide. There are three sets of closed shutters with spyholes bored through them looking across the street to the embassy. One is occupied by the latest model of camera, a modified Kodak bought in London for eighteen pounds sterling, with a film-roll canister and a set of variable lenses, mounted on a tripod; another aperture has a telescope pushed up against it; beside the third stands the desk at which Ducasse logs the times of visitors entering and leaving the embassy. Pinned to the walls are studio photographs of various characters of interest to us, including Esterhazy, von Schwartzkoppen, Count Münster, the elderly German ambassador, and the Italian military attaché, Major Panizzardi.

Desvernine, looking out through the third spyhole, signals to me to join him at the window, then stands aside to let me see. Four men, elegantly dressed in frock coats, are crossing the street below. They have their backs to us, walking away. They pause at the embassy gates and two of them shake hands with a third before strolling on into the courtyard: German diplomats, presumably. The two who are left on the pavement watch them go, then turn away to continue their conversation.

Ducasse, who is focusing the telescope, says, "That's Schwartz-koppen on the left, Georges; the one on the right is the Italian, Panizzardi."

"Use the telescope, Colonel," suggests Desvernine.

Viewed through the lens, the two men loom shockingly close—I might almost be standing with them. Schwartzkoppen is slim, fine-featured, attractively animated, beautifully tailored: a dandy. He throws back his head as he laughs, showing beneath his wide mous-tache a row of perfect white teeth. Panizzardi has his hand on his shoulder and seems to be telling him a funny story. The Italian is handsome in a different way—rounder-faced, with curly dark hair swept back off a wide forehead—but there is the same lively amuse-ment in his features. Another gust of laughter seizes them. Panizzar-di's hand is still on the German's shoulder. They are staring straight into each other's eyes, oblivious to the world.

"My God," I exclaim, "they're in love!"

Ducasse simpers, "You should have heard them the other after-noon, in the bedroom downstairs."

"Filthy buggers!" mutters Desvernine.

I wonder if Madame de Weede knows of her lover's predilections—it's possible, I suppose: nothing much surprises me now.

Finally the laughter on the pavement opposite dwindles to smiles. Panizzardi's face expresses a shrug and the two men lean for-ward and embrace, first one side and then the other. To my left, the camera clicks as Desvernine takes a photograph; he winds the film. Observed casually by someone passing in the street, the embrace would seem no more than a social gesture between good friends, but the pitiless magnification of the telescope reveals how each man whispers into the ear of the other. The clinch is broken. They stand apart. Panizzardi raises his hand in farewell, turns and moves out of vision. Schwartzkoppen remains stationary for several seconds watching him go, a half-smile hovering on his lips, before pivoting on his heel and heading into the embassy courtyard. As he walks, he fans out the tails of his frock coat behind him—a rather magnifi-cent gesture: strutting, virile—then thrusts his hands deep into his trouser pockets.

I take my eye away from the lens and step back in astonishment.

The German and Italian military attachés! "And you say they use the apartment downstairs to meet?"

"'Meet' is one word for it!" Desvernine has draped a black cloth over the back of the camera and is removing the canister of exposed film.

"How are the photographs turning out?"

"Good, as long as the subject doesn't move suddenly. That last one will be a blur, unfortunately."

"Where do you develop the pictures?"

"We have a darkroom in the second bedroom."

"Is the arrangement of the apartment on the ground floor the same as it is up here?"

Ducasse says, "As far as I can tell."

Desvernine asks, "What are you thinking, Colonel?"

"I'm thinking how good it would be to be able to hear what they're actually saying." I cross to the fireplace and run my hands over the plasterwork above the chimneypiece. "If the layout is the same, then presumably the flue from their fireplace would run next to ours?"

Desvernine agrees: "It would."

"Then what if we were to take out a few bricks and lower a speaking-tube down it?"

Ducasse laughs nervously. "Good heavens, Georges, what an idea!"

"You disapprove?"

"They'd be certain to discover it."

"Why?"

"Well . . ." He casts around for reasons. "Supposing they light a fire . . ."

"The weather's warmer. They won't be lighting fires until the autumn."

"It might be possible," agrees Desvernine, nodding slowly, "although it wouldn't be anything like the same quality as if they were actually talking into it."

"Maybe not, but it would be an improvement on what we're picking up now."

Ducasse persists: "But how could you install a speaking-tube in the first place? At the very least you'd need to gain access to their apartment. You'd be breaking the law . . ."

I look at Desvernine, the policeman among us. "It could be arranged," he says.

Reluctant as I am to involve the General Staff, even I recognise that I will need to have Gonse's authority to embark upon an operation as fraught with risk as this, so the next morning I go to see him in his office with a memorandum outlining my plan. I sit opposite him watching as he reads it with his usual infuriating thoroughness, lighting a fresh cigarette from the old one without lifting his eyes from the page. Nowhere in my memo do I mention Esterhazy: I still want to keep Benefactor to myself for the time being.

"You come to me seeking my approval," says Gonse, looking up with irritation when he finishes reading, "but you've already rented the apartment and equipped it."

"I needed to move quickly, while the lease was still available. It was a rare opportunity."

Gonse grunts. "And what do you think we'll get out of it?"

"It will help us discover whether Schwartzkoppen is running any other agents. And it might enable us to turn up the extra evidence about Dreyfus that General Boisdeffre requested."

"I don't think we need to worry about Dreyfus anymore." Gonse starts reading again. His inability to reach a decision is legendary. I wonder how long I will have to sit here until he makes up his mind. His tone softens. "But is it really worth the risk, my dear Picquart? That's what I ask myself. It's quite a provocation to set up shop on the Germans' doorstep like this. If they find out, they will kick up the devil of a fuss."

"On the contrary: if they find out, they won't say a word. It would make them look like fools. Besides, Schwartzkoppen will be terrified we'll expose him as a pansy, which we could—you know it carries a sentence of five years' imprisonment in Germany? That would pay him back for employing Dreyfus."

"Good God, I couldn't possibly countenance that! Von Schwartz-koppen is a gentleman. It would be contrary to all our traditions."

I anticipated his objections, and I have come prepared. "Do you remember what you told me when you first offered me this job, General?"

"What's that?"

"You said that espionage was the new front line in the war against the enemy." I lean forward and tap my report. "Here we have an opportunity to push that front line right into the heart of German territory. In my view this sort of audacious enterprise is very much in the tradition of the French army."

"My goodness, Picquart, you really hate the Germans, don't you?"

"I don't hate them. They're just occupying my family's home."

Gonse sits back and regards me through his cigarette smoke—a long, evaluating look, as if he is recalculating all his previous assumptions—and for a few moments I wonder if I have gone too far. Then he says, "Actually, I do remember when I appointed you, Colonel; I remember it very well. I was worried by your reluctance to accept. I feared you might be too scrupulous for this kind of work. It seems I was wrong." He stamps my memorandum, signs it and holds it out to me. "I won't stop you. But if it all goes wrong, the blame will rest with you."

8

We decide that if we are going to install one listening-tube, we might as well put in a second, in the bedroom, where Schwartzkoppen and Panizzardi are more likely to discuss their most intimate matters. Desvernine has to smuggle in the necessary equipment: the tubes, a saw, cutters, a hammer and chisel, sacks for the rubble. The work of breaking into the chimney flues can only be undertaken when the ground-floor apartment is empty, usually at night. Ducasse is also worried about the couple who live upstairs, who have already started to ask him suspicious questions about the noises they can hear, and what he does all day. So the work must be undertaken with agonising slowness: a ringing blow from the hammer, and then a pause; a blow from the hammer, another pause. Loosening a single brick can take all night. There is a constant risk of dislodging a fall of soot into the Germans' fireplaces. It is also filthy work. Nerves become strained. Desvernine reports that Ducasse is starting to drink heavily: another occupational hazard of the spying business.

There is also the problem of gaining access to the Germans' premises. Desvernine first suggests that we simply break in. He comes to my office with a small leather tool roll, which he opens out on my desk. It contains a set of steel lock-picking instruments, designed for the Sûreté by a master locksmith. They look like a surgeon's scalpels. He explains what they do: double-ended picks for various types of locks—trunk, wafer, bit key and disc tumbler; rakes for loosening tumblers that are stuck . . . The very sight of them, and the thought of one of our agents getting caught while burglarising a property rented by the Germans, makes me feel queasy.

"But it's very simple, Colonel," he insists. "Look. Show me any-thing here that's locked."

"Very well." I indicate the top right-hand drawer of my desk.

Desvernine kneels, inspects the lock and selects a couple of his tools. "You need two, do you see? You insert your tension tool to put pressure on the racking stump, like this . . . Then you insert the pick and you feel for the first tumbler and raise that to the unlocking posi-tion . . ." He grimaces with concentration. "Then you do the same for any other tumblers . . . And then . . ." He smiles and opens the drawer. "It's done!"

"Leave them with me," I say. "Let me think about it."

After he's gone, I lock the tools in my desk. From time to time I take them out and look at them. No, I decide: it's too risky, too criminal. Instead I come up with a plan of my own, one that has the merit of being perfectly legal. I put it to Desvernine a day or two later.

"All we need is access to their fireplaces, correct?"

"Yes."

"And this is exactly the time of year when fires are no longer needed and chimneys are swept, is it not?"

"Yes."

"Then why don't you simply disguise a couple of your men as chimney sweeps, and have them offer to clean the Germans' flues?"

In the middle of May, Desvernine comes to see me in my office wearing a rare smile. It turns out that a friend of his wife's brother knows a chimney sweep, a patriot, who happened to be in the same regiment of dragoons when Desvernine was a sergeant. It was the pleasure of this man, whose father was killed in '70, to do something to help the Republic, no questions asked. That lunchtime, says Des-vernine, when the Germans were drinking before sitting down to eat, he knocked on the door of the ground-floor apartment, announced himself as the sweep, and was admitted without a question being asked. Under the very noses of those stiff-necked Prussians, he went back and forth to the first floor, lowering the tubes while pretending to clean the flues, and then secured both in place. At the end, when he left his card, one of the Germans actually gave him a tip.

"And can you hear much?" I ask.

"Plenty, especially if whoever is speaking is sitting or standing near to the fireplace. Well, let's put it this way—you can get the sense of a conversation."

"That's good work. Well done."

"And there's something else, Colonel."

From his pocket, Desvernine produces an envelope and a magnifying glass. Inside the envelope is a photograph, ten centimetres by thirteen. I take it over to the window, for the light.

Desvernine says, "It was exposed yesterday afternoon, just after three o'clock."

Without magnification the figure of a man leaving through the embassy gates is difficult to distinguish, and even with it one has to concentrate hard: his forward momentum has slightly blurred the image; the shadow cast behind him by the bright May sun is sharper. However, a prolonged examination leaves little doubt. On this occasion the distinctive round eyes and the extravagant ram's-horn moustache prove to be the traitor's own betrayers: it is Esterhazy.

On the Friday of that week Bachir comes creaking and gasping up the stairs to my office with a personal telegram addressed to me care of the ministry. It has taken a while to reach me, and even before he hands it over I have a premonition that it concerns my mother, which can only mean bad news. In some private corner of our minds, from the moment we first become conscious of mortality, are we not all waiting secretly for our parents' deaths? Or is this constant state of dread unique to those of us who have already been bereaved in childhood? In any case, the telegram is from Anna, my sister, and announces that our mother has fallen and broken her hip. To reset the joint, the doctors have decided to anaesthetise her, to spare her the pain and distress. "She is bewildered and hysterical. If possible, please come at once."

I walk along the corridor and tell Henry. He offers friendly sympathy: "I know exactly how you feel, Colonel. Don't worry about things here. I'll make sure the office runs efficiently in your absence."

His warmth is clearly genuine, and I feel an unexpected pang of affection for the old brute. I say I shall let him know how long I'll be away. He wishes me luck.

By the time I reach the hospital in Versailles, the operation has been done. Anna is sitting at Maman's bedside with her husband, Jules Gay. Both are more than ten years older than I am: good family people, capable, with two grown-up children and two still teenaged. Jules is a professor at a Paris lycée, a booming, red-faced Lyon man, devoutly Catholic and conservative, who, by all the laws of logic, I should dislike and yet who, by some strange alchemy, for over a quarter of a century I have always loved. Even as they rise to greet me, I can tell from their faces things are not good.

"How is she?"

In reply, Anna moves aside so I can see the bed. My mother is shrunken, tiny, grey. Her face is turned away from me. The lower side of her body is encased in plaster, which seems weirdly bigger and more substantial than she is. She looks like a sickly fledgling, halfway out of its egg.

"When will she come round from the chloroform?"

"She has come round, Georges."

"What?" At first I don't understand. I put my hand gently under her cheek and turn her head towards me. "Maman?" Her eyes are indeed open, but watery and vacant; they peer into mine without a sign of recognition. It is not uncommon, the doctor tells me, for patients in her condition, if given anaesthetic, to leave part of their minds behind in sleep. I start to shout at him—"Why didn't you tell us that before?"—but Anna calms me: what alternative did we have?

The following day we take her home. On Sunday morning the bells of Saint-Louis ring for Mass, but if she hears them she no longer knows what they mean. She even seems to have forgotten how to eat.

We hire a nurse to look after her during the day, and from now on every evening I leave the office early and return to Versailles to sleep in the spare bedroom. I am not alone in this vigil, of course. Anna and Jules travel out from Paris most days. My cousin Edmond Gast and his wife, Jeanne, drive over from Ville-d'Avray. And one night I arrive back later than usual to find Pauline by the bed reading aloud a novel to her unresponsive audience. When she puts down the book and rises to embrace me, I hold on to her.

I say, "This time I don't think I'm ever going to let you go."

"Georges," she whispers primly, "your mother . . ."

We glance down at her. She is lying on her back with her eyes closed. The muscles of her face have relaxed; her expression is impassive, almost regal in its indifference; she is beyond all convention now, I think, all stupid narrow morality . . .

I say, "She can't see us, and if she could, she'd be delighted. You know she could never understand why we weren't married."

"She is not alone in that . . ."

She says it wryly. She has never reproached me. We grew up together in Alsace. We survived the siege together. We clung to each other when we were both in exile, when everything else had gone. I was her first lover. I should have proposed to her before I left to join my regiment in Algeria. But I always thought there would be plenty of time for that later. As it was, when I finished my foreign soldiering and came home from Indochina, she had given up on me, and had already produced one daughter and was pregnant with a second. I didn't even mind very much, especially as we soon resumed our love affair where we had left it. "We have something better than a future together," I used to tell her. "We have the past." I'm not sure I entirely believe it anymore.

"You realise," I say, taking her hand, "that we've been together, in one way or another, for more than twenty years? It practically is a marriage."

"Oh Georges," she says wearily, "I can assure you this is nothing like a marriage."

The front door opens, we hear my sister's voice, and immediately she pulls away her hand.

My mother lingers on in this state for a month. It is astonishing how long the body can last without nourishment. Occasionally, as I jolt back and forth on the crowded Versailles train, I remember Henry's remark: *There aren't many easy ways out of this life* . . . Her path, though, seems to be a smooth and gentle descent into oblivion.

Henry is solicitous throughout. One day he asks me if I might have a moment to step down to the waiting room to meet his wife, who has something for me. I have never before considered what sort of a woman Henry might be married to; I assume she will be a female version of him—large, red-faced, loud, coarse. Instead I find a tall and slender young woman, barely half his age, with thick dark hair, a clear complexion and lively brown eyes. He introduces her as Berthe. Like Henry, she has the accent of the Marne. In one hand she proffers a bunch of flowers, which she has brought for me to pass on to my mother; with the other she is holding on to a boy of two or three, dressed in a sailor suit. It seems strange to see a child in this gloomy building. Henry says, "This is my boy, Joseph." "Hello, Joseph." I pick him up and whirl him around for a bit while his parents look on smiling (we bachelors learn to be good with children). Then I set him down and thank Madame Henry for the flowers. She lowers her eyes flirtatiously. As I walk back upstairs, I reflect that Henry may be a more complex character than I appreciated. His pride in his pretty young wife is understandable, and I can see why he wants to show her off; but in Madame Henry I sense ambition, and I wonder what that does to him.

My mother receives the last rites on the afternoon of Friday, 12 June 1896. It is a hot summer's day outside, full of the noise of the street; the sunlight, fierce beyond the drawn curtains, beats down on the glass regardless as if demanding entrance. I watch as the priest anoints her ears, eyes, nostrils, lips, hands and feet while he intones his Latin spells. His handshake when he leaves is moistly repulsive. She dies in my arms that night, and when I kiss her goodbye, I taste the residue of his oil.

The event has long been anticipated; the arrangements are all in place; but the shock is somehow as great as if she had dropped dead out of the blue. After the requiem Mass in Saint-Louis's and the interment in a corner of the cemetery, we walk back to her apartment for the wake. It is an uncomfortable occasion. The weather is too warm; the tiny rooms are too crowded and full of tensions. My sister-in-law, Hélène, widow of my brother, Paul, has turned up: for some reason she has always disliked me, and we take pains to avoid each other—no easy feat in that cramped space—so much so that in the end I find myself in my mother's old bedroom, its mattress stripped, talking to, of all people, Pauline's husband.

Monnier is a decent enough sort, devoted in his way to his wife and daughters. If he were a brute, our deception would be easier. Instead he is simply dull. Professionally, his role in the Foreign Ministry, as far as I can make out, seems to be that of the senior bureaucrat brought in to pick holes in the bright ideas of younger colleagues. Socially, he has the bore's trick of seeking one's opinion on something—in this case he asks my view of the impending state visit of the Russian tsar—and listening to it with barely disguised impatience, until he is at last able to interrupt and launch into his own prepared monologue. It turns out he has been appointed to the Franco-Russian planning commission for the trip—apparently His Imperial Highness's official train, at four hundred and fifty tons, is two hundred tons heavier than our railways can cope with, and he has had to speak firmly to the ambassador on the matter . . .

Over his shoulder I can see Pauline talking to Louis Leblois. Her gaze meets mine. Monnier glances behind him, irritated not to have my complete attention, then resumes his speech.

"As I was saying, it's not so much a question of protocol as of basic good manners . . ."

I try to concentrate on his diplomatic platitudes; it seems the least I can do.

Throughout this time, Operation Benefactor has continued running like an untended machine, churning out intelligence, almost all of it useless: stacks of blurry photographs and lists of visitors to the rue de Lille (*unidentified male, mid-fifties, walks with slight limp, ex-military?*) and fragmentary transcripts of conversations (*I saw him at the manoeuvres in Karlsruhe and he offered [unintelligible] but I told him we already had [unintelligible] from our source in Paris*). By July I have spent thousands from the secret fund bequeathed to me by Sandherr, risked a serious diplomatic crisis, concealed a potential traitor from my superiors, and I have nothing of tangible value to show for it except that one picture of Esterhazy leaving the embassy.

And then, quite unexpectedly, all of this changes, and with it my life and career and everything else.

It is a broiling summer's evening. I am out of Paris for once, accompanying General Boisdeffre on a staff tour in the Burgundy region. Our advance scouts have found us a good restaurant beside a canal in Venarey-les-Laumes, and we dine out of doors, to the sound of bullfrogs and cicadas, washed by the scent of the citronella candles that are driving away the mosquitoes. I am seated a little way down the table from Boisdeffre, beside his orderly officer, Major Gabriel Pauffin de Saint Morel. Moths dart in and out of the gleam of the lanterns; stars have just started to appear above the hillside vineyards to the east. What could be more agreeable? Pauffin is an exquisitely handsome, vaguely dim aristocrat, exactly my age, give or take a couple of weeks, who I have known since we were cadets at Saint-Cyr. His profile in the candlelight is flushed with the effects of the wine and the heat, and he is in the act of spooning some soft and pungent Époisses de Bourgogne onto his plate when suddenly quite out of the blue he says, "Oh, by the way, I'm sorry, Picquart, I clean forgot—the chief wants you to have a word with Colonel Foucault when we get back to Paris."

"Yes, of course I will. Do you know what it's about?" Foucault is our military attaché in Berlin.

Still concentrating on his cheese, without lowering his voice or even turning to look at me, Pauffin replies, "Oh, I believe he's picked up some story in Berlin about the Germans having another spy in the army. He sent the chief a letter about it."

"What?" I set down my glass with enough force to spill some wine. "My God, when was this exactly?"

The tone of my voice causes him to glance in my direction. "A few days ago. Sorry, Georges. Slipped my mind."

There is nothing I can do that evening, but the following morning I seek out Boisdeffre over breakfast in the chateau where we are staying and ask permission to return at once to Paris to interview Colonel Foucault.

Boisdeffre takes a corner of his napkin and wipes a speck of egg from his moustache. "Why the urgency? You think there might be something in it?"

"Perhaps. I'd like to check."

Boisdeffre seems surprised by my keenness to depart, even mildly offended: an invitation to join him on one of these leisurely tours of inspection to our finer gastronomic regions is regarded as a mark of favour. "As you wish," he says, dismissing me with a flourish of his napkin. "Keep me informed."

By early afternoon I am back in the Ministry of War, sitting in Foucault's office, listening to his report. Our military attaché in Berlin is a competent, straightforward professional, hardened by years of dealing with liars and fantasists. His hair is iron-grey, thick, cut short; it fits him like a helmet. He says, "I was wondering when General Boisdeffre would get around to responding to my letter." Wearily he retrieves a file from his drawer and opens it. "You remember our agent in the Tiergarten, Richard Cuers?"

The Tiergarten is the district in Berlin where German army intelligence has its headquarters.

"Yes, of course. He was working for German intelligence in Paris until we turned him. Sandherr briefed me about him when I took over."

"Well, he's been dismissed."

"That's a pity. When did this happen?"

"Three weeks ago. Did you ever meet Cuers?"

I shake my head.

"He's a nervy fellow at the best of times, but when he came to tell me what had happened, he was in a truly terrible state. He's scared the German General Staff are going to arrest him for treason. He thinks his friend Lajoux in Brussels ratted him out for money, which may well be true. In any case, he wants to make sure we'll protect him. Otherwise, he says, he'll have no choice except to go to Hauptmann Dame—that's his section chief—and sing his heart out about us."

"Does he know much?"

"A little."

"So he's trying to blackmail us?"

"I don't think so. Not really. He just wants reassurance."

"Then let's give it to him. Reassurance doesn't cost a sou—he can have all the reassurance he wants. Tell him he can be certain nothing will leak about him from our end."

"I told him he had nothing to worry about. But it's rather more complicated than that." Foucault sighs and rubs his forehead: I realise he is under some strain. "He wants to hear it man to man—a personal meeting with someone from the section itself."

"But that's just an unnecessary risk for both of us. What if he's followed?"

"I made exactly that point. He was quite insistent. That was when I began to realise there was more to it than he was telling me. So I fetched out a bottle of absinthe—he likes absinthe because he says it reminds him of a French girl he was once in love with—and gradually I got him to tell me the whole story."

"Which is what?"

"He's scared and wants to meet someone from the section because he says the Germans have a spy in the French army we don't know about."

Here it is. I try to put on a show of nonchalance. "Does this spy have a name?"

"No. The best he can offer are some details that he's picked up here and there." Foucault checks the file. "This agent is said to be at the level of a battalion commander. He's between forty and fifty years old. He's been passing information to Schwartzkoppen for roughly two years, mostly about artillery, and most of it not of high quality—he recently handed over details of a gunnery course at Châlons, for example. The intelligence has gone right up the chain of command to von Schlieffen[*] himself, who apparently doesn't like the smell of it—thinks the source could be a hoaxer, or an agent provocateur—and has told Schwartzkoppen to have nothing more to do with him." He looks up from the file. "I put all this in my letter to General Boisdeffre. Does it ring any bells for you?"

---

[*] Field Marshal Count Alfred von Schlieffen (1833–1913), Chief of the Imperial German General Staff.

I pretend to think. "Not immediately." In truth, it is all I can do not to leap from my chair. "Is that all there is?"

Foucault laughs. "Do you mean: was there a second bottle?" He closes the file and returns it to his drawer. "Yes, there was. In fact I ended up having to clean him up and put him to bed. See how I suffer for my country!"

I join in the laughter. "I'll arrange a medal."

Foucault's smile dies away. "The truth is, Colonel Picquart, our friend Cuers is a neurotic, and like most neurotics he is a fantasist. So let's be clear: when I pass on to you what he tells me, I'm not endorsing it, you understand? There are some agents I might vouch for; Cuers isn't one of them. That's why I haven't put the rest of his story in writing."

"I know entirely what you mean." I wonder what is coming next. "I shall treat everything you tell me in an appropriate spirit of scepticism."

"Good." Foucault pauses. He frowns at his desk and then looks at me—a very straight, level gaze, soldier to soldier. "Here it is then: Cuers says German intelligence is still very angry about the Dreyfus business."

"You mean about the fact that we caught him?"

"No. About the fact that they'd never even heard of him—or so Cuers says."

I hold the colonel's gaze. His eyes are dark, and unwavering. "Then presumably," I reply carefully, "they're still covering up for him."

"What? Even in private?" Foucault winces and shakes his head. "No. I accept in public one has to go on denying these things for ever—that's the diplomatic game. But why carry on denying it behind closed doors to one another, year after year?"

"Perhaps no one in Berlin wants to admit to running Dreyfus—given how badly it ended?"

"We both know that's not how these things work, though, don't we? According to Cuers, the Kaiser personally demanded the truth from Schlieffen: 'Did the Imperial army ever employ this Jew, yes or no?' Schlieffen in turn asked the question of Dame, who swore he knew nothing of any Jewish spy. On Schlieffen's orders, Dame recalled Schwartzkoppen to Berlin for consultation—Cuers saw him in the Tiergarten with his own eyes—and Schwartzkoppen insisted that the first time he ever heard the name Dreyfus was when he opened his newspaper after the spy had been arrested. Cuers told me Dame has since made discreet inquiries of every other friendly European intelligence agency, to see if any of them had ever employed Dreyfus. Again: nothing."

"And they feel angry about this?"

"Yes, of course—you know how touchy our ponderous Prussian neighbours are about being taken for fools. They think the whole thing is some sophisticated French trick designed to make them look bad in the eyes of the world."

"But that's absurd!"

"No doubt. But it's what they believe—or so Cuers says."

Without realising it, I have been gripping my armrests like a man in a dentist's chair. I make a conscious effort to relax. I cross my legs, adjust the crease of my trousers, affect a coolness I don't feel, and which I'm sure doesn't fool Foucault—a professional connoisseur of dissembling—for a second.

"It seems to me," I say after a long pause, "that we should approach this business one step at a time, and the first step should be to take Cuers up on his suggestion of a meeting and debrief him thoroughly."

"I agree with that."

"And in the meantime we should keep it to ourselves."

"I agree with that even more."

"How soon can you return to Berlin?"

"Tomorrow morning."

"Might I suggest that you contact Cuers and tell him we want to talk, as early as possible?"

"I'll do it the moment I get back."

"The question is: where can we meet him? It can't really be on German soil."

"Absolutely not—too risky." Foucault thinks it over. "What about Switzerland?"

"That would be safe enough. Basel perhaps? It's full of visitors at this time of year. He could pretend to be on a walking holiday; we could meet him there."

"I'll put it to him and let you know. You'll pay his expenses? Sorry to bring it up, but I know it'll be the first question he asks."

I smile. "Ah, the people with whom we work! Of course we will."

I stand and salute. Foucault does the same. Then we shake hands. No further words are exchanged; none is needed—we both understand the potentially staggering import of what we have just discussed.

So I have found one spy, at least. On that score any vestige of doubt is gone. Major Charles Ferdinand Walsin Esterhazy—"Count Esterhazy," as he likes to style himself—walks the streets of Rouen and Paris, gambles, drinks champagne in nightclubs, fucks most nights with Four-Fingered Marguerite in an apartment near Montmartre, and funds his squalid lifestyle by trying to sell his country's secrets to a foreign power with all the dignity of a door-to-door pedlar.

Yes, Esterhazy is a simple matter: an open-and-shut case, in point of fact if not in law. But Dreyfus? My God, that is a much bigger question—that is a nightmare, actually—and as I walk back from the ministry to the Statistical Section, my mind begins to race with the implications, so much so that I have to make another deliberate effort to calm down. I issue orders to myself: Take it one step at a time, Picquart! Approach the matter dispassionately, Picquart! Avoid a rush to judgement! Confide in nobody until there is hard evidence!

Still, when I reach the front door, I cast a wistful look down the rue de l'Université towards the apartment of Louis Leblois—what wouldn't I give for a chance to talk it over with him . . .

When I get upstairs to my office, I find a message waiting for me from Desvernine asking if he can see me tonight: same time, same place. Thanks to my travels with Boisdeffre, it is ten days since I last met him, and by the time I arrive at the café of the gare Saint-Lazare, a quarter of an hour late, he is already sitting waiting with a glass of beer set up for me and, unprecedentedly, one for himself.

"This is a first," I say, as we touch glasses. "Do we have something to celebrate?"

"Perhaps." Desvernine wipes the foam from his moustache, reaches into his inside pocket, places a photograph upside down on the table and slides it across to me. I pick it up and turn it over. No magnifying glass is needed this time. It is as sharp as a studio portrait: Esterhazy in a grey bowler coming out of the German embassy gates. I can even make out a half-smile on his face. He must have paused to enjoy the warmth of the sun.

"So he's been back," I say. "That's significant."

"No, Colonel, what's significant is what's in his hand."

I look at the image again. "His hand is empty."

Desvernine slides over another facedown photograph and sits back to enjoy his beer while he watches my reaction. This picture shows a figure in three-quarters profile, in blurry motion, turning from the street to enter the embassy. In his right hand he carries something white: an envelope, perhaps, or a package. I lay the photographs side by side. It is the grey bowler that gives him away: that and the height and the build.

"How long between the two?"

"Twelve minutes."

"He's careless."

"Careless? He's *shameless* is what he is. You want to be careful of this one, Colonel. I've come across his type before." He taps the face with an oily thumbnail. "There's nothing he isn't capable of."

Two nights later, I receive a cipher telegram from Colonel Foucault in Berlin: Cuers is willing to meet our representatives in Basel on Thursday, 6 August.

My first instinct is to go myself. I even consult the railway timetable. But then I pause to weigh the risks. Basel straddles the German border: I have visited it a couple of times on my way to the Wagner festival in Bayreuth. The population speaks German; the buildings are Gothic, half-timbered, shuttered: it feels exactly like a city in the Reich; I shall be surrounded by unfriendly faces. And I have to assume that after more than a year in post, there is a chance that Berlin has now discovered my identity as Sandherr's successor. I am not afraid for my personal safety, but I can't afford to be self-indulgent: there is too much at stake. If I were to be spotted, the consequences for the rendezvous could be disastrous.

Accordingly, on the morning of Monday, 3 August, three days before the scheduled meeting, I invite Major Henry and Captain Lauth to come into my office. They arrive together, as usual. I sit at the head of the conference table, Henry to my left and Lauth to my right. I have the Benefactor file in front of me. Henry looks at it suspiciously.

"Gentlemen," I begin, opening the file, "I feel this is an appropriate time for me to brief you on an intelligence operation that has been running now for several months and which has finally started to bear fruit."

I take them through it stage by stage, starting with a recap of what they already know. I produce the *petit bleu* addressed to Esterhazy and the draft letter from Schwartzkoppen complaining that he is not getting value for money from "the house of R." I remind them of my visit to Rouen and of my conversation with my friend Major Curé. "After that," I say, "I took the decision to commission a thorough investigation." I read out Desvernine's reports on Esterhazy: his debts, his gambling, his four-fingered mistress and the rest. They listen in a silence that becomes increasingly tense. When I describe how we have taken the apartment opposite the German Embassy, I notice how they briefly glance at each other in surprise. Then, with a conjuror's flourish, I pull out the photographs of Esterhazy's two visits.

Henry puts on his spectacles and scrutinises them for a while. "Does General Gonse know about this?"

"He knows about the surveillance operation, yes."

"But not specifically about Esterhazy?"

"Not yet. I wanted to wait until we had enough evidence to pick him up."

"I understand." Henry passes the photographs over to Lauth and removes his spectacles. He sucks on one of the stems in the manner of a scholar appraising a colleague's research. "This is very interest-ing, Colonel, although of course we're not there yet. It's impressive circumstantial detail, no question of that. But show all this to Ester-hazy and he'll simply say he was dropping off a visa application. And we can't prove otherwise."

"I agree. But in the last few days there's been a significant new development, which is why I want to widen the scope of the opera-tion." I pause. This is the decisive moment. A few words from me now and everything will be different. Henry taps his glasses against his teeth, waiting. "We have a source with information from inside German military intelligence. He says they've been running an agent in France for several years. This agent holds the rank of major. He's between forty and fifty years old. He's been on the gunnery course at Châlons."

Lauth says, "That must be Esterhazy!"

"I don't think there can be much doubt. Our source is offering to meet us in Basel on Thursday to tell us all he knows."

Henry emits a low whistle of surprise, and for the first time I see in his expression a trace of something like respect. It makes me want to go even further, to confide everything ("And you know what else? He also claims Dreyfus was never a German spy!"), but I don't want to venture that far yet. *Take it one step at a time, Picquart!*

Henry says, "Who is this source?"

"Richard Cuers—do you remember, the Germans used him here a few years ago? He's been employed by Hauptmann Dame in Berlin. Now Dame has let him go, probably because he suspects him, and he's come running to us."

"Do we trust him?"

"Do we trust anybody? But I don't see why he should lie, do you? At the very least, we should find out what he has to say." I turn to Lauth. "Captain, I'd like you to take charge of his debriefing."

"Of course, Colonel." Lauth bows quickly in his Teutonic man-ner. If he were standing up, I think, he would click his heels.

Henry says, "Why my good friend Lauth here, might I ask?"

"Because he's known about the case since we retrieved the *petit bleu*, but above all because he speaks German."

Henry objects: "If Cuers worked here, he must have decent

French. Why don't I go? I'm more experienced in dealing with these rogues."

"Yes, but I think he'll talk more freely in his native language. Is that all right with you, Lauth?" Lauth's German is perfect, almost accentless.

"Yes." He glances at Henry for approval. "Yes, I'm sure I can handle it."

"Good. You'll need at least one man as backup, possibly two, just to make sure Cuers comes on his own and this isn't all a trap. I'm proposing to assign Louis Tomps to the mission. He knows Cuers from Paris days." Tomps is another of the Sûreté officers, like Guénée and Desvernine, who does work for the section: a competent, reliable fellow who also has the advantage of speaking good German; I've used him before. "We'll discuss the operational details later. Thank you, gentlemen."

Lauth jumps up. "Thank you, Colonel!"

Henry stays seated for a moment or two, contemplating the table, then pushes back his chair and rises heavily to his feet. He tugs his tunic down over his commodious belly. "Yes, thank you, Colonel." There is a wistful look in his eyes: I can tell he's still not reconciled to being excluded from the Basel meeting, but can't come up with a way to convince me to let him go. "Interesting," he repeats, "very interesting. I must say, though, if I were you—if you'll allow me to make a suggestion—I'd tell General Gonse what's going on. It's a serious matter—a French officer meeting a German spy on foreign soil to discuss a traitor in our own ranks. You wouldn't want him finding out from someone else."

After he's gone, I wonder if that was a threat. If so, then in the chess game of military bureaucracy, I have the perfect countermove. I walk over to the ministry, climb the stairs to the office of the Chief of the General Staff, and ask for an appointment to see General Boisdeffre.

Queen takes bishop!

Unfortunately, his orderly officer tells me that the general has gone straight from Burgundy to Vichy.

I send Boisdeffre a telegram asking to speak to him urgently.

The following morning—the Tuesday—I receive a weary reply: *My dear Colonel Picquart, Is it really as pressing a matter as all that? I am on vacation taking the waters, and then going home to Normandy for my annual leave. What is this about?*

I respond in guarded terms that *it concerns a matter similar to that of 1894*—meaning the Dreyfus affair.

Within an hour I have an answer: *Very well, if you insist. My train arrives tomorrow, Wednesday, 5 August, 18:15 hours gare de Lyon. Meet me. Boisdeffre.*

Henry does not give up easily, however.

On the same day that I receive Boisdeffre's summons to see him, I hold a final meeting in my office with Lauth and Tomps to discuss the arrangements for the Basel interview. The plan is straightforward. The two men—plus Inspector Vuillecard, police commissioner in Vassy, whom Tomps has chosen as his assistant—will catch the sleeper train tomorrow night from the gare de l'Est, arriving in Basel at six o'clock on Thursday morning. All three will be armed. In Basel, they will split up. Lauth will go directly to a private room in the Schweizerhof hotel, which is right next to the station, and wait. Tomps will go to the city's other main railway terminus, the Badischer Bahnhof, on the opposite side of the Rhine, where the German trains arrive. Meanwhile Vuillecard will position himself in Munsterplatz, in front of the cathedral, which is where the initial rendezvous is to take place at nine o'clock. Tomps, who knows Cuers by sight, will watch as Cuers comes through passport control from the Berlin train to make sure he is not being followed, and will then tail him all the way to Munsterplatz, where Vuillecard will be holding a white handkerchief as a signal. Cuers will approach the inspector and say, in French, "Are you Monsieur Lescure?" (Lescure was the name of the doorkeeper in the rue Saint-Dominique for many years), to which Vuillecard will reply, "No, but I am supposed to take you to him," whereupon Vuillecard will conduct the German agent to his meeting with Lauth in the hotel.

"I want you to extract absolutely every last scrap of information you can out of him," I order Lauth, "however long it takes. Continue into the following day if necessary."

"Yes, Colonel."

"The main focus is Esterhazy, but don't feel you have to confine yourself to him."

"No, Colonel."

"Whatever leads come up, however outlandish, follow them."

"Of course, Colonel."

At the end of the meeting we shake hands and I wish them luck. Tomps leaves but Lauth lingers. He says, "I want to make a request, Colonel, if I may?"

"Go ahead."

"I think it would be useful to take Major Henry with me, as backup."

At first I think he must be suffering from stage fright. "Come now, Captain Lauth! You don't need any backup! You're perfectly capable of handling Cuers on your own."

But Lauth holds his ground. "I really feel the mission would benefit from Major Henry's experience, Colonel. There are matters he knows about which I don't. And he's good with people. They let their guard down with him, whereas I tend to be rather . . . formal."

"Has Major Henry asked you to say all this to me? Because I don't take kindly to officers questioning my authority behind my back."

"No, Colonel. Certainly not!" Lauth's pale neck flushes candy pink. "It's not for me to interfere in matters above my grade. But sometimes I sense that Major Henry needs to be made to feel . . . *valued*—if I can put it that way."

"And by not sending him to Basel I've hurt his feelings—is that what you're trying to say?"

Lauth doesn't reply. He hangs his head. As well he might, I think, for there is something preposterous about Henry's desire to insinuate himself, like a nosy concierge, into every aspect of the section's work. On the other hand, putting aside my irritation—*Approach the matter dispassionately, Picquart!*—I can see that there are certain potential advantages to me in letting Henry feel that he is an equal partner in the investigation into Esterhazy. The first rule of survival in any bureaucracy is safety in numbers, and I have no desire to turn into a lone voice—on this issue especially. If it does transpire, God forbid, that we have to look again at the Dreyfus case, I will need to have Henry at my side.

I tap my foot in irritation. "Very well," I say at length. "If you both feel strongly about it, then Major Henry can accompany you to the meeting."

"Yes, Colonel. Thank you, Colonel." Lauth is almost pathetic in his gratitude.

I jab my finger at him to emphasise the point. "But the interview with Cuers should be in German, you understand?"

This time Lauth really does click his heels. "It will be."

9

At five o'clock the following afternoon, the Swiss expedition assembles in the lobby, kitted out in stout walking boots, high socks, sports jackets and knapsacks. The cover story is that they are four friends on a hiking holiday in the Baselbiet. Henry's jacket is of an unfortunate broad-check design; his felt hat sprouts a feather. He is red-faced and grumpy in the heat. It makes one wonder why he has schemed so hard to join the party.

"My dear Major Henry," I laugh, "this is taking disguise too far—you look like a Tyrolean innkeeper!" Tomps and Vuillecard and even Lauth all join in the amusement, but Henry remains sullen. He likes teasing others but can't abide to be teased himself. I say to Lauth, "Send me a telegram from Basel to let me know how the meeting goes, and what time you'll be back—in coded terms, of course. Good luck, gentlemen. I must say, I wouldn't let you into my country dressed like that, but then I'm not Swiss!"

I walk with them out of the door and see them into their cab. I wait until the landau is out of sight before setting off on foot towards my own rendezvous. I have plenty of time, enough to make the most of this perfect late summer afternoon, and so I stroll along the embankment, past the big construction site on the quai d'Orsay, where a new railway terminus and grand hotel are rising beside the river. The first great international event of the twentieth century will be held here in Paris in less than four years' time—the Universal Exhibition of 1900—and the giant skeleton of the building swarms with workers. There is a definite energy in the air; there is even, dare one say it, optimism—not a quality that has been in wide supply in France over the past couple of decades. I amble along the Left Bank

and on to the pont de Sully, where I stop and lean against the para-
pet, looking west along the Seine to Notre-Dame. I am still trying to
work out how best to deal with the coming meeting.

Such are the vagaries of public life that General de Boisdeffre,
firmly in Mercier's shadow barely a year and a half ago, has now
emerged as one of the most popular men in the country. Indeed, for
the past three months it has scarcely been possible to open a newspaper without reading a story about him, whether as head of the
French delegation at the coronation of the Tsar in Moscow, or relay-
ing the President's respects to the Tsarina while she vacationed on the
Côte d'Azur, or watching the Grand Prix de Paris at Longchamps
in the company of the Russian ambassador. Russia, Russia, Russia—
that is all one hears, and Boisdeffre's strategic alliance is considered
the diplomatic triumph of the age, although privately I have reser-
vations about fighting the Germans alongside an army of serfs.

Still, there is no denying Boisdeffre's celebrity. His schedule has
been printed in the newspapers, and when I arrive at the gare de
Lyon, the first thing I encounter is a crowd of admirers waiting to
catch a glimpse of their idol disembarking from the Vichy train.
When at last it pulls into the platform, several dozen run along its
entire length trying to spot him. Eventually he emerges and pauses
in the doorway for the photographers. He is in civilian dress but
unmistakable nonetheless, his tall and erect figure made even loftier
by a beautiful silk top hat. He doffs it politely to the applauding
throng, then descends to the platform, followed by Pauffin de Saint
Morel and a couple of other orderlies. He progresses slowly towards
the ticket barrier, like a great stately battleship passing in a naval
review, raising his hat and smiling faintly at the cries of *"Vive Boisdeffre!"* and *"Vive l'armée!,"* until he sees me. His expression clouds
briefly while he tries to remember why I am there, then he acknowledges my salute with a friendly nod. "Ride with me in my automobile, Picquart," he says, "although I'm afraid I'm only going as far
as the hôtel de Sens, so it will have to be brief."

The automobile, a Panhard Levassor, has no roof. We sit up on
the cushioned bench seat, the general and I, behind the driver,
and trundle shakily over the cobblestones towards the rue de Lyon,

watched by a small group of passengers queuing for taxis, who recognise the Chief of the General Staff and break into cheers.

Boisdeffre says, "I think that's enough for them, don't you?" He takes off his hat and places it in his lap, and runs his hand through his thinning white hair. "So what is all this about another 1894?"

Although this is hardly the kind of interview I had rehearsed, there is at least no danger of our being overheard: he has to turn and shout his question into my ear and I respond in a similar way. "We believe we've found a traitor in the army, General, passing information to the Germans!"

"Not another! What sort of information?"

"So far it seems to be mainly about our artillery."

"Important information?"

"Not particularly, but there might be other matters we don't know about."

"Who is he?"

"A so-called 'Count Walsin Esterhazy,' a major with the Seven-four."

Boisdeffre makes a visible effort of memory, then shakes his head. "Not a name I would have forgotten if I'd met him. How did we get onto him?"

"The same way we did with Dreyfus, though our agent in the German Embassy."

"My God, I only wish my wife could find a cleaner half as thorough as that woman!" He laughs at his own joke. He seems remarkably relaxed; perhaps it is the effects of his hydrotherapy. "What does General Gonse say?"

"I haven't told him yet."

"Why not?"

"I thought it best to talk to you first. With your permission, I'd like to brief the minister next. I hope to know more about Esterhazy in a day or two. Until then, I would prefer not to tell General Gonse."

"As you wish."

He pats his pockets until he finds his snuff box, and offers it to me. I refuse. He takes a couple of pinches. We round the place de la

Bastille. In a minute or two we'll be at our destination and I need a decision.

"So do I have your permission," I ask, "to notify the minister?"

"Yes, I think you should, don't you? However, I would dearly love," he adds, tapping my knee to emphasise each word, "to avoid another public scandal! One Dreyfus is quite enough for a generation. Let us try to deal with this case more discreetly."

I am spared the need to reply by our arrival at the hôtel de Sens. For once, that gloomy medieval pile is a scene of activity. An official reception of some sort is in progress. People are arriving in evening dress. And there, waiting on the doorstep, smoking a cigarette, I see none other than Gonse. Our automobile pulls up a few metres away. Gonse drops his cigarette and heads towards us, just as the driver jumps out to lower the steps for Boisdeffre. Gonse halts and salutes—"Welcome back to Paris, General!"—then looks at me with undisguised suspicion. "And Colonel Picquart?" The statement is delivered as a question.

I say quickly, "General Boisdeffre was kind enough to give me a ride from the station." It is neither a blatant lie nor the full truth, but hopefully it is enough to cover my exit. I salute and wish them a good evening. When I reach the street corner I risk a look back, but the two men have gone inside.

I don't want to tell Gonse about Esterhazy yet, for three reasons: first, because I know that once that consummate old bureaucrat gets his hands on the case he will want to take control of it and information will start to leak; second, because I know how the army works and I wouldn't put it past him to go behind my back to Henry; and third, and above all, because if I can armour myself with the prior backing of the Chief of the General Staff and the Minister of War, then Gonse will be unable to interfere and I shall be free to follow the trail wherever it leads me. I am not entirely without cunning: how else did I become the youngest colonel in the French army?

Accordingly, on Thursday morning, at the same time as the team in Basel should be making its first contact with the double agent, Cuers, I take the Benefactor file and my private key—the token of my privileged access—and let myself through the wooden door into the garden of the hôtel de Brienne. The grounds, which appeared so magical to me under snow on the day of Dreyfus's degradation, have a different kind of charm in August. The foliage on the big trees is so thick that the ministry might not exist; the distant sounds of Paris are as drowsy as the drone of bees; the only other person around is an elderly gardener watering a flower bed. As I cross the scorched brown turf I promise myself that if I am ever minister, I shall move my desk out here in the summer, and run the army from under a tree, as Caesar did in Gaul.

I reach the edge of the lawn, cross the gravel, and trot up the shallow pale stone steps that lead to the glass doors of the minister's residence. I let myself in and ascend the same marble staircase that I climbed at the beginning of my story, pass the same suits of armour and the bombastic painting of Napoleon. I put my head around the door of the minister's private office and ask one of his order-lies, Captain Robert Calmon-Maison, if it would be convenient for me to have a word with the minister. Calmon-Maison knows bet-ter than to ask what it is about, for I am the keeper of his master's secrets. He goes off to check and returns to tell me that I can be seen immediately.

How quickly one accommodates to power! Not many months ago, I would have been awed at finding myself in the minister's inner sanctum; now it is just a place of work, and the minister himself merely another soldier-bureaucrat passing through the revolving door of government. The present occupant, Jean-Baptiste Billot, is nudging seventy, and is on his second stint in the office, having held it fourteen years before. He is married to a wealthy and sophisti-cated woman and his politics are left-radical, yet he looks like an idiot general out of a comic opera—all barrel chest and bristling white moustaches and outraged bulging eyes: naturally, the cartoon-ists adore him. There's one other detail about him I know, and is of interest: he dislikes his predecessor, General Mercier, and has done ever since the grand army manoeuvres of 1893, when the younger man commanded the opposing corps and defeated him—a humilia-tion he has never forgiven.

As I enter, he is standing at the window with his broad back to the room. Without turning round he says, "When I watched you coming across that lawn just now, Picquart, I thought to myself: well, here he comes, that bright young colonel with another damn problem! And then I asked myself: why do I need such tribulations at my age? I should be at my country place on a day like this, playing with my grandchildren, not wasting it by talking to you!"

"We both know, Minister, that you would be bored to death within five minutes, and complaining that we were ruining the country in your absence."

The massive shoulders shrug. "That's true enough, I suppose. Someone sane must oversee this madhouse." He pivots on his heel and waddles across the carpet towards me: an alarming sight for those not used to it, like a charging bull walrus. "Well, well, what is it? You look very tense. Sit down, my boy. Do you want a drink?"

"No, thank you." I occupy the same chair that I did when I described the degradation ceremony to Mercier and Boisdeffre. Billot settles himself opposite me and regards me with a piercing eye. The old buffer routine is all an act: he is as sharp and ambitious as a man of half his age. I open the Benefactor file. "I'm afraid we appear to have discovered a German spy operating in the army . . ."

"Oh God!"

Yet again I describe Esterhazy's activities and the operation we have mounted to watch him. I give Billot a few more details than I did Boisdeffre; in particular I tell him about the debriefing mission that is under way in Basel. I show him the *petit bleu* and the surveillance photographs. But I don't mention Dreyfus: I know that if I did, it would blot out everything else.

Billot interjects a number of shrewd questions. How valuable is this material? Why didn't Esterhazy's commanding officer notice something strange about him? Are we sure he's operating alone? He keeps returning to the image of Esterhazy emerging empty-handed from the embassy. At the end he says, "Perhaps we should try to do something clever with the scum? Rather than simply lock him up, couldn't we use him to feed false information to Berlin?"

"I've been thinking about that. The trouble is, the Germans are already suspicious of him. It's unlikely they'd simply swallow whatever he told them without checking it for themselves. And of course—"

Billot finishes my argument for me. "And of course, to get him to play along, we'd have to give him immunity from prosecution, whereas the only place for the likes of Esterhazy is behind bars. No, you've done well, Colonel." He shuts the file and hands it back to me. "Keep on with the investigation until we've nailed him once and for all."

"You'd be willing to take it all the way to a court-martial?"

"Absolutely! What's the alternative? To allow him to retire on half pay?"

"General Boisdeffre would prefer it if there were no scandal . . ."

"I'm sure he would. I don't relish one myself. But if we allowed him to get away with it—that really would be a scandal!"

I return to my office well satisfied. I have the approval of the two most powerful men in the army to continue my investigation. Effectively Gonse has been cut out of the chain of command. All I can do now is to wait for news from Basel.

The day drags on with routine work. The drains stink more than usual in the heat. I find it hard to concentrate. At half past five, I ask Captain Junck to book a telephone call to the Schweizerhof hotel for seven o'clock. At the appointed time I stand by the receiver in the upstairs corridor, smoking a cigarette, and when the bell sounds I snatch the instrument from its cradle. I know the Schweizerhof: a big, modern place overlooking a city square crossed by tramlines. I give Lauth's cover name to the front desk and ask to speak to him. There is a long wait while the undermanager goes off to check. When he returns, he announces that the gentleman has just checked out and has left no forwarding address. I hang up, wondering what I should read into this. It may be that they are continuing the debriefing into a second day and have taken the precaution of changing hotels, or it could be that the meeting is over and they are rushing to catch the overnight train back to Paris. I hang around for another hour in the hope of receiving a telegram, then decide to leave for the evening.

I would welcome some company to distract me, but everyone seems to be away for August. The de Commingeses have closed up their house and decamped to their summer estate. Pauline is on holiday in Biarritz with Philippe and her daughters. Louis Leblois has gone home to Alsace to be with his gravely ill father. I am suffering from a pretty bad dose of what the gentlemen in the rue de Lille would call *Weltschmerz*: I am world weary. In the end, I dine alone in a restaurant near the ministry and return to my apartment intending to read Zola's new novel. But its subject, the Roman Catholic Church, bores me, and it also runs to seven hundred and fifty pages. I am willing to accept such prolixity from Tolstoy but not from Zola. I set it aside long before the end.

I am at my desk early the next morning, but no telegrams have come in overnight and it isn't until early in the afternoon that I hear Henry and Lauth coming upstairs. I rise from my seat and stride across my office. Flinging open the door, I am surprised to find them both wearing uniform. "Gentlemen," I say with sarcasm, "you have actually *been* to Switzerland, I take it?"

The two officers salute, Lauth with a certain nervousness it seems to me, but Henry with a nonchalance that borders on insolence. He says, "I'm sorry, Colonel. We stopped off at home to change."

"And how was your trip?"

"I should say it was a pretty good waste of time and money, wouldn't you agree, Lauth?"

"It proved to be disappointing, I'm afraid, yes."

I look from one to the other. "Well, that's unexpectedly depressing news. You'd better come in and tell me what happened."

I sit behind my desk with my arms folded and listen while they relate their story. Henry does most of the talking. According to him, he and Lauth went directly from the railway station to the hotel for breakfast, then upstairs to the room, where they waited until nine-thirty, when Inspector Vuillecard brought in Cuers. "He was pretty shifty from the start—nervous, couldn't sit still. Kept going over to the window and checking the big square in front of the station. Mostly what he wanted to talk about was him—could we guarantee the Germans would never find out what he'd done for us?"

"And what could he tell you about the Germans' agent?"

"Just a few bits and scraps. He reckoned he'd personally seen four documents that had come in via Schwartzkoppen—one about a gun and another about a rifle. Then there was something about the lay-out of the army camp at Toul, and the fortifications at Nancy."

I ask, "What were these? Handwritten documents?"

"Yes."

"In French?"

"That's it."

"But he didn't have a name for this agent, or any other clue to his identity?"

"No, just that the German General Staff decided he wasn't to be trusted and ordered Schwartzkoppen to break off relations with him. Whoever he is, he was never very important and he's no longer active."

I turn to Lauth. "Were you talking in French or German?"

He flushes. "French to start with, in the morning, then we switched to German in the afternoon."

"I told you to encourage Cuers to speak in German."

"With respect, Colonel," cuts in Henry, "there wasn't much point in my being there unless I had a chance to talk to him myself. I take responsibility for that. I stuck it for about three hours then I left it to Captain Lauth."

"And how long did you talk to him in German, Lauth?"

"For another six hours, Colonel."

"And did he say anything else of interest?"

Lauth meets my gaze and holds it. "No. We just went over the same old ground again and again. He left at six to catch the train back to Berlin."

"He left at six?" I can no longer suppress my exasperation. "You see, gentlemen, this just doesn't make any sense to me. Why would a man risk travelling seven hundred kilometres to a foreign city to meet intelligence officers from a foreign power in order to say almost nothing? In fact to say *less* than he'd already told us in Berlin?"

Henry says, "It's obvious, surely? He must have changed his mind. Or he was lying in the first place. What a fellow blurts out when he's drunk at home at night with someone he knows is different to what he might say in the cold light of day to strangers."

"Well why didn't you take him out and get him drunk then?" I bang my fist down on the desk. "Why didn't you make some effort to get to know him better?" Neither man answers. Lauth looks at the floor, Henry stares straight ahead. "It seems to me that you both couldn't wait to get back on that train to Paris." They start to protest but I cut them off. "Save your excuses for your report. That will be all, gentlemen. Thank you. You may leave."

Henry halts at the door and says, with quivering and affronted dignity, "No one has ever questioned my professional competence before."

"Well I'm very surprised to hear it."

After they have gone, I lean forward and put my head in my hands. I know that a decisive moment has just been reached, in terms of both my relationship with Henry and my command of the section. Are they telling the truth? For all I know, they might be. Perhaps Cuers really did clam up when he got into their hotel room. Of one thing I am sure, however: that Henry went to Switzerland determined to wreck that meeting, and succeeded, and that if Cuers told them nothing it was because Henry willed it to be so.

Among the files demanding my attention that day is the latest batch of censored correspondence of Alfred Dreyfus, sent over as usual by the Colonial Ministry. The minister wishes to know if I have any observations to make "from an intelligence perspective." I untie the ribbon and flick open the cover and begin to read:

> A gloomy day with ceaseless rain. The air full of tangible darkness. The sky black as ink. A real day of death and burial. How often there comes to my mind that exclamation of Schopenhauer at the thought of human iniquity: "If God created the world, I would not care to be God." The mail from Cayenne has come, it seems, but has not brought my letters! Nothing to read, no avenue of escape from my thoughts. Neither books nor magazines come to me any-

more. I walk in the daytime until my strength is exhausted, to calm
my brain and quiet my nerves . . .

The quotation from Schopenhauer leaps out at me from the file.
I know it; I have used it often. It never occurred to me that Dreyfus
might read philosophy, let alone harbour a blasphemous thought.
Schopenhauer! It is as if someone who has been trying to attract
my attention for a long while has finally succeeded. Other passages
catch my eye:

Days, nights, are all alike. I never open my mouth. I no longer ask
for anything. My speech used to be limited to asking if my mail had
come or not. But I am now forbidden to ask even that, or at least,
which is the same thing, the guards are forbidden to answer even
such commonplace questions. I wish to live until the day of the
discovery of the truth, that I may cry aloud my grief at the torture
they inflict on me . . .

And again:

That they should take all possible precautions to prevent escape,
I understand; it is the right, I will even say the strict duty, of the
administration. But that they bury me alive in a tomb, prevent
all communication with my family, even via open letters—this is
against all justice. One would readily believe one is thrown back
several centuries . . .

And on the back of one intercepted and retained letter, written out
several times as if he is trying to commit it to memory, is a quotation
from Shakespeare's *Othello*:

Who steals my purse steals trash. 'Tis something, nothing:
'Twas mine, 'tis his, and has been slave to thousands.
But he that filches from me my good name
Robs me of that which not enriches him
And makes me poor indeed.

As I turn the pages, I feel as if I am reading a novel by Dostoyevsky. The walls of my office seem to melt; I hear the ceaseless crash and roar of the sea on the rocks beneath his prison hut, the strange cries of the birds, the deep silence of the tropical night broken by the endless clumping of the guards' boots on the stone floor and the rustle of the venomous spider crabs moving in the rafters; I feel the saturating furnace of the humid heat and the raw itch of the mosquito bites and ant stings, the doubling-over stomach cramps and blinding headaches; I smell the mouldiness of his clothes and his books destroyed by damp and insects, the stink of his latrine and the eye-watering clinging pale smoke of the cooking fire built from wet green wood; above all I am hollowed by his loneliness. Devil's Island is twelve hundred metres long by four hundred wide at its maximum point; it has a surface area of just one-sixth of a square kilometre. It wouldn't take long to map it. I wonder if he remembers what I taught him.

After I have finished reading the file, I take up my pen and write a note to the Colonial Minister informing him that I have no comments to make.

I place it in my out-tray. I sink back in my chair and think about Dreyfus.

I became professor of topography at the École Supérieure de Guerre in Paris when I was thirty-five. Some friends thought I was mad to take the post—I was already a battalion commander in Besançon—but I saw the opportunity: Paris is Paris, after all, and topography is the fundamental science of war. *Could a battery at A bring fire to bear on N? Would the churchyard, village Z, be under fire of a battery at G? Could a picket be posted in the fields immediately east of N, unseen by an enemy's vedette at G?* I instructed my students in how to measure distances by counting their paces (the more rapid, the more accurate); how to survey terrain using a plane table or a prismatic compass; how to sketch the contours of a hill in red pencil using a Watkins clinometer or Monsieur Fortin's mercurial barometer; how to bring the sketch alive by mixing in green or blue chalk scraped from a pencil in imitation of a flat wash of watercolour; how to use a pocket sextant, a theodolite, a sketching protractor; how to make an accurate representation from the saddle under fire. Among the students to whom I taught these skills was Dreyfus.

However hard I try, I cannot recall our first meeting. I looked down from the lecture podium week after week at the same eighty faces and only gradually did I learn to distinguish his from the others: thin, pale, solemn, myopic in his pince-nez. He was barely thirty but his lifestyle and appearance made him seem much older than his contemporaries. He was a husband among bachelors, a man of means among the perennially hard up. In the evenings when his comrades went out drinking he returned home to his smart apartment and his wealthy wife. He was what my mother would have called "a regular Jew," by which she meant such things as "new money," pushiness, social climbing and a fondness for expensive ostentation.

Twice Dreyfus tried to invite me to social functions: on the first occasion to dinner at his apartment on the avenue du Trocadéro and on the second to what he called "some top-class shooting" he had rented out near Fontainebleau; on both occasions I declined. I didn't much care for him, even less so when I discovered that the rest of his family had elected to remain in occupied Alsace, and that Germany was where his money came from: blood money, I thought it. At the end of one term, when I failed to award him the high marks for cartography he believed he deserved, he actually confronted me.

"Have I done something to offend you?" His voice was his least attractive feature: nasal and mechanical, with a grating trace of Mulhouse German.

"Not at all," I replied. "I can show you my marking scheme if you like."

"The point is, you are the only one of my tutors who has given me a low mark."

"Well," I said, "perhaps I don't share your high opinion of your own abilities."

"So it's not because I'm a Jew?"

The bluntness of the accusation took me aback. "I am scrupulous not to let any personal prejudices affect my judgement."

"Your use of the word 'scrupulous' suggests it might be a factor." He was tougher than he looked. He stood his ground.

I replied coldly, "If you are asking, Captain, whether I like Jews particularly, the honest answer I suppose would be no. But if you are implying that because of that I might discriminate against you in a professional matter, I can assure you—never!"

That concluded the conversation. There were no more private approaches after that; no further invitations to dinner or to shooting, top-class or otherwise.

At the end of three years' teaching, my gamble paid off and I was transferred from the École to the General Staff. There was talk even then of sending me to the Statistical Section: the skills of topography are a useful grounding for secret intelligence. But I fought hard to avoid becoming a spy. Instead I was made deputy chief of the Third Department (Training and Operations). And here I ran across Dreyfus again.

Those who graduate in the highest places from the École Supérieure are rewarded by a two-year attachment to the General Staff, consisting of six months in each of the four departments. It was part of my job to supervise the placement of these *stagiaires*, as they are called. Dreyfus had passed out ninth in his year. Therefore he was fully entitled to come into the Ministry of War. It fell to me to determine where he should go. He would be the only Jew on the General Staff.

It was a time of growing anti-Semitic agitation within the army, whipped along by that poisonous rag *La Libre Parole*, which alleged that Jewish officers were being given preferential treatment. Despite my lack of sympathy towards him, I took some care to try to protect Dreyfus from the worst of it. I had an old friend, Armand Mercier-Milon, a major in the Fourth Department (Movement and Railways), who was entirely free of prejudice. I had a word with him. The upshot was that Dreyfus went to the Fourth for his initial placement at the start of 1893. In the summer he moved on to the First (Administration); then at the beginning of 1894 to the Second (Intelligence); and finally in July he came to my department, the Third, to complete his rotation on the General Staff.

I saw very little of Dreyfus throughout that summer and autumn of 1894—he was often away from Paris—although we would nod civilly enough to each other if we happened to pass in the corridor. From the reports of his section chiefs I knew that he was regarded as hardworking and intelligent but uncongenial, a loner. Some also spoke of him as cold and arrogant to his equals and obsequious to his superiors. During a General Staff visit to Charmes he monopolised General Boisdeffre over dinner and took him off for an hour to smoke cigars and discuss improvements in artillery, much to the annoyance of the more senior officers present. Nor did he make any effort to disguise his wealth. He had a wine cellar built in his apartment, employed three or four servants, kept horses in livery, collected pictures and books, hunted regularly and bought a Hamerless shotgun from Guinard & Cie on the avenue de l'Opéra for five hundred and fifty francs—the equivalent of two months' army salary.

There was something almost heroic in his refusal to play the part of the grateful outsider. But looking back, one can see it was a foolish way to behave, especially in that climate.

A regular Jew . . .

Operation Benefactor languishes in the August heat. There are no fresh sightings of Esterhazy in the rue de Lille. Schwartzkoppen seems to be away on leave. The Germans' apartment is shuttered up for the summer. I write to Boisdeffre on his estate in Normandy asking for permission to obtain a sample of Esterhazy's handwriting, in case it matches any scrap of evidence retrieved by Agent Auguste. My request is turned down on the grounds that this would represent "a provocation." If Esterhazy has to be removed from the army, Boisdeffre reiterates that he wants it done quietly, without a scandal. I raise it with the Minister of War. He is sympathetic, but on this issue he refuses to overrule the Chief of the General Staff.

Meanwhile the atmosphere inside the Statistical Section is as noxious as the drains. Several times when I step out of my office I hear doors close along the corridor. The whispering starts up again. On the fifteenth there is a small party in the waiting room to say goodbye to Bachir, who is retiring as concierge, and to welcome his successor, Capiaux. I say a few words of thanks: "The building will not be the same without the presence of our old comrade, Bachir," to which Henry remarks into his glass, just loud enough for everyone to hear, "Well why did you get rid of him then?" Afterwards the others all go off to continue drinking at the Taverne Royale, a favourite bar nearby. I am not asked to go with them. Sitting alone at my desk with a bottle of cognac, I remember Henry's remark on his return from Basel: *Whoever he is, he was never very important and he's no longer active.* Have I caused all this ill feeling in pursuit of an agent who in any case was never much more than a chancer and a fantasist?

On the twentieth, Henry departs on a month's leave to his family's home on the Marne. Normally before he goes away he puts his head round my door to say goodbye. On this occasion, he slips away without a word. In his absence the building sinks even further into the August torpor.

And then, on the twenty-seventh, a Thursday afternoon, I receive a message from Billot's orderly Captain Calmon-Maison asking if he might have a word with me as soon as is convenient. I have cleared my in-tray so I decide I might as well walk over right away: through the garden and up the stairs and into the office of the minister's secretariat. The windows are open. The room is light and airy. Three or four young officers are working together congenially. I feel a stab of envy: how much better to be here than across the street in my dank and rancorous warren! Calmon-Maison says, "I have something here that General Billot thinks you ought to see." He goes to a filing cabinet and takes out a letter. "It came in yesterday. It's from Major Esterhazy."

The letter is handwritten, addressed to Calmon-Maison, dated Paris two days earlier. It is a request to be transferred to the General Staff. The implications of this hit me with a force that is almost physical. *He's trying to get into the ministry. He's trying to get access to secret material he can sell . . .*

Calmon-Maison says, "My colleague Captain Thévenet has received a similar appeal."

"May I see it?"

He gives me the second letter. It is couched in almost identical terms to the first: *I am writing to request an immediate transfer from the headquarters of the 74th Infantry Regiment in Rouen . . . I believe I have demonstrated the qualities necessary for work on the General Staff . . . I have served in the Foreign Legion and in the intelligence department as a German translator . . . I would be most grateful if you could bring this request to the attention of the appropriate authority . . .*

"Have you replied?"

"We've sent him a holding letter—'your request is being considered by the minister.'"

"Can I borrow these?"

Calmon-Maison responds as if reciting a legal formula: "The minister has asked me to tell you that he can see no objection to your making use of these letters as part of your inquiry."

Back in my office, I sit at my desk with the letters in front of me. The writing is neat, regular, well spaced. I am almost sure I have seen it before. At first I think it must be because the script is quite similar to that of Dreyfus, whose correspondence I have spent so many hours studying lately.

And then I remember the *bordereau*—the covering note that was retrieved from Schwartzkoppen's wastepaper basket and that convicted Dreyfus of treason.

I look at the letters again.

No, surely not . . .

I rise from my seat like a man in a dream and take the few steps across the carpet to the safe. My hand shakes very slightly as I insert the key. The envelope containing the photograph of the *bordereau* is still there, where Sandherr left it: I have been meaning for months to take it upstairs to Gribelin so he can file it away in his archive.

The *bordereau*, in facsimile, is a column of thirty narrow lines of handwriting—undated, unaddressed, unsigned:

I am forwarding to you, sir, several interesting items of information . . .

> 1. *A note on the hydraulic brake of the 120 and how that part performed*

2. *A note on covering troops (several modifications will be introduced by the new plan)*

3. *A note on the change to artillery formations*

4. *A note concerning Madagascar*

5. *The draft Field Artillery Firing Manual (14 March 1894)*

The last paragraph explains that the Ministry of War will not permit individual officers to keep possession of the Field Artillery Firing Manual for very long, therefore *if you would like to take from it what interests you and afterwards leave it at my disposal, I will collect it. Otherwise I can copy it verbatim and send you the copy. I am off to manoeuvres.*

The leading handwriting expert in Paris swore that this was written by Dreyfus. I carry the photograph over to my desk and place it between the two letters from Esterhazy. I stoop for a closer look.

The writing is identical.

10

For several minutes I sit motionless, holding the photograph. I might be made of marble, a sculpture by Rodin: *The Reader*. What really freezes me, even more than the matching handwriting, is the content—the obsession with artillery, the offer to have a manual copied out verbatim, the obsequious salesman's tone—it is Esterhazy to the life. Briefly, just as I did when the *petit bleu* came in, I consider marching over to the minister's office and laying the evidence in front of him. But again I know that would be folly. My four golden principles are more important now than ever: take it one step at a time; approach the matter dispassionately; avoid a rush to judgement; confide in nobody until there is hard evidence.

I pick up the two letters, straighten my tunic and walk along the corridor to Lauth's office. For a moment I hesitate outside his door, then I knock and go straight in.

The captain of dragoons is leaning back in his chair, long legs outstretched, eyes closed. There is something quite angelic about that blond head in repose. No doubt he is a success with women, although he has a young wife, I believe; I wonder if he has affairs. I am on the point of leaving when suddenly he opens his blue eyes and sees me. And in that unguarded instant something flickers in them that is beyond surprise: it is alarm.

"I'm sorry," I say. "I didn't mean to disturb you. I'll come back when you're ready."

"No, no." Embarrassed, Lauth scrambles to his feet. "Pardon me, Colonel, it's just so infernally hot, and I've been indoors all day . . ."

"Don't worry, my dear Lauth, I know precisely how you feel. This really is no life for a soldier, to be trapped in an office day after day.

Sit, please. I insist. Do you mind if I join you?" And without waiting for a reply I pull up a chair on the other side of his desk. "I wonder: could you do something for me?" I push the two letters towards him. "I'd like to have these both photographed, but with the signature and the name of the addressee blocked out."

Lauth examines the letters then glances at me in shock. "Esterhazy!"

"Yes, it seems our minor spy has ambitions to become a major one. But thank goodness," I can't resist adding, "we had our eye on him, otherwise who knows what damage he might have done."

"Indeed." Lauth gives a reluctant nod and shifts in his seat uncomfortably. "Might I ask, Colonel, why you need photographs of the letters?"

"Just photograph them, if you don't mind, Captain." I stand and smile at him. "Shall we say four prints of each by first thing tomorrow? And just for once let's try to keep this strictly between ourselves."

Upstairs, Gribelin has only recently returned from his annual leave—not that you would think it to look at him. His face is pallid; his eyes, beneath a green celluloid eyeshade, carry dark pouches of exhaustion. His only concession to the summer heat is shirtsleeves rolled back to his bony elbows, exposing arms as thin and white as tubers. He is bent over a file as I enter, and quickly closes it. He takes off his eyeshade.

"I didn't hear you coming up the stairs, Colonel."

I hand him the photograph of the *bordereau*. "I think you should be in charge of this."

He blinks at it in surprise. "Where did you find it?"

"Colonel Sandherr had it in his safe."

"Ah yes, well, he was very proud of it." Gribelin holds the photograph at arm's length to admire it. His tongue moistens his top lip as if he's studying a pornographic print. "He told me he would have had it framed, and hung it on his wall, if regulations had allowed."

"A hunting trophy?"

"Exactly."

Gribelin unlocks the bottom left-hand drawer of his desk and fishes out his immense bunch of keys. He carries the *bordereau* across to a heavy old fireproof filing cabinet, which he opens. I look around. I hardly ever venture up here. Two large tables are pushed together in the centre of the room. Laid out across the scuffed brown leather surfaces are half a dozen stacks of files, a blotting pad, a strong electric lamp, a rack of rubber stamps, a brass inkstand, a hole-puncher and a row of pens—all precisely aligned. Around the walls are the locked cabinets and safes that contain the section's secrets. There is a map of France, showing the *départements*. The three windows are narrow, barred and dusty, their sills encrusted with the excrement of the pigeons I can hear cooing on the roof.

"I wonder," I say casually, "do you keep the original *bordereau* up here?"

Gribelin does not turn round. "I do."

"I'd like to see it."

He glances over his shoulder at me. "Why?"

I shrug. "I'm interested."

There is nothing he can do. He unlocks another drawer in the cabinet and retrieves one of his ubiquitous manila files. He opens it, and with some reverence retrieves from it the *bordereau*. It is not at all what I expected. It weighs almost nothing. The paper is flimsy onionskin, semitransparent, written on both sides, so that the ink from one bleeds through and shows on the other. The most substantial thing about it is the adhesive tape holding together the six torn pieces.

I say, "You'd never guess it looked like this from the photograph."

"No, it was quite a process." Gribelin's normally astringent tone is softened by a touch of professional pride. "We had to photograph both sides and then retouch them, and then stick them together and finally rephotograph the whole image. So it came out looking like a continuous sheet of writing."

"How many prints did you make?"

"Twelve. It was necessary to disguise its original state so that we could circulate it around the ministry."

"Yes, of course. I remember." I turn the *bordereau* back and forth, marvelling once again at Lauth's skill. "I remember it very well."

It was the first week of October 1894 when word began to spread that there might be a traitor in the Ministry. All four chiefs of department were required to check the handwriting of every officer in their section, to see if anyone's matched the photograph. They were sworn to secrecy, allowed only to tell their deputies. Colonel Boucher devolved the job to me.

Despite the restricted circle, it was inevitable that news would leak, and soon a miasma of unease infiltrated the rue Saint-Dominique. The problem lay in that five-point list of the documents betrayed, which set us all chasing our own tails. A "note on the hydraulic brake of the 120" and the "draft Field Artillery Firing Manual" suggested the spy must be in the artillery. But the "new plan" mentioned in point two was the very phrase we used in the Third Department for the revised mobilisation schedule. Of course, the "new plan" was also being studied by the railway timetable experts in the Fourth, so the spy could work there perhaps. But then the "note on the change to artillery formations" was most likely to have come from the First. Whereas the plan to occupy Madagascar had been worked on by the intelligence officers in the Second . . .

Everyone suspected everyone else. Old incidents were dredged up and picked over, ancient rumours and feuds revived. The ministry was paralysed by suspicion. I went through the handwriting of every officer on our list, even Boucher's; even mine. I found no match.

And then someone—it was Colonel d'Aboville, deputy chief of the Fourth—had a flash of inspiration. If the traitor could draw on current knowledge of all four departments, wasn't it reasonable to assume that he had recently worked in all four? And unlikely as it seemed, there *was* a group of officers on the General Staff of whom that was true: the *stagiaires* from the École Supérieure de Guerre— men who were relative strangers to their long-serving comrades. Suddenly it was obvious: the traitor was a *stagiaire* with a background in artillery.

Eight captains of artillery on the *stagiaire* programme fitted that particular bill, but only one of them was a Jew: a Jew moreover who spoke French with a German accent, whose family lived in the Kaiser's Reich and who always had money to throw around.

Gribelin, watching me, says, "I'm sure you remember the *bordereau*, Colonel." He gives one of his rare smiles. "Just as I remember that you were the one who provided us with the sample of Dreyfus's handwriting that matched it."

It was Colonel Boucher who brought me the request from the Statistical Section. Normally he was loud and cheerfully red-faced, but on this occasion he was sombre, even grey. It was a Saturday morning, two days after we had started hunting for the traitor. He closed the door behind him and said, "It looks like we might be getting close to the bastard."

"Really? That's quick."

"General Gonse wants to see some handwriting belonging to Captain Dreyfus."

"Dreyfus?" I repeated, surprised.

Boucher explained d'Aboville's theory. "And so," he concluded, "they've decided the traitor must be one of your *stagiaires*."

"One of *my stagiaires*?" I did not like the sound of that!

I had skimmed through Dreyfus's file the previous day and eliminated him as a suspect. Now I pulled it out again and compared the handwriting of a couple of his letters to the *bordereau*. And on second glance, looking at them more closely, perhaps there were similarities: the same small lettering; the same slope to the right; similar spacing between both words and lines . . . A terrible feeling of certainty began to seize hold of me. "I don't know, Colonel," I said. "What do you think?" I showed the letters to Boucher.

"Well, I'm no expert either, but they look pretty much alike to me. You'd better bring them along."

Ten minutes earlier, Dreyfus had been no more of a suspect to me than anyone else. But the power of suggestion is insidious. As the colonel and I walked together along the corridors of the ministry, my imagination began to fill with thoughts of Dreyfus—of his family still living in Germany, of his solitariness and cleverness and arro-

gance, of his ambition to enter the General Staff and his careful cul-
tivation of senior officers—so much so that by the time we reached
General Gonse's office I had all but convinced myself: *Of course he
would betray us, because he hates us; he has hated us all along because he
isn't like us, and knows he never will be, for all his money; he is just . . .*

A regular Jew!

Waiting for us, along with Gonse himself, were Colonel
d'Aboville, Colonel Fabre, the chief of the Fourth Department,
Colonel Lefort, head of the First, and Colonel Sandherr. I laid Dreyfus's letters out on Gonse's desk and stepped back while my superiors
crowded around to look. And from that huddle of uniformed backs
arose a growing exclamation of shock and conviction: "Look how
he forms the capital 's' there, and the 'j' . . . And the small 'm' and
the 'r,' do you see? And the gap between the words is exactly the
same . . . I'm no expert, but . . . No, I'm no expert either, but . . . I'd
say they're identical . . ."

Sandherr straightened and slapped his forehead with the heel of
his hand. "I should have known! How many times have I seen him
loitering round, asking questions?"

Fabre said, "I predicted exactly this in my report on him, do you
remember, Major Picquart?" He pointed at me. "'An incomplete
officer, lacking the qualities of character necessary for employment
on the General Staff . . .' Were those not my very words?"

"They were, Colonel," I agreed.

Gonse said to me, "Where is Dreyfus exactly?"

"He's at infantry camp outside Paris until the end of next week."

"Good." Sandherr nodded. "Excellent. That gives us some time.
We need to get all this to a handwriting expert."

Gonse said: "So you really think it's him?"

"Well, if not him—who?"

No one responded. That was the nub of it. If the traitor wasn't
Dreyfus, then who was it? You? Me? Your comrade? Mine? Whereas
if it was Dreyfus, this debilitating hunt for an enemy within would
come to an end. Without saying it, or even thinking it, collectively
we willed it to be so.

Gonse sighed and said, "I'd better go and tell General Mercier.

He may have to speak to the Prime Minister." He glanced at me, as if I were the one responsible for introducing this contagion into the ministry, and said to Boucher, "I don't think we need detain Major Picquart any longer, do you, Colonel?"

Boucher said, "No, I don't believe so. Thank you, Picquart."

"Thank you, General."

I saluted and left.

I have been silent for a while. Suddenly I am aware of Gribelin, still staring at me.

"Strange," I say, flourishing the *bordereau*. "Curious how it brings it all back."

"Yes, I can imagine."

And that might well have been the end of it, as far as my own involvement was concerned. But then to my surprise, a week later I received a telegram at my apartment summoning me to a meeting in the office of the Minister of War at six o'clock on the evening of Sunday, 14 October.

I presented myself at the hôtel de Brienne at the appointed time. I could hear voices as I climbed the stairs, and when I reached the first floor I discovered a small group waiting in the corridor to go in: General Boisdeffre, General Gonse, Colonel Sandherr and a couple of men I didn't recognise—a corpulent, claret-faced major who, like me, wore the red ribbon of the Legion of Honour, and a superintendent from the Sûreté. There was one other officer. He was standing further along the passage next to the window, rather self-importantly wearing a monocle and flicking through a file, and I realised it was Colonel du Paty de Clam, Blanche's former lover. He saw me looking at him, closed his file, removed his monocle, and strutted towards me.

"Picquart," he said, returning my salute. "What an appalling business this is."

"I didn't know you were involved in it, Colonel."

"Involved!" Du Paty laughed and shook his head. "My dear Major, I've been put in charge of the entire investigation! I'm the reason you're here!"

I always found something disconcerting about du Paty. It was as if he were acting the central part in a play for which no one else had been shown the script. He might laugh abruptly, or tap his nose and adopt an air of great mystery, or disappear from a room in the middle of a conversation without explanation. He fancied himself a detective in the modern scientific manner and had made a study of graphology, anthropometry, cryptography and secret inks. I wondered what role in his drama he had chosen for me to play.

I said, "May I ask how the investigation is going?"

"You are about to hear." He patted the file and nodded to the minister's door, which at that moment was being opened by one of his staff officers.

Inside, Mercier was seated at his desk, signing a pile of correspondence. "Please, gentlemen," he said in that quiet voice of his without looking up, "take a seat. I shan't be a moment."

We arranged ourselves around the conference table in order of rank, leaving the place at the head free for Mercier, with Boisdeffre to the right and Gonse to the left, then Sandherr and du Paty facing each other, and finally we three junior officers at the far end.

"Henry," said the burly officer, leaning across the table to extend his hand to me.

"Picquart," I replied.

The commissioner from the Sûreté also introduced himself: "Armand Cochefort."

For a minute we sat in awkward silence while the minister finished signing his papers, then gave them to his aide, who saluted and left.

"So," said Mercier, taking his seat at the table, and placing a sheet of paper in front of him, "I have informed the President and the Prime Minister of where things stand, and this is the warrant for Dreyfus's arrest; all it needs is my signature. Have we received the results of the handwriting expert? I gather the first man, from the Banque de France, concluded that the writing wasn't Dreyfus's after all."

Du Paty opened his file. "We have, Minister. I have consulted Alphonse Bertillon, head of the identification branch of the Préfecture of Police. He says the *bordereau* contains strong elements of Dreyfus's handwriting, and where it differs, the discrepancies are deliberate. If I might spare you the technical detail and just read you his conclusion: 'It appears clear to us that it was the same person who wrote the various items submitted and the incriminating document.'"

"So one says yes and one says no? That's experts for you!" Mercier turned to Sandherr. "Is Dreyfus back in Paris yet?"

Sandherr said, "He's having dinner with his wife's parents, the Hadamards: his father-in-law is a diamond merchant—you know how they specialise in portable property. We have the building under watch."

Boisdeffre interrupted: "Isn't it quite tempting, Colonel, if we know where he is, simply to have him arrested tonight?"

"No, General," replied Sandherr, shaking his head emphatically, "with the greatest respect, absolutely not. You don't know these people as well as I do. You don't know the way they operate. The moment they discover we have Dreyfus in custody, the whole force of upper Jewdom will swing into action to agitate for his release. It's essential that he simply disappears with the minimum of fuss and we have him to ourselves for at least a week. I think Colonel du Paty's plan is a good one."

Mercier turned his impassive, masklike face to du Paty. "Go on."

"I have concluded that the most secure location in which to arrest Dreyfus is inside the ministry itself. General Gonse has already sent him a telegram ordering him to attend a duty inspection in General Boisdeffre's office at nine o'clock tomorrow morning . . ."

"In civilian dress," put in Gonse, "so that if anyone sees him afterwards, when he arrives at the prison, they won't realise he's an army officer."

". . . so we'll arrest him here in the rue Saint-Dominique, in the Chief of the General Staff's office."

Mercier said, "What if he suspects a trap?"

"Ah well, this is where Major Picquart comes in," said du Paty.

I felt all eyes turn in my direction. I tried to stare ahead as if I knew what was coming.

"Major Picquart," explained Gonse to Mercier, "was one of Dreyfus's tutors at the École Supérieure. He runs the *stagiaire* programme."

"I know that." Mercier regarded me through his eye slits; it was impossible to tell what he was thinking.

Du Paty continued: "I propose that Major Picquart waits for Dreyfus in the main entrance at nine o'clock and personally conducts him to General Boisdeffre's office. Dreyfus knows him and trusts him. That should allay any suspicions."

There was a silence while the minister considered this.

Mercier said, "And what do you think of this plan, Major Picquart?"

"I am not sure Captain Dreyfus regards me as a particularly reassuring figure," I replied carefully, "but if Colonel du Paty believes my presence will be useful, then of course I shall play my part."

Mercier trained his eye slits back on du Paty. "So we have him in General Boisdeffre's office. And then what do we do with him?"

"General Boisdeffre will not be there . . ."

"I should hope not!" cut in Boisdeffre.

". . . instead, I'll greet Dreyfus, explain that the Chief of the General Staff has been delayed, and ask him to take a seat. My right hand will be bandaged—I'll say it's injured—and I'll ask Dreyfus to take down a letter for me, which I'll dictate. By catching him unawares, I'll make it hard for him to disguise his writing. Once I have sufficient evidence, I'll give the signal and we'll confront him."

"Who is 'we'?" asked Mercier.

"With me in the room will be Superintendent Cochefort of the Sûreté—who is with us here—along with one of his men, and Monsieur Gribelin, archivist of the Statistical Section, who will make a verbatim record. Major Henry of the Statistical Section will be concealed behind a screen."

"So it will be five against one?"

"Exactly, Minister. I believe with the benefit of numbers and surprise there is an excellent chance he will be break down and confess on the spot. In which case, I wish to make a further suggestion."

"Go on."

"That we offer him the honourable way out—I show him a service revolver with a single bullet, and he can finish it there and then."

There was a silence while Mercier considered this, then he inclined his head slightly. "Yes."

Boisdeffre said, "Good heavens! I would be grateful if he could do it away from my carpet—it's an Aubusson."

Grateful laughter relieved the tension. Only Mercier didn't smile. "And if he doesn't take the traditional course, what then?"

"Then Major Henry will escort him to Cherche-Midi prison," said du Paty, "while Cochefort and I go to the Dreyfus apartment and search it for evidence. I'll warn his wife to say nothing of what has happened to her husband, or she'll make it far worse for him. At Cherche-Midi, the governor has agreed to keep Dreyfus in solitary confinement twenty-four hours a day—no letters, no visitors, no lawyers. Nobody will know where he is, not even the commander of the Paris garrison. As far as the world is concerned, Captain Alfred Dreyfus will have vanished from the face of the earth."

Having delivered himself of this masterpiece, du Paty closed his file and sat back in his chair.

I glanced around the table. Mercier and Boisdeffre were impassive, Gonse lighting a cigarette, Sandherr gripping the arms of his chair and shaking slightly, Henry watching him with concern, Cochefort looking at the floor with his arms folded.

Mercier said, "Does anyone have any questions?"

I hesitated, and then tentatively I raised my hand. I never could resist the opportunity to goad du Paty whenever I had the chance.

"Yes, Major . . . Picquart, is it?"

"It is. Thank you, Minister. I wondered," I said, turning towards du Paty, "what happens if Dreyfus doesn't confess?"

Du Paty gave me a cold look. "He will confess. He has no choice."

"But if he doesn't . . . ?"

"If he doesn't," interrupted Sandherr, staring down the table at me and apparently trembling with emotion, "we have plenty of other evidence, apart from his handwriting, that demonstrates his guilt."

I decided not to press it further. I nodded. "Thank you."

A long pause followed.

"Anyone else?" asked Mercier, the eye slits sweeping past each of us in turn. "No? Chief? No? In that case, gentlemen, you are authorised to proceed with the plan, as outlined by Colonel du Paty, at nine o'clock tomorrow morning."

And with that he signed the arrest warrant and tossed it down the table towards du Paty.

The next day was the most perfect crystalline autumn morning one could ever wish for—cool, with a clear sky and a promise of warmth to come, the early sun already starting to part the layers of mist draped across the Seine.

When I arrived at the ministry soon after eight, I found du Paty in the main lobby, in a state of high nervous excitement, marshalling his troops. Three were in civilian dress—Cochefort and his deputy, and a cadaverous clerk whom I took to be Gribelin, even though we were not introduced. Henry and I were both in uniform. Henry looked bemused, and at one point, as du Paty outlined for the second or third time what he wanted us to do, he caught my eye and gave me the tremor of a wink.

"So, Picquart, make sure you arrive with Dreyfus at the Chief of Staff's office on the stroke of nine" were du Paty's parting words to me. "Not a minute either side, understood? I want this thing to go off like clockwork!"

Du Paty and the others disappeared upstairs and I settled down on one of the green leather benches to wait. I had a commanding view of the courtyard leading to the rue Saint-Dominique. I pretended to read a newspaper. The minutes dragged by. The whole of the army seemed to pass before me—doddery and white-whiskered old generals, gallant colonels of dragoons flushed by the cold after an early morning canter in the Bois de Boulogne, keen-faced young captains carrying stacks of files for their masters—and then suddenly, in the midst of this parade, came Dreyfus: incongruous, hesitant, frowning, already looking like an outcast, shorn of his uniform, wearing an immaculate black frock coat, striped trousers and a bowler hat. He might have been a stockbroker. I glanced at my watch and cursed. He was fifteen minutes early.

I folded my newspaper and rose as he came through the door. Obviously he was taken aback to meet me. He touched his bowler in salute.

"Major Picquart, good morning." And then, glancing around the crowded lobby, he added, "I fear some of the fellows may be playing a joke on me. I had a telegram on Saturday, supposedly from General Boisdeffre's office, telling me to report for a staff review wearing civilian clothes, but nobody else seems to have received it."

"That sounds odd," I said. "May I see?"

Dreyfus pulled the telegram out of his pocket book and handed it over: *Summons. The Division General, Chief of the Army General Staff, will conduct an inspection of the officers on duty with the Staff during the day of Monday, 15 October. M. Captain Dreyfus, currently with the 39th Regiment of the Infantry in Paris, is invited to be present on that date at 9 a.m., in the office of the Chief of the Army General. Civilian dress . . .*

I pretended to read it through carefully. I was playing for time. "I don't understand," I said. "Come to my office. Let's get to the bottom of this."

"No, Major, please don't concern yourself with it . . ."

"Nonsense, I insist."

"I don't want to put you to any inconvenience . . ."

"Really, I have plenty of time."

It seemed an endless walk to the Third Department, during which I could think of nothing to utter except banalities about the weather and his family. "And how is your wife?"

"She's very well, thank you, Major."

"And do you have children? I'm sorry, I can't remember."

"Yes, Major—two."

"What sort?"

"A boy and a girl."

"And how old are they?"

"Pierre is three and Jeanne is one and a half . . ."

And so on and so forth. It was a relief when we reached my door. "Why don't you wait in here," I said, "while I check what's going on."

"Thank you, Major."

He went inside and I closed the door. I checked my watch again. Ten to nine. For several minutes I paced up and down the corridor like a sentry, repeatedly glancing at my closed door, willing the time to pass, wondering if perhaps he had climbed out of the window and shinned down the drainpipe, or was at that moment rifling through my desk for secrets. At last, at two minutes to the hour, I went in to fetch him. He was sitting on the edge of a chair with his bowler hat on his knees. The papers on my desk were undisturbed. It didn't look as if he'd moved a centimetre.

"Your telegram is quite correct," I said brightly. "There is an inspection."

"What a relief!" exclaimed Dreyfus, getting to his feet. "I really thought some of the fellows were playing a joke on me—they sometimes do, you know."

"I need to see the general myself. I'll walk over with you."

Off we set again.

Dreyfus said, "I hope I get the opportunity to have a word with General Boisdeffre. We had a really good talk about artillery formations in the summer. There are one or two additional points that have occurred to me since." I made no reply. Then he said, "You don't happen to know how long this inspection is likely to take, do you, Major?"

"I'm afraid I don't."

"The thing is, I told my wife I'd be home for lunch. Well, it doesn't matter."

We had reached the wide, high-ceilinged passage leading to the office of the Chief of the General Staff.

Dreyfus said, "I say, it's awfully quiet, isn't it? Where is everyone?"

The double doors were up ahead. His pace was slowing. I willed him to complete the distance.

I said, "I think they must all be inside waiting for you." I placed my hand in the small of his back and gently pressed him forward.

We reached the door. I opened it. He turned to me, puzzled. "Aren't you coming in as well, Major?"

"I'm sorry. I just remembered something I have to do. Goodbye."

I turned on my heel and walked away. Behind me I heard the

click of a lock, and when I looked back the door was closed and Dreyfus was gone.

"Tell me," I say to Gribelin, "what exactly happened that morning after I delivered Dreyfus to you and Colonel du Paty?"

"I don't understand what you mean, Colonel."

"You were there to act as a witness?"

"Yes."

"Well, what was it you witnessed?" The archivist stares at me as I pull out a chair. "Forgive all these questions, Monsieur Gribelin. I'm simply trying to fill in the gaps in my knowledge. It is a continuing case, after all." I indicate the chair opposite. "Sit down with me for a moment."

"If that is what you want, Colonel." Without taking his eyes off me, as if he suspects I might make a sudden lunge at him, Gribelin lowers his bony frame into the seat. "What do you want to know?"

I light a cigarette, and make a great show of pulling the ashtray towards me. "We wouldn't want a stray spark up here!" I say with a smile, shaking out the match and placing it carefully in the ashtray. "So Dreyfus comes through the door, and then what?"

It is as difficult as pulling teeth, but gradually I extract the story from him: how Dreyfus walked in, looked around and asked where General Boisdeffre was; how du Paty replied that he had been delayed, invited Dreyfus to sit down, indicated his gloved hand, and inquired if he wouldn't mind taking down a letter for him as he had sprained his wrist; how Dreyfus did as he was asked, watched by Cochefort and his assistant, and by Gribelin, who was sitting opposite him.

"He must have started to get nervous," I suggest. "He must have wondered what was happening."

"He did, most definitely. You can see it in his handwriting. I can show you, in fact." Gribelin goes once again to his filing cabinet and returns with a bulging folder, several centimetres thick. He opens it. "The first item is the actual document Dreyfus wrote down at Colonel du Paty's dictation." He pushes the file over to me. "You can see how his writing changes halfway through, as he realises he's been trapped and tries to disguise it."

It starts like an ordinary letter: *Paris, 15 October 1894. Having the most serious reasons, sir, for temporarily retaking possession of the documents I had passed on to you before taking off on manoeuvres . . .*

I say, "I don't see any change halfway through . . ."

"Yes, there is, it's obvious. Here." Gribelin leans across and taps the letter. He sounds exasperated. "Exactly here, where the colonel made him write *the hydraulic brake of the 120 millimetre cannon*—that was when he understood what was happening. You can see the way his writing suddenly gets larger and less regular."

I look again. I still don't see it. "Perhaps, if you say so . . ."

"Believe me, Colonel, we all noticed the change in his demeanour. His foot began to tremble. Colonel du Paty accused him of changing his style. Dreyfus denied it. When the dictation was finished, the colonel told him he was under arrest for treason."

"And then what happened?"

"Superintendent Cochefort and his assistant seized him and searched him. Dreyfus continued to deny it. Colonel du Paty showed him the revolver and offered him the honourable course."

"What did Dreyfus say to that?"

"He said, 'Shoot me if you want to, but I am innocent!' He was like a character in a play. At that moment Colonel du Paty called out for Major Henry, who was hidden behind the screen, and Major Henry took him away to prison."

I start to turn the pages of the file. To my astonishment, every sheet is a copy of the *bordereau*. I open it at the midpoint. I flick to the end. "My God," I murmur, "how many times did you make him write it out?"

"Oh, a hundred or more. But that was over the course of several weeks. You'll see they're labelled: 'Left hand,' 'right hand,' 'standing up,' 'sitting down,' 'lying down . . .'"

"You made him do this in his cell, presumably?"

"Yes. Monsieur Bertillon, the handwriting expert from the Préfecture of Police, wanted as large a sample as possible so that he could demonstrate how he managed to disguise his writing. Colonel du Paty and I would visit Dreyfus at Cherche-Midi, usually around midnight, and interrogate him throughout the night. The colonel had the idea of surprising him while he was asleep—springing in and shining a powerful lantern in his face."

"And what was his mental state during all this?"

Gribelin looks shifty. "It was rather fragile, to be frank with you, Colonel. He was held in solitary confinement. He was not allowed any letters or visitors. He was often quite tearful, asking after his family and so forth. I remember he had some abrasions on his face." Gribelin touches his temple lightly. "Around here. The warders told us he used to hit his head against the wall."

"And he denied any involvement in espionage?"

"Absolutely. It was quite a performance, Colonel. Whoever trained him taught him very well."

I continue to leaf through the file. *I am forwarding to you, sir, several interesting items of information . . . I am forwarding to you, sir, several interesting items of information . . . I am forwarding to you, sir, several interesting items of information . . .* The writing deteriorates as the days pass. It is like a record from a madhouse. I start to feel my own head reeling. I close the file and push it back across the table.

"That's fascinating, Gribelin. Thank you for your time."

"Is there anything else I can assist you with, Colonel?"

"I don't think so, no. Not just at the moment."

He cradles the file tenderly in his arms and takes it over to the filing cabinet. I pause at the door and look back at him. "Do you have any children, Monsieur Gribelin?"

"No, Colonel."

"Are you married, even?"

"No, Colonel. It never fitted with my work."

"I understand. I'm the same. Good night, then."

"Good night, Colonel."

I trot down the stairs to the first floor, picking up speed as I go, past the corridor to my office, down the stairs to the ground floor, across the lobby and out into the sunshine, where I fill my lungs with reviving draughts of clean fresh air.

11

I sleep very little that night. I sweat and turn and twist on my narrow bed, corrugating the sheets until it feels as if I am lying on stones. The windows are open to try to circulate some air, but all they admit is the noise of the city. In my insomnia I end up counting the distant chimes of the church clocks every hour from midnight until six. Finally I drop off to sleep, only to be woken thirty minutes later by the hoarse horn blasts of the early morning tramway cars. I dress and go downstairs and walk up the street to the bar on the corner of the rue Copernic. I have no appetite for anything more substantial than black coffee and a cigarette. I look at *Le Figaro*. An area of high pressure off the southwest coast of Ireland is moving across the British Isles, the Netherlands and Germany. The details of the Tsar's forthcoming visit to Paris have yet to be announced. General Billot, the Minister of War, is attending the cavalry manoeuvres in Gâtinais. In other words, in these dog days of August, there is no news.

By the time I reach the Statistical Section, Lauth is already in his office. He wears a leather apron. He has produced four prints of each of the two Esterhazy letters: damp and glistening, they still reek of chemical fixer. He has done his usual excellent job. The addresses and signatures have been blocked out but the lines of handwriting are sharp and easily legible.

"Good work," I say. "I'll take them with me—and the original letters, too, if you don't mind."

He puts them all in an envelope and hands it to me. "Here you are, Colonel. I hope they lead you somewhere interesting." There is an imploring spaniel's look in his pale blue eyes. But he has already asked me once what I want with them, and I have refused to answer. He dare not ask again.

I take great pleasure in ignoring the implied question and wishing him a jaunty "Good day, Lauth," before strolling back to my office. I remove one print of each of the letters and slip them into my brief-case; all the rest go into my safe. I lock my office door behind me. In the lobby I tell the new concierge, Capiaux, that I'm not sure when I'll be back. He's an ex-trooper in his late forties. Henry dredged him up from somewhere and I'm not entirely sure I trust him: to me he has the glassy-eyed, broken-veined look of one of Henry's drinking companions.

It takes me twenty minutes to walk to the Île de la Cité, to the headquarters of the Préfecture of Police, a gloomy fortress rising over the embankment beside the pont Saint-Michel. The building is the old municipal barracks, as dark and ugly inside as out. I give my visit-ing card to the porter—*Lt. Col. Georges Picquart, Ministry of War*—and tell him I wish to see Monsieur Alphonse Bertillon. The man is immediately respectful. He asks me to come with him. He unlocks a door and ushers me through it, then locks it behind us. We climb a narrow, winding stone staircase, floor after floor of steps so steep I am bent half double. At one point we have to stop and press ourselves against the wall to let past a dozen prisoners descending in single file. They trail a stench of sweat and despair in their wake. "Mon-sieur Bertillon has been measuring them," explains my guide, as if they have been to visit their tailor. We resume our ascent. Finally he unlocks yet another door and we emerge onto a hot and sunny corridor with a bare wooden floor. "If you wait in here, Colonel," he says, "I'll find him."

We are at the very top of the building, looking west. It swelters like a greenhouse with the trapped heat. Beyond the windows of Bertillon's laboratory, past the chimneypots of the Préfecture, the massive roofs of the Palace of Justice rise and plunge, a blue slate sea, pierced by the dainty gold and black spire of the Sainte-Chapelle. The lab's walls are papered with hundreds of photographs of crimi-nals, full-face and profile. Anthropometry—or "Bertillonage," as our leading practitioner modestly calls it—holds that all human beings can be infallibly identified by a combination of ten different measurements. In one corner is a bench with a metal ruler set into it and an adjustable gauge for measuring the length of forearms and fingers; in another, a wooden frame like a large easel, for recording height, both seated (torso length) and standing; in a third, a device with bronze calipers for taking cranial statistics. There is a huge camera, and a bench with a microscope and a magnifying glass mounted on a bracket, and a set of filing cabinets.

I wander around examining the photographs. It reminds me of a vast natural science collection—of butterflies, perhaps, or beetles, pinned and mounted. The expressions on the prisoners' faces are variously frightened, shamed, defiant, disinterested; some look badly beaten up, half starved or crazy; no one smiles. Amid this dismal array of desperate humanity I suddenly come across Alfred Dreyfus. His bland accountant's face stares out at me from above his torn uniform. Without his habitual spectacles or pince-nez his face looks naked. His eyes bore into mine. There is a caption: *Dreyfus 5.1.95.*

A voice says, "Colonel Picquart?" and I turn to find Bertillon holding my card. He is a squat, pale figure in his early forties with a thick pelt of black hair. His stiff beard is cut square, like the blade of an axe: I feel that if I ran my finger along the edge, it would draw blood.

"Good day, Monsieur Bertillon. I was just noticing that you have Captain Dreyfus here among your specimens."

"Ah yes, I recorded him myself," replies Bertillon. He comes over to stand beside me. "I photographed him when he arrived at La Santé prison, straight from his degradation."

"He looks different to how I remember him."

"The man was in a trance—a somnambulist."

"How else could one endure such an experience?" I open my briefcase. "Dreyfus in fact is the reason for my visit. I've replaced Colonel Sandherr as chief of the Statistical Section."

"Yes, Colonel, I remember you from the court-martial. What new is there to say about Dreyfus?"

"Would you be so good as to examine these?" I hand him the

photographs of the two Esterhazy letters. "And tell me what you think."

"You know that I never give instant judgements?"

"You might want to in this case."

He looks as if he might refuse. But then curiosity overcomes him. He goes to the window and holds up the letters to the light, one in either hand, and inspects them. He frowns and gives me a puzzled look. He returns his attention to the photographs. "Well," he says; and then again: "Well, well . . . !"

He crosses to a filing cabinet, slides open a drawer and takes out a thick green folder bound with black ribbon. He carries it over to his bench. He unties it, and pulls out a photograph of the *bordereau* and various sheets and charts. He lays the *bordereau* and the letters in a row. Then he takes three identical sheets of squared transparent paper and lays one over each of the three documents. He switches on a lamp and pulls the magnifying glass into position and starts to examine them. "A-ha," he mutters to himself, "a-ha, yes, yes, a-ha . . ." He makes a series of rapid notes. "A-ha, a-ha, yes, yes, a-ha . . ."

I watch him for several minutes. Eventually I can't stop myself. "Well? Are they the same?"

"Identical," he says. He shakes his head in wonder. He turns to me. "Absolutely identical!"

I can scarcely believe he can be so certain so quickly. The main prop in the case against Dreyfus has just vanished: kicked away by the very expert who put it there in the first place. "Would you be willing to sign an affidavit to that effect?"

"Absolutely."

Absolutely? The photographs of the criminals on the walls seem to whirl around me. "What if I told you that those letters weren't written by Dreyfus at all, but here in France this very summer?"

Bertillon shrugs, unconcerned. "Then I would say that obviously the Jews have managed to train someone else to write using the Dreyfus system."

———

I head back from the Île de la Cité to the Left Bank. I try to track down Armand du Paty at the Ministry of War. I am told he is not expected in that day, but he may be found at home. A junior staff officer gives me his address: 17, avenue Bosquet.

I set off yet again on foot. At some point I seem to have ceased to be an army officer and become a detective. I pound pavements. I interview witnesses. I collect evidence. If and when this is all over, perhaps I should apply to join the Sûreté.

The avenue Bosquet is pleasant and prosperous, close to the Seine, sun-dappled beneath its trees. Du Paty's apartment is on the second floor. I knock several times without receiving a reply, and I am on the point of leaving when I notice a shadow shifting slightly in the gap below the door. I knock again. "Colonel du Paty? It's Georges Picquart."

There is a silence, and then a muffled command: "A moment, if you please!" Bolts are drawn back, a lock turns, and the door opens a crack. A distorted eye blinks at me through a monocle. "Picquart? Are you alone?"

"Yes, of course. Why wouldn't I be?"

"True." The door opens fully to reveal du Paty dressed in a long red silk dressing gown covered in Chinese dragons; on his feet are pale blue Moroccan slippers; on his head a crimson Turkish fez. He is unshaven. "I was working on my novel," he explains. "Come in."

The apartment smells of incense and cigar smoke. Dirty plates are piled beside a chaise longue. Manuscript pages are stacked on an escritoire and strewn across the rug. Above the fireplace hangs a painting of a naked slave girl in a harem; on the table is a photograph of du Paty and his aristocratic new wife, Marie de Champlouis. He married her just before the Dreyfus affair began. In the picture she holds a baby in its christening robes.

"So you have become a father again? Congratulations."

"Thank you. Yes, the boy is one year old.* He's with his mother

---

* Charles du Paty de Clam (1895–1948), subsequently Head of Jewish Affairs in Vichy France.

on her family's estate for the summer. I've stayed behind in Paris to write."

"What are you writing?"

"It's a mystery."

Whether he is referring to the genre of his composition or its current state I am not sure. He seems to be in a hurry to get back to it: at any rate he doesn't invite me to sit. I say, "Well, here is another mystery for you." I open my briefcase and give him one of the Esterhazy letters. "You'll recognise the handwriting, perhaps."

He does, immediately—I can tell by the way he flinches, and then by the effort he makes to conceal his confusion. "I don't know," he mutters. "Perhaps it could be familiar. Who is the author?"

"I can't tell you that. But I can tell you it definitely wasn't our friend on Devil's Island, because it was written in the last month."

He thrusts it back at me: it's clear he doesn't want any part of it. "You should show this to Bertillon. He's the graphologist."

"I already have. He says it's identical to the *bordereau*—'identical,' that was his word."

There is an awkward silence, which du Paty tries to cover by breathing on both sides of his monocle, polishing it on the sleeve of his dressing gown, screwing it back into his eye and staring at me. "What exactly are you about here, Georges?"

"I'm just about doing my duty, Armand. It's my responsibility to investigate potential spies and I seem to have found another—a traitor who somehow escaped detection when you were leading the Dreyfus investigation two years ago."

Du Paty folds his arms defensively inside the wide sleeves of his robe. He looks absurd, like a wizard in a cabaret at Le Chat Noir. "I'm not infallible," he says. "I've never pretended otherwise. It's possible there were others involved. Sandherr always believed Dreyfus had at least one accomplice."

"Did you have any names?"

"Personally I suspected that brother of his, Mathieu. So did Sandherr, as a matter of fact."

"But Mathieu wasn't in the army at the time. He wasn't even in Paris."

"No," replies du Paty with great significance, "but he was in Germany. And he's a Jew."

I have no desire to be drawn into any of du Paty's crazy theories. It is like becoming lost in a maze with no exits. I say, "I must allow you to get back to your work." I rest my briefcase on the escritoire for a moment so that I can put away the photograph. As I do so, my eye falls unavoidably on a page of du Paty's novel. *"You shall not deceive me with your beauty for a second time, mademoiselle," cried the duc d'Argentin, with a flourish of his poisoned dagger . . .*

Du Paty watches me. He says, "The *bordereau* wasn't the only evidence against Dreyfus, you know. It was the intelligence we had that actually convicted him. The secret file. *As you remember.*" There is a definite threat in this last remark.

"I do remember."

"Good."

"Are you trying to imply something?"

"No. Or at least only that I hope you don't forget, as you pursue your investigations, that you were part of the whole prosecution as well. Let me show you out."

At the door I say, "Actually, that's not entirely accurate, if you'll allow me to correct you. You and Sandherr and Henry and Gribelin were the prosecuting authority. I was never anything more than an observer."

Du Paty emits a whinny of laughter. His face is close enough to mine for me to smell his breath: there's a whiff of decay about it that seems to come from deep within him and reminds me of the drains beneath the Statistical Section. "Oh, is that what you think? An observer! Come, my dear Georges, you sat through the entire court-martial! You were Mercier's errand boy throughout the whole thing! You advised him on his tactics! You can't turn round now and say it was nothing to do with you! Why else do you think you've ended up chief of the Statistical Section?" He opens the door. "Will you give my regards to Blanche, by the way?" he calls after me. "She's still not married, I believe? Tell her I would call upon her, but you know how it is: my wife wouldn't approve."

I am too angry to think of a reply, and so I leave him with the satisfaction of the last word, imagining himself a wit: smiling after me insufferably from his doorstep in his dressing gown and slippers and fez.

I walk back towards the office slowly, thinking over what I have just been told.

Is this what people say about me—that I was Mercier's errand boy? That I only got my present job because I knew how to tell him the things he wanted to hear?

I feel as if I have walked into a mirrored room and glimpsed myself from an unfamiliar angle for the first time. Is that really what I look like? Is that who I am?

Two months after Dreyfus's arrest, in the middle of December 1894, General Mercier summoned me to see him. I was not told what it was about. I assumed it must be in connection with the Dreyfus affair and that others would be present. I was right on the first point, wrong on the second. This time Mercier received me alone.

He was sitting behind his desk. A weak fire of brownish coal hissed in the grate. The bare facts of Dreyfus's arrest had been leaked to the press six weeks earlier, at the beginning of November—*High Treason. Arrest of the Jewish Officer A. Dreyfus*—and people were agog to know what he was guilty of, and what the government planned to do about him; I was curious myself. Mercier told me to take a seat and then played his favourite trick of making me wait while he finished annotating whatever document he was bent over, giving me a long opportunity to study the top of his narrow, close-cropped, balding skull and speculate on what schemes and secrets it contained. Eventually he set down his pen and said, "Before I go any further, let me just be certain—you haven't taken any part in the investigation of Captain Dreyfus since his arrest?"

"None, Minister."

"And you haven't spoken about the case to Colonel du Paty or Colonel Sandherr or Major Henry?"

"No."

There was a pause while Mercier scrutinised me through his eye slits. "You have literary interests, I believe?"

I hesitated. This was the sort of admission that could ruin one's prospects of promotion. "To some degree; in private, General; yes, I take an interest in all the arts."

"There's no need to be ashamed of it, Major. I simply want someone who can make a report for me that would contain more than just the bare facts. Do you think you can do that?"

"I would hope so. Naturally, it would depend on what it's about."

"Do you remember what you said in this office on the eve of Dreyfus's arrest?"

"I'm not sure what you mean, General."

"You asked Colonel du Paty: 'What happens if Dreyfus doesn't confess?' I made a note of it at the time. It was a good question. 'What happens if he doesn't confess?' Colonel du Paty assured us he would. But now it transpires he hasn't, despite being held in prison for the past two months. In confidence, Major, I must tell you I feel let down."

"I can understand that." *Poor old du Paty*, I thought. I found it hard to keep a straight face.

"Now Captain Dreyfus is going to stand trial next week in front of a military court, and the very same people who assured me he would confess are promising me with equal certainty that he will be found guilty. But I have learned to be more cautious, you understand?"

"Absolutely."

"The government will be roasted alive if this trial goes wrong. You've seen the press already: 'the case will be hushed up because the officer is a Jew . . .' So this is what I want you to do." He put his elbows on his desk and spoke very quietly and deliberately. "I want you, Major Picquart, to attend the court-martial every day on my behalf and report back to me each evening on what you've seen. I don't just want 'He said this, he said that . . .'—any secretary with shorthand could give me that. I want the very nub of the thing." He rubbed his thumb and forefinger together. "Describe it to me like a writer. Tell me how the prosecution sounds. Look at the judges, study the witnesses. I can't attend the court myself. That would make the whole thing seem like a political trial. So you'll have to be my eyes and ears. Can you do that for me?"

"Yes, General," I said, "I would be honoured."

I withdrew from Mercier's office maintaining a suitably solemn expression. But as soon as I reached the landing I tipped my cap to the painting of Napoleon. A personal assignment from the Minister of War! But not just that—I was to be his "eyes and ears"! I trotted down those marble steps with a broad smile on my face.

Dreyfus's court-martial was scheduled to start on Wednesday, 19 December in the military courthouse, a grim old building directly across the street from the Cherche-Midi prison, and to last three or four days. I very much hoped it would be over by Saturday night: I had tickets to the Salle d'Harcourt, to attend the first public performance of Monsieur Debussy's *Prélude à l'après-midi d'un faune*.

I made sure to be at the court building early. It was not yet light when I made my way into the crowded vestibule. The first person I met was Major Henry: when he saw me, he jerked his head back in surprise.

"Major Picquart! What are you doing here?"

"The minister has asked me to attend as his observer."

"Has he, by God?" Henry pulled a face. "Aren't we grand these days? So you're to be his stool pigeon? We'll have to watch what we say when you're around!" He tried to make it sound as if he was making a joke, but I could tell he was affronted, and from that moment on he was always wary of me. I wished him good luck and climbed the stone staircase to the courtroom on the first floor.

The building was a former convent with low, thick arched doors and roughly plastered whitewashed walls that had little nooks built into them for icons. The chamber set aside for the hearing was barely larger than a classroom and already packed with reporters, gendarmes, soldiers and those peculiar members of the general public whose pastime is attending trials. At the far end, on a platform erected beneath a mural of the Crucifixion, was a long table for the judges, covered with green baize. Carpets had been nailed up over the windows—whether to shut out prying eyes or the December cold I never did discover, but the effect was claustrophobic and curiously sinister. There was a plain wooden chair facing the judges for the accused, a small desk behind it for his lawyer and another nearby for the prosecutor. A chair just to the side of and behind the judges was reserved for me. There was nowhere for the spectators to sit; they could only press themselves against the walls. I took out my notebook and pencil and sat down to wait. At one point du Paty pushed his way in briefly, followed by General Gonse. They surveyed the scene, then left.

Soon afterwards the main players began to appear. There was Maître Edgar Demange, Dreyfus's attorney, exotic in his black robes and cylindrical black cap but otherwise the epitome of a dull middle-aged farmer with a broad, clean-shaven face and straggling wispy sideburns. The prosecutor was Brisset, thin as a sabre, in the uniform of a major. And finally there came the seven military judges, also in uniform—a colonel, three majors and two captains, led by the president of the court, Colonel Émilien Maurel. He was a shrivelled and unhealthy-looking elderly figure: I learned later he was suffering from piles. He took his place in the centre of the long table and addressed the court in a peevish voice: "Bring in the accused!"

All eyes went to the back of the court and the door opened and in he came. He was slightly bent from lack of exercise, grey from exhaustion and the darkness of his cell, thin from his poor diet: in ten weeks he had aged ten years. And yet, as he advanced into the room, escorted by a lieutenant of the Republican Guard, he held his head at a defiant angle. I even detected a hint of anticipation in his step. Perhaps Mercier was right to be worried. *Quite the grand seigneur*, I noted, *& eager to begin.* He halted in front of Colonel Maurel and saluted.

Maurel coughed to clear his throat and said, "State your name."

"Alfred Dreyfus."

"Place of birth?"

"Mulhouse."

"Age?"

"Thirty-five."

"You may sit."

Dreyfus lowered himself into his place. He took off his cap and placed it under his seat. He adjusted his pince-nez and glanced around. I was in his direct line of sight. Almost at once his gaze settled on me. I must have held his stare for perhaps half a minute. What was in his expression? I couldn't tell. But I sensed that to look away would be to concede that I had played a shabby trick on him, and so I wouldn't do it.

In the end, it was the prosecutor, Brisset, who made us break our contest and look away at the same time. He rose and said, "Monsieur President, in view of the sensitive nature of this case, we would like to request that this hearing be held in private."

Demange immediately lumbered to his feet. "Monsieur President, we object strongly. My client has the right to be treated the same as anyone else who is accused."

"Monsieur President, under normal circumstances, nobody would argue with that. But the evidence against Captain Dreyfus necessarily includes important matters of national defence."

"With all due respect, the only actual *evidence* against my client consists of just one sheet of disputed writing . . ."

A murmur of surprise went round the room. Maurel gavelled it away. "Maître Demange! Be silent, please! You are too experienced an advocate to be excused that type of trick. This court will stand adjourned while we retire to make our decision. Take the accused back to his cell."

Dreyfus was led away again. The judges filed out after him. Demange looked content with this first exchange. As I later warned Mercier, whatever happened, he had smuggled out to the public a message about the thinness of the prosecution's case.

Fifteen minutes later the judges returned. Maurel ordered that Dreyfus should be retrieved from his cell. He was conducted back to his place, apparently as unperturbed as ever. Maurel said, "We have considered the matter carefully. This case is highly unusual in that it touches on the gravest and most sensitive issues of national security. In these matters one simply cannot be too careful. Our ruling therefore is that all spectators should be excluded immediately and that these hearings should proceed in private." A great groan of complaint and disappointment arose. Demange tried to object, but Maurel brought down his gavel. "No, no! I have made my decision, Maître Demange! I shall not debate it with you. Clerk, clear the court!"

Demange slumped back. Now he looked grim. It took barely two minutes for the press and public to be ushered out by the gendarmes. When the clerk closed the door, the atmosphere was completely altered. The room was hushed. The carpeted windows seemed to seal us off from the outside world. Only thirteen remained: Dreyfus and his defender and prosecutor; the seven judges; the clerk, Vallecalle; a police official and me.

"Good," said Maurel. "Now we can begin to consider the evidence. Would the prisoner please stand? Monsieur Vallecalle, read the indictment . . ."

For the next three afternoons, at the end of each day's session, I would hurry down the stairs, past the waiting journalists—whose questions I would ignore—stride out into the winter dusk, and pace along the icy pavements for seven hundred and twenty metres exactly—I counted them each time—from the rue du Cherche-Midi to the hôtel de Brienne.

"Major Picquart to see the Minister of War . . ."

My briefings of the minister always followed the same pattern. Mercier would listen with close attention. He would ask a few terse and pertinent questions. Afterwards he would send me off to Boisdeffre to repeat what I had just said. Boisdeffre, only recently returned from the funeral of Tsar Alexander III in Moscow, his noble head no doubt stuffed full of matters Russian, would hear me through to the end courteously and mostly without comment. From Boisdeffre I would be taken in a War Ministry carriage to the Élysée Palace. There I would brief the President of the Republic himself, the lugubrious Jean Casimir-Perier—an uncomfortable assignment, as the President had long suspected his Minister of War of scheming behind his back. In fact Casimir-Perier was by this time something of a prisoner himself—cut off in his gilded apartments, ignored by his ministers, reduced to a purely ceremonial role. He made clear his contempt for the army by not once inviting me to sit. His response to my narrative was to punctuate it throughout with sarcastic remarks and snorts of disbelief: "It sounds like the plot of a comic opera!"

Privately I shared his misgivings, and they grew as the week progressed. On the first day the witnesses were the six key men who had put together the case against Dreyfus: Gonse, Fabre and d'Aboville, Henry, Gribelin and du Paty. Gonse explained how easily Dreyfus could have got access to the secret documents handed over with the *bordereau*. Fabre and d'Aboville described his suspicious behaviour while serving in the Fourth Department. Henry testified to the genuineness of the *bordereau* as evidence retrieved from the German Embassy. Gribelin—drawing on police reports compiled by Guénée—painted a picture of Dreyfus as a womaniser and gambler, which I found frankly unbelievable. But du Paty insisted Dreyfus was driven by "animal urges" and that he was *canaille*—lowlife—despite his rather prim appearance (Dreyfus simply shook his head at this). Du Paty also alleged the accused had made conscious changes to disguise his handwriting during dictation—an accusation gravely undermined when Demange showed him samples of Dreyfus's hand, asked him to point out where these transitions occurred, and du Paty was unable to do so.

Taken together, it was not impressive.

At the end of my first report, when Mercier asked me how I thought the prosecution case was looking, I hemmed and hawed. "Now then, Major," he said softly, "your honest opinion, please. That's why I put you in there."

"Well, Minister, in my honest view, it's all very circumstantial. We have shown beyond doubt that the traitor *could* have been Dreyfus; we have not proved definitely that it *was* him."

Mercier grunted but made no further comment. However, the next day when I turned up at the court building for the start of the second day's evidence, Henry was waiting for me.

He said in an accusing tone, "I hear you've told the minister our case is looking thin."

"Well, isn't it?"

"No, I don't think so."

"Now, Major Henry, don't look so offended. Will you join me?" I offered him a cigarette, which he took grudgingly. I struck a match and lit his first. "I didn't say it was thin, exactly, just not specific enough."

"My God," replied Henry, exhaling a jet of smoke in a sigh of frustration, "it's easy enough for you to say that. If only you knew how much specific evidence we have against that swine. We even have a letter from a foreign intelligence officer in which he's identified as the traitor—can you believe it?"

"Then use it."

"How can we? It would betray our most secret sources. It would do more damage than Dreyfus has caused already."

"Even with the hearing behind closed doors?"

"Don't be naïve, Picquart! Every word uttered in that room will leak one day."

"Well, then I don't know what to suggest."

Henry drew deeply on his cigarette. "How would it be," he asked, glancing around to check he was not being overheard, "if I came back into court and described some of the evidence we have on file?"

"But you've already given your evidence."

"Couldn't I be recalled?"

"On what pretext?"

"Couldn't you have a word with Colonel Maurel and suggest it?"

"What reason could I give him?"

"I don't know. I'm sure we could come up with something."

"My dear Henry, I'm here to observe the court-martial, not interfere in it."

"Fine," said Henry bitterly. He took a last drag from his cigarette then dropped it on to the flagstone floor and ground it out with the toe of his boot. "I'll do it myself."

That second morning was devoted to a parade of officers from the General Staff. They queued up to denigrate their former comrade, to his face. They described a man who snooped around their desks, refused to fraternise with them and always acted as if he was their intellectual superior. One claimed Dreyfus had told him he didn't care if Alsace was under German occupation because he was a Jew, and Jews, having no country of their own, were indifferent to changes of frontier. Throughout all this, Dreyfus's expression betrayed no emotion. One might have thought him stone deaf or wilfully not listening. But every so often he would raise his hand to signal he wished to speak. Then he would calmly correct a point of fact in his toneless voice: this piece of testimony was wrong because he had not been in the department then; that statement was an error because he had never met the gentleman concerned. He seemed to have no anger in him. He was an automaton. Several officers did say a word or two in his defence. My old friend Mercier-Milon called him "a faithful and scrupulous soldier." Captain Tocanne, who had attended my topography classes with Dreyfus, said he was "incapable of a crime."

And then, at the start of the afternoon session, one of the judges, Major Gallet, announced he had an important issue to bring to the court's attention. It was his understanding, he said gravely, that there had been an earlier inquiry into a suspected traitor on the General Staff, even before the investigation into Dreyfus began in October. If true, he regretted that this fact had been withheld from the court. He suggested that the matter should be cleared up right away. Colonel Maurel agreed, and told the clerk to recall Major Henry. A few minutes later, Henry appeared, apparently embarrassed and buttoning his tunic, as if he had been dragged from a bar. I made a note of the time: 2:35.

Demange could have objected to Henry's recall. But Henry was putting on such a virtuoso performance of being a reluctant witness— standing bareheaded before the judges, fidgeting nervously with his cap—he must have gambled that whatever was coming might work to Dreyfus's advantage.

"Major Henry," said Maurel severely, "the court has received information that your evidence yesterday was less than frank, and that you neglected to tell us about an earlier inquiry you made into the existence of a spy on the General Staff. Is that correct?"

Henry mumbled, "It is true, Monsieur President."

"Speak up, Major! We can't hear you!"

"Yes, it's true," replied Henry, loudly. He glanced along the row of judges with a look of defiant apology. "I wished to avoid revealing any more secret information than was necessary."

"Tell us the truth now, if you please."

Henry sighed and stroked his hand through his hair. "Very well," he said. "If the court insists. It was in March of this year. An honourable person—a very honourable person—informed us that there was a traitor on the General Staff, passing secrets to a foreign power. In June he repeated his warning to me personally, and this time he was more specific." Henry paused.

"Go on, Major."

"He said the traitor was in the Second Department." Henry turned to Dreyfus and pointed at him. "The traitor is that man!"

The accusation detonated in that little room like a grenade. Dreyfus, hitherto so calm he had seemed scarcely human, jumped up to protest at this ambush. His pale face was livid with anger. "Monsieur President, I demand to know the name of this informer!"

Maurel banged his gavel. "The accused will sit!"

Demange grabbed the back of his client's tunic and tried to tug him down into his seat. "Leave it to me, Captain," I heard him whisper. "That's what you're paying me for." Unwillingly, Dreyfus sat. Demange rose and said, "Monsieur President, this is hearsay evidence—an outrage to justice. The defence absolutely demands that this informant be called so that he can be cross-examined. Otherwise, none of what has just been said has any legal weight whatsoever. Major Henry, at the very least you must tell us this man's name."

Henry looked at him with contempt. "It's obvious you know nothing about intelligence, Maître Demange!" He waved his cap at him. "There are some secrets an officer carries in his head that even his cap isn't allowed to know!"

That brought Dreyfus to his feet again—"This is outrageous!"—and once again Maurel gavelled for order.

"Major Henry," said Maurel, "we will not demand the name, but do you affirm on your honour that the treasonous officer referred to was Captain Dreyfus?"

Henry slowly raised a fat and stubby forefinger and pointed to the picture of Christ above the judges' heads. In a voice as fervent as a priest's he proclaimed: "I swear it!"

I described the exchange to Mercier that evening.

He said, "You make it sound highly dramatic."

"I think one may safely say that if Major Henry ever leaves the army, the Comédie-Française will stand ready to receive him."

"But will his evidence have the desired effect?"

"In terms of theatre it was first-class. Whether it carries much weight legally is another question."

The minister sat back low in his chair and made a steeple of his fingers. He brooded. "Who are the witnesses tomorrow?"

"In the morning, the handwriting expert, Bertillon; in the afternoon, the defence is producing witnesses to Dreyfus's good character."

"Who?"

"Family friends—a businessman, a doctor, the Chief Rabbi of Paris—"

"Oh, good God!" cried Mercier. It was the first time I had seen him display emotion. "How absurd is this? Do you imagine the Germans would permit such a circus? The Kaiser would simply have a traitor in his army put against a wall and shot!" He propelled himself out of his chair and went over to the fireplace. "This is one of the reasons why we lost in '70—we completely lack their *ruthlessness*." He picked up the poker and stabbed viciously at the coals, sending a spray of orange sparks whirling up the chimney. I was unsure how to respond, so I stayed silent. I confess I had some sympathy for his predicament. He was fighting a life-or-death battle, but without being able to deploy his best troops. After a while, still staring into the flames, he said quietly, "Colonel Sandherr has put together a file for the court-martial. I've seen it. So has Boisdeffre. It proves the extent of Dreyfus's crimes beyond any doubt. What do you think I should do with it?"

I replied without hesitation, "Show it to the court."

"We can't—that would mean showing it to Dreyfus. We could,

perhaps, show it to the judges, in confidence, so that they can see what we're dealing with."

"Then I would do it."

He glanced at me over his shoulder. "Even though it breaks all the rules of legal procedure?"

"I can only say that if you don't, there's a chance he may be acquitted. Under the circumstances, some would say it is your duty."

I was telling him what he wanted to hear. Not that it would have made any difference. He would have done it anyway. I left him still poking at his fire.

The following morning Bertillon gave his evidence. He came in laden with various charts and handwriting samples which he passed out to the judges, and to the defence and the prosecution. He set up an easel with a complicated diagram involving arrows. "Two handwriting experts," he said, "have maintained that Dreyfus wrote the *bordereau*; two have pointed out discrepancies and concluded he did not. I, Monsieur President, shall reconcile these different opinions."

He paced up and down the confined space, dark and hirsute, like a small ape in a cage. He talked very rapidly. Occasionally he pointed at the chart.

"Gentlemen, you will see that I have taken the *bordereau* and ruled vertical and horizontal lines over it at a distance of five millimetres. What do we find? We find that the words that occur twice—*manoeuvres, modifications, disposal, copy*—all begin, within a millimetre, in exactly the same part of one of the squares I have ruled. There is a one-in-five chance that this might happen in any single case. The odds of it happening in all these cases are sixteen in ten thousand. The odds of it occurring with all the other words I have analysed are one hundred million to one! Conclusion: this could not happen with a naturally written document. Conclusion: the *bordereau* is forged.

"Question: who forged it, and why? Answer: look again at the polysyllables repeated within the *bordereau*—*manoeuvres, modifications*. When you place one over the other, you find that the beginnings coincide while the ends do not. But shift the word that comes earliest a millimetre and a quarter to the right, and the ends coincide also. Gentlemen, the writing of Alfred Dreyfus supplied to me by the Ministry of War exhibits exactly the same peculiarities! And as for the differences between the culprit's hand and the *bordereau*—the 'o' and the double 's,' most obviously—imagine my astonishment when I found exactly these letter formulations in correspondence seized from the culprit's wife and brother! Five millimetres reticulation, twelve point five centimetres gabarit and a millimetre and a quarter imbrication! Always you find it—always—always! Final conclusion: Dreyfus forged his own handwriting to avoid detection, by modifying it with formulations taken from his family!"

Dreyfus interrupted: "So the *bordereau* must have been written by me, both because it resembles my handwriting and because it doesn't?"

"Exactly!"

"Then how can you ever be refuted?"

A good point. I had to suppress a smile. But although Bertillon may have seemed to Dreyfus and indeed to me an impostor, I could see he had impressed the judges. They were soldiers. They liked facts and diagrams and ruled squares and words like "reticulation." One hundred million to one! Here was a statistic they could grasp.

At the lunchtime adjournment, du Paty approached me in the corridor. He was rubbing his hands. "I gather from several of the judges that Bertillon did well this morning. I do believe we have the scoundrel where we want him at last. What will you tell the minister?"

"That Bertillon appears unhinged, and that I'm still not sure I would put the odds of a conviction at better than fifty-fifty."

"The minister told me of your pessimism. Of course it's always easy to complain from the sidelines." Tucked beneath his arm he had a large manila envelope. He gave it to me. "This is from General Mercier for you."

It wasn't heavy. It felt as if it might contain perhaps a dozen sheets of paper. In the top right-hand corner was written in blue pencil a large letter "D."

I said, "What am I supposed to do with this?"

"You are to give it to the president of the court before the end of the day, as discreetly as possible."

"What is it?"

"You don't need to know what it is. Just give it to him, Picquart, that's all. And do try to be less defeatist."

I took the envelope in with me to the afternoon session. I didn't know where to put it. Under my seat? Beside it? In the end, I sat with it awkwardly on my lap as the defence called their character witnesses—a handful of officers, an industrialist, a physician, the Chief Rabbi of Paris in his Hebrew garb. Colonel Maurel, plainly feeling the effects of his piles, dealt with them briskly, especially the rabbi.

"Your name?"

"Dreyfuss—"

"Dreyfus? You are a relative?"

"No, a different family. We are Dreyfuss with two s's. I am the Chief Rabbi of Paris."

"Fascinating. What do you know about this case?"

"Nothing. But I have known the family of the accused for a long time and I consider it to be an honest family . . ."

Maurel fidgeted throughout his testimony. "Thank you. The witness may stand down. That concludes all the evidence in this case. Tomorrow we shall hear closing arguments. The court stands adjourned. Take the prisoner back to his cell."

Dreyfus picked up his cap, stood, saluted, and was escorted out of the room. I waited until the judges began to file down from their platform, then approached Maurel. "Excuse me, Colonel," I said quietly, "I have something for you, from the Minister of War."

Maurel glanced at me irritably. He was a small, hunched figure, his complexion greenish-grey. He said, "That's right, Major, I've been expecting it." He slipped the envelope between his other papers and walked on without another word. As I turned to watch him go, I discovered Dreyfus's attorney studying me. Demange frowned and pursed his lips, and for a moment I thought he was going to challenge me. I put my notebook away in my pocket, nodded at him, and walked straight past him.

When I recounted the episode to Mercier, he said, "I believe we did the right thing."

"In the end it will be for the judges to evaluate," I replied. "All you can do is to give them the full facts."

"I presume I don't need to remind you that no one outside our small group should know about this." I half expected him to tell me what was in the file, but instead he picked up his pen and went back to his papers. His parting words were: "Be sure to inform General Boisdeffre I have done as we agreed."

The following morning when I arrived in the rue du Cherche-Midi, a small crowd had already gathered. Extra gendarmes guarded the gate in case of trouble. Inside the courthouse twice the usual number of reporters milled around: one told me they had been promised that they would be allowed back into the courtroom to hear the verdict. I squeezed through the throng and went upstairs.

At nine, the final day's session opened. Each of the seven judges was given a magnifying glass, a copy of the *bordereau* and a sample of Dreyfus's writing. Brisset made an interminable speech for the prosecution. "Take your magnifying glass," he instructed them, "and you will be certain that Dreyfus has written it." The court rose for lunch. In the afternoon, an attendant turned on the gaslights, and in the encroaching dusk Demange began summing up for the defence. "Where is the proof?" he demanded. "No single shred of direct evidence links my client to this crime." Maurel invited Dreyfus to make a short statement. He delivered it staring fixedly ahead: "I am a Frenchman and a man of Alsace above all else: I am no traitor." And with that it was over, and Dreyfus was led away to await the verdict in a different part of the building.

Once the judges had retired, I went out into the courtyard to escape the oppressive atmosphere. It was just before six, desperately cold. Shadowed in the dim gaslight was a company of soldiers from the Paris garrison. By this time the authorities had closed the gates to the street. It felt like a fortress under siege. I could hear the crowd beyond the high wall, talking and moving in the darkness. I smoked a cigarette. A reporter said, "Did you notice the way Dreyfus missed every other step when they brought him downstairs? He doesn't know where he is, poor wretch." Another said, "I hope they're done in time for the first edition." "Oh, they will be, don't worry—they'll want their dinners."

At half past six, an aide to the judges announced that the doors to the courtroom had been reopened. There was a stampede for places. I followed the reporters back upstairs. Gonse, Henry, du Paty and Gribelin stood in a row together beside the door. Such was the nervous tension that their faces seemed scarcely less white than the wall. We nodded but didn't speak. I reclaimed my seat and took out my notebook for the final time. There must have been close to a hundred people jammed into that confined space, yet they made barely a sound. The silence seemed subaqueous—to exert a physical pressure on one's lungs and eardrums. I wanted desperately for it to be over. At seven, there was a shout from the corridor—"Shoulder arms! Present arms!"—followed by a thump of boots. The judges filed back in, led by Maurel.

"All rise!"

The clerk, Vallecalle, read the verdict. "In the name of the people of France," he said, at which point all seven judges raised their hands to their caps in salute, "the first permanent court-martial of the military government of Paris, having met in camera, delivered its verdict in public session as follows . . ." When he pronounced the word "Guilty!" there was a shout from the back of the court of *"Vive la patrie!"* Reporters began running from the room.

Maurel said, "Maître Demange, you may go and inform the condemned man."

The lawyer didn't move. He had his head in his hands. He was crying.

A strange noise seemed to blow in from outside—an odd pattering and howling. I mistook it at first for rain or wind. Then I realised it was the crowd in the street reacting to the verdict with applause and cheering. "Down with the Jews!" "Death to the Jewish traitor!"

"Major Picquart to see the Minister of War . . ."

Past the sentry. Across the courtyard. Into the lobby. Up the stairs.

Mercier was standing in the middle of his office, wearing full dress uniform. His chest was armour-plated with medals and decorations. His English wife stood beside him in a blue velvet gown with diamonds at her throat. They both looked very small and dainty, like a pair of mannequins in an historical tableau.

I was breathless from my run, sweating despite the cold. "Guilty," I managed to stammer out. "Deportation for life to a fortified enclosure."

Madame Mercier's hand flew straight to her breast. "The poor man," she said.

The minister blinked at me but made no comment except to say, "Thank you for letting me know."

I found Boisdeffre in his office, similarly bemedalled in dress uniform, about to depart for the same state banquet at the Élysée Palace as the Merciers. His only remark was, "At least I shall be able to dine in peace."

Duty done, I ran out into the rue Saint-Dominique and managed, by the skin of my teeth, to hail a taxi. By eight-thirty I was slipping into my seat beside Blanche de Comminges at the Salle d'Harcourt. I looked around for Debussy but couldn't see him. The conductor tapped his baton, the flautist raised his instrument to his lips, and those first few exquisite, plangent bars—which some say are the birth of modern music—washed Dreyfus clean from my mind.

12

I wait deliberately until the day is almost over before I go upstairs to see Gribelin. He looks startled to see me standing in his doorway for the second time in two days. He gets creakily to his feet. "Colonel?"

"Good evening, Gribelin. I want to see the secret file on Dreyfus, if you please."

Is it my imagination or do I detect, as with Lauth, a pinprick of alarm in his eyes? He says, "I don't have that particular file, Colonel, I'm afraid."

"In that case I believe Major Henry must have it."

"What makes you say that?"

"Because when I took over the section, Colonel Sandherr told me that if I ever had any questions about the Dreyfus file, I should consult Henry. I took that to mean that Henry was the one who had retained custody of it."

"Well, obviously, if *Colonel Sandherr* said that . . ." Gribelin's voice trails off. Then he adds hopefully, "I wonder, Colonel—given that Henry is on leave—I wonder, wouldn't it be better to wait until he returns . . . ?"

"Absolutely not. He won't be back for several weeks and I need it right away." I pause, waiting for him to move. "Come along, Monsieur Gribelin." I hold out my arm to him. "I'm sure you have the keys to his office."

I sense he would like to lie. But that would mean disobeying a direct order from a superior. And that is an act of rebellion of which Gribelin, unlike Henry, is congenitally incapable. He says, "Well, I suppose we can check . . ." He unlocks the bottom right-hand drawer of his desk and takes out his bunch of keys. Together we go downstairs.

Henry's office overlooks the rue de l'Université. The smell of the drains seems stronger in the unaired room. A large fly knocks itself dementedly against the grimy window. There is the usual War Ministry–issue desk, chair, safe, filing cabinet and thin square of brown carpet. The only personal touches are a carved wooden tobacco jar in the shape of a dog's head on the desk, an elaborately hideous German regimental beer stein on the windowsill and a photograph of Henry with some comrades in the uniform of the 2nd Zouaves in Hanoi: he was there at the same time as I was, although if we met I've forgotten it. Gribelin crouches to unlock the safe. He searches through the files. When he finds what he wants, he locks it again. As he straightens, his knees make a sound like snapping twigs. "Here you are, Colonel."

It appears to be the same manila envelope with the letter "D" written in the corner that I handed to the president of the court-martial twenty months earlier, except that the seal has been broken. I weigh it in my hand. I remember thinking how light it was when du Paty gave it to me originally; it feels the same. "This is all there is?"

"That's all. If you let me know when you've finished with it, I can lock it up again."

"Don't worry. I'll take care of it from now on."

Back in my office I lay the envelope on my desk and contemplate it for a moment. Odd that such a dreary-looking object should assume such significance. Do I really want to do this? Once one has read a thing, there is no un-reading it. There could be consequences—legal and ethical—that I can't even guess at.

I lift the flap and pull out the contents. There are five documents.

I start with a handwritten deposition from Henry, providing the context for his theatrical testimony at the court-martial:

Gentlemen,

In June 1893, the Statistical Section came into possession of a note written by the German military attaché Colonel von Schwartzkoppen. This note showed that he was in receipt, via an unknown

informant, of the plans of the fortifications at Toul, Reims, Lan-
gres and Neufchâteau.

In January 1894, another intercepted note revealed that he had
paid this informant an advance of six hundred francs for the plans
of Albertville, Briançon, Mézières and the new embankments on
both sides of the Moselle and the Meurthe.

Two months later, in March 1894, an agent of the Sûreté,
François Guénée, acting on our behalf, met the Spanish military
attaché, the marquis de Val Carlos, a regular informant of the
Statistical Section. Among other intelligence, the marquis warned
M. Guénée of a German agent employed on the General Staff.
His exact words were: "Be sure to tell Major Henry on my behalf
(and he may repeat it to the colonel) that there is reason to intensify
surveillance at the Ministry of War, since it emerges from my last
conversation with the German attachés that they have an officer
on the General Staff who is keeping them admirably well informed.
Find him, Guénée: if I knew his name, I would tell you!"

I subsequently met the marquis de Val Carlos myself in June
1894. He told me that a French officer who worked specifically in
the Second Department of the General Staff—or at any rate had
worked there in March and April—had supplied information to
the German and Italian military attachés. I asked for the name of
this officer, but he could not tell me. He said: "I am sure of what I
say but I do not know the officer's name." Following my report of
this conversation to Colonel Sandherr, new orders were issued for
a much more rigorous surveillance. It was during this period, on
25 September, that the bordereau that forms the basis of the Drey-
fus case came into our possession.

(Signed)

Henry, Hubert-Joseph (Major)

The next three documents are original, glued-together papers
purloined from Schwartzkoppen's wastepaper basket: raw intelligence presumably included to buttress Henry's statement. The first
is written in German, in Schwartzkoppen's own hand, and appears
to be a draft memorandum, either for his own use or for his superiors

in Berlin, jotted down after he was first approached by the would-be traitor. He has torn it into extra fine pieces; there are tantalising gaps:

> *Doubt . . . Proof . . . Letter of service . . . A dangerous situation for myself with a French officer . . . Must not conduct negotiations personally . . . Bring what he has . . . Absolute . . . Intelligence Bureau . . . no relation . . . Regiment . . . only importance . . . Leaving the ministry . . . Already elsewhere . . .*

The second reassembled document is a letter to Schwartzkoppen from the Italian military attaché, Major Alessandro Panizzardi. It is written in French, dated January 1894, and begins *My dear Bugger.*

> *I have written to Colonel Davignon again, and that is why, if you have the opportunity to broach this question with your friend, I ask you to do so in such a way that Davignon doesn't come to hear of it . . . for it must never be revealed that one has dealings with another.*
>
> > *Goodbye my good little dog,*
> > *Your A*

Davignon is the deputy head of the Second Department—the officer responsible for briefing the various foreign military attachés and arranging their invitations to manoeuvres, receptions, lectures and so forth. I know him well. His integrity is, as they say, above reproach.

The third reconstituted letter is a note from Schwartzkoppen to Panizzardi:

> *P 16.4.94*
>
> *My dear friend,*
> *I am truly sorry not to have seen you before I left. Anyway, I will be back in eight days. I am enclosing twelve master plans of Nice which that lowlife D gave me for you. I told him that you did not*

intend to resume relations. He claims there was a misunderstand-
ing and that he would do his utmost to satisfy you. He says that he
had insisted you would not hold it against him. I replied that he was
crazy and that I did not think you would resume relations with him.
Do as you wish! I am in a hurry.

Alexandrine

Don't bugger too much!!!

The final document, again handwritten, is a commentary on Dreyfus's alleged career as a spy signed by du Paty. It attempts to draw together all these various scraps of evidence into a coherent story:

Captain Dreyfus began his espionage activities for the German General Staff in 1890, aged thirty, while undergoing instruction at the École Centrale de Pyrotechnie Militaire in Bourges, where he purloined a document describing the process for filling shells with melinite.

In the second half of 1893, as part of the *stagiaire* system, Captain Dreyfus was attached to the First Department of the General Staff. While there he had access to the safe containing the blueprints of various fortifications, including those at Nice. His behaviour throughout his attachment was suspicious. Inquiries have established that it would have been an easy matter for him to remove these plans when the office was unattended. These were passed to the German Embassy, and later forwarded to the Italian military attaché (see attached document: "that lowlife D").

At the beginning of 1894 Dreyfus joined the Second Department. The presence there of a German spy was drawn[*] to the attention of M. Guénée in March (see attached report by Major Henry) . . .

And that is all. I take the envelope and shake it out again, just to make sure. Can that really be it? I feel a sense of anticlimax, and even some anger. I have been duped. There is nothing in the so-called "secret file" but circumstance and innuendo. Not one document or witness directly names Dreyfus as a traitor. The nearest it comes to incriminating him is an initial letter: "that lowlife D."

I reread du Paty's compilation of breezy non sequiturs. Does it actually make sense? I know the layout and procedures of the First Department. It would have been practically impossible for Dreyfus to have smuggled out undetected something the size of architectural plans. And even if he had, their absence would have been noticed immediately. And yet there have never been, to my knowledge, any complaints about stolen documents. So presumably Dreyfus must have copied them and then replaced them—is that the suggestion? But how did he have so many copies made so quickly? And how did he manage to smuggle the originals back into the safe again without being seen? The dates don't fit, either. Dreyfus only joined the First in July 1893, yet according to Henry, Schwartzkoppen already had some stolen plans in his possession by June. And the German attaché's description of D as "crazy": is that a word one would apply to the meticulous Dreyfus, any more than one would call him "lowlife"?

I lock the file away in my safe.

Just before I go home, I call in at the ministry to make an appointment to see Boisdeffre. Pauffin de Saint Morel is the officer on duty. He tells me the Chief is not in until Tuesday. "Can I tell him what it's about?"

"I'd prefer not."

"Secret stuff?"

"Secret stuff."

"Say no more." He enters my name in the diary for ten o'clock. "By the way," he asks, "did you follow up that business with old Foucault, about some German spy story?"

"Yes I did, thank you."

"Nothing in it?"

"Nothing in it."

I spend Saturday in my office writing a report for Boisdeffre: "Intelligence Service note on Major Esterhazy, 74th Infantry." It requires some delicate drafting. I make several false starts. I describe in guarded terms the interception of the *petit bleu*, the investigation into Esterhazy's suspicious character, the information from Cuers that the Germans (whom I describe by the unoriginal code name "X") still have a spy in the French army, and the similarity between the writing of the *bordereau* and that of Esterhazy (*striking even to the least expert eye*). The report runs to four closely written pages. I conclude:

> The facts indicated seem serious enough to merit a more detailed inquiry. Above all it is necessary to seek some explanations from Major Esterhazy about his relations with Embassy X and the use he made of the documents that he copied. But it is vital to operate by surprise, with both firmness and caution, because the major is known as a man of unequalled audacity and trickery.

I burn my notes and discarded drafts in the fireplace, then lock the completed report away in my safe along with the secret file. It is much too explosive to entrust to the internal post. I shall deliver it by hand.

The following morning I take the train out to Ville-d'Avray to join my cousins the Gasts for Sunday lunch. The red-roofed house, La Ronce, sits prettily in its own land on the main road to Versailles. The day is fine. Jeanne has prepared a picnic patriotically redolent of childhood days in Alsace—*rillettes de canard*, and *flammekueche* and sauerkraut with Munster cheese. All should be well. Yet I can't shake off the shadows of the rue de l'Université. I feel agitated and pale beside my relaxed and suntanned friends, although I try not to show it. Edmond fetches an old pram from the stable and loads it up with a wicker hamper, blankets and wine, then wheels it down the lane while we follow in a procession.

I keep a lookout for Pauline, and ask my sister, in an offhand way, if she happens to know if she's coming, but Anna tells me she has decided to stay an extra week in Biarritz with Philippe and the girls. She scrutinises my complexion and says, "You look as though you could do with a vacation yourself."

"I'm fine. Anyway, it isn't possible at the moment."

"But Georges, you simply have to *make* it possible!"

"Yes, I know. I will, I promise."

"You wouldn't work half so hard if you had a wife and family of your own to go home to."

"Oh my God," I laugh, "not this again!" I light a cigarette to forestall further conversation.

We leave the sandy track and walk on into the wood. Suddenly Anna says, "It's really very sad. You do understand that Pauline will never leave Philippe? Because of the girls?"

I glance at her, startled. "What are you talking about?" She stares at me and I realise there's no point in maintaining the pretence: she's always been able to see right through me. "I didn't think you knew."

"Oh, Georges, everybody knows! Everybody's known for years!"

Everybody! Years! I feel a spasm of irritation.

"In any case," I mutter, "what makes you think I *want* her to leave him?"

"No," she agrees. "No, you don't. *That's* what's sad."

She walks on ahead of me.

We spread the blankets in a clearing, on the edge of a slope leading down to a rocky stream. We exiles love the woods, I have noticed. Trees are trees, after all: it is easier to pretend one is still in one's homeland, collecting mushrooms and insects in the forest of Neudorf. The children slither down with the bottles of wine and lemonade to chill in the water. They splash around in the mud. It's hot. I take off my hat and jacket. Someone says, "Look at the colonel, stripping down for action!" I smile and pretend to salute. I have been in my job for more than a year and still no one knows what I do.

Over lunch, Edmond wants to talk about the impending visit of the Tsar. He takes the radical view. "I just think it is plain wrong," he says, "for our democratic republic to roll out the carpet for an absolute monarch who locks up people who disagree with him. That's not what France exists for."

"France may not exist at all," I point out, "if we don't have an ally who can help us defeat the Germans."

"Yes, but what if it's the *Russians* who fight the Germans and *we're* the ones who end up getting dragged in?"

"It's hard to imagine the scenario in which that might happen."

"Well, I hate to break it to a soldier, but things have a habit of not going according to plan."

Jeanne says, "Oh do shut up, Ed! Georges has come out to relax on his day off, not listen to a lecture from you."

"Very well," grumbles Edmond, "but you can tell your General Boisdeffre from me that alliances work both ways."

"I am sure the Chief of the General Staff will be fascinated to receive a lecture in strategy from the Mayor of Ville-d'Avray . . ."

Everyone laughs, including Edmond. "Touché, Colonel," he says, and pours me some more wine.

After we have eaten, we play hide-and-seek with the children. When it's my turn I walk a hundred paces into the trees and search around until I find the perfect spot. I lie down in a small hollow behind a fallen tree and cover myself with dead leaves and twigs, just as I used to teach my topography students to do at the École Supérieure de Guerre. It is amazing how completely a human being can disappear if he is prepared to take the trouble. In the summer after my father died I would lie out in the forest like this for hours. I listen to the sounds of the children calling my name. After a while they get bored and move off; soon I can no longer hear them. There is only the cooing of the wood pigeons and the scent of the rich, dry earth and the softness of the moss against my neck. I savour the solitude for ten minutes, then brush myself down and go back smiling to join the others. They have already packed up the picnic and are waiting to leave.

I say, "You see, that's how a soldier learns to hide! Would you like me to teach you?"

They look at me as if I have gone mad.

Anna says irritably, "Where in heaven's name have you been?"

One of the children starts to cry.

13

At precisely ten o'clock on the morning of Tuesday, 1 September, I present myself in General Boisdeffre's outer office, carrying my briefcase.

Pauffin de Saint Morel says, "You can go straight in, Colonel. He's expecting you."

"Thank you. Would you make sure we're not disturbed?"

I enter to find Boisdeffre leaning over his conference table, studying a map of Paris and making notes. He acknowledges my salute with a smile and a wave and then returns to the map. "Excuse me, Picquart, will you? I shan't be a moment."

I close the door behind me. Boisdeffre is tracing the route of the Tsar's ceremonial parade, marking it on the map in red crayon. For security reasons, Their Imperial Majesties will pass through a succession of wide-open spaces—the Jardins du Ranelagh, the Bois de Boulogne, the Champs-Élysées and the place de la Concorde—where all the houses are screened by trees and stand well back from the road. Nevertheless, every occupant is being given a background check: the Statistical Section has been brought in to advise; Gribelin has been busy with our lists of aliens and potential traitors. Given our urgent need for an alliance with the Russians, if the Tsar were to be assassinated on French soil it would be a national disaster. And the threat is real: it is only fifteen years since his grandfather was blown in half by socialists, only two years since our own president was stabbed to death by an anarchist.

Boisdeffre taps the map and says, "It's this initial stretch here, between the Ranelagh railway station and the porte Dauphine, that causes me most concern. The First Department tells me we shall need thirty-two thousand men, including cavalry, simply to keep the crowd at a safe distance."

"Let's hope the Germans don't choose that moment to attack us in the east."

"Indeed." Boisdeffre finishes writing and looks at me with his full attention for the first time. "So, Colonel, what do we need to talk about? Please." He sits, and indicates that I should take the chair opposite him. "Is it about the Russian visit?"

"No, General. It's about the matter we discussed in the automobile on your return from Vichy—the suspected traitor, Esterhazy."

It takes him a moment to search back through his memory. "Ah yes, I remember. Where do we stand on that?"

"If I could just clear some space . . ."

"By all means."

I roll up the map. Boisdeffre takes out his silver snuff box. He places a pinch on the back of his hand and takes two quick sniffs, one in either nostril. He watches as I open my briefcase and extract the documents I need for my presentation: the *petit bleu*, a photograph of the *bordereau*, Esterhazy's letters requesting a transfer to the General Staff, the surveillance photographs of Esterhazy outside the German Embassy, the secret dossier on Dreyfus and my four-page report on the investigation to date. His expression grows increasingly astonished. "Good heavens, my dear Picquart," he says, half amused, "what *have* you been doing?"

"We have quite a serious problem to confront, General. I feel it's my duty to bring it to your attention right away."

Boisdeffre winces and casts a wistful look at the rolled map: plainly, he would prefer not to be dealing with this. "Very well, then," he sighs. "As you wish. Proceed."

I take him through it step by step: the interception of the *petit bleu*, my initial inquiries into Esterhazy, Operation Benefactor. I show him the pictures taken from the apartment in the rue de Lille. "Here you can see he takes an envelope into the embassy, and here he leaves without it."

Boisdeffre peers short-sightedly at the photographs. "My God, the things you fellows can do nowadays!"

"The saving grace is that Esterhazy has no access to important classified material: what he offers them is so trivial even the Germans want to sever their connection with him. However," I say, sliding over the two letters, "Esterhazy is now trying to turn himself into a much more valuable agent, by applying for a position in the ministry—where of course he would have ready access to secrets."

"How did you get hold of these?"

"General Billot instructed his staff to give them to me."

"When was this?"

"Last Thursday." I pause to clear my throat. *Here goes,* I think. "I noticed almost immediately a striking similarity between Esterhazy's two letters and the writing of the *bordereau.* You can see it for yourself. Naturally, I am no handwriting expert, so I took them the next day to Monsieur Bertillon. You remember . . ."

"Yes, yes." Boisdeffre's voice is suddenly faint, dazed. "Yes, of course I remember."

"He confirmed that the writing is identical. It then seemed to me, in the light of this, that I should review the rest of the evidence against Dreyfus. Accordingly, I consulted the secret file that was shown to the judges at the court-martial—"

"Just a moment, Colonel." Boisdeffre holds up his hand. "Wait. When you say you consulted the file, do you mean to tell me it *still exists?*"

"Absolutely. This is it." I show him the envelope with "D" written on it. I empty out the contents.

Boisdeffre looks at me as if I have just vomited over his table. "My God, what have you got there?"

"It's the secret file from the court-martial."

"Yes, yes—I can see what it is. But what is it doing *here?*"

"I'm sorry, General? I don't understand . . ."

"It was supposed to have been dispersed."

"I didn't know that."

"Yes, of course! The whole episode was highly irregular." He pokes gingerly at the pieced-together letters with a long, slim forefinger. "There was a meeting in the minister's office soon after Dreyfus was convicted. I was present with Colonel Sandherr. General Mercier specifically ordered him to break up the file. The intercepted letters were to be returned to the archive, the commentaries destroyed—he was absolutely clear about it."

"Well, I don't know what to say, General." Now I am the one who is bewildered. "Colonel Sandherr didn't disperse it, as you can see. In fact he was the one who told me where to find it if I ever needed it. But if I may say so, perhaps the existence of the file is not the main issue we have to worry about."

"Meaning what?"

"Well, the *bordereau*—the handwriting—the fact that Dreyfus is innocent . . ." My voice trails away.

Boisdeffre blinks at me for a few moments. Then he starts gathering together all the papers and photographs that are spread across the table. "I think what you need to do, Colonel, is to go and see General Gonse. Don't let us forget he is the head of the intelligence department. Really you should have gone to him rather than me. Ask his advice on what needs to be done."

"I shall do that, General, absolutely. But I do think we need to move quickly and decisively, for the army's own sake . . ."

"I know perfectly well what's good for the army, Colonel," he says curtly. "You don't need to worry on that account." He holds out the evidence. "Go and talk to General Gonse. He's on leave at the moment, but he's only just outside Paris."

I take the papers and open my briefcase. "May I at least leave my report with you?" I search through the bundle. "It's a summary of where matters stand at the moment."

Boisdeffre eyes it as if it's a snake. "Very well," he says reluctantly. "Give me twenty-four hours to consider it." I stand and salute. When I am at the door he calls to me: "Do you remember what I told you when we were in my motorcar, Colonel Picquart? I told you that I didn't want another Dreyfus case."

"This isn't another Dreyfus case, General," I reply. "It's the same one."

The next morning I see Boisdeffre again briefly, when I go to retrieve my report. He hands it back to me without a word. There are dark semicircles under his eyes. He looks like a man who has been punched.

"I'm sorry," I say, "to bring you a potential problem at a time when you have issues of such immense importance to deal with. I hope it isn't too much of a distraction."

"What?" The Chief of the General Staff lets out his breath in a gasp of exasperated disbelief. "Do you really think, after what you told me yesterday, that I got a moment's sleep last night? Now go and talk to Gonse."

The Gonse family house lies just beyond the northwest edge of Paris, in Cormeilles-en-Parisis. I send a telegram to the general announcing that Boisdeffre would like me to brief him on an urgent matter. Gonse invites me to tea on Thursday.

That afternoon I take the train from the gare Saint-Lazare. Half an hour later I alight in a village so rural I might be two hundred kilometres from the centre of Paris rather than twenty. The departing train dwindles down the track into the distance and I am left entirely alone on the empty platform. Nothing disturbs the silence except birdsong and the distant clip-clop of a carthorse pulling a wagon with a squeaking wheel. I walk over to the porter and ask for directions to the rue de Franconville. "Ah," he says, taking in my uniform and briefcase, "you'll be wanting the general."

I follow his instructions along a country lane out of the village and up a hill, through wooded country, then down a drive to a spacious eighteenth-century farmhouse. Gonse is working in the garden in his shirtsleeves, wearing a battered straw hat. An old retriever lopes across the lawn towards me. The general straightens and leans on his rake. With his tubby stomach and short legs he makes a more plausible gardener than he does a general.

"My dear Picquart," he says, "welcome to the sticks."

"General." I salute. "My apologies for interrupting your vacation."

"Think nothing of it, dear fellow. Come and have some tea." He takes my arm and leads me into the house. The interior is crammed with Japanese artefacts of the highest quality—antique silkscreens, masks, bowls, vases. Gonse notices my surprise. "My brother's a collector," he explains. "This is his place for most of the year."

Tea has been laid out in a garden room full of wicker furniture: petits fours on the low table, a samovar on the sideboard. Gonse pours me a cup of lapsang souchong. The cane seat squeaks as he sits down. He lights a cigarette. "Well then. Go ahead."

Like a commercial traveller, I unlock my briefcase and lay out my wares among the porcelain. It is an awkward moment for me: this is the first time I have even mentioned my investigation of Esterhazy to Gonse, the Chief of Intelligence. I show him the *petit bleu,* and in an attempt to make it seem less of an insult, I pretend that it arrived in late April rather than early March. Then I repeat the presentation I made to Boisdeffre. As I hand him the documents, Gonse studies each in turn, in his usual methodical manner. He spills cigarette ash onto the surveillance photographs, makes a joke of it—"Covering up the crime!"—and blows it away calmly. Even when I produce the secret file he looks unperturbed.

I suspect Boisdeffre must have warned him beforehand of what I was planning to tell him.

"In conclusion," I say, "I had hoped to find something in the file that would establish Dreyfus's guilt beyond doubt. But I'm afraid there's nothing. It wouldn't withstand ten minutes' cross-examination by a halfway decent attorney."

I lay down the last of the documents and sip my tea, which is now stone cold. Gonse lights another cigarette. After a pause he says, "So we got the wrong man?"

He says it matter-of-factly, as one might say, "So we took the wrong turning?" or "So I wore the wrong hat?"

"I'm afraid it looks like it."

Gonse plays with a match as he considers this, flicking it around and between his fingers with great dexterity, then snaps it. "And yet how do you explain the contents of the *bordereau?* None of this changes our original hypothesis, does it? It must have been written by an artillery officer who had some experience of all four departments of the General Staff. And that's not Esterhazy. That's Dreyfus."

"On the contrary, this is where we made our original error. If you look at the *bordereau* again, you'll see it always talks about *notes* being handed over: a *note* on the hydraulic brake . . . a *note* on covering troops . . . a *note* on artillery formations . . . a *note* on Madagascar . . ." I point out what I mean on the photograph. "In other words, these aren't the original documents. The only document that *was* actually handed over—the firing manual—we know that Esterhazy acquired by going on a gunnery course. Therefore I'm afraid the *bordereau* indicates precisely the opposite of what we thought it did. The traitor wasn't on the General Staff. He didn't have access to secrets. He was an outsider, a confidence trickster if you like, picking up gossip, compiling notes and trying to sell them for money. It was Esterhazy."

Gonse settles back in his chair. "May I make a suggestion, dear Picquart?"

"Yes please, General."

"Forget about the *bordereau*."

"Excuse me?"

"Forget about the *bordereau*. Investigate Esterhazy if you like, but don't bring the *bordereau* into it."

I take my time responding. I know he is dim, but this is absurd. "With respect, General, the *bordereau*—the fact that it's in Esterhazy's handwriting, and the fact that we know he took an interest in artillery—the *bordereau is* the main evidence against Esterhazy."

"Well you'll have to find something else."

"But the *bordereau*—" I bite my tongue. "Might I ask why?"

"I should have thought that was obvious. A court-martial has already decided who wrote the *bordereau*. That case is closed. I believe it's what the lawyers call res judicata: 'a matter already judged.'" He smiles at me through his cigarette smoke, pleased to have remembered this piece of schoolroom Latin.

"But if we discover Esterhazy was the traitor and Dreyfus wasn't . . . ?"

"Well we won't discover that, will we? That's the point. Because, as I have just explained to you, the Dreyfus case is over. The court has pronounced its verdict and that is the end of that."

I gape at him. I swallow. Somehow I need to convey to him, in the words of the cynical expression, that what he is suggesting is worse than a crime: it is a blunder. "Well," I begin carefully, "*we* may wish it to be over, General, and our lawyers may indeed tell us that it is over. But the Dreyfus family feel differently. And putting aside any other considerations, I am worried, frankly, about the damage to the army's reputation if it were to emerge one day that we knew his conviction was unsafe and we did nothing about it."

"Then it had better not emerge, had it?" he says cheerfully. He is smiling, but there is a threat in his eyes. "So there we are. I've said all I have to say on the matter." The arms of the wicker chair squeak in protest as he pushes himself to his feet. "Leave Dreyfus out of it, Colonel. That's an order."

On the train back to Paris I sit with my briefcase clutched tightly in my lap. I stare out bleakly at the rear balconies and washing lines of the northern suburbs, and the soot-caked stations—Colombes, Asnières, Clichy. I can hardly believe what has just occurred. I keep going over the conversation in my mind. Did I make some mistake in my presentation? Should I have laid it out more clearly— told him in plain terms that the so-called evidence in the secret file crumbles into the mere dust of conjecture compared to what we know for sure about Esterhazy? But the more I think of it, the more certain I am that such frankness would have been a grave error. Gonse is utterly intransigent: nothing I can say will shift his opinion; there is no way on earth, as far as he's concerned, that Dreyfus will be brought back for a retrial. To have pushed it even further would only have led to a complete breakdown in our relations.

I don't return to the office: I cannot face it. Instead I go back to my apartment and lie on my bed and smoke cigarette after cigarette with a relentlessness that would impress Gonse, even if nothing else about me does.

The thing is, I have no wish to destroy my career. Twenty-four years it has taken me to get this far. Yet my career will be pointless to me—will lose the very elements of honour and pride that make it worth having—if the price of keeping it is to become merely one of the Gonses of this world.

Res judicata!

By the time it is dark and I get up to turn on the lamps, I have concluded that there is only one course open to me. I shall bypass Boisdeffre and Gonse and exercise my privilege of unrestricted access to the hôtel de Brienne: I shall lay the case personally before the Minister of War.

Things are starting to stir now—cracks in the glacier; a trembling under the earth—faint warning signs that great forces are on the move.

For months there has been nothing in the press about Dreyfus. But on the day after my visit to Gonse, the Colonial Ministry is obliged to deny a wild rumour in the London press that he has escaped from Devil's Island. At the time I think nothing of it: it's just journalism, and English journalism at that.

Then on the Tuesday *Le Figaro* appears with its lead story, "The Captivity of Dreyfus," spread across the first two and a half columns of the front page. The report is an accurate, well-informed and sympathetic account of what Dreyfus is enduring on Devil's Island ("forty to fifty thousand francs a year to keep alive a French officer who, since the day of his public degradation, has endured a death worse than death"). I presume the information has come from the Dreyfus family.

It is against this background that the next day I go to brief the minister.

I unlock the garden gate and make my way, unseen by any curious eyes in the ministry, across the lawn and into the rear of his official residence.

The old boy has been on leave for a week. This is his first day back. He seems to be in good spirits. His bulbous nose and the top of his bald head are peeling from exposure to the sun. He sits up straight in his chair, stroking his vast white moustaches, watching with amusement as yet again I bring out all the paperwork associated with the case. "Good God! I'm an old man, Picquart. Time is precious. How long is all this going to take?"

"I'm afraid it's partly your fault, Minister."

"Ah, do you hear him? The cheek of the young! My fault? And pray, how is that?"

"You very kindly authorised your staff to show me these letters from the suspected traitor, Esterhazy," I say, passing them over, "and then I'm afraid I noticed their distinct similarity to this." I give him the photograph of the *bordereau*.

Once again I am surprised by how quick on the uptake he is. Ancient he may be—a captain of infantry before I was even born— yet he looks from one to the other and grasps the implications immediately. "Well I'll be blessed!" He makes a clicking sound with his tongue. "You've had the handwriting checked, I presume?"

"By the original police expert, Bertillon, yes. He says it is identical. Naturally I'd like to get other opinions."

"Have you shown this to General Boisdeffre?"

"Yes."

"What's his opinion?"

"He referred me to General Gonse."

"And Gonse?"

"He wants me to abandon my investigation."

"Does he, indeed? Why's that?"

"Because he believes, as do I, that it would almost certainly set in train a process that would lead to an official revision of the Dreyfus affair."

"Heavens! That would be an earthquake!"

"It would, Minister, especially as we would have to reveal the existence of this . . ."

I hand him the secret file. He squints at it. " 'D'? What the hell is this?" He has never even heard of it. I have to explain. I show him the contents, item by item. Once again he goes straight to the heart of the matter. He extracts the letter referring to "that lowlife D" and holds it close to his face. His lips move as he reads. The backs of his hands are flaking like his scalp, and mottled with liver spots: an old lizard who has survived more summers than anyone could believe possible.

When he gets to the end he says, "Who's 'Alexandrine'?"

"That's von Schwartzkoppen. He and the Italian military attaché call each other by women's names."

"Why would they do that?"

"Because they are buggers, Minister."

"Good God!" Billot pulls a face. He holds the letter gingerly between finger and thumb and passes it back to me. "You have a pretty tawdry job, Picquart."

"I know that, General. I didn't ask for it. But now I have it, it seems to me I must do it properly."

"I agree."

"And in my view, that means investigating Esterhazy thoroughly for the crimes he's committed. And if it transpires that we have to fetch Dreyfus back from Devil's Island—well, I say it's better for us in the army to rectify our own mistake rather than be forced to do it by outside pressure later."

Billot stares into the middle distance, his right thumb and forefinger smoothing down his moustaches. He grunts as he thinks. "This secret file," he says after a while. "Surely it's against the law to pass evidence to the judges without letting the defence have a chance to challenge it first?"

"It is. I regret having been a party to it."

"So whose decision was it?"

"Ultimately, it was General Mercier's, as Minister of War."

"Ha! Mercier? Really? I suppose I might have guessed he'd be in there somewhere!" The staring and the moustache-smoothing and the grunting resume. Eventually he gives a long sigh. "I don't know, Picquart. It's a devil of a problem. You're going to have to let me think about it. Obviously, there would be consequences if it turned out we had locked up the wrong man for all this time, especially having made such a public spectacle out of doing it—profound consequences, for both the army and the country. I'd have to talk to the Prime Minister. And I can't do that for at least a week—I've got the annual manoeuvres in Rouillac starting on Monday."

"I appreciate that, General. But in the meantime do I have your permission to continue my investigation of Esterhazy?"

The massive head nods slowly. "I should think so, my boy, yes."

"Wherever the investigation leads me?"

Another heavy nod: "Yes."

Filled with renewed energy, that evening I meet Desvernine in our usual rendezvous at the gare Saint-Lazare. It's the first time I've seen him since the middle of August. I am slightly late. He is already sitting waiting for me in a corner seat, reading *Le Vélo*. He has stopped drinking beer, I notice, and gone back to mineral water. As I slip into the chair opposite him, I nod to his newspaper. "I didn't know you were a cyclist."

"There's a lot you don't know about me, Colonel. I've had a machine for ten years." He folds the paper up small and stuffs it into his pocket. He seems to be in a bad mood.

I say, "No notebook today?"

He shrugs his shoulders. "There's nothing to report. Benefactor's still on leave at his wife's place in the Ardennes. The embassy's quiet, half shut up for the summer—no sign of either of our men for weeks. And your friend Monsieur Ducasse has had enough and gone to Brittany for a holiday. I tried to stop him but he said if he stayed in the rue de Lille much longer he'd go crazy. I can't say I blame him."

"You sound frustrated."

"Well, Colonel, it's been five months since I started investigating this bastard—if you'll excuse me—and I don't know what else we're supposed to do. Either we pick him up and sweat him for a bit, see if we can make him admit something, or we suspend the operation: that would be my proposal. Either way, the weather's turning colder and we ought to pull those speaking-tubes out within a day or two. If the Germans decide to light a fire, we'll be in trouble."

"Well, for once let *me* show *you* something," I say, and pass the photographs of Esterhazy's letters face-down across the table. "Benefactor is trying to get a position on the General Staff."

Desvernine looks at the letters and immediately his expression brightens. "The bastard!" he repeats happily, under his breath. "He must owe more than we thought."

I wish I could tell him about the *bordereau* and Dreyfus and the secret file, but I daren't, not yet—not until I have official clearance from Billot to broaden the scope of my inquiry.

Desvernine says, "What do you propose to do about him, Colonel?"

"I think we need to become much more active. I'm going to suggest to the minister that he actually agrees to Benefactor's request and gives him a position on the General Staff, in a department where we can monitor him round the clock. We should let him believe he has access to secret material—something apparently valuable, but which we've forged—and then we should follow him and see what he does with it."

"That's good. And I'll tell you what else we could do, if we're indulging in a little forgery. Why don't we send him a fake message from the Germans inviting him to a meeting to discuss the future? If Benefactor turns up, that's incriminating in itself. But if he turns up carrying secret material, we'll have caught him red-handed."

I think this over. "Is there a forger we could use?"

"I'd suggest Lemercier-Picard."

"Is he trustworthy?"

"He's a forger, Colonel. He's about as trustworthy as a snake. His real name is Moisés Lehmann. But he did a lot of work for the section when Colonel Sandherr was there, and he knows we'll come looking for him if he tries to pull any tricks. I'll find out where he is."

Desvernine leaves looking much happier than he did when I arrived. I stay to finish my drink, then take a taxi home.

The next day it suddenly starts to feel like autumn—a threatening dark grey sky, windy, the first leaves blowing off the trees and chasing down the boulevards. Desvernine is right: we need to get those sound-tubes out of the apartment in the rue de Lille as soon as possible.

I arrive at the office at my usual time and quickly scan the day's papers laid out ready for me by Capiaux on my table. *Le Figaro*'s description of Dreyfus's conditions on Devil's Island has stirred up the sediment of opinion again, and everywhere Dreyfus is widely denounced: "Make him suffer even more" seems to be the collective view. But it is a story in *L'Éclair* that brings me up short—an anonymous article headlined "The Traitor" which alleges that Dreyfus's guilt was proved beyond doubt by "a secret file of evidence" passed to the judges at his court-martial. The author calls on the army to publish the contents in order to put an end to the "inexplicable sense of pity" surrounding the spy.

This is the first time the existence of the secret file has been mentioned in the press. The coincidence that it should happen now, of all times, just as I have taken possession of the dossier, makes me uneasy. I march down the corridor to Lauth's office and drop the newspaper on his desk. "Seen this?"

Lauth reads it and looks up at me, alarmed. "Somebody must be talking."

"Find Guénée," I order him. "He's supposed to be monitoring the Dreyfus family. Tell him to come over here now."

I walk back to my office, unlock my safe and take out the secret file. I sit at my desk and make a list of everyone who knows about it: Mercier, Boisdeffre, Gonse, Sandherr, du Paty, Henry, Lauth, Gribelin, Guénée; to these nine, thanks to my briefing yesterday, can now be added Billot—that's ten; and then there are the seven judges, starting with Colonel Maurel—seventeen—and President Fauré, and the President's doctor, Gibert—that's nineteen—who was the man who told Mathieu Dreyfus—who makes twenty; and after that—who knows how many more Mathieu has told?

There is no such thing as a secret—not really, not in the modern world, not with photography and telegraphy and railways and newspaper presses. The old days of an inner circle of like-minded souls communicating with parchment and quill pens are gone. Sooner or later most things will be revealed. That is what I have been attempting to make Gonse understand.

I massage my temples, trying to think it through. The leak ought to vindicate my position. But I suspect it is more likely to make Gonse and Boisdeffre panic and strengthen their determination to limit the investigation.

Guénée arrives in my office towards the end of the morning, jaundice-yellow as usual and smelling like the inside of an old tobacco pipe. He has brought with him the Dreyfus surveillance file. He looks around nervously. "Is Major Henry here?"

"Henry's still on leave. You'll have to deal with me."

Guénée sits and opens his file. "It's the Dreyfus family who are behind it, Colonel, almost certainly."

"Even though the tone of the *L'Éclair* article is hostile to Dreyfus?"

"That's just to cover their tracks. The editor, Sabatier, has been got at by them—we've monitored him meeting both Mathieu and Lucie. This is part of a pattern of increased activity by the family lately—you may have noticed. They've hired the Cook Detective Agency in London to dig for information."

"And have they got anywhere?"

"Not that we know of, Colonel. That may be why they've changed their tactics and decided to become more public. It was a journalist employed by the detective agency who planted the false story that Dreyfus had escaped."

"Why would they do that?"

"I suppose, to get people talking about him again."

"Well then, I'd say they've succeeded, wouldn't you?"

Guénée lights a cigarette. His hands are shaking. He says, "You remember a year ago, I told you about a Jewish journalist the family were talking to—Bernard Lazare? Anarchist, socialist, Jewish activist?"

"What about him?"

"He now seems to be writing a pamphlet in defence of Dreyfus."

He searches through the file and gives me a photograph of a heavyset, youngish man in pince-nez with a huge balding forehead and a heavy beard. Clipped to it is a selection of newspaper cuttings authored by Lazare: "The New Ghetto," "Anti-Semitism and Anti-Semites," a series of recent articles in *La Voltaire* attacking Drumont of *La Libre Parole* (*you are not invulnerable, neither you nor your friends* . . .).

"Quite the polemicist," I say, flicking through it. "And now he's working with Mathieu Dreyfus?"

"No doubt of it."

"So he's another who must know about the secret file?"

Guénée hesitates. "Yes, presumably."

I add Lazare's name to the list; that makes twenty-one; this is becoming hopeless. "Do we know when this pamphlet is likely to appear?"

"We haven't picked up anything from our sources in the French printing trade. They may be planning to publish abroad. We don't know. They've become much more professional."

"What a mess!" I toss the photograph of Lazare back across the desk towards Guénée. "This secret file is going to become a real embarrassment. You were involved in its compilation, isn't that right?"

I don't ask the question in an interrogatory way, but entirely casually. To my surprise Guénée frowns and shakes his head, as if making a great effort at memory. "Ah no, Colonel, not I."

The stupid lie puts me on immediate alert. "No? But surely you provided Major Henry with a statement from the Spanish military attaché? It was a central part of the case against Dreyfus."

"Did I?" Suddenly he looks less sure.

"Well, did you or didn't you? Major Henry says you did."

"Then I must have."

"I have it here, in fact: what you said Val Carlos told you." I take the secret file from my desk drawer, open it and extract Henry's deposition. Guénée's eyes widen in amazement at the sight of it. " '*Be sure to tell Major Henry on my behalf (and he may repeat it to the colonel)*'—that's Colonel Sandherr, I presume—'*that there is reason to intensify surveillance at the Ministry of War, since it emerges from my last conversation with the German attachés that they have an officer on the General Staff who is keeping them admirably well informed. Find him, Guénée: if I knew his name, I would tell you!*' "

"Yes, that sounds about right."

"And he actually said this to you roughly six months before Dreyfus was arrested?"

"Yes, Colonel—in March."

Something in his demeanour tells me he is still lying. I look again at the statement. It doesn't sound much like a Spanish marquis to me; it reads more like a policeman making up evidence.

"Wait a moment," I say. "Let me be clear about this. If I go to see the marquis de Val Carlos and say to him, 'My dear Marquis, between you and I, is it true that you said these words to Monsieur Guénée that helped send Captain Dreyfus to Devil's Island?' he will reply, 'My dear Major Picquart, that's absolutely correct'?"

Panic flickers in Guénée's face. "Well I don't know about that, Colonel. Remember, he said that to me in confidence. Given all this stuff in the press about Dreyfus now—how can I swear to what he'd say today?"

I stare at him. *My God,* I think. *What in the name of heaven were they up to?* If Val Carlos didn't say it to Guénée, it stands to reason he didn't say it to Henry either. Because it wasn't just Guénée whom the Spaniard was supposed to have warned about a German spy on the General Staff: it was Henry. It was their alleged conversation that provided the basis for Henry's theatrical testimony at the court-martial: *The traitor is that man!*

A long pause is ended by a knock at the door. Lauth thrusts his blond head into the room. I wonder how long he has been listening. "General Boisdeffre would like you to go over and see him straight away, Colonel."

"Thank you. Tell his office I'm on my way." Lauth withdraws. I say to Guénée, "We'll talk about this some other time."

"Yes, Colonel." He leaves, looking—or so it seems to me—mightily relieved to have escaped without any further interrogation.

Boisdeffre is seated behind his grand desk, his elegant hands palm-down on the surface; a copy of *L'Éclair* lies between them. He says, "I gather you saw the minister yesterday." His tone is one of a calmness that is only being maintained with great difficulty.

"Yes, I see him most days, General."

Boisdeffre has left me standing to attention on the carpet, the first time this has happened.

"And you showed him the secret file on Dreyfus?"

"I felt he needed to be aware of the facts—"

"I will *not* have it!" He lifts one of his hands and brings it down hard on his desk. "I told you to speak to General Gonse and to no one else! Why do you think you can disobey my orders?"

"I'm sorry, General, I wasn't aware your order applied to the minister. If you remember, last month you gave me permission to brief General Billot about the Esterhazy investigation."

"About Esterhazy, yes! But not about Dreyfus! I thought it was made absolutely clear to you by General Gonse that you were to keep the two matters separate?"

I continue to stare straight ahead, at a particularly hideous oil painting by Delacroix hanging just above the Chief of Staff's scanty white hair. Only occasionally do I risk a brief glance at the general himself. He seems to be under tremendous stress. The Virginia creeper–like mottling on his cheeks has ripened from crimson to purple.

"Frankly, I don't believe it's possible to keep the two matters separate, General."

"That may be your opinion, Colonel, but you have no business trying to create dissension in the high command." He picks up the newspaper and waves it at me. "And where did this come from?"

"The Sûreté believe the story may have originated with the Dreyfus family."

"And did it?"

"It's impossible to say. A considerable number of people have knowledge of the file." I pull out my list. "I count twenty-one so far."

"Let me see that." Boisdeffre holds out his hand. He runs his eye down the column of names. "So you are saying that one of these must be behind the leak?"

"I can't see where else it could have come from."

"I notice you haven't put your own name on it."

"I know that I'm not a suspect."

"You might know that, but I don't. A casual observer might find it a curious coincidence that just as you begin agitating for a reopening of the Dreyfus case, revelations about it start to appear in the press."

There is a loud crack from somewhere beyond the tall windows. It sounds as though a tree has blown down. Rain slashes against the glass. Boisdeffre, still staring at me, doesn't seem to notice.

"I deny that insinuation absolutely, General. These stories do nothing to help my investigation, as you have just made clear. They only make it more difficult."

"That's one view. Another is that you are seeking every possible means to reopen the Dreyfus case, whether by going to the minister behind my back, or fomenting an agitation in the press. Did you know that a member of the Chamber of Deputies has announced he is seeking to question the government about the whole affair?"

"I give you my word I had nothing to do with this."

The general bestows on me a look of deep suspicion. "Let us hope this is the end of these disclosures. It's bad enough for the press to report the existence of the file. If they were to describe its actual contents, it would become much more serious. I'll keep this list, if I may."

"Of course." I bow my head in a way that I hope indicates contrition, even though I don't feel it.

"Very well, Colonel." He flicks his fingers, as if dismissing a waiter at the Jockey Club. "You may go."

I step out into the rue Saint-Dominique to find a hurricane blowing: a freak system that moves across Paris between noon and three. I have to clutch the railings to prevent myself being knocked off my feet; by the time I reach our building I am drenched to the skin. The wind takes roofs off the Opéra-Comique and the Préfecture of Police. It blows out the windows on one side of the Palace of Justice. Riverboats are torn from their moorings and dashed against the quays. Some of the laundrywomen on the banks of the Seine are blown into the water and have to be rescued. The stalls in the flower market in the place Saint-Sulpice are entirely whisked away. Walking home that evening I pass through streets that lie ankle-deep in shredded vegetation and broken tiles. The havoc is terrible, but privately I am relieved: the press will have other things to talk about for the next few days apart from Captain Dreyfus.

14

The respite is brief. On Monday, *L'Éclair* publishes a second and longer article. Its headline couldn't be worse from my point of view: "The Traitor: The Guilt of Dreyfus Demonstrated by the Dossier."

Feeling sick, I carry it over to my desk. The story is grossly inaccurate but it includes some telling details: that the secret dossier was passed to the judges in the room where they were deliberating; that the dossier contained confidential letters between the German and Italian military attachés; and that one of these letters referred specifically to "that animal Dreyfus"—not exactly "that lowlife D" but close enough. "It was this irrefutable proof," concludes the article, "that determined the verdict of the judges."

I drum my fingers. Who is revealing all this detail? Guénée says it is the Dreyfus family. I'm not so sure. Who stands to gain from the leaks? From where I sit, the most obvious beneficiaries are those who want to create a siege mentality within the Ministry of War and curtail my inquiry into Esterhazy. It is the phrase "that animal Dreyfus" that strikes a chord in my memory. Isn't that what du Paty always claimed about Dreyfus: that he had "animal urges"?

I take a pair of scissors from my desk and carefully cut out the article. Then I write a letter to Gonse, who is still on leave: *Recently I took the liberty of telling you that in my opinion we were going to have a major problem on our hands if we did not take the initiative. The attached article in* L'Éclair *unfortunately confirms me in my opinion. I feel obliged to repeat that in my view it is imperative to act without delay. If we wait any longer, we will be overwhelmed, locked into an inextricable position, and unable either to defend ourselves or ascertain the real truth.*

I hesitate before I post it. I am putting my opinion formally on the record. Gonse is a consummate soldier of the filing cabinet, if not the battlefield. He will recognise this for what it is: an escalation of hostilities.

I send it anyway.

The next day he summons me. He has cut short his vacation. He is back in his office. I can sense his panic at a range of two hundred metres.

The corridors of the ministry are quieter than usual. Billot and Boisdeffre are both away in the southwest, accompanying President Fauré as he inspects the autumn manoeuvres. Most General Staff officers with career ambitions—and that is nearly all of them—have made sure they are in the field. As I walk down those empty, echoing passages I am reminded of the atmosphere at the time of the traitor hunt two years ago.

"I got your letter," says Gonse, waving it at me as I settle down in a chair in front of his desk, "and don't think I'm not sympathetic to your point of view. If I could put back the clock to the start of this whole damned business, believe me, I would. Cigarette?" He pushes a box towards me. I hold up my hand to decline. He takes one, lights it. His tone could not be friendlier. "Let's face it, dear Picquart: the investigation into Dreyfus was not handled as professionally as it should have been. Sandherr was a sick man, and du Paty—well, we all know what Armand is like, despite his many fine qualities. But we have to proceed from where we are, and really we can't go back over it all again. It would reopen too many wounds. You've seen the press these past few days, the potential hysteria there is about Dreyfus. It would tear the country apart. We just have to shut it down. You must appreciate that, surely?"

There is a look of such entreaty on his face—such yearning for me to agree—that for a few fleeting moments I am almost tempted to give in. He is not a bad man, just a weak one. He wants a quiet life, pottering back and forth between the ministry and his garden.

"I do see that, General. But these leaks to the press are a warning to us in another way. We have to recognise that an inquiry into the Dreyfus case is already going on as we speak. Unfortunately, it's organised by the Dreyfus family and their supporters. The process is slipping out of our control. The point I was trying to make in my letter is a basic military principle: that we should be the ones taking the initiative, while there's still time."

"And we do that—how? By surrendering? By giving them what they want?"

"No, by abandoning a position that is frankly becoming indefensible and establishing a new line on higher ground."

"Yes—as I say—by giving them what they want! Anyway, I don't agree with you. Our present position is highly defensible, just as long as we all stand together. It shelters behind an iron wall of law. We simply say: 'Seven judges considered all the evidence. They reached a unanimous verdict. The case is closed.'"

I shake my head. "No, I'm sorry, General, but that line won't hold. The judges only reached a unanimous verdict because of the secret file. And the evidence in the secret file is, well . . ." I stop, unsure how to proceed. I am remembering Guénée's expression when I started to question him about his supposed conversation with Val Carlos.

Gonse says quietly, "The evidence is what, Colonel?"

"The evidence in the file is"—I spread my hands—"*weak*. If the proofs it contained were cast-iron, we might be able to excuse the fact that they weren't seen by the defence. But as it is . . ."

"I completely understand what you're saying, my dear Picquart— believe me, I do!" He leans forward, imploring. "But that's precisely why the integrity of the secret file must be protected at all costs. Suppose we follow your route to this higher ground of yours, and we say to the French people: 'Oh look, Esterhazy wrote the *bordereau* after all, let's bring back Dreyfus, let's hold some great new trial'—what will happen next? People will want to know how the original judges—all seven of them, mark you—could have got the whole thing so wrong. That will lead straight to the secret file. Some very senior figures are going to be gravely embarrassed. Do you want that? Can you imagine the damage it will do to the reputation of the army?"

"I accept there would be damage, General. But we would also

gain credit for cleaning out our own stables. Whereas it seems to me that we will only compound that damage if we pile fresh lies on top of the old—"

"Nobody's talking about lying, Colonel! I'm not asking you to lie! I'd never do that. I know you are a man of honour. I'm not asking you to *do* anything, in point of fact. I'm merely asking you *not* to do something—not to go near the Dreyfus case. Is that so unreasonable, Georges?" He risks a little smile. "After all, I know your views on the Chosen Race—really, when all is said and done, what does it matter to you if one Jew stays on Devil's Island?"

It is as if he has leaned across his desk and offered me a secret handshake. I say carefully, "I suppose it matters to me because he is an innocent man."

Gonse laughs; there is an edge of hysteria to it. "Well, how very sentimental!" He claps his hands. "A beautiful thought! Newborn lambs and kittens and Alfred Dreyfus—all innocent!"

"With respect, General, you make it sound as if I have some emotional attachment to the man. I can assure you I have no feelings for him one way or the other. Frankly, I wish he *were* guilty—it would make my life a great deal easier. And until quite recently I was certain that he was. But now I look at the evidence and it seems to me that he can't be. The traitor is Esterhazy."

"Perhaps it's Esterhazy and perhaps it's not. You can't be sure. The fact is, however, *if you say nothing, nobody will ever know.*"

So we have reached the dark heart of the matter at last. Suddenly the room seems even quieter than before. He stares at me quite frankly. I take a moment before replying.

"That is an abominable suggestion, General. You cannot expect me to carry this secret with me to my grave."

"Most certainly I can, and I do! Taking secrets to the grave is the essence of our profession."

Another silence, and then I try again. "All I ask is that the whole case be thoroughly investigated—"

"*All* you ask!" Gonse finally erupts. "*All!* I like that! I don't understand you, Picquart! So what are you saying? That the entire army—the entire nation come to that!—is supposed to revolve around your tender conscience? You have a pretty good conceit of yourself, I must say!" His neck is fat and flushed bright pink, like some unspeakable pneumatic rubber tube. It bulges against the collar of his tunic. He is terrified, I realise. Abruptly his manner becomes businesslike. "Where is the secret file now?"

"In my safe."

"And you haven't discussed its contents with anyone else?"

"Of course not."

"You have made no copies?"

"No."

"And you are not the source of these leaks to the newspapers?"

"If I were, I would hardly admit it, would I?" I can no longer keep the contempt out of my voice. "But for what it's worth, the answer is no."

"Don't be insolent!" Gonse stands. I follow suit. "This is an army, Colonel, not a society for debating ethics. The Minister of War gives orders to the Chief of Staff, the Chief of Staff gives orders to me, and I give orders to you. I now order you formally, and for the final time, not to investigate anything connected with the Dreyfus case, and not to disclose anything about it to anyone who isn't authorised to receive such information. Heaven help you if you disobey. Understand?"

I cannot even bring myself to reply to him. I salute, turn on my heel, and walk out of the room.

When I get back to the office, Capiaux tells me Desvernine is in the waiting room with the forger Lemercier-Picard. After my encounter with Gonse, interviewing such a creature is the last thing I feel like doing, but I don't want to send him away.

The moment I enter, I recognise him as another of that little group, along with Guénée, who were playing cards and smoking pipes on my first morning. Moisés Lehmann suits him better as a name than Lemercier-Picard. He is small and Jewish-looking, plump with charm and confidence, smelling of eau de cologne and eager to impress me with his skill. He persuades me to write out three or four sentences in my own handwriting—"Go on, Colonel: what harm can it do, eh?"—and then after a couple of practice attempts he produces a passable copy. "The trick is speed," he explains. "One must capture the essence of the line and inhabit its character and then write naturally. You have a very artistic hand, Colonel: very secretive, very *introspective*, if I may say so."

"That's enough, Moisés," says Desvernine, pretending to cuff his ear. "The colonel has no time for your nonsense. You can get out of here now. Wait for me in the lobby."

The forger grins at me. "A pleasure to meet you, Colonel."

"It's mutual. And I'd like my sheet of handwriting back, if you please."

"Oh yes," he says, pulling it out of his pocket. "I almost forgot."

After he's gone, Desvernine says, "I thought you ought to know that Esterhazy seems to have done a runner. He and his wife have moved out of the apartment in the rue de la Bienfaisance—and left in a hurry, by the look of it."

"How do you know?"

"I've been inside. Don't worry—I didn't have to do anything illegal. It's up for rent. I pretended I was looking for a place. They've taken away most of their furniture, just left a few bits of rubbish. He burned a lot of paper in the hearth. I found this."

It is a visiting card, singed at the edges:

ÉDOUARD DRUMONT
Editor
La Libre Parole

I turn it back and forth. "So Esterhazy's a contributor to that anti-Jewish rag?"

"Apparently. Or perhaps he just gives them information—plenty in the army do. The thing is, Colonel—he's gone to ground. He's not in Paris. He's not even in Rouen anymore. He's moved out to the Ardennes."

"Do you think he knows we're on to him?"

"I'm not sure. But I don't like the smell of it. I think if we're going to lay our trap we need to do it quickly."

"Have we done anything about those speaking-tubes yet?"

"They came out yesterday."

"Good. And how soon before the flues can be bricked up again?"

"We have a man going in tonight."

"All right. Leave it with me."

Billot is my only hope now. Billot: the old lizard, the old survivor, the two times Minister of War—surely he will realise not just the immorality but the political insanity of the General Staff's policy?

He is due to return from the manoeuvres in the southwest on Friday. That morning *Le Figaro* publishes on its front page the text of a petition sent by Lucie Dreyfus to the Chamber of Deputies, pointing out that the government hasn't denied the stories about the secret file:

And so it must be true that a French officer has been convicted by a court-martial on a charge produced by the prosecution without his knowledge, which therefore neither he nor his counsel was able to discuss.

It is the denial of all justice.

I have been the victim of the most cruel martyrdom for almost two years—like the man in whose innocence I have absolute faith. I have remained silent despite the odious and absurd slanders propagated amongst the public and the press.

Today it is my duty to break that silence, and without comment or recriminations I address myself to you, gentlemen, the only power to whom I can have recourse—and I demand justice.

In the narrow, gloomy passages and stairwells of the Statistical Section there is silence. My officers shut themselves away in their rooms. Hourly I expect to be summoned over the road by Gonse for an explanation of this latest bombshell, but the telephone never rings. From my office I keep half an eye on the back of the hôtel de Brienne. Finally, just after three o'clock, I glimpse uniformed orderlies with dispatch cases passing behind its tall windows. The minister must be back. The topography works in my favour: Gonse, sitting in the rue Saint-Dominique, will not yet know he has returned. I go down into the rue de l'Université, cross the street and take out my key to let myself into the minister's garden.

And then something odd happens. My key does not fit. I try it three or four times, dully refusing to believe it won't work. But the shape of the lock is entirely different to what it used to be. Eventually I give up and walk the long way round, via the place du Palais Bourbon, like any ordinary mortal.

"Colonel Picquart to see the Minister of War . . ."

The sentry lets me through the gate but the captain of the Republican Guard in the downstairs lobby asks me to wait. After a few minutes, Captain Calmon-Maison comes downstairs.

I hold up my key to show him. "It doesn't work anymore." I try to make a joke of it. "Like Adam, I appear to have been expelled from the garden for an excess of curiosity."

Calmon-Maison's face is deadpan. "I'm sorry, Colonel. We have to change the locks occasionally—security, you understand."

"You don't have to explain, Captain. But I still need to brief the minister."

"Unfortunately, he's only just returned from Châteauneuf. He has a lot to do, and he's really rather exhausted. Could you possibly come back on Monday?" At least he has the grace to look embarrassed as he says this.

"It won't take long."

"Nevertheless . . ."

"I'll wait." I resume my place on the red leather banquette.

He looks at me dubiously. "Perhaps I'd better go and have another word with the minister."

"Perhaps you should."

He clatters off up the marble staircase, and shortly afterwards calls down to me, his voice echoing off the stone walls. "Colonel Picquart!"

Billot is sitting behind his desk. "Picquart," he says, wearily raising his hand, "I'm afraid I'm very busy"—although there is no sign of any activity in his office, and I suspect he has simply been staring out of the window.

"Forgive me, Minister. I shan't detain you. But in the light of the newspaper stories this week, I feel the need to press you now for a decision about the Esterhazy investigation."

Billot peers at me warily from beneath his bushy white brows. "A decision about what aspect of it, exactly?"

I begin to describe the idea I have devised with Desvernine, of luring Esterhazy to a meeting by means of a message purporting to come from Schwartzkoppen, but he cuts me off very quickly. "No, no, I don't like that at all—that's far too crude. In fact, you know, I'm starting to think that the quickest way to deal with this swine is actually not to prosecute him at all but to pension him off. Either that, or send him somewhere a long way away—Indochina or Africa: I don't know—preferably somewhere he can contract a very nasty local disease, or take a bullet in the back without too many questions being asked."

I'm not sure how to respond to this suggestion, so I ignore it. "And what do we do about Dreyfus?"

"He'll just have to stay where he is. The law has pronounced and that's an end of it."

"So you've reached a final decision?"

"I have. I had the opportunity before the parade in Châteauneuf to discuss the matter privately with General Mercier. He motored over specially from Le Mans to talk about it."

"I bet he did!"

"Be careful, Colonel . . . !" Billot points a warning finger at me. Up till now he has always encouraged me to tiptoe to the edge of insubordination: it has amused him to play the indulgent paterfamilias. Clearly, like access to his garden, that privilege has been withdrawn.

Still, I can't stop myself. "This secret file—you do know that it proves nothing against Dreyfus? That it may even contain downright lies?"

Billot puts his hands over his ears. "There are things I shouldn't hear, Colonel."

He looks absurd, in the way that stubborn old men sometimes do: a sulky child in a nursery.

"I can shout quite loudly," I warn him.

"I mean it, Picquart! I mustn't hear it!" His voice is sharp. Only when he is satisfied that I won't pollute his ears any further does he lower his hands. "Now don't be such an arrogant young fool and listen to me." His voice is conciliatory, reasonable. "General Boisdeffre is about to welcome the Tsar to Paris in a diplomatic coup that will change the world. I have a six-hundred-million-franc budget estimate to negotiate with the Finance Committee. We simply can't allow ourselves to be distracted from these great issues by the sordid matter of one Jew on a rock. It would tear the army to pieces. I would be hounded out of this office—and rightly so. You must keep the whole matter in proportion. Do you understand what I'm saying, Colonel?"

I nod.

He rises from behind his desk with surprising grace and comes round to stand in front of me. "Calmon-Maison tells me we've had to change the locks on the garden. It's such a bore. I'll make sure you get a new key. I do so greatly value your intelligence, dear boy." He offers me his hand. His grip is hard, dry, calloused. He clamps his other hand around mine, imprisoning it. "There's nothing easy about power, Georges. One needs the stomach to take hard decisions. But I've seen all this before. Today the press is Dreyfus, Dreyfus, Dreyfus; tomorrow, without some new disclosure, they'll have forgotten all about him, you'll see."

Billot's prediction about Dreyfus and the press proves correct. As abruptly as they took him up again, the newspapers lose all interest in the prisoner on Devil's Island. He is replaced on the front pages by stories about the Russian state visit, in particular by speculation about what the Tsarina will be wearing. But I do not forget him.

Although I have to tell Desvernine we will not be requiring the services of Monsieur Lemercier-Picard, and that our request to lay a trap has been refused, I continue to pursue my investigation of Esterhazy as best I can. I interview a retired noncommissioned officer, Mulot, who remembers copying out portions of an artillery manual for the major; I also meet Esterhazy's tutor at gunnery school, Captain le Rond, who calls his former pupil a blackguard: "If I met him in the street I would refuse to shake his hand." All this goes into the Benefactor file, and occasionally at the end of the day as I leaf through the evidence we have so far collected—the *petit bleu*, the surveillance photographs, the statements—I tell myself that I will see him in prison yet.

But I am not offered a new key to the garden of the hôtel de Brienne: if I want to see the minister, I have to make an appointment. And although he always receives me cordially, there is an unmistakable reserve about him. The same is true of Boisdeffre and Gonse. They no longer entirely trust me, and they are right.

One day towards the end of September, I climb the stairs to my office at the start of the morning and see Major Henry standing further along the corridor, deep in conversation with Lauth and Gribelin. His back is to me, but those broad and fleshy shoulders and that wide neck are as recognisable as his face. Lauth glances past him, notices me and darts him a warning look. Henry stops talking and turns round. All three officers salute.

"Gentlemen," I say. "Major Henry, welcome back. How was your leave?"

He is different. He has caught the sun—like everyone else apart from me—but he has also changed his haircut to a short fringe so that he looks less like a sly farmer and more like a crafty monk. And there's something else: a new energy in him, as if all the negative forces that have been swirling around our little unit—the suspicion and disaffection and anxiety—have coalesced in his capacious frame and charged him with a kind of electricity. He is their leader. My jeopardy is his opportunity. He is a danger to me. All this passes through my mind in the few seconds it takes him to salute, grin and say, "My leave was good, Colonel, thank you."

"I need to brief you on what's been happening."

"Whenever you wish, Colonel."

I am on the point of inviting him into my office, and then I change my mind. "I tell you what, why don't we have a drink together at the end of the day?"

"A drink?"

"You look surprised."

"Only because we've never had a drink before."

"Well, that is a poor state of affairs, is it not? Let us rectify it. Shall we walk somewhere together? Let us say at five o'clock?"

Accordingly at five he knocks on my door, I pick up my cap and we go out into the street. He asks, "Where do you want to go?"

"Wherever you like. I don't frequent the bars round here very often."

"The Royale, then. It saves us from having to think."

The Taverne Royale is the favourite bar of the General Staff. I haven't been in it for years. The place is quiet at this hour: just a couple of captains drinking near the door, the barman reading a paper, a waiter wiping down the tables. On the walls are regimental photographs; on the bare wooden floor, sawdust; the colours are all brown and brass and sepia. Henry is very much at home. We take a table in the corner and he orders a cognac. For want of a better idea I do the same. "Leave us the bottle," Henry tells the waiter. He offers me a cigarette. I refuse. He lights one for himself and suddenly I realise that an odd part of me has actually missed the old devil, just as one occasionally grows fond of something familiar and even ugly. Henry *is* the army, in a way that I, or Lauth, or Boisdeffre will never be. When soldiers break ranks and want to run away on the battle-field, it is the Henrys of this world who can persuade them to come back and keep fighting.

"Well," he says, raising his glass, "what shall we drink to?"

"How about something we both love? The army."

"Very well," he agrees. We touch glasses: "The army!"

He downs his tumbler in one, tops up mine then refills his own. He sips it, staring at me over the rim. His small eyes are a muddy colour, and opaque: I can't read them. "So—things seem to be in a bit of a mess back at the office, Colonel, if you don't mind me saying."

"I'll have that cigarette after all, if I may." He pushes his cigarette case across the table towards me. "And whose fault is that, do you think?"

"I point no fingers. I'm just saying, that's all."

I light my cigarette and toy with my glass, moving it around the table as if it is a chess piece. I feel a curious desire to unburden myself. "Man to man, I never wanted to be chief of the section, did you know that? I had a horror of spies. I only achieved the position by accident. If I hadn't known Dreyfus, I wouldn't have been involved in his arrest, and then I wouldn't have attended the court-martial and the degradation. Unfortunately, I think our masters have got the entirely wrong idea about me."

"And what would the right idea be?"

Henry's cigarettes are very strong, Turkish. The back of my nose feels as if it's on fire. "I've been having another look at Dreyfus."

"Yes, Gribelin told me you'd taken the file. You seem to have stirred things up."

"General Boisdeffre was convinced the dossier no longer existed. He said that General Mercier ordered Colonel Sandherr to get rid of it."

"I didn't know that. The colonel just told me to keep it nice and safe."

"Why did Sandherr disobey, do you think?"

"You'd have to ask him that."

"Perhaps I shall."

"You can ask him all you want, my Colonel, but you won't get much of an answer." Henry taps the side of his head. "He's under lock and key in Montauban. I went all the way down to visit him. It was pitiful." He looks mournful. He suddenly raises his glass. "To Colonel Sandherr: one of the best!"

"To Sandherr," I respond, and pretend to drink his health. "But why did he retain the file, do you think?"

"I suppose because he thought it might be useful—it was the file that convicted Dreyfus after all."

"Except you and I both know that Dreyfus is innocent."

Henry's eyes open wide in warning and alarm. "I wouldn't talk like that too loudly, Colonel, especially not in here. Some of the fellows wouldn't like it."

I look around. The bar is beginning to fill. I lean in closer and lower my voice. I'm not sure whether I'm seeking a confession or offering one, only that some kind of absolution is required. "It wasn't Dreyfus who wrote the *bordereau*," I say quietly. "It was Esterhazy. Even Bertillon says his writing is a perfect match. That's the central part of the case against Dreyfus demolished right there! As for your secret file of evidence—"

A gust of laughter from the neighbouring table interrupts me. I glance at them in irritation.

Henry says, very seriously now, studying me intently, "What were you going to say about the secret file?"

"With the best will in the world, my dear Henry, the only thing in it that points to Dreyfus is the fact that the Germans and the Italians were receiving plans of fortifications from someone with the initial 'D.' I'm not blaming you, incidentally: once Dreyfus was in custody, your job was to make the most convincing case you could. But now that we have the facts about Esterhazy, it changes everything. Now we know that the wrong man was condemned. So you tell me: what are we supposed to do in the light of that? Simply ignore it?"

I sit back. After a long silence, during which he continues to scan my face, Henry says, "Are you asking me for my advice?"

I shrug. "By all means, if you have any."

"You've mentioned this to Gonse?"

"I have."

"And Boisdeffre, and Billot?"

"Yes."

"And what do they say?"

"They say drop it."

"Then for God's sake, Colonel," he hisses, "drop it!"

"I can't."

"Why not?"

"I'm just not made that way. It's not what I joined the army to do."

"Then you've chosen the wrong profession." Henry shakes his head in disbelief. "You have to give them what they want, Colonel— they're the chiefs."

"Even though Dreyfus is innocent?"

"There you go, saying it again!" He looks around. Now it's his turn to lean over the table and talk quietly. "Listen, I don't know whether he's innocent or guilty, Colonel, and quite frankly I don't give a shit, if you'll excuse me, either way, and neither should you. I did as I was told. You order me to shoot a man and I'll shoot him. You tell me afterwards you got the name wrong and I should have shot someone else—well, I'm very sorry about that, but it's not my fault." He pours us both another cognac. "You want my advice? Well here's a story. When my regiment was in Hanoi, there was a lot of thieving in the barracks. So one day my major and I, we laid a trap and we caught the thief red-handed. It turned out he was the son of the colonel—God knows why he needed to steal from the likes of us, but he did it. Now my major—he was a bit like you, a little bit of the idealistic type, shall we say—he wanted this man prosecuted. The top brass disagreed. Still, he went ahead and brought the case anyway. But at the court-martial it was my major that was broken. The thief went free. A true story." Henry raises his glass to me. "That's the army we love."

15

The following morning when I go into the office, the Dreyfus file is on my desk—not the secret dossier but the Colonial Office record, which continues to be sent over regularly for my comments.

There have been two security scares about Dreyfus in recent weeks. First there was the English newspaper report that the prisoner had escaped. Then there was a letter addressed to him posted in the rue Cambon and signed with a name that looked like "Weiler" that contained a message supposedly written in invisible ink: *Impossible to decipher last communication. Return to the former procedure in your answer. Indicate precisely where the documents are and how the cupboard can be unlocked. Actor ready to move immediately.* Dreyfus's guards were ordered to observe him closely after he was handed this letter. He merely frowned and put it aside. Manifestly he had never heard of "Weiler." Both we and the Sûreté were in agreement that this was just a malicious hoax.

Yet as I turn the pages of the file I see that the episodes have been used by the Colonial Ministry as a pretext to make Dreyfus's confinement much harsher. For the past three weeks he has been clapped in irons every night. There is even an illustration of the contraption shipped over from the penal colony in Cayenne that is used to restrain him. Two U-shaped irons are fixed to his bed. His ankles are put into these at sundown. A bar is then inserted through the irons and padlocked. He is left in this position until dawn. In addition, a double perimeter fence of heavy timber is being erected around his hut to a height of two and a half metres. The inner fence is only half a metre from his window. Therefore his view of the sea is entirely cut off. And during the day he is no longer allowed access to the island beyond the second perimeter fence. The bare narrow space of rock and scrub between the two walls, in which there are no trees or shade, is now the entirety of his world.

As usual, the file contains an appendix of Dreyfus's confiscated writings:

Yesterday evening I was put in irons. Why, I know not. Since I have been here, I have always scrupulously observed the orders given me. How is it I did not go crazy during the long, dreadful night? (7 September 1896)

These nights in irons! I do not even speak of the physical suffering, but what moral ignominy, and without any explanation, without knowing why or for what cause! What an atrocious nightmare is this in which I have lived for nearly two years! (8 September)

Put in irons when I am already watched like a wild beast night and day by a guard armed with rifle and revolver! No, the truth should be told. This is not a security precaution. This is a measure of hatred and torture, ordered from Paris by those who, not being able to strike a family, strike an innocent man, because neither he nor his family will accept submissively the most frightful judicial error that has ever been made. (9 September)

I am disinclined to read any further. I have seen what the chafing of leg irons can do to a prisoner's flesh: cut it to the bone. In the insect-infested heat of the tropics, the torment must be unendurable. For a moment my pen hovers over the file. But in the end I simply mark it "Return to the Colonial Ministry" and sign the circulation slip without comment.

Later that day I attend a meeting in Gonse's office to settle last-minute security details for the Tsar's visit. Sombre-faced men from the Interior and Foreign Ministries, the Sûreté and the Élysée Palace—men full of the grand self-importance of those who handle such issues—sit around the table and discuss the minutiae of the Imperial itinerary.

The Russian flotilla will be escorted into Cherbourg harbour on Monday at 1 p.m. by twelve ironclads. The President of the Republic will meet the Tsar and Tsarina. There will be a dinner for seventy in the Arsenal at 6:30, General Boisdeffre to be seated at the Tsar's table. On Tuesday morning the Russian Imperial train will arrive in Versailles at 8:50 a.m. The Imperial party will transfer to the President's train, which will arrive at the Ranelagh railway station at 10 a.m. It will take one and a half hours for the procession to cover the ten-kilometre route into Paris: 80,000 soldiers will be deployed for protection. All suspected terrorists have either been detained or turned away from Paris. After luncheon at the Russian Embassy, the Tsar and Tsarina will visit the Russian Orthodox church in the rue Daru. At 6:30 there will be a state banquet for two hundred and seventy at the Élysée, and at 8:30 fireworks in the Trocadéro followed by a gala performance at the Opéra. On Wednesday . . .

My mind keeps wandering eight thousand miles to the shackled figure on Devil's Island.

When the meeting is finished and everyone is filing out, Gonse asks me to stay for a moment. He could not be friendlier. "I've been thinking, my dear Picquart. When all this Russian fuss is over, I want you to undertake a special mission to the eastern garrison towns."

"To do what, General?"

"Inspect and report on security procedures. Recommend improvements. Important work."

"How long will I be away from Paris?"

"Oh, just a few days. Perhaps a week or two."

"But who will run the section?"

"I'll take it over myself." He laughs and claps my shoulder. "If you'll trust me with the responsibility!"

On Sunday, I see Pauline at the Gasts': the first time I have set eyes on her in weeks. She wears another dress she knows I like, plain yellow with white lace cuffs and collar. Philippe is with her and so are their two little girls, Germaine and Marianne. Usually I can cope perfectly well seeing the family all together, but on this day it is agony. The weather is cold and wet. We are confined indoors. So there is no escaping the sight of her immersed in her other life—her real life.

After a couple of hours I can't keep up the pretence any longer. I go out on to the veranda at the back of the house to smoke a cigar. The rain is coming down cold and hard and mixed with hail like a northern European monsoon, stripping the few remaining leaves from the trees. The hailstones bounce off the saturated lawn. I think of Dreyfus's descriptions of the incessant tropical downpours.

There is a soft chafing of silk behind me, a scent of perfume, and then Pauline is at my side. She doesn't look at me but stands gazing out across the gloomy garden. I have my cigar in my right hand, my left hangs loosely. The back of her right hand barely brushes against it. It feels as if only the hairs are touching. To anyone coming up behind us we are just two old friends watching the storm together. But her proximity is almost overwhelming. Neither of us speaks. And then the door to the passage bangs open and Monnier's voice booms out: "Let's hope it's not like this next week for Their Imperial Majesties!"

Pauline casually moves her hand up to her forehead to brush away a stray hair. "Are you very much involved in it, Georges?"

"Not much."

"He's being modest, as usual," cuts in Monnier. "I know the part you fellows have played to make the whole thing secure."

Pauline says, "Will you actually have an opportunity to meet the Tsar?"

"I'm afraid you have to be at least a general for that."

Monnier says, "But surely you could watch the parade, couldn't you, Picquart?"

I puff hard on my cigar, wishing he would go away. "I could, if I could be bothered. The Minister of War has allocated places for my officers and their wives at the Bourbon Palace."

"And you're not going!" cries Pauline, pretending to punch my arm. "You miserable republican!"

"I don't have a wife."

"That's no problem," says Monnier. "You can borrow mine."

And so on Tuesday morning, Pauline and I edge along the steps of the Bourbon Palace to our allotted places, whereupon I discover that every officer of the Statistical Section has accepted the minister's invitation and has brought his wife—or in Gribelin's case his mother. They make no attempt to hide their curiosity when we appear and I realise, too late, how we must look in their eyes—the bachelor chief with his married mistress on his arm. I introduce Pauline very formally, emphasising her social position as the wife of my good friend Monsieur Monnier of the quai d'Orsay. That only makes it sound more suspicious. And although Henry bows briefly and Lauth nods and clicks his heels, I notice that Berthe Henry, the innkeeper's daughter, with her parvenu's snobbery, is reluctant even to take Pauline's hand, while Madame Lauth, her mouth tightly crimped in disapproval, actually turns away.

Not that Pauline seems to care. We have a perfect view, looking straight down the bridge, across the Seine, half a kilometre to the obelisk in the place de la Concorde. The weather is sunny but windy. The vast tricolours hanging off the buildings—the red, white and blue stripes vertical for France, horizontal for Russia—snap and billow against their moorings. The crowds on the bridge are ten or twelve deep and have been waiting since dawn. It is reported to be the same all across the city. According to the Préfecture of Police, one and a half million spectators are lining the route.

From the place de la Concorde comes the faint roar of thousands of voices cheering, and then gradually at first but increasing in volume, as in a symphony, an underlying percussion of horses' hooves on cobbles. A shimmering line of light appears spread across the wide thoroughfare, and then more lines behind it, which gradually resolve into helmets and breastplates glinting in the bright sun— wave after wave of lancers and cuirassiers, bobbing up and down on their horses, banners streaming, twelve abreast, riding across the bridge. On and on they come, heading straight for us at a stiff trot, until it seems they will mount the steps and charge right through us. But then abruptly at the last moment they sweep round to our right, down the boulevard Saint-Germain. Behind them come the native cavalry—the Chasseurs d'Afrique, the Algerian Saphis, the Arab caids and chiefs, their horses shying at the racket of the crowd—and then after these is the procession of open state carriages—the President, the Russian ambassador, the leaders of the Senate and the Chamber of Deputies, and all the other prominent figures of the Republic, including General Billot. There is a particularly loud cheer for Boisdeffre in his plumed helmet, which he doffs from side to side: the gossip is that after this he could be Foreign Minister.

There is a gap, and then the Russian state coach appears, surrounded by a mounted bodyguard. Pauline gasps and clutches my arm.

After all the talk of alliances and armies, it is the *smallness* of the Imperial couple that makes the most impression on me. Tsar Nicholas II might be mistaken for a frightened fair-headed boy wearing a false beard and his father's uniform. He salutes mechanically every few seconds, touching the edge of his astrakhan cap in rapid gestures—more nervous tic than acknowledgement of applause. Sitting by his side the Tsarina Alexandra appears even younger, a girl who has raided the dressing-up box. She wears a swansdown boa and clutches a white parasol in one hand and an immense bouquet in the other. She bows rapidly to right and left. I am close enough to see her clenched smile. They both look apprehensive. Their carriage swings sharply rightwards and they sway gently over to one side with the motion then disappear—sucked out of sight into a funnel of noise.

Still holding my arm, Pauline turns to speak to me. I can't quite hear her voice above the tumult. "What?" She pulls me closer, her lips so close I can feel her breath in my ear, and as I strain to listen, I see Henry, Lauth and Gribelin all staring at us.

Afterwards I follow the trio back to the office along the rue de l'Université. They are perhaps fifty metres ahead of me. The street is empty. Most people, including our womenfolk, have decided to stay where they are in order to catch a glimpse of the Imperial couple driving back across the bridge after lunch to the Russian Orthodox church. Something about the way Henry is gesturing with his hand and the other two are nodding tells me they are talking about me. I can't resist quickening my step until I am right behind them. "Gentlemen!" I say loudly. "I'm glad to see you're not neglecting your duties!"

I had expected guilty laughter, even embarrassment. But the three faces that turn to meet mine are surly and defiant. I have offended their bourgeois sensitivities even more than I realised. We complete the journey to the Statistical Section in silence and I keep to my office for the rest of the day.

The sun sets over Paris shortly after seven. By eight it is too gloomy to read. I don't switch on my lamp.

The timbers of the old building shrink and creak as the day cools into evening. The birds in the minister's garden fall silent. The shadows achieve a solid geometry. I sit at my desk, waiting. If ever there was a time for the ghosts of Voltaire and Montesquieu to materialise, this is it. At eight-thirty when I open my door I half expect to see a periwig and velvet coat floating down the corridor. But the ancient house seems deserted. Everyone has gone off to watch the fireworks in the Trocadéro, even Capiaux. The front door will be locked. I have the place to myself.

From my drawer I take the leather roll of lock-picking tools that Desvernine left behind months earlier. As I climb the stairs I am aware of the ludicrousness of my situation: the chief of the secret intelligence section obliged to break into the archives of his own department. But I have considered the problem rationally from every angle and I can see no better solution. At the very least, it is worth a try.

I kneel in the passage outside Gribelin's door. My first discovery is that lock-picking is easier than it looks. Once I have the hang of which instrument to use I am able to find the notch in the underside

of the bolt. All I have to do next is press. Then it is a matter of maintaining the pressure with the left hand while with the right I insert
the pick and manipulate it to raise the tumblers. One rises, then
a second, and finally the third; the racking stump slides forwards;
there is a well-oiled click and the door opens.

I turn on the electric light. It would take me hours to pick all the
locks in Gribelin's archive. But I remember he keeps his keys in the
bottom left-hand drawer of his desk. After ten minutes of patient
trial and error, it yields to my pick. I open the drawer. The keys are
there.

Suddenly there is a bang that makes my heart jump. I glance
out of the window. Searchlights on top of the Eiffel Tower a kilometre away are shining across the Seine to the place de la Concorde. The beams are surrounded by bursting stars which pulse and
flash in silence and then a second or two later come the explosions,
loud enough to vibrate the glass panes in their ancient mouldings.
I glance at my watch. Nine o'clock. They are running half an hour
late. The fireworks are scheduled to last thirty minutes.

I take Gribelin's bunch of keys and start trying to open the nearest filing cabinet.

Once I have worked out which key fits which lock, I open all the
drawers. My first priority is to collect every scrap of Agent Auguste
material I can find.

The glued-together documents are already beginning to yellow
with age. They rustle like dried leaves as I sort them into piles: letters and telegrams from Hauptmann Dame in Berlin, signed with
his *nom de guerre*, "Dufour"; letters to Schwartzkoppen from the
German ambassador, Count Münster, and to Panizzardi from the
Italian ambassador, Signor Ressmann, and to the military attaché
of the Austro-Hungarian Empire, Colonel Schneider. There is an
envelope full of cinders dated November 1890. There are letters to
Schwartzkoppen from the Italian naval attaché, Rosselini, and the
British military attaché, Colonel Talbot. Here are the forty or fifty
love letters from Hermance de Weede—*My dear adored friend* . . .
My Maxi . . .—and perhaps half that many from Panizzardi: *My dear
little one* . . . *My big cat* . . . *My dear big bugger* . . .

There was a time when I would have felt uncomfortable—grubby, even—handling such intimate material; no longer.

Mixed in with all this is a cipher telegram from Panizzardi to the General Staff in Rome, dispatched at three o'clock on the morning of Friday, 2 November 1894:

> *Commando Stato Maggiore Roma*
> *913 44 7836 527 3 88 706 6458 71 18 0288 5715 3716 7567*
> *7943 2107 0018 7606 4891 6165*
>
> > *Panizzardi*

The decoded text is clipped to it, written out by General Gonse: *Captain Dreyfus has been arrested. The Ministry of War has evidence of his dealings with Germany. We have taken all necessary precautions.*

I copy it down in my notebook. Beyond the window, the Eiffel Tower is a cascade of tumbling light. There is one last final thunderous explosion and slowly it fades into darkness. I hear a faint roar of applause. The display is over. I estimate it would take someone roughly thirty minutes to escape from the crowds in the Trocadéro gardens and get back to the section.

I return my attention to the glued-together documents.

Much of the material is incomplete or pointless, its sense tantalisingly out of reach. It suddenly strikes me as madness to try to read so much meaning into such detritus: that we are little better than the haruspices of the ancient world who decided public policy by scrutinising animal livers. My eyes feel gritty. I have been stuck in my office without food since noon. Perhaps that explains why, when I do come to the crucial document, I miss it at first, and move on to the next. But it nags at my mind, and then I go back and look at it again.

It is a short note, in thin black ink, on squared white paper, torn into twenty pieces, a few of which are missing. The writer is offering to sell Schwartzkoppen "the secret of smokeless powder." It is signed *your devoted Dubois* and dated 27 October 1894—two weeks after Dreyfus's arrest.

I delve a little further into the file. Two days later, Dubois writes to the German attaché again: *I can procure for you a cartridge from the Lebel rifle that will enable you to analyse the secret of the smokeless powder.* Schwartzkoppen does not seem to have done anything about it. Why should he? The letter looks cranky and I guess he could go into almost any bar in any garrison town in France and pick up a Lebel cartridge for the price of a beer.

It is the name of the signatory that interests me. Dubois? I am sure I have just read that name. I go back to the pile of letters from Panizzardi to Schwartzkoppen. *My beautiful little girl . . . My little green dog . . . Dear Top Bugger . . . Your devoted bugger 2nd class . . .* And here it is: in a note of 1893, the Italian writes to Schwartzkoppen: *I have seen M. Dubois.*

Attached to the letter is a cross-reference to a file. It takes me several minutes to work out Gribelin's system and track it down. In a folder I find a brief report addressed to Colonel Sandherr by Major Henry dated April 1894 regarding the possible identity of the agent referred to as "D" who has provided the Germans and Italians with "twelve master plans of Nice." Henry's conclusion is that he is one Jacques Dubois, a printer who works for a factory that handles Ministry of War contracts: it is he who has probably also provided the Germans with large-scale drawings of the fortifications at Toul, Reims, Langres, Neufchâteau and the rest. When he sets the printing machine for a run, it is a simple matter for him to print off extra copies for his own use. *I interviewed him yesterday,* relates Henry, *and found him to be a miserable fellow, a criminal fantasist with limited intelligence and no access to classified material. The plans he has handed over are publicly available. Recommendation: no further action necessary.*

So there it is. "D" is not Dreyfus; he is Dubois.

You order me to shoot a man and I'll shoot him . . .

I have made a careful note of where every document and folder originated and now I start the laborious process of putting each one back in its proper place. It takes me perhaps ten minutes to return it all exactly to where it was, to lock up the filing cabinets and wipe down the table surfaces. By the time I finish it is just after ten. I replace Gribelin's keys in his desk drawer, kneel, and set about the tricky business of locking it again. I am conscious of the minutes passing as I try to manipulate the two thin metal tools. My hands are clumsy with tiredness and slippery with sweat. For some reason it seems much harder to close a lock than open one, but at last I manage it. I turn off the lights.

My only remaining task is to relock the door to the archive. I am still on my knees in the corridor fiddling with the tumblers when I think I hear the front door slam downstairs. I pause, straining to hear. I can't pick out any suspicious noises. I must be imagining things. I resume my frustrating efforts. But then comes the definite creak of a footstep on the first-floor landing and someone begins to mount the stairs to the archive. I am so close to shifting the final tumbler I am reluctant to abandon the attempt. Only when I hear a much louder creak do I realise I am out of time. I dart across the passage, try the nearest door—locked—and then the next one—open—and slip inside.

I listen to the slow, deliberate tread of someone approaching along the corridor. Through the gap between the door and the jamb I see Gribelin come into view. My God, is there anything in this wretched man's life apart from work? He stops outside the entrance to the archive and takes out his key. He inserts it in the lock and tries to turn it. I can't see his face, but I see his shoulders stiffen. What is this? He tries the handle and opens the door cautiously. He doesn't go in but stands on the threshold, listening. Then he throws the door wide open, turns on the light and moves inside. I can hear him checking his desk drawers. A moment later he returns to the corridor and glances up and down it. He ought to be an absurd little figure—a small dark-suited troll. But somehow he isn't. There is a malevolence about him as he stands there, alert and suspicious—he is a danger to me, this man.

Finally—satisfied presumably that he must have made a mistake in locking up—he goes back into the archive and closes the door. I wait another ten minutes. Then I take off my shoes and creep past his lair in my stockinged feet.

On my walk back to my apartment I stop in the middle of the bridge and drop the roll of lock-picking tools into the Seine.

———

Over the next few days the Tsar tours Notre-Dame, names a new bridge after his father, banquets in Versailles.

While he goes about his business, I go about mine.

I walk over the road to see Colonel Foucault, who has come back from the Berlin embassy to witness the Imperial visit. We exchange a few pleasantries and then I ask him, "Did you ever hear anything from Richard Cuers after that meeting we arranged in Basel?"

"Yes, he came and complained about it bitterly. I gather you fellows decided to give him some rough treatment. Who on earth did you send?"

"My deputy, Major Henry; another of my officers, Captain Lauth; and a couple of policemen. Why? What did Cuers say?"

"He said he'd made the journey in good faith, to reveal what he knew about the German agent in France, but when he got to Switzerland he felt he was treated as if he was a liar and a fantasist. There was one French officer in particular—fat, red-faced—who merely bullied him: interrupted him all the time; made it clear he didn't believe a word of what he was saying. That was a deliberate tactic, I assume?"

"Not that I'm aware of; not at all."

Foucault looks at me in consternation. "Well, whether it was intentional or not, you won't be hearing from Cuers again."

I go to see Tomps at the headquarters of the Sûreté. I tell him, "It's about your trip to Basel." Immediately he looks anxious. He doesn't want to land anyone in any trouble. But it's clear the episode has been preying on his mind.

"I won't quote you," I promise him. "Just tell me what happened."

He doesn't take much prompting. He seems to be relieved to get it off his chest.

"Well, Colonel," he says, "you remember our original plan? It worked to the letter. I followed Cuers from the German railway station to the cathedral, saw him make contact with my colleague Vuillecard, then followed the pair of them to the Schweizerhof, where Major Henry and Captain Lauth were ready for him upstairs. After that I went back to the bar at the station to wait. I guess it must have been about three hours later that Henry suddenly came in and ordered a drink. I asked him how it was going and he said,

'I've had enough of this bastard'—you know how he talks—'there's nothing we can learn from him, I'll bet a month's salary on it.' I said, 'Well, what are you doing back here so early?' And he said, 'Oh, I played Mr. Big, pretended to get angry and finally walked out of there. I left him with Lauth: let the young fellow have a try!' Obviously I was disappointed with the sound of how this was going, so I said, 'You know I'm an old acquaintance of Cuers? You know he likes a lot of absinthe? He really loves a drink. That might have been a better approach. If Captain Lauth can't get anywhere, do you want me to have a try?'"

"And what did Major Henry say to that?"

Tomps continues his passable impersonation of Henry. "'No,' he says, 'it's not worth the trouble. Forget it.' Then at six, when Captain Lauth had finished his session and turned up at the station, I asked Henry again: 'Listen, I know Cuers well. Why don't you let me take him out for a drink?' But he just repeated what he'd said before: 'No, it's useless. We're wasting our time here.' So we caught the night train to Paris and that was that."

Back in my office, I open a file on Henry. That Henry is the man who framed Dreyfus I have no doubt.

Code-breaking isn't the province of the Statistical Section, or even the Ministry of War. It is run out of the Foreign Ministry by a seven-man team whose presiding genius is Major Étienne Bazeries. The major is famous in the newspapers for having broken the Great Cipher of Louis XIV and revealed the identity of the Man in the Iron Mask. He conforms to every cliché of the eccentric prodigy—unkempt, abrupt, forgetful—and is not an easy man to get to see. Twice I visit the quai d'Orsay on the pretext of other business and try to find him, only to be told by his staff that no one knows where he is. It is not until the end of the month that I track him to his office. He is in his shirtsleeves, bent over his desk with a screwdriver and a cylindrical enciphering device which lies all around him in pieces. In theory I am his superior officer, but Bazeries doesn't salute or even stand; he has never believed in rank, just as he doesn't believe in haircuts or shaving or even, to judge by the atmosphere in his office, washing.

"The Dreyfus affair," I say to him. "The telegram from the Italian military attaché, Major Panizzardi, sent to the General Staff in Rome on the second of November 1894."

He squints up at me through greasy spectacles. "What about it?"

"You broke it?"

"I did. It took me nine days." He resumes tinkering with his machine.

I take out my notebook and open it to a double page. On one side is the coded text that I copied down from the file in the archive, on the other the solution as written out by Gonse: *Captain Dreyfus has been arrested. The Ministry of War has evidence of his dealings with Germany. We have taken all necessary precautions.* I offer it to Bazeries. "Is this your solution?"

He glances at it. Immediately his jaw tenses with anger. "My God, you people don't give up, do you?" He pushes back his chair, strides across the office, throws open his door and shouts, "Billecocq! Bring me the Panizzardi telegram!" He turns to me. "Once and for all, Colonel, that is not what it says, and wishing it did will not make it otherwise."

"Wait," I say, holding up my hand to pacify him, "there's obviously some history here that I'm not aware of. Let me be clear: you're telling me that this is not an accurate transcription of the decoded telegram?"

"The only reason it took us nine days to arrive at the solution was because your ministry kept refusing to believe the facts!"

A young, nervous-looking man, presumably Billecocq, arrives bearing a folder. Bazeries snatches it off him and flicks it open. "Here it is, you see—the original telegram?" He holds it up for me to see. I recognise the Italian attaché's handwriting. "Panizzardi took it to the telegraph office on the avenue Montaigne at three o'clock in the morning. By ten, thanks to our arrangement with the telegraph service, it was here in our department. By eleven, Colonel Sandherr was standing exactly where you are now demanding we decipher it as a matter of extreme urgency. I told him it was impossible—this particular cipher was one of great complexity, which we'd never before managed to break. He said, 'What if I could guarantee you that it contained a particular word?' I told him that would be a different matter. He said that the word was 'Dreyfus.'"

"And how did he know that Panizzardi would mention Dreyfus?"

"Well, that was very clever, I must concede. Sandherr said that the previous day he had arranged for the name to be leaked to the newspapers as the identity of the man arrested for espionage. He reasoned that whoever was employing Dreyfus would panic and contact their superiors. When Panizzardi was followed to the telegraph office in the middle of the night, naturally Colonel Sandherr was sure his tactic had worked. Unfortunately, when I succeeded in breaking the cipher, the text of the message was not as he wished. You can read it yourself."

Bazeries shows me the telegram. The solution is written out neatly under the numerals of the encoded text: *If Captain Dreyfus has had no dealings with you it would be appropriate to instruct the ambassador to publish an official denial in order to avoid comments by the press.*

I read it through twice to make sure I understand the implications. "And so what this suggests is that Panizzardi was actually in the dark about Dreyfus—the direct opposite of what Colonel Sandherr believed?"

"Exactly! Sandherr wouldn't accept it, though. He insisted we must have got a word wrong somewhere. He took it to the highest levels. He even arranged for one of his agents to feed Panizzardi some fresh information about an unrelated matter, so that he would be obliged to send a second cipher message to Rome incorporating certain technical terms. When we broke that as well, we demonstrated beyond doubt that this was the correct decryption. Nine days this whole procedure took us, from beginning to end. So please, Colonel—don't let us go over it again."

I perform the calculation in my head. Nine days from 2 November takes us to 11 November. The court-martial began on 19 December. Which means that for over a month before Dreyfus even stood trial, the Statistical Section were aware that the phrase "that lowlife D" could not possibly refer to Dreyfus, because they knew Panizzardi had never even heard of him—unless he was lying to his superiors, and why would he do that?

"And there is no doubt, is there," I ask, "that at the end of the whole process you provided the correct version to the Ministry of War?"

"No doubt at all. I gave it to Billecocq to hand-deliver."

"Can you remember who you gave it to?" I ask Billecocq.

"Yes, Colonel, I remember it very well, because I gave it to the minister himself. I gave it to General Mercier."

When I get back to the Statistical Section, I can smell cigarette smoke emanating from my office, and when I open the door, I find General Gonse sitting at my desk. Henry is resting his ample backside against my table.

Gonse says cheerfully, "You've been out a long time."

"I didn't know we had an appointment."

"We didn't. I just thought I'd drop by."

"You've never done that before."

"Haven't I? Perhaps I should have done it more often. What a separate little operation you have running over here." He holds out his hand. "I'll take that secret file on Dreyfus, if I may."

"Of course. Might I ask why?"

"Not really."

I'd like to argue. I glance at Henry. He raises his eyebrows slightly. *You have to give them what they want, Colonel—they're the chiefs.*

Slowly I bend to unlock my safe, searching my brain for some excuse not to comply. I take out the file marked "D." Reluctantly I hand it over to Gonse. He opens the flap and quickly thumbs through the contents.

I ask pointedly, "Is it all there?"

"It had better be!" Gonse smiles at me—a purely mechanical adjustment of his lower face, devoid of all humour. "Now then, we need to make a few administrative changes, in view of your imminent departure on your tour of inspection. Henceforth, Major Henry will bring all the Agent Auguste material direct to me."

"But that's our most important source!"

"Yes, so it's only right that it comes to me, as head of the intelligence department. Is that all right with you, Henry?"

"Whatever you wish, General."

"Am I being dismissed?"

"Of course not, my dear Picquart! This is simply a reshuffle of responsibilities to improve our efficiency. Everything else remains with you. So that's settled then." Gonse stands and stubs out his cigarette. "We'll talk soon, Colonel." He clasps the Dreyfus file to his chest with crossed arms. "I'll look after our precious baby very well, don't you worry."

After he has gone, Henry looks at me. He shrugs apologetically. "You should have taken my advice," he says.

I have heard it claimed by those who have attended the public executions in the rue de la Roquette that the heads of the condemned men after they have been guillotined still show signs of life. Their cheeks twitch. Their eyes blink. Their lips move.

I wonder: do these severed heads also briefly share the illusion that they are alive? Do they see people staring down at them and imagine, for an instant or two before the darkness rushes in, that they can still communicate?

So it is with me after my visit from Gonse. I continue to come into the office at my usual hour as if I am still alive. I read reports. I correspond with agents. I hold meetings. I write my weekly *blanc* for the Chief of the General Staff: the Germans are planning military manoeuvres in Alsace-Moselle, they are making increasing use of dogs, they are laying a telephone cable at Bussang close to the border. But this is a dead man talking. The real direction of the Statistical Section has passed over the road to the ministry, where regular meetings now take place between Gonse and my officers Henry, Lauth and Gribelin. I hear them leaving. I listen to them coming back. They are up to something, but I cannot work out what.

My own options seem nonexistent. Obviously I cannot report what I know to my superiors, since I must assume they already know it. For a few days I consider appealing directly to the President, but then I read his latest speech, delivered in the presence of General Billot—*The army is the nation's heart and soul, the mirror in which France perceives the most ideal image of her self-denial and patriotism; the army holds the first place in the thoughts of the government and in the pride of the country*—and I realise that he would never take up arms on behalf of a despised Jew against "the nation's heart and soul." Obviously also I cannot share my discoveries with anyone outside the government—senator, judge, newspaper editor—without betraying our most secret intelligence sources. The same applies to the Dreyfus family; besides, the Sûreté is watching them night and day.

Above all, I recoil from the act of betraying the army: *my* heart and soul, *my* mirror, *my* ideal.

Paralysed, I wait for something to happen.

I notice it on a newsstand on the corner of the avenue Kléber early one morning in November, when I am on my way to work. I am just about to step off the kerb and it stops me dead: a facsimile of the *bordereau* printed slap in the middle of the front page of *Le Matin*.

I glance around at the people reading it in the street. My immediate instinct is to snatch their newspapers off them: don't they realise this is a state secret? I buy a copy and retreat into a doorway. The full-size illustration is plainly taken from one of Lauth's photographs. The article is headlined "The Proof"; its tone is unremittingly hostile to Dreyfus. Immediately it reads to me like the work of one of the prosecution's handwriting experts. The timing is obvious. Lazare's pamphlet, *A Judicial Error: The Truth About the Dreyfus Affair*, was published three days ago. It contains a violent attack on the graphologists. They have a professional motive to want everyone still to believe that Dreyfus was the author of the *bordereau;* more to the point, they have all hung on to their facsimiles.

I hail a cab to get to the office as quickly as possible. The atmosphere is funereal. Even though the report appears to vindicate Dreyfus's conviction, it is a calamity for our section. Schwartzkoppen, like the rest of Paris, will be able to read the *bordereau* over his breakfast table; when he realises his private correspondence is in the hands of the French government he will choke, and then presumably he will try to work out how it reached them. The long career of Agent Auguste may well be over. And what of Esterhazy? The thought of how he will react to seeing his handwriting emblazoned over the newsstands is the only aspect that gives me any pleasure, especially when Desvernine comes to see me late in the morning to report that he has just observed the traitor rushing bare-headed out of the apartment of Four-Fingered Marguerite into a rainstorm, "looking as if all the hands of hell were after him."

I am summoned by General Billot. He sends a captain with a message that I am to come to his office at once.

I would like time to prepare for this ordeal. I say to the captain, "I'll be there directly. Tell him I'm on my way."

"I'm sorry, Colonel. My orders are to escort you to him now."

I collect my cap from the hatstand. When I step into the corridor I notice Henry loitering outside his office with Lauth. Something about their stance—some combination of shiftiness and curiosity and triumph—tells me that they knew beforehand that this summons was coming and wanted to watch me leave. We nod to one another politely.

The captain and I walk round to the street entrance of the hôtel de Brienne.

I have Colonel Picquart to see the Minister of War . . .

As we climb the marble staircase, I recall how I trotted up here so eagerly after Dreyfus's degradation—the silent garden in the snow, Mercier and Boisdeffre warming the backs of their legs at the blazing fire, the delicate fingers smoothly turning the globe and picking out Devil's Island . . .

Boisdeffre once again waits in the minister's office. He is seated at the conference table with Billot and Gonse. Billot has a closed file in front of him. The three generals side by side make a sombre tribunal—a hanging committee.

The minister smooths his walrus moustaches and says, "Sit down, Colonel."

I assume I am to be blamed for the leak of the *bordereau*, but Billot takes me by surprise. He begins without preliminaries: "An anonymous letter has been passed to us. It alleges that Major Esterhazy will shortly be denounced in the Chamber of Deputies as an accomplice of Dreyfus's. Have you any idea where the author of this letter could have obtained the information that Esterhazy was under suspicion?"

"None."

"I presume I don't have to tell you that this represents a serious breach in the confidentiality of your inquiry?"

"Of course not. I'm appalled to hear of it."

"It's intolerable, Colonel!" His cheeks redden, his eyes pop. Suddenly he has become the choleric old general beloved of the cartoonists. "First the existence of the dossier is revealed! Then a copy of the *bordereau* is printed on the front page of a newspaper! And now this! Our inescapable conclusion is that you have developed an obsession—in fact a dangerous fixation—with substituting Major Esterhazy for Dreyfus, and that you are willing to go to any lengths to fulfil it, including leaking secret information to the press."

Boisdeffre says, "It's a very poor business, Picquart. Very poor. I'm disappointed in you."

"I can assure you, General, I have never disclosed the existence of my inquiry to anyone, certainly not to Esterhazy. And I've never leaked information to the press. My inquiry is not a matter of personal obsession. I have simply followed a logical trail of evidence which leads to Esterhazy."

"No, no, no!" Billot shakes his head. "You have disobeyed specific orders to keep clear of the Dreyfus business. You have gone around acting like a spy in your own department. I could call one of my orderlies now and have you taken to Cherche-Midi on a charge of insubordination."

There is a pause, and then Gonse says, "If it really is a question of logic, Colonel, what would you do if we showed you cast-iron proof that Dreyfus was a spy?"

"If it were cast-iron, then obviously I'd accept it. But I don't believe such proof can be found."

"That is where you are wrong."

Gonse glances at Billot, who opens the file. It appears to contain only a single sheet of paper.

Billot says, "We have recently intercepted a letter, via Agent Auguste, from Major Panizzardi to Colonel Schwartzkoppen. This is the relevant passage: *I have read that a deputy is going to ask questions about Dreyfus. If someone asks in Rome for new explanations, I will say that I have never had any dealings with this Jew. If someone asks you, say the same, for no one must ever know what happened to him.* It's signed 'Alexandrine.' There," says Billot, closing the file with great satisfaction, "what do you say about *that?*"

It is a forgery, of course. It has to be. I keep my composure. "When exactly did this reach us, may I ask?"

Billot turns to Gonse, who says, "Major Henry collected it in the usual way about two weeks ago. It was in French, so he pieced it together."

"Could I see the original?"

Gonse bridles. "Why is that necessary?"

"Only that I would be interested in seeing what it looks like."

Boisdeffre says, with great chilliness, "I would sincerely hope, Colonel Picquart, that you are not doubting the integrity of Major Henry. The message was retrieved and reconstructed—and that is that. We are sharing it with you now in the expectation that its existence will not be disclosed to the press, and that finally you will drop your pernicious insistence that Dreyfus is innocent. Otherwise the consequences for you will be grave."

I stare from one general to the next. So this is what the army of France has sunk to. Either they are the greatest fools in Europe or the greatest villains: for the sake of my country I am not sure which is worse. But some instinct for self-preservation warns me not to fight them now; I must play dead.

I bow my head slightly. "If you are satisfied that it is authentic, then naturally I accept that it must be."

Billot says, "Therefore you also must accept that Dreyfus is guilty?"

"If the document is authentic, then yes—he must be."

There. It is done. I do not know what else I could have said at that moment that would have made any difference to Dreyfus's plight.

Billot says, "In view of your previous record, Colonel, we are willing to suspend taking legal action against you, at least for the time being. We do, however, expect you to turn over all documents connected with the investigation of Major Esterhazy, including the *petit bleu,* to Major Henry. And you will proceed immediately to the depot at Châlons to begin your tour of inspection with the Sixth and Seventh Corps."

Gonse is smiling again. "I'll take all your office keys now, my dear Picquart, if I may. There's no need for you to return to the section. Major Henry can take over the day-to-day running. You go straight home and pack."

I fill a suitcase with enough clothes for three or four days. I ask the concierge to forward my mail to the Ministry of War. Then I just have sufficient time before my train leaves at seven to call on a few people to say goodbye.

Pauline is in the family's apartment on the rue de la Pompe, supervising tea for the girls. She looks alarmed to see me. "Philippe will be back from the office any minute," she whispers, half closing the door behind her.

"Don't worry, I'm not coming in." I stand on the landing with my suitcase beside me and tell her that I'm going away.

"For how long?"

"It should only be for a week or so, but if it turns out to be longer and you need to make contact, write to me care of the ministry— only be careful what you say."

"Why? Is something the matter?"

"No, but precautions are always wise." I kiss her hand and press it to my cheek.

"Maman!" shrills a voice behind her.

"You'd better go," I say.

I take a cab to the boulevard Saint-Germain and ask the driver to wait. By now it is dark and the lights of the great house are bright in the November gloom; there is an atmosphere of activity: Blanche will be holding one of her musical soirées later in the evening. "Stranger!" she greets me. "You're far too early."

"I won't come in," I say. "I'm afraid I have to leave Paris for a few days." I repeat the instructions I've just given Pauline: if she needs to get in touch she should do so via the ministry, but she should try to be discreet. "Give my love to Aimery and Mathilde."

"Oh, Georges!" she cries in delight, pinching my cheek and kissing the tip of my nose. "You are a mystery!"

When I climb back into my cab, I see her in the downstairs window, showing the musicians where to set up. I retain one final impression of chandeliers and a profusion of indoor plants, of Louis XIV chairs covered in rose-pale silk and of light gleaming on the polished spruce and maple of the instruments. Blanche is smiling at one of the violinists, pointing out where he should sit. The cabman flicks his whip and this vision of civilisation jerks out of sight.

My final call is on Louis Leblois. Again the driver waits; again I do not go in but stay on the landing to say my goodbyes. He has only just returned from court. He sees my anguish immediately.

"I suppose you can't talk about it?"

"I fear not."

"I'm here if you need me."

As I get back into the cab, I glance along the rue de l'Université to the offices of the Statistical Section. The building is a patch of gloom even in the darkness. I notice that a taxi has parked about twenty paces behind us with the yellow light of the Poissonnière-Montmartre depot. It pulls away as we do, and when we arrive at the gare de l'Est, it stops a discreet distance away. I guess I must have been followed ever since I left my apartment. They aren't taking any chances.

On a Morris column outside the station, amid the adverts and the multicoloured playbills of the Opéra-Comique and the Comédie-Française, is a poster showing the facsimile of the *bordereau* from *Le Matin* beside a sample of Dreyfus's writing: placed together the two look very different. Mathieu has already paid for these posters to be plastered all over Paris. That was quick work! "Where Is the

Proof?" demands the headline. A reward is offered for anyone who recognises the original.

He is not going to give up, I think, *not until his brother is either free or dead.* As I stow my suitcase in the overhead rack and settle into my seat on the crowded eastbound train, that thought, at least, gives me some hope.

Part Two

16

The Sousse Military Club looks out from behind a screen of dusty palms across an unpaved square, past a modern customs shed to the sea. The glint from the Gulf of Hammamet is particularly fierce this afternoon, like sunlight on tin: I have to shield my eyes. A boy in long brown robes passes, leading a goat on a length of rope. The glare melts both figures into tarry black silhouettes.

Inside its heavy brick walls, the Military Club's decor makes no concession to North Africa. The wooden panelling, stuffed armchairs and tasselled standard lamps are of the type that might be seen in any garrison town in France. As is my custom after lunch, I am seated alone beside the window while my brother officers of the 4th Tunisian Rifles play cards or doze or read the four-day-old French newspapers. Nobody approaches me. Although they are always careful to treat me with the deference owed to my rank, they keep their distance—and who can blame them? After all, there must be *something* wrong with me—some unspeakable disgrace must have ruined my career: otherwise why would the youngest colonel in the army have been transferred to a dump like this? Against the sky-blue tunic of my new regiment, the scarlet ribbon of my Legion of Honour draws their fascinated eyes like a bullet wound.

As usual, at about three o'clock, through the high glass-panelled door comes a young orderly carrying the afternoon's post. He is a pretty boy in a rough street-urchin sort of way, a musician in the regimental band who goes by the name of Flavian-Uband Savignaud. He arrived in Sousse a few days after I did: dispatched, I am fairly sure, by the Statistical Section, with orders from Henry or Gonse to spy on me. It is not the spying I resent as much as the incompetence with which he goes about it. "Look," I want to tell him, "if you're going to search my belongings, make sure you put them back as you found them: try to make a mental picture in your mind before you start. And if your job is to ensure my mail is intercepted, at least go through the pretence of putting it in the box normally rather than handing it direct to the post office official—I have followed you twice now and observed your sloppiness on both occasions."

He stops beside my chair and salutes. "Your mail, Colonel. Do you have anything to send?"

"Thank you. Not yet."

"Is there anything else at all I can do for you, Colonel?" The remark carries a hint of suggestion.

"No. You may go."

He sways slightly at the waist as he walks away. One of the younger captains puts down his paper to watch him pass. This is something else I resent: not the fact that Henry and Gonse think I might be tempted to go to bed with a man, but that I'd be tempted to go to bed with a man like Savignaud.

I inspect my mail: a letter from my sister and another from my cousin Edmond; both have been opened by the Statistical Section and then resealed with telltale over-firmness using glue. Like my fellow exile Dreyfus, I suffer the intrusion of having my correspondence monitored—although not, as in his case, actually censored. There are a couple of agents' reports of the type that continue to be forwarded to me as part of the fiction that I am only temporarily seconded from my job; these too have been opened. And then there is a letter from Henry: his schoolroom handwriting is familiar—we have exchanged messages often since I left Paris more than half a year ago.

Until recently the tone of our correspondence has been friendly (Here, *the sky is blue and the heat is sometimes too much in the afternoons; it is certainly nothing like Paris*). But then in May I was ordered by the High Command in Tunis to take the regiment to Sidi El Hani for three weeks and instruct them in target practice. This entailed a day's march southwest to pitch camp in the desert. The native troops were difficult to teach, and the heat and the boredom of the featureless stony landscape stretching in every direction, and above all the constant presence of Savignaud, combined to wring from me at last a cry of protest: *My dear Henry, Let it be publicly admitted once and for all that I have been relieved of my duties. I have no reason to be embarrassed by that fact; what embarrasses me are all the lies and mysteries that have been spread about me in the course of the last six months.*

I assume Savignaud has brought me Henry's reply. I open it quite casually, expecting the usual soothing reassurances that I shall be returning to Paris very soon. Instead, the tone could not be colder. He has the honour to inform me that "an inquiry" within the Statistical Section has concluded that the only "mysteries" I can be referring to in my letter are the three I perpetrated, to wit: (1) running an illicit operation "unconnected to the service"; (2) suborning false testimony from serving officers "that a classified document had been seized at the post office and came from a known individual"; and (3) "the opening of a secret dossier and examination of its contents, leading to certain indiscretions taking place." Henry ends with sarcasm: *As for the word "lies," the investigation was unable to determine where, how and to whom this word should be applied. Yours respectfully, J. Henry.*

And this man is supposed to be my subordinate! The letter is dated a week ago, Monday, 31 May. I check the envelope for the postmark: Thursday, 3 June. I guess at once what will have happened: Henry will have written this letter and then sent it over the road to Gonse for his approval before dispatching it. So his clumsy threat almost certainly carries behind it the force of the General Staff. I feel a momentary chill on my skin, despite the African heat. I read the letter again. But then my anxiety slowly vanishes and in its place a tremendous feeling of anger begins to build within me (*Yours respectfully?*), reaching such a level of intensity that it is all I can do not to cry out loud and kick the furniture. I stuff my mail into my trouser pocket, jam my cap back on my head, and stride towards the door with such fury that I am aware of a sudden silence and of heads turning to follow my progress.

I clump across the wooden veranda, almost knocking aside two majors who are smoking cigars, down the club steps, past the flaccid tricolour, across the wide boulevard and into the Marine Garden, where every Sunday afternoon the regimental band plays familiar melodies to the French expatriate community in a tuneless parody of home. Here I pause to gather myself. The two majors are staring after me from the veranda in open bewilderment. I turn and walk on through the little park towards the sea, past the bandstand and the broken fountain, and along the harbour front.

For months I have been going into the Military Club at lunchtime and scanning the stale newspapers in the hope of finding fresh revelations about the Dreyfus affair. In particular I have counted on the likelihood that sooner or later someone will recognise Esterhazy's handwriting from the *bordereau* and approach the Dreyfus family direct. But there has been nothing: the case is not even mentioned anymore. As I walk past the fishing boats, my head down and my hands clasped behind me, I reproach myself furiously for my cowardice. I have left it to others to do my duty. And now Henry and Gonse believe I am so broken down by exile, so crushed by their ruthlessness, that they can intimidate me into complete submission.

There is a fish market on the dockside at the southern end of the quay, close to the walls of the old Arab city, and I stop for a minute to watch as a catch is brought in and tipped over the counter: red mullet, sea bream, hake, mackerel. In a nearby pen are half a dozen turtles, their jaws tied shut with string, still alive, but blinded to prevent them escaping. They make a noise like cobbles being cracked together as they clamber over one another, desperate to regain the water they can sense but no longer see.

My quarters are in the military camp on the other side of the medina—a single-storey brick-built hut on the edge of the parade ground, with two rooms, their windows blanked by mosquito mesh, and a veranda with two chairs, a table and a kerosene lamp. In the torpid heat of the late afternoon the parade ground is deserted. Satisfied that I am unobserved, I drag the table to the edge of the veranda, climb up onto it, and reach up to push aside a loose rafter. The great advantage of being watched by an incompetent spy, and the reason I haven't asked for Savignaud's removal, is that he misses things, such as this. I move my fingers in the empty space until they encounter metal—an old cigarette tin.

I pull out the tin, replace the rafter, drag the table back to its original place, and go into my quarters. The larger room serves as a sitting room–cum–office; the curtains are drawn against the sun. I pass through this into my bedroom, sit on the edge of my narrow iron cot, and open the tin. It contains a photograph of Pauline taken five years ago and a bundle of letters from her: *Darling Georges . . . My dearest Georges . . . I yearn for you . . . I miss you . . .* I wonder how many hands they have been through; not as many as the Dreyfuses' correspondence, but doubtless quite a few.

I have visited your apartment several times. All is well. Mme Guerault tells me you are on a secret mission! Sometimes I lie on your bed and your smell is still on the pillow and I imagine where you are and what you are doing. That is when I want you most. In the afternoon light I could scream with wanting you. It is a physical pain . . .

I don't need to read them again; I know them off by heart.

Also in the tin is a photograph of my mother, seven hundred francs in cash and an envelope on which I have written: *In case of the death of the undersigned, please deliver this letter to the President of the Republic, who alone should know of its contents. G. PICQUART.* Inside is a sixteen-paragraph report of my investigation into Esterhazy, written in April. It goes through all the evidence in detail, relates the attempts of Boisdeffre, Gonse and Billot to block my researches, and comes to three conclusions:

1. *That Esterhazy is an agent for Germany.*
2. *That the only tangible facts blamed on Dreyfus are attributable to Esterhazy.*
3. *That the trial of Dreyfus was handled in an unprecedentedly superficial manner, with the preconceived idea that Dreyfus was guilty, and with a disregard for due legal forms.*

From the minarets of the Arab town comes the wail of the muezzin calling the faithful to prayer. It is Asr, the time when a man's shadow is twice his height. I slip the letter into the inside pocket of my tunic and go back out into the heat.

Early the following morning, Savignaud brings me hot water in my bedroom as usual so that I can shave. Naked above the waist, I bend to my mirror and lather my face. Instead of leaving, he lingers, watching me from behind.

I look at him in the mirror. "Yes, soldier? What is it?"

"I understand you've made an appointment to see General Leclerc in Tunis, Colonel."

"Do I need your permission?"

"I wondered if you wanted me to accompany you."

"It's not necessary."

"Will you be back in time for dinner?"

"Go away, Savignaud."

He hesitates, salutes and sidles out of the room. I return to my shaving, but with greater urgency: I have little doubt that he has gone off to telegraph Paris the news of my trip to Tunis.

An hour later, suitcase in hand, I wait beside the railway line in the central town square. A mining company has recently laid the track from Sousse to Tunis. There is no station: the locomotive simply passes through the streets. The first sign of its approach is a column of black smoke which I see rising in the distance above the flat roofs against the brilliant blue sky. A steam whistle shrieks nearby and a crowd of children erupts around the corner, scattering in all directions, screaming with excitement, pursued by an engine pulling two flatbed trucks and three carriages. It slows to a crawl until its momentum expires altogether in a loud exhalation of steam. I heave my suitcase into the carriage and clamber up the ladder after it, glancing over my shoulder to check if I am followed. But there is no sign of men in uniforms, just Arabs and Jews and a lot of livestock—chickens in crates, a sheep and a small goat with its hooves tethered, which its owner crams beneath his seat.

We pull away, gathering speed until our escort of excited children is left behind. Dust blows through the open sides of the carriage as we rattle out into the monotonous landscape—olive groves and hazy grey mountains to the left of us, the flat glare of the Mediterranean to the right. Every quarter of an hour or so we stop to pick up figures, always accompanied by animals, who seem to rise out of nowhere, shimmering up ahead beside the tracks. I slip my hand inside my tunic and feel the sharp edges of my posthumous letter to the President.

When at last we arrive in Tunis, around the middle of the afternoon, I push my way across the crowded platform to the taxi rank. The heat in the city feels almost solid. The air holds soot and spices—cumin, coriander, paprika—and tobacco and horse dung in a humid suspension. Beside the taxis a boy is selling *La Dépêche tunisienne*, which for five centimes offers an overnight compilation of the previous day's news as telegraphed from Paris. I skim it on the drive to army headquarters. Yet again there is nothing about Dreyfus. But it is within my power to change all that. For the twentieth time I touch the letter, like an anarchist checking his dynamite.

Leclerc is too busy to see me, so I am left to sweat in an anteroom for half an hour. Then an aide approaches me: "The general would like to know what this is about."

"It's a personal matter."

He goes away and comes back a couple of minutes later. "The general suggests you discuss all personal issues with General de Chizelle." De Chizelle is the senior officer of the 4th Tunisian Rifles, my direct superior.

"I am sorry, but this is a personal matter that I can only disclose to the Supreme Commander."

Once again he withdraws, but this time he is only gone for a few moments. "The general will see you now."

I leave my suitcase and follow him.

Jérôme Leclerc is on the veranda of his office, in his shirtsleeves, seated at a portable card table, working his way through a pile of letters. An electric fan above his head lifts the edges of the pages, which are weighted down by his revolver. He is in his middle sixties, square-jawed and -shouldered; he has been in Africa so long his skin is almost the same light brown as the natives'.

"Ah," he says, "the exotic Colonel Picquart: our very own man of mystery, sent to us under cover of darkness!" The sarcasm is not entirely unfriendly. "So tell me, Colonel, what is the latest secret about you that can't be divulged to your commanding officer?"

"I would like permission to go on leave to Paris."

"And why can't you make this application to General de Chizelle?"

"Because he would refuse it."

"And how do you know that?"

"Because I have reason to believe there is a standing instruction from the War Ministry that I should not be allowed to leave Tunisia."

"If that is true—and I am not confirming that it is—then why have you come to me?"

"Because I believe you are more likely to ignore an order from the General Staff than General de Chizelle."

Leclerc blinks at me for a moment, and I wonder if he might have me thrown out, but then abruptly he laughs. "Yes, well, that's probably true. I'm past caring. But I'd need a damned good reason, mark you. It can't just be that there's some woman in Paris you want to see."

"I have unfinished business there."

"Do you, by God!" He folds his arms and tilts back in his chair and looks me up and down a couple of times. "You're a funny fish, Colonel Picquart. I don't know what to make of you. I'd heard you were supposed to be the next Chief of the General Staff but four, and instead suddenly you're out here in our little backwater. Tell me, what did you do? Embezzle funds?"

"No, General."

"Screw the minister's wife?"

"Certainly not that."

"Then what?"

"I can't tell you."

"Then I can't help you."

He sits back straight in his chair and picks up a sheaf of papers. I feel a sudden desperation. "I'm in a kind of imprisonment out here, General. My mail is read. I'm followed. I'm not allowed to leave. It's really very effective. If I protest, it's been made clear to me I'll be disciplined on trumped-up charges. Short of desertion, I'm not sure how I can escape. And of course if I do desert I really would be finished."

"Oh no, don't desert—if you desert I'd have to shoot you." He gets up to stretch his legs—a big, lithe man, despite his years. A fighter, I think, not a desk man. He prowls up and down the veranda, frowning, and then stops to look out across the garden. I can't name all the flowers—jasmine I recognise, and cyclamen, and dianthus. He notices me looking. "You like it?"

"It's very fine."

"I planted it myself. Prefer this country to France now, oddly. Don't think I'll go back when I retire." He falls silent and then says fiercely, "You know what I can't stand, Colonel? I can't abide the way the General Staff dump their rubbish out here. No offence to you, but every malcontent and deviant and well-bred cretin in the army gets sent my way, and I can tell you that I'm just about sick of it!" He taps his foot on the wooden boards, thinking things over. "Do you give me your word that you've done nothing criminal or immoral—that you've simply fallen foul of those desk generals in the rue Saint-Dominique?"

"On my honour."

He sits down at his desk and starts writing. "Is a week enough?"

"A week is all I need."

"I don't want to know what you're up to," he says, still writing, "so don't let's talk about it. I shan't inform the ministry that you've left Tunisia. If and when they find out, I propose to tell them that I'm a soldier, not a gaoler. But I won't lie, you understand?" He finishes his writing, blows on the ink and hands the letter to me. It is official permission for Lieutenant Colonel Picquart of the 4th Tunisian Rifles to leave the country on compassionate leave, signed by the General Officer Commanding, Tunisia. It is the first official help I have been offered. I have tears in my eyes, but Leclerc affects not to notice.

———

The passenger ferry for Marseille is scheduled to leave Tunis at noon the next day. A clerk at the steamship company's office tells me ("with profound regret, my Colonel") that the list is already full; I have to bribe him twice—first to allot me a tiny two-berth cabin all to myself, and then to keep my name off the passenger manifest. I stay overnight in a *pension* near the docks and go aboard early, dressed in civilian clothes. Despite the sweltering African midsummer I can't linger on deck and risk being recognised. I go below and lock my door, strip naked and lie on the lower bunk, dripping sweat. I am reminded of Dreyfus and his description of his warship anchoring off Devil's Island: *I had to wait nearly four days in this tropical heat, shut close in my cell, without once going upon deck.* By the time the engines start, my own metal cell is as hot as a Turkish bath. The surfaces vibrate as we slip our moorings. Through the porthole I watch the coast of Africa recede. Only when we are out at sea and I can see nothing except the blue of the Mediterranean do I wrap a towel around my waist, summon the steward and ask him to bring me some food and drink.

I have packed a Russian–French dictionary, and a copy of Dostoyevsky's *Notes from Underground*, which I set to work translating, propped up on my bunk bed, the two books balanced on my knees, my pencil and paper beside me. The work soaks up the time and even the heat. *To care only for well-being seems to me positively ill-bred. Whether it's good or bad, it is sometimes very pleasant, too, to smash things . . .*

At midnight, when the vessel seems quiet, I venture up the iron staircase and step cautiously out onto the deck. The momentum of the ship provides a warm northerly breeze of thirteen knots. I walk to the prow and raise my face to it, drinking it in. There is blackness ahead and to either side. The only light is above: a wash of stars and a moon that scuds in and out of cloud and seems to be racing us. A male passenger stands nearby, leaning over the rail, talking quietly to one of the crew. Behind me I hear footsteps and turn to see the glowing red tip of a cigar approaching. I move on quickly, down the other side of the ship to the stern, where I watch our wake for a while, flickering like a comet's tail. But when I see the cigar again, disembodied in the dark, I go below and make my way along the passageway to my cabin, where I stay for the remainder of the voyage.

We dock in Marseille in the late afternoon of the following day in a summer downpour. It seems an ominous welcome home. I hurry straight to the gare Saint-Charles and buy a ticket on the first available train to Paris, conscious that this is my moment of maximum vulnerability. I must assume that Savignaud has reported my visit to Tunis, and also by now my subsequent failure to return to Sousse. Therefore it's possible that Gonse and Henry will have worked out that I am on my way back to Paris. All they need to do is ask Leclerc. If I were Henry, I would have telegraphed the Prefécture of Police in Marseille and asked him to keep watch at the station, just in case.

I linger under the station clock with my head buried in a newspaper until just before seven, when I hear the whistle blow and the Paris train begins to move. I grab my suitcase, run through the ticket barrier, weave past the guard, who tries to stop me, and sprint along the platform. I wrench open the rearmost door of the train, feeling the strain on my arm socket as the locomotive gathers momentum. I throw in my suitcase, increase my pace and narrowly manage to scramble aboard and slam the door behind me. I lean out of the window and look back. There is a man fifty metres behind on the platform, a thickset, bare-headed fellow in a brown suit, who has just missed the train and is leaning forward with his hands on his knees, recovering his breath, being reproached by the guard. But whether he is an ordinary passenger who arrived too late or an agent of the Sûreté who was on my tail I have no way of knowing.

The carriages are crowded. I have to walk almost the entire length of the train to find a compartment where I can squeeze into a corner seat. My fellow passengers are businessmen, mostly, and a priest, and an army major who keeps glancing in my direction, even though I am not wearing my uniform, as if he recognises a fellow soldier. I don't stow my suitcase overhead but keep it on my lap as a precaution should I fall asleep. And indeed, despite my nervous tension, as the day fades, lulled by the motion of the train, I do drop off, only to be jerked awake repeatedly throughout the night whenever we pull into a gas-lit station or someone enters or leaves the compartment. Eventually it is the early June daybreak that rouses me, the light falling drab and grey, like a film of ash spread over the southern outskirts of the city.

I move towards the very front of the train, so that at five in the morning, as we pull into the gare de Lyon, I am the first to disembark. I hurry across the deserted concourse, my eyes darting in all directions, but all I can see are a few ragged men, *les ramasseux de mégots*, gathering cigarette butts in order to sell the tobacco. I tell the taxi driver, "Sixteen, rue Cassette," and sink down low in my seat. A quarter of an hour later we are skirting the Jardin du Luxembourg and turning into the narrow street. As I pay the fare, I glance in either direction: no one is about.

On the second floor I knock on the apartment door: loudly enough to wake the occupants but not so loud, I hope, that I terrify them. Unfortunately no one can be roused from their bed at five-thirty in the morning without experiencing dread. I see it in my sister's eyes the moment she opens the door, clutching her nightdress to her throat, and finds me there exhausted and engrimed with the dust and smell of Africa.

Jules Gay, my brother-in-law, boils a kettle to make coffee while Anna fusses around in the children's old bedroom, making it fit for me to sleep in. They are a couple on their own together now, pushing sixty; I can tell they are glad to take me in, to have someone to look after.

Over coffee I say, "I'd prefer it if no one knew I was here, if that's all right with you both?"

They exchange glances. Jules replies, "Of course. We can be discreet."

"If anyone comes to the door asking for me, you should tell them you don't know where I am."

Anna says, only half jokingly, "Good heavens! You haven't deserted, have you, Georges?"

"The one person I do need to see is Louis Leblois. Would you be kind enough to take a message to him, asking if he could call round as soon as possible? But tell him he mustn't mention to anyone that I'm here."

"So you only want to talk to your lawyer?" Jules laughs. "That's not a good sign." It's the closest he comes to an expression of curiosity.

After breakfast he goes off to work, and then later Anna leaves to find Louis. I prowl around the apartment, examining its contents—the crucifix above the marital bed, the family Bible, the Meissen porcelain figures that used to belong to my grandmother in Strasbourg and which somehow survived the siege. I peer out of the windows at the front of the apartment, which overlook the rue Cassette, and then at the rear, where there is a public garden: that is where I would station a man if I were watching the house—with a small pocket telescope he could record every movement. I am unable to sit still. The most quotidian sounds of Parisian life—children playing in the park, the clip-clop of traffic, the cry of a hawker—seem charged with menace.

Anna returns and says that Louis will come as soon as he can get away from court. She cooks me an omelette for lunch and I tell her about life in Sousse as if I have been on some exotic grand tour—the narrow stone alleyways of the old Arab town unaltered since the days of the Phoenicians, the hot stink of tethered sheep on the street corners waiting to be slaughtered, the foibles of the tiny French community, only eight hundred souls out of nineteen thousand. "No culture," I complain. "No one to talk to. Nothing Alsatian to eat. My God, how I hate it!"

She laughs. "And I suppose you'll tell me next they've never even heard of Wagner." But she doesn't ask how I ended up there.

At four, Louis arrives. He crosses the carpet on his dainty feet and we embrace. The mere sight of him helps restore my nerve. His trim figure and beard, his neat appearance, his mild voice, his economical gestures—all convey an air of supreme competence. "Leave it to me," his personage seems to say. "I have made a study of all that is difficult in this world, I have mastered it, and I am ready to place my mastery at your disposal for an appropriate fee." Even so, I feel I have a duty to warn him what he might be getting into. So after I have fetched my suitcase from the children's bedroom, and Anna has made tea and discreetly withdrawn from the sitting room, I sit with the case on my lap and my thumbs poised on the locks and say, "Listen, Louis, before I go any further, you ought to be aware that for us merely to have this conversation could put you in some danger."

"Physical danger?"

"No, not that—I'm sure not that. But professional danger—political danger. It could become all-consuming." Louis frowns at me. "I suppose what I'm trying to say is that once you start on this I can't promise you where it may end. And you need to be aware of that now."

"Oh do shut up, Georges, and tell me what all this is about."

"Well, if you're quite certain." I press my thumbs on the locks and open the suitcase. "It's difficult to know where to start. You remember I came to see you in the middle of November, to tell you I was going away?"

"Yes, for a couple of days or so you said."

"It was a trap." From a false compartment at the bottom of the case I take out a wedge of papers. "First of all I was sent by the General Staff to Châlons to inspect intelligence procedures in the Sixth Corps. Then I was told I would have to go straight on to Nancy to write a report on the Seventh as well. Naturally I asked for permission to return to Paris, for a few hours at least, just to pick up some clean clothes. That was turned down flat by telegram—you see?" I hand it over. "All these letters I've kept are from my immediate superior, General Charles-Arthur Gonse, ordering each move—there are fourteen. From Nancy I was sent to Besançon. Then to Marseille. Then to Lyon. Then to Briançon. Then back to Lyon again, where I fell ill. This is the letter I received from Gonse while I was there: *I'm sorry that you are suffering, but I hope that after resting in Lyon you will regain your strength. Meanwhile prepare yourself to depart for Marseille and Nice . . .*"

"And all this time you were not permitted to return to Paris, not even for a day?"

"See for yourself."

Louis takes the handful of letters and scans them, frowning. "But this is ridiculous . . ."

"I was told I would be meeting the Minister of War over Christmas in Marseille, but he didn't turn up. Instead I was ordered to sail directly for Algeria—that was at the end of last year—to reorganise intelligence. And then a month after I got to Algeria I was ordered to Tunisia. Once I was in Tunisia I was transferred out of my old regiment and into a native outfit. Suddenly it wasn't an inspection trip anymore: it was a permanent posting to the colonies."

"You must have complained, I assume?"

"Of course. Gonse simply wrote back telling me to stop sending him so many letters: *You just have to let things go and gain satisfaction from serving a regiment in Africa.* Effectively, I'd been exiled."

"Did they give you a reason?"

"They didn't have to. I knew what it was. I was being punished."

"Punished for what?"

I take a breath. It still feels almost sacrilegious to say it aloud. "For having discovered that Captain Dreyfus is innocent."

"Ah." Louis looks at me, and for once even his mask of professional detachment seems to crack very slightly. "Ah, yes, I can see that would do it."

I hand Louis the envelope that is to be delivered to the President in the event of my death. He pulls a face as he reads the inscription. I suppose he considers it melodramatic, the sort of device one might encounter in a railway "thriller." I would have felt the same until a year ago. Now I have come to see that thrillers may sometimes contain more truths than all Monsieur Zola's social realism put together.

I say, "Go ahead." I light a cigarette and watch his expression as he takes out the letter. He reads the opening paragraph aloud: "*I, the undersigned Marie-Georges Picquart, Lieutenant Colonel with the 4th Colonial Infantrymen, formerly head of the secret intelligence service at the Ministry of War, certify on my honour the accuracy of the following information, which in the interests of truth and justice it is impossible to 'stifle,' as has been attempted . . .*" His voice trails off. He frowns, and then glances at me.

I say, "There's still time to stop, if you don't want to get involved. I wouldn't blame you for a moment. But I warn you: if you continue beyond that paragraph, you will be in the same predicament I am."

"Well now you make it sound quite irresistible." He continues reading, but silently, his eyes moving rapidly back and forth as he scans the lines. When he's finished, he blows out his cheeks in a sigh, then leans back in his chair and closes his eyes. "How many copies of this letter exist?"

"Only that one."

"God! Only this? And you carried it all the way from Tunisia?" He shakes his head in dismay. "Well, the first thing you'll have to do is to copy it out at least twice more. We shall need three copies as an absolute minimum. What else do you have in that old suitcase of yours?"

"There's this," I say, giving him my original report to Boisdeffre: "Intelligence Service note on Major Esterhazy, 74th Infantry." "And there are these"—my earlier exchange of letters with Gonse, after I had been out to see him in the country, in which he urges me not to extend my inquiries from Esterhazy to Dreyfus. "There's also this"—the letter from Henry revealing the existence of an inquiry into my behaviour as chief of the Statistical Section.

Louis reads them quickly and with complete absorption. When he has finished, he sets them aside and looks at me with great seriousness. "The question I ask all my clients at the outset, Georges—and that is what you are now, by the way, although heaven knows how I'm ever going to be paid—the question I always ask my clients is: what do you want to achieve from this?"

"I want to see justice done—that above all. I'm anxious that the army should emerge from this scandal with as little damage as possible: I still love the army. And on a selfish note, I'd like to have my career restored."

"Ha! Well, you might conceivably achieve one of those, or by a miracle two, but three is quite impossible! I assume there's no one in the military hierarchy who would take up the struggle alongside you?"

"That's not the way the army works. Unfortunately, we are dealing with four of the most senior officers in the country—the Minister of War, the Chief of the General Staff, the Head of Military Intelligence and the Commander of the Fourth Army Corps—that's Mercier's command these days—and all four of them are implicated in this affair to a greater or lesser extent, not to mention the entire secret intelligence section. Don't misunderstand me, Louis. The army isn't completely rotten. There are plenty of good and honourable men in the High Command. But if it came to it they would all put the interests of the army first. Certainly none of them is going to want to bring the temple crashing down around their ears, just for the sake of a—well . . ." I hesitate.

"A Jew?" suggests Louis. I make no response. "Well," he continues, "if we can't approach someone in the army with the facts, then what else can we do?"

I am about to reply when there is a loud knocking at the door. Something about the force of it, the implied sense of entitlement, warns me this is official: police. Louis opens his mouth to speak, but I hold up a silencing hand. I walk quietly over to the sitting-room door, which is glass-paned with lace curtains, and peer round the edge, just as Anna, smoothing her skirts, walks down the passage from the kitchen. She catches my eye, nods to show she knows what she has to do, then opens the front door.

I can't see who is standing there, but I can hear him—a heavy male voice: "Excuse me, madame, is Colonel Picquart here?"

"No. Why would he be? This isn't his apartment."

"Do you happen to know where he is?"

"The last letter I had was posted in Tunisia. And who are you, may I ask?"

"Forgive me, madame—I'm just an old army friend."

"Do you have a name?"

"Let's just leave it at that, shall we? You can tell him 'an old army friend' was looking for him. Goodbye."

Anna closes the door and locks it. She glances at me. I smile. She has done well. I turn to Louis. "They know I'm in Paris."

Louis leaves soon afterwards, taking with him all my papers apart from the letter to the President, which he tells me to copy out twice. I stay up late after Jules and Anna have gone to bed, sitting at the kitchen table with pen and ink—the anarchist again, assembling his bomb. *The trial of Dreyfus was handled in an unprecedentedly superficial manner, with the preconceived idea that Dreyfus was guilty, and with a disregard for due legal forms . . .*

Louis returns the following day at the same time, late in the afternoon. Anna shows him into the sitting room. I embrace him and then go over to the window and peer down into the street. "Do you think you might have been followed?"

"I haven't the faintest idea."

I crane my neck to look up and down the rue Cassette. "I can't actually see anyone watching the house. But these people are good, unfortunately. I think it would be wise to assume that you were."

"I agree. Now, my dear friend, did you make those copies of your letter? Excellent." He takes them from me and puts them in his briefcase. "One copy can remain in my safe and the other can go to a safe deposit box in Geneva." He smiles at me. "Cheer up, my dear Georges! Now, even if they kill you and then go on to kill me, they'll still have to invade Switzerland!"

But another day cooped up in my sister's apartment has not put me in the mood for jokes. "I don't know, Louis. I wonder if the safest course isn't just to give everything to the newspapers and have done with it."

"Oh no, no, no!" replies Louis in great alarm. "That would be fatal—both for yourself and for Dreyfus. I've been doing some hard thinking about the whole matter. This letter from Major Henry," he says, pulling it out, "is really very interesting, you know—very cunning, actually. They've obviously prepared contingency plans in case you make public what you know, but not only that—they want you to understand broadly what those contingency plans are."

"In order to frighten me off?"

"Yes, it's good logic, if you think about it. Their primary objective is that you should do nothing. Therefore they want to show you how unpleasant they are willing to make your life if you *do* try to do something." He studies the letter. "As I understand it, Major Henry is alleging here, in effect, that you conspired to frame Esterhazy: first by mounting an illegal operation against him, secondly by attempting to suborn from your associates false testimony about the incriminating evidence, and thirdly by leaking classified information to undermine the case against Dreyfus. Clearly, that will be their line of defence if you go to the newspapers: that you have been working for the Jews all along."

"Absurd!"

"Absurd, I agree. But a great many people will be eager to believe it."

I can see the truth of this. "Well then," I say, "if I don't go openly to the newspapers, perhaps I should go privately to the Dreyfus family, and at least give them the name of Esterhazy?"

"I have thought about that as well. Plainly the family are admirably loyal to their unfortunate captain. But I have to ask myself, as your lawyer, would they feel a similar loyalty to you? To have the name of Esterhazy would of course be immensely useful to their cause. But the real prize for them would be the fact that his name came to them from you—from the chief of the secret intelligence service himself."

"You think they would reveal me as their source?"

"If their objective is to free their brother, they would be almost bound to. And I wouldn't blame them if they did, would you? In any case, even if they didn't release your name themselves, I'm sure it would leak within a day or two. You are being watched and so are they. And unfortunately, once your name is known, it will provide the General Staff with all the evidence they need to convince most people that you have been conspiring to free Dreyfus all along. That is why I say this letter of Henry's is very cunning."

"So I'm trapped?"

"Not entirely. We must think tactically. What do you soldiers call it when you go around the side of your opponent rather than charging him head-on?"

"Outflanking?"

"Outflanking—exactly—we need to outflank them. You should not talk to anyone: that only plays into their hands. You should leave all that to me. I shall take your information and give it not to the newspapers or to the Dreyfus camp, but to a public figure of unimpeachable integrity."

"And who might this paragon be?"

"I spent a good part of last night thinking about exactly that, and this morning while I was shaving the answer came to me. With your permission, I shall go and see the Vice President of the Senate, Auguste Scheurer-Kestner."

"Why him?"

"To begin with, he's an old family friend—my father taught him mathematics—so I know him. He's a man of Alsace, which is always reassuring. He's rich, which gives him independence. But above all, he's a patriot. He's never done a sordid or selfish thing in his life. Let your friend Major Henry try to smear old Auguste as a traitor!"

I sit back and consider this. The other advantage of Scheurer-Kestner is that he is a member of the moderate left but with plenty of friends on the right. He is by temperament emollient but determined. "And what will the senator do with the information?"

"That will be up to him. Knowing his instinct for compromise, I would guess he'll approach the government to begin with, and try to sort it out that way. He'll only go to the press if the authorities won't listen. But one thing I'll absolutely insist on beforehand is that your name is not to be mentioned as the source of the information. No doubt the General Staff will guess you're behind it, but they'll be hard pushed to prove it."

"And what about me? What shall I do during this process?"

"Nothing. You will return to Tunisia and lead a blameless life—let them follow you all they want: they will observe nothing untoward. That alone will drive them mad. In short, my dear Georges, you just sit in the desert and wait for things to happen."

On the final day of my leave, after Jules has gone to work and my suitcase is packed ready for the evening train, there is another knock on the door—but softer this time, and tentative. I put down my book and listen as Anna lets in the visitor. A moment later the sitting-room door opens and there is Pauline. She looks at me without speaking. Behind her, Anna is putting on her hat. "I have to go out for an hour," she says briskly, before adding, with a mixture of fondness and disapproval, "and *only* for an hour, mind you."

We make love in the children's bedroom, under the watchful eyes of a row of my nephew's old toy soldiers. Afterwards, lying in my arms, she says, "You were really going to go back to Africa without trying to see me?"

"Not by choice, my darling."

"Without even sending me a note?"

"I'm worried I'm going to bring disaster down on you if we carry on like this."

"I don't care."

"I promise you, you will care, because it won't be just you who is damaged: it will be the girls as well."

Suddenly she sits up straight. She is so angry she doesn't bother to cover herself with a sheet in the way that she normally does. Her hair is tousled, loose, and for the first time I notice a few strands of grey among the blonde. Her skin is flushed rose pink. There is sweat between her breasts. She looks magnificent. "You have no right," she says, "after all these years, to make decisions that affect the two of us without even telling me what's in your mind! And don't you dare use the girls as an excuse!"

"Darling, wait—"

"No! Enough!"

She moves to get out of bed but I grasp her shoulders. She tries to shrug me off. I push her down and hold her. She gasps and struggles beneath me. But she is weaker than she looks, even in her anger, and I restrain her easily. "Listen, Pauline," I say quietly, "I'm not talking about gossip—we're already common gossip among our circle. I wouldn't be surprised if it turns out Philippe actually guessed about us years ago—even a man who works at the Foreign Ministry can't be as blind to the obvious as all that."

"Don't talk about him! You know nothing about him!" Pinioned, she beats the back of her head against the pillow in helpless frustration.

I press on. "Gossip is one thing—if it's just gossip, it can be ignored. But I'm talking about exposure and humiliation. I'm talking about the power of the state being used to crush us—to parade us through the newspapers and the courts, to invent things about us and pass them off as true. Nothing is going to withstand that. Do you think I've been away from home for the past seven months by choice? And that's only a tiny foretaste of what they can do to us."

I clamber off her and sit on the edge of the bed with my back to her. She doesn't move. After a while she says, "It's useless, I suppose, to ask what exactly it is that has brought this foulness into our lives?"

"I can't speak of it to anyone, apart from Louis. And I've only talked to him because he's my lawyer. If anything happens, he's the one you should go to. He's wise."

"And how long is this going to continue—for the rest of our lives?"

"No, a few more weeks—perhaps a couple of months. And then the storm will break, and you will be able at last to see what it has all been about."

She is silent for a while, and then she says, "Can we still write to each other, at least?"

"Yes, but we need to take precautions." I rise from the bed and walk naked into the sitting room to fetch a pencil and paper. It is a relief to be doing something practical. When I return, she is sitting up with her arms wrapped around her knees. "I've arranged with Louis to set up a poste restante with a friend in the avenue de la Motte-Picquet—here's the address. I'll send my letters to you there: have someone else pick them up on your behalf. I won't put your name on the envelope or use it in the letter itself, and I won't add a signature. And you shouldn't sign your letters to me, or put anything in them that would give anyone a clue as to who you are."

"Are people in the government really going to read our letters?"

"Yes, almost certainly: many people—ministers, army officers, policemen. There's one precaution you can take, although it may mean the letter doesn't get through. Use a double envelope; the inner one you should cover entirely with glue, so that when you insert it into the outer envelope it sticks to it. That way it can't be opened and then resealed. So if they do tamper with it they'll have to keep it and they may not want to be as blatant as that. I don't know—it's worth a try."

She tilts her head to one side and looks at me in a kind of puzzled wonder, as if seeing me properly for the first time. "How do you come to *know* all this?"

I put my arms around her. "I'm sorry," I say. "It was my job."

17

Four months pass.

The Sousse Military Club still looks out from behind its screen of dusty palms across the unpaved square to the sea. The glare off the Mediterranean remains as fiercely metallic as ever. The same boy in long brown robes still passes at the same time in the middle of the afternoon, leading a goat on a length of rope. The only difference these days is that the boy gives me a wave and I wave back, for I have become a familiar sight. As usual when lunch is over I am seated alone beside the window while my brother officers continue to play cards or doze or read the four-day-old French newspapers. Nobody approaches me.

It is Friday, 29 October 1897, and I have checked those stale newspapers every day since my return from Paris, without once coming across the word "Dreyfus." I am beginning to worry that something may have happened to Louis.

In time-honoured fashion, at about three o'clock, through the high glass-panelled door comes a young orderly carrying the afternoon's post. It is no longer Savignaud—he has gone, arrested for immoral conduct with a local olive oil trader, sentenced to nine days' detention and shipped off to God knows where. His replacement is an Arab, Jemel, and if he is a spy, as I assume he must be, he is too good for me to catch him out; in consequence, I rather miss Savignaud and his familiar, clumsy ways.

Jemel glides to a stop alongside my chair and salutes. "You have a telegram, Colonel."

It is from army headquarters in Tunis: *The Ministry of War today orders Colonel Picquart to proceed immediately to El-Ouatia to investi-*

gate and if possible verify reports of hostile Bedouin cavalry massing in the vicinity of Tripoli. Please report to me to discuss the implications of your mission before your departure. Cordially yours, Leclerc.

Jemel says, "Will there be a reply, Colonel?"

For a moment I am too surprised to speak. I read the telegram again, just to make sure I am not hallucinating.

"Yes," I say eventually. "Will you please telegraph General Leclerc and tell him that I shall report to him tomorrow?"

"Of course, Colonel."

After Jemel has shimmied off into the afternoon heat, I study the telegram again. *El-Ouatia?*

The following morning I catch the train to Tunis. In my briefcase I have a file: "Intelligence report on the assassination of the marquis de Morès." I know it well: I wrote it—one of the few real accomplishments of my time in Africa.

Morès, a fanatical anti-Semite and the most celebrated duellist of the day, came to Tunisia two years ago with a madcap plan to lead an Arab revolt against the British Empire, starting with a trek across the Tunisian Sahara—an area beyond law and civilisation, where Bedouin caravans still occasionally pass trailing columns of Negro slaves chained at the neck. Nevertheless, ignoring all warnings, he set off with a party of thirty, following the coast before heading south from Gabes into the desert.

Riding a camel, escorted by six Tuareg whom he saw as the nucleus of his private army, Morès struck camp on the morning of 8 June last year. He was a mile ahead of the rest of his followers when Bedouin fighters began to appear all around him. At that instant his escort fell upon him and attempted to seize his Winchester rifle and revolver. Morès shot two of his assailants dead with his revolver, mortally wounded a third and then ran forty metres to a nearby tree, shooting two more of the pursuing Tuareg. Dropping to his knees, he reloaded and awaited rescue from the remainder of his expedition. But they, too frightened or treacherous to move, had halted a kilometre away. The heat of the day grew fierce. One Tuareg went forward to pretend to parley with the marquis; in reality he wanted to find out how many bullets he had left. Desperate, Morès seized him round the throat as a hostage. Soon afterwards the man broke free, whereupon Morès shot him dead. But the distraction had lasted long enough for his assassins to get closer. The marquis was hit by a rifle bullet in the back of the neck. His money belt was cut open and a hundred and eighty gold pieces were stolen. His corpse was stripped and mutilated.

The Second Department wanted to know if the British secret service had organised the murder. I was able to assure them that was not the case. Instead, the real lesson of the episode was clear: to venture so far south with anything less than a full infantry brigade plus cavalry and artillery would be suicidal. The name of the place where Morès died was El-Ouatia.

The train pulls into Tunis in the middle of the afternoon. As usual I have to push through the crowd on the platform to reach the taxi rank; as usual there is a boy beside it selling *La Dépêche tunisienne*. I give him five centimes and settle back in the cab, and suddenly I catch my breath, for there it is—the explanation for my suicidal mission—in the middle of the front page. I should have guessed it:

> DREYFUS CASE. Paris, 8h 35m. Vice President of the Senate M. Scheurer-Kestner last night created a sensation by informing *L'Agence Nationale*: "I am firmly convinced of Captain Dreyfus's innocence and I will do everything to prove it, not only by obtaining a verdict of acquittal at the revision of his trial, but by doing him full justice and rehabilitating him completely." 10h 15m. *Le Matin* reports further comments of M. Scheurer-Kestner: "What methods will I use to reveal the truth? And at what time will I use them? For now that remains my secret. I have not passed the file which is in my possession to anyone, not even, as has been suggested, the President of the Republic."

A single paragraph, that is all. *Last night created a sensation . . .* It is like catching the faint shock wave of some immense but distant explosion. As the taxi clip-clops along the avenue de France I stare out at the facades of the official buildings and the apartment blocks gleaming white and ochre in the afternoon sun, and I am amazed that they look so *normal.* I cannot absorb what has happened. I feel a great sense of dislocation from my surroundings, as if I am in a dream.

At army headquarters, Leclerc's aide-de-camp comes to fetch me. I follow him down a wide corridor past an office where a sergeant sits bent over a typewriter, picking out the letters with excruciating slowness. Leclerc himself appears equally oblivious to the enormity of what has occurred in Paris. Evidently he doesn't read *La Dépêche*—or if he does, he hasn't associated the story with me. But then why should he?

He greets me cheerfully. I hand him my report on the murder of Morès. He glances through it quickly, eyebrows raised. "Well don't worry, Picquart," he says, handing it back to me, "I'll make sure you have a perfectly decent funeral. You can choose the hymns before you go."

"Thank you, General. I appreciate that."

He goes over to the map of the French protectorate hanging on his office wall. "It's a hell of a trek, I must say. Don't they keep any charts these days in Paris?" He traces the route from Tunis in the north due south, past Sousse, Sfax and Gabès, all the way down into the vast desert area towards Tripoli, where the map is blank of roads or settlements. "That must be eight hundred kilometres. And at the end of it: a whole region swarming with hostile Bedouin."

"It is somewhat daunting. May I ask where the order came from?"

"Yes, I dare say you can—it was from General Billot himself." Leclerc sees my grim expression; it only increases his amusement. "I think perhaps you must have slept with his wife after all!" And then when I still don't smile, he becomes serious. "Look, don't worry about it, my dear fellow. Obviously it's a mistake. I've already sent him a telegram reminding him that this was the very spot where Morès was ambushed barely a year ago."

"And has he responded?"

"Not yet, no."

"General, I don't think this is a mistake." He looks at me and cocks his head, puzzled. I continue, "When I was in Paris, I had command of the secret intelligence section of the General Staff. In that capacity I made certain discoveries that revealed there was a traitor in the army, and that it was he who had committed the crimes for which Captain Dreyfus was condemned."

"Did you, by God?"

"I brought this to the attention of my superiors, including General Billot, with a recommendation that we should arrest the real spy. They refused."

"Even though you had proof?"

"It would have meant admitting that Dreyfus was innocent. And that would have exposed—well, let us say certain *irregularities* in the way his case was handled."

Leclerc holds up his finger to stop me. "Hold on. I'm a slow fellow—too many years in the sun. Let me be clear about this. Are you suggesting that the minister wants to send you on this hazardous mission because he hopes to get rid of you?"

In reply I hand him *La Dépêche tunisienne*. Leclerc stares at the paper for a long time. Eventually he says, "You are the person who supplied Monsieur Scheurer-Kestner with his information, I take it?"

I reply with the formula agreed with Louis. "I have not given him any facts myself, General."

"And presumably this was why you were so keen to go to Paris in the summer?"

Again I seek refuge in evasion. "I am profoundly sorry if I've caused you embarrassment. I was being threatened with disciplinary action if I dared to protest at my treatment. I felt I had to go back to Paris to talk to my lawyer."

"This is completely unacceptable behaviour, Colonel."

"I understand, General, and I apologise. I didn't know what else I could do."

"No, not your behaviour—*Billot's* behaviour is unacceptable. And these people have the nerve to feel superior to the Africans!"

He gives me back my newspaper. "Unfortunately I can't countermand a direct order from the head of the army, but I can obstruct it. Go back to Sousse and pretend to get yourself ready to go south. In the meantime I'll see what I can do. In any case, if what you say about Billot is true, he may not be minister for very much longer."

The next day, a Sunday, the orderly who runs the Sousse Military Club brings in the newspapers soon after eleven. The rest of the garrison is at church. I have the place to myself. I order a cognac, pick up one of the club's two copies of La Dépêche tunisienne and retreat with it to my customary window seat.

> DREYFUS CASE. Paris, 8h 35m. Newspapers maintain their belief that M. Scheurer-Kestner was hoodwinked by the family of the former captain Dreyfus, but they are now calling for a prompt and full investigation. An editor of Figaro interviewed M. Scheurer-Kestner, who repeated his conviction that Dreyfus is innocent. But he said he would not reveal anything until he had laid the case before the competent ministers. Le Figaro says M. Scheurer-Kestner will see the President and the Ministers of War and Justice.

It's a nightmare to sit here idly not knowing what is going on. I resolve to send a telegram to Louis. I finish my cognac and walk as far as the new post office building beside the harbour. Then my nerve fails me and I linger for ten minutes smoking a cigarette in the Bar de la Poste, watching a dozen of my fellow expatriates play boules in the dusty square. The truth is that any message I send or receive is certain to be intercepted, just as any code I might invent would not fool the experts for more than a few minutes.

On Tuesday, the actual Paris newspapers that were published the previous Friday finally arrive in Sousse. They carry the first stories of Scheurer-Kestner's intervention in the Dreyfus affair. Le Figaro, Le Matin, La Libre Parole, Le Petit Parisien and the rest are passed around the club and provoke outrage among my fellow officers. From my window seat I hear them talking. "Do you think this fellow Scheurer-Kestner is also a Jew?" "Well, with a name like that, if he's not a Jew he must be a German . . ." "It's a contemptible slur on the army—let's hope someone seeks satisfaction . . ." "Yes, say what you like about Morès but he would have known how to deal with the scoundrel . . ." "What do you think of it all, Colonel, if you don't mind us asking?"

I am so unused to being addressed in the club, it takes me a moment to realise they are talking to me. I put down my novel and turn round in my chair. Half a dozen tanned and moustached faces are looking at me. "I'm sorry," I say. "What do I think about . . . ?"

"This canard that Dreyfus might have been innocent?"

"Oh, that? That's a bad business, don't you think? A very bad business." This gnomic utterance seems to satisfy them and I return to my book.

Wednesday is quiet. Then on Thursday *La Dépêche* reports new developments:

DREYFUS CASE. Paris, 8h 25m. The Dreyfus affair appears to be entering a decisive phase. M. Scheurer-Kestner attended the Ministry of War yesterday to convey to General Billot the information concerning Captain Dreyfus which he had in his possession. The meeting was long and kept very secret . . . 9h 10m. *Le Figaro* announces that M. Scheurer-Kestner saw the Prime Minister, M. Méline, yesterday on the subject of the Dreyfus affair.

I lie awake that night with my door locked and my revolver under my pillow, listening to the predawn call to prayer from the nearby minaret. I entertain myself by picturing the crisis meetings in Billot's office: the minister raging, Gonse nervously spilling cigarette ash down his tunic, Boisdeffre frozen, Henry drunk; I think of Gribelin scuttling back and forth between his files in an effort to fish up new scraps of evidence against Dreyfus, and Lauth steaming open my letters and trying to decipher the hidden code by which I am somehow controlling events. I exult in this imagined confounding of my enemies.

And then my enemies begin returning fire.

The opening shot is a telegram. Jemel brings it to my office first thing. It was dispatched from the Bourse post office in Paris the previous day: *We have proof that the* bleu *was forged by Georges. Blanche.*

Blanche?

It is like a threat whispered by a stranger in a crowd who has melted away before one has time to look round. I am conscious of Jemel studying my reaction. The thing is meaningless and yet sinister, especially the use of Blanche's name. "I can't make sense of this," I tell him. "Perhaps it's been garbled in transmission. Would you mind going back to the telegraph office and asking them to repeat it?"

He returns later in the morning. "There is no doubt, Colonel," he says. "They checked in Paris: the text is accurate. Also, this has just arrived for you, redirected from Tunis." He gives me a letter. On the envelope, which is marked "urgent," my name is misspelt "Piquart." I vaguely recognise the handwriting. Here it comes: the second shot.

"Thank you, Jemel."

I wait until he has gone before I open it.

Colonel,

I have received an anonymous letter informing me that you have organised an abominable plot to substitute me for Dreyfus. The letter alleges, among other things, that you have bribed junior officers to obtain samples of my handwriting; I know this to be true. It is also alleged that you took from the Ministry of War documents entrusted to you in good faith in order to compose a secret dossier which you have passed to friends of the traitor. This I also know to be true, as I have today been given a document from this file.

Despite the evidence I still hesitate to believe that a senior officer in the French army could be party to such a monstrous conspiracy against one of his comrades.

It is unthinkable that you will not provide me with a frank and clear explanation.

Esterhazy

A letter of complaint from the traitor, in the same hand in which he wrote the *bordereau*—one almost has to admire the impudence of the fellow! And then the questions start to assail me. How does he know my name? Or that I am in Tunis? Or that I have obtained samples of his handwriting? Presumably from the author of this alleged "anonymous letter." And who could be the author of such a letter? Henry? Is this where the logic of the General Staff's position has led them—actually to helping the guilty man evade justice as the only means of keeping the innocent man imprisoned? I fetch out the telegram. *We have proof that the* bleu *was forged by Georges. Blanche.* What are they up to?

The next day Jemel brings me another telegram, another menacing riddle: *Stop the Demigod. Everything is discovered. Extremely serious matter. Speranza.* This message was sent from the rue la Fayette post office in Paris, and actually on the same day as the Blanche telegram, but it has taken an extra twenty-four hours to reach me because, like Esterhazy's letter, it was wrongly addressed to me in Tunis.

I have never met anyone called Speranza—I know it only as the Italian word for "hope"—but "the Demigod" is Blanche's nickname for our mutual friend and fellow Wagnerian Captain William Lallemand. And the only person connected to the Statistical Section who is likely to know that obscure fact from our circle is Blanche's former lover, du Paty.

Du Paty. Yes—of course—the moment the name comes into my mind it is obvious: du Paty has been drafted in to help devise this sinister production; his decayed Gothic style, part Dumas, part *Fleurs du Mal*, is inimitable. But whereas a year or two ago I would have laughed off any threat from so ludicrous a figure, now I know differently. Now I have seen what he is capable of. And that is when I realise I am being fitted for the same convict's outfit as Dreyfus.

———

The echo of the next detonation, on Wednesday, 17 November, is sufficient to shake even the sleepy palms of the Sousse Military Club:

DREYFUS'S BROTHER NAMES "THE REAL TRAITOR." Paris, 2h. Here is the text of the letter which the brother of Dreyfus has sent to the Minister of War: "Monsieur le Minister, The only basis for the accusation against my brother is an unsigned, undated letter establishing that confidential documents were delivered to an agent of a foreign power. I have the honour to inform you that the author of that document is M. le comte Walsin Esterhazy, an infantry major suspended from active service since last spring for reasons of temporary ill health. The handwriting of Major Esterhazy is identical with that of this document. I cannot doubt, Minister, that once you know the perpetrator of the treason for which my brother has been convicted you will act swiftly to see that justice is done. With the deepest respect, Mathieu Dreyfus."

I read it after lunch and then retreat to the window, where I pretend to be immersed in my novel. Behind me the *Dépêche* is passed from hand to hand. "Well," says one officer, "there you go—that's the Jews for you—they stick together and they don't let up." Another says, "I must say, I feel sorry for this fellow Esterhazy." Then a third, the captain who lusted after Savignaud, chimes in: "You see here it says that Esterhazy has written to General Billot? 'I have read in this morning's papers the infamous accusation brought against me. I ask you to order an inquiry, and I am ready to reply to all the charges.'" "Good for him," rejoins the first, "but what chance does he stand against all that Jewish gold?" The captain: "That's true enough— perhaps we should raise a subscription for poor old Esterhazy? Put me down for twenty francs."

The following day I go for a long ride along the coast to clear my head. Far out to sea, immense clouds are rolling north, trailing funeral draperies of rain. It is the start of the wettest season. I spur my mount and gallop towards the thousand-year-old watchtower of the Ribat in Monastir, a distance of perhaps fifteen kilometres. As I come closer, it stands out pale against the darkening sea. I consider riding into the little fishing port. But the sky is now as black as squid's ink, and sure enough, as I turn for home the cloud overhead splits like a slashed sac and a drenching cold rain begins to fall.

When I reach the base I go straight to my quarters to change. The door, which I had made sure to lock, is open and I enter to find Jemel standing guiltily in the middle of my sitting room. A few seconds earlier and I would have caught him mid-search, but now I look around and can see nothing out of place.

I say curtly, "Fetch me some water; I need a bath."

"Yes, Colonel."

By the time I reach the Military Club I am too late for lunch, and I can tell from the instant I enter that something momentous has happened. Conversations cease as I walk towards my normal place. Several of the older officers quickly finish their drinks and leave. Today's *Dépêche* has been placed carefully, pointedly, on my armchair, folded to a story on the front page.

ESTERHAZY ACCUSES COLONEL PICQUART. Paris, 10h 35m. In an interview in *Le Matin*, Esterhazy says: "Everything that has happened is the responsibility of Colonel Picquart. He is a friend of the Dreyfus family. He opened an investigation against me fifteen months ago when he was in the Ministry of War. He wanted to destroy me. M. Scheurer-Kestner has been given all his information by Picquart's lawyer, Maître Leblois, who went to the colonel's office and was shown secret files. The colonel's behaviour was considered so appalling by his superiors he was sent in disgrace to Tunisia."

I have never before had my name printed in a newspaper. I picture all the people I know, my friends and family in France, coming upon it unawares. What will they think? I am supposed to be a spy, a man in the shadows. Now a searchlight has picked me out.

And there is more:

CHEZ MAÎTRE LEBLOIS. According to *Le Matin:* "At midnight, after our interview with Major Esterhazy, we go to the door of Maître Leblois, advocate of the court of appeal—96, rue de l'Université—but the door is closed. We ring again. The door doesn't open. But from the interior comes a voice: 'Who's there? What do you want?' We explain the reason for our visit: that Major Esterhazy has formally alleged that he, Maître Leblois, provided the dossier to M. Scheurer-Kestner based on documents furnished by Colonel Picquart. The voice becomes more menacing: 'What can I tell you? I am bound by a professional vow of silence. I have nothing to say, absolutely nothing. But I recommend you do not name Colonel Picquart. Now, good night and don't come back!'"

By the time I finish reading and look round, the clubroom is empty.

That evening I receive another telegram: I find it pushed under my door. But this one is quite unambiguous: *Evacuate your quarters in Sousse immediately on assumption you will not be returning and report to me at General Headquarters. Signed Leclerc.*

In Tunis I am given a small room on the second floor of the main barracks. I lie on the bed and listen to the symphony of male institutional life—the shouts and sudden bursts of whistling, the clanging of doors and heavy footsteps. I think about Pauline. She has gone very quiet over the last few weeks. I wonder what she will have made of the references to me in the press—that I am in the pay of the Jews; that I was shipped off to Tunisia "in disgrace." I write her a letter.

Tunis   *20 November 1897*

Ma chérie,
What with all my comings and goings between Sousse and here, I receive mail very irregularly. Perhaps there are other causes for this. Anyway, it's boring and sad not to hear from you. Don't be

afraid to write to me even if it's only two words. I'm fine, but I have to make sure your life is not compromised. Poor little girl—here I am for the first time with my life laid out in the papers! I have the disadvantage that I am attacked without having the right or the will to defend myself through the same medium. Finally all this will end. I shall write no more now, but I hold you in my heart with all my love.

I set down my pen and read the letter through. It seems to me very stilted. But then how inhibiting it is to know that one's love letters will by steamed open and read by men in offices, and copied and placed on file.

PS I am very calm and will not be hurt. You see that grave circum-stances cannot scare me. The only thing that concerns me is your emotion while reading this.

I don't sign it or write her name on the envelope, and I pay a soldier a franc to post it for me.

Leclerc receives me in his office at the end of the day. His garden is in darkness. He looks weary. He has a stack of telegrams on one side of his desk and a pile of newspapers on the other. He invites me to sit. "I have a list of questions I have been instructed to ask you, Colonel, sent to me by the Minister of War. Such as: have you ever given any secret information to a person or persons outside the army?"

"No, General."

He makes a note.

"Have you ever forged or otherwise altered any confidential documents?"

"No, General."

"Have you ever asked a subordinate, or subordinates, to forge or alter confidential documents?"

"No, General."

"Have you ever allowed a woman access to secret documents?"

"A woman?"

"Yes. Apparently this Major Esterhazy has claimed he was passed secret information by an unknown woman wearing a veil."

A veiled lady! Another du Paty touch . . .

"No, General, I have not shown documents to a woman, veiled or unveiled."

"Good. I shall telegraph Paris accordingly. In the meantime I am to inform you that the Minister of War has ordered an internal inquiry into this whole affair, under General de Pellieux, Military Commander of the Département of the Seine. You are instructed to return to France to give evidence. An official from the Colonial Ministry will escort you." He closes the file. "And that, I think, concludes our business together, Colonel."

He stands. I follow suit.

He says, "I wouldn't describe it as having been a pleasure exactly to have you under my command, but it has certainly been interesting." We shake hands. He puts his arm around my shoulders and escorts me to the door. He smells strongly of eau de cologne. "I was talking to Colonel Dubuch the other night. He says this Esterhazy character is a thoroughly bad lot. He was out here in '82 and was charged with embezzlement in Sfax. There was a board of inquiry, but somehow he got off."

"It doesn't surprise me, General."

"You must be up against some pretty desperate opposition, Picquart, if they're willing to tie themselves to a character like that. May I give you some advice?"

"Please."

"Don't stand too close to the railings on the ship back to France."

18

The passage across the Mediterranean in November is much rougher than in June. One moment the porthole shows grey sky, the next grey waves. My Russian books slide off my little table and splay out on the floor. As before, I keep mostly to my cabin. Occasionally I am visited by my escort, Monsieur Périer of the Colonial Ministry, but he is very green and prefers to keep to his own quarters. On my rare excursions above decks I follow Leclerc's advice and keep well away from the edge. I enjoy the lash of the sea across my face, the smell of the coal smoke mingled with the salt spray. Occasionally I am aware of some of the other passengers staring at me, but I am not sure whether they are police agents, or have merely heard that a person whose name is in the news is aboard.

We leave Africa on the Tuesday. On the Thursday afternoon the coast of France comes into view—a watery line in the mist. I have just finished packing when someone knocks on my door. I pick up my revolver and call out, "Who's there?"

A voice replies, "It's the captain, Colonel Picquart."

"Just a moment." I slip the gun into my pocket and open the door.

He's a morose-looking fellow in his early fifties; a drinker to judge by the filigree of blood vessels in his eyes: I should guess that plying back and forth between Tunis and Marseille three times a week must become tedious after a while. We exchange salutes. He says, "Arrangements have been made to take you and Monsieur Périer off the ship before we dock."

"Is that really necessary?"

"Apparently there's a crowd of reporters on the quayside, and some protesters. The Ministry of War feels it would be safer to transfer you to a tug while we're still at sea and then land you ahead of us in a different part of the harbour."

"What an absurd idea."

"Maybe so," replies the captain with a shrug, "but those are my orders."

A half-hour later the throb of the engines ceases and we heave to. I climb up to the deck carrying my suitcase. We have come to a stop about a kilometre outside the harbour entrance. A tugboat lies alongside us. The weather is cold and squally but that doesn't deter several dozen passengers from lining the rails in sullen silence to watch me depart. It is my first experience of my new celebrity, and a singularly uncomfortable one. There is a strong swell on the sea and the two vessels pitch against each other, their decks rising and falling in opposite directions. My suitcase is taken from me, flung down into the tug and caught, and then I am lowered after it. Strong arms stretch up to lift me aboard. Behind me I hear someone shout an insult; the word "Jew" is whipped away in the wind. Monsieur Périer is handed down along with his luggage. He staggers to the other side of the tug and throws up. The ropes are cast off and we pull clear.

We pass behind the harbour wall and swing to port, moving between the towering hulls of a pair of anchored ironclads, towards the western end of the harbour. Over the tug's stern, gathered in the place where the ferries berth, I can see a crowd of people, at least a hundred or two. And this is the instance when I realise the hold that the Dreyfus affair is beginning to exert on the imagination of my fellow countrymen. The tug manoeuvres alongside a military dock, where a cab is waiting. Next to it stands a young officer. As the crew jump off to tie up the boat, he steps forward and takes my suitcase. He passes it up to the taxi driver, then offers his hand to help me ashore.

He salutes. His manner is cold but impeccable. In the back of the cab, facing me and Périer, he says, "If I might make a suggestion, Colonel, it would perhaps be advisable to crouch down as low as possible, at least until we are some distance clear of the port."

I do as he asks. And so, like a hunted criminal, I return to France.

At the railway station, a first-class compartment at the rear of the train has been reserved for our exclusive use. Périer pulls down the blinds on the doors and the windows and refuses to allow me out to buy a newspaper. If I so much as visit the lavatory he insists on accompanying me and standing outside the door until I have finished. Occasionally I wonder what he would do if I disobeyed his orders, which invariably are delivered in a nervous, embarrassed, almost pleading tone. But in truth I am afflicted by a curious fatalism. I surrender myself to events, and to the rocking cocoon of our journey, which begins in the darkness of Marseille at five in the afternoon and ends in the darkness of Paris at five in the morning.

I am asleep when we arrive at the gare de Lyon. The jolting of the compartment awakens me and I open my eyes to see Périer peering around the edge of the window blind. He says, "We shall wait here, Colonel, if you don't mind, until the other passengers have disembarked." Ten minutes later we step down onto the deserted platform. A porter wheels our cases ahead of us and we walk the length of the train to the ticket barrier, where a dozen men are waiting, holding notebooks. Périer warns me, "Don't say anything," and we hold on to our hats and hunch forward slightly, as if stepping into a headwind. Their shouted questions all come at once so that it is impossible to distinguish more than a few words: "Esterhazy . . . ? Dreyfus . . . ? Veiled lady . . . ? Search . . . ?" There is a brilliant lightning flash and the *whumph* of a magnesium tray igniting, but we are hurrying too fast, I am sure, for any photograph to be usable. Ahead of us a couple of railway officials have their arms outstretched and they steer us into an empty waiting room and close the door. Inside, my old friend Armand Mercier-Milon, now a colonel, salutes me very formally.

"Armand," I say, "I cannot tell you how pleased I am to see you," and I hold out my hand, but instead of offering me his, he merely gestures me towards the door.

"There's a motorcar waiting," he says. "We need to leave before they run round to the front of the station."

Drawn up outside is a big modern vehicle in the livery of the Compagnie Paris–Lyon Méditerranée. I am squeezed onto the back seat between Périer and Mercier-Milon. The luggage is stowed and the car pulls away just as the reporters come pouring out of the station towards us. Mercier-Milon says, "I have a letter here for you from the Chief of Staff."

It is awkward to open the envelope in the cramped space. *Colonel Picquart, I order you very strictly not to communicate with anyone until you have given your evidence to General de Pellieux's inquiry. Boisdeffre.*

We pass quickly and in silence through the darkened, rainy streets. There is no traffic at this hour; hardly anyone is about. We head west along the boulevard Saint-Martin and I wonder if they might be taking me back to my apartment, but then suddenly we turn off north and pull up on the rue Saint-Lazare outside the giant hôtel Terminus. A porter opens the door. Périer gets out first. He says, "I'll go in and register us."

"Am I staying here?"

"For now."

He disappears inside. I haul myself out of the car and contemplate the vast facade. It occupies an entire city block—five hundred bedrooms: a temple of modernity. Its electric lights glisten in the rain. Mercier-Milon joins me. Out of earshot of anyone else for the first time he says, "You are a bloody fool, Georges. What can you have been thinking of?" He speaks quietly but with force and I can tell he's been bursting to say this since we left the railway station. "I mean, I feel sorry for Dreyfus myself—I was one of the few prepared to defend him at that charade of a court-martial. But you? Passing secret information to an outsider, so that he can use it against your own commanders? That's a crime in my book. I doubt you'll find a soldier in the whole of France who'll defend what you've done."

His vehemence both shakes and angers me. I say coldly, "What happens next?"

"You go to your room and change into your uniform. You speak to no one. You write to no one. You open no letters. I'll wait in the lobby. At nine I'll come and fetch you and escort you to the place Vendôme."

Périer appears in the doorway. "Colonel Picquart? Our room is ready."

"*Our* room? You mean we are to share one?"

"I am afraid so."

I try to make light of this humiliating arrangement—"Your devotion to your duties really is exemplary, Monsieur Périer"—but that is when I realise that of course he is not an official of the Colonial Ministry at all; he is a secret policeman of the Sûreté.

The only time he lets me out of his sight is when I take a bath. Lying in the tub I listen to him moving around in the bedroom. Someone knocks on the outer door and he lets them in. I hear low male voices and I think how vulnerable I would be if two men were to enter quickly and grab my ankles. A simple case of drowning in the bath: it would be over in minutes with barely a mark to show.

Périer—if that is his name—calls through the door, "Your breakfast is here, Colonel."

I step out of the bath, dry myself and put on the sky-blue tunic and the red trousers with grey stripe that make up the uniform of the 4th Tunisian Rifles. In the mirror it seems to me that I cut an incongruous figure—the colours of North Africa in the winter of northern Europe. They have even dressed me up to look a motley fool. *I doubt you'll find a soldier in the whole of France who'll defend what you've done*. Well then. So be it.

I drink black coffee. I eat *tartine*. I translate another page of Dostoyevsky. *What makes a hero? Courage, strength, morality, withstanding adversity? Are these the traits that truly show and create a hero?* At nine, Mercier-Milon comes to collect me and we ride down in the lift to the lobby without exchanging a word. Outside on the pavement the pack of journalists surges towards us. "Damn it," says Mercier-Milon, "they must have followed us from the station."

"If only our soldiers were as resourceful."

"This isn't funny, Georges."

The same chorus of questions: "Dreyfus . . . ? Esterhazy . . . ? Search . . . ? Veiled lady . . . ?"

Mercier-Milon pushes them out of the way and opens the door to our carriage. "Jackals!" he mutters.

Over my shoulder I glimpse some of the reporters jumping in taxis to follow us. Our journey is short, barely half a kilometre. We arrive to find a dozen more already lying in wait in the corner of the place Vendôme. They block the huge, worm-eaten old door that leads to the headquarters of the military governor of Paris. Only when Mercier-Milon draws his sword and they hear the scrape of steel do they fall back and let us pass. We enter a chilly vaulted chamber, like the nave of an abandoned church, and climb a stair-case lined with plaster statues. In this quasi-religious house I perceive that I have become something beyond a mere dangerous nuisance to my masters: I am a heretic to the faith. We sit in silence in a waiting room for a quarter of an hour until Pellieux's aide comes to fetch me. As I stand to go, Mercier-Milon's expression is one of pity mixed with a kind of dread. He says, very quietly, "Good luck, Georges."

I know Pellieux by reputation only as a monarchist and a strict Catholic. I suspect that he despises me on sight. In response to my salute he simply points to a chair where I may sit. He is in his middle fifties, handsome, vain: his dark hair, which matches the blackness of his tunic, is brushed back carefully into a severe widow's peak; his moustaches are full and splendid. He presides at a table flanked by a major and a captain whom he does not introduce; a uniformed secretary sits at a separate desk to take notes.

Pellieux says, "The purpose of this inquiry, Colonel, is to estab-lish the facts regarding your investigation of Major Esterhazy. To that end I have already interviewed Major Esterhazy himself, Mon-sieur Mathieu Dreyfus, and Senator Auguste Scheurer-Kestner and Maître Louis Leblois. At the end of my inquiry I will recommend to the minister what, if any, disciplinary action needs to be taken. Do you understand?"

"Yes, General." Now I know why they have taken such pains to prevent me speaking to anyone: they have already interviewed Louis and they don't want me to know how much he has told them.

"Very well, let us begin at the beginning." Pellieux's voice is cold and precise. "When did Major Esterhazy first come to your attention?"

"When the Statistical Section intercepted a *petit bleu* addressed to him from the German Embassy."

"And this was when?"

"In the spring of last year."

"Be more precise."

"I'm not sure of the precise date."

"You told General Gonse that it was in 'late April.'"

"Then that is when it must have been."

"No, in fact it was in early March."

I hesitate. "Was it?"

"Come, Colonel. You know perfectly well it was in March. Major Henry was on compassionate leave at the bedside of his dying mother. He remembers the date. He returned to Paris on a flying visit, met Agent Auguste and received a consignment of documents, which he then handed over to you. So why did you falsify the date in your report?"

The aggression of his manner and the detail of his research catch me off guard. All I can remember is that by the time I came to submit my report I had been investigating Esterhazy for nearly six months without Gonse's knowledge: an act of insubordination which I thought I might make slightly more palatable by pretending it was only four. At the time the lie didn't seem important—it *isn't* important—but suddenly now in this room, under the hostile eye of this Grand Inquisitor, it looks inexplicably suspicious.

Pellieux says sarcastically, "Take all the time you need, Colonel."

After a long pause I reply, "I must have been confused about the dates."

"'Confused about the dates'?" Pellieux turns mockingly to his aides. "But I thought you were supposed to be a soldier of scientific precision, Colonel—part of the modern-thinking generation that would replace such reactionary old fossils as me!"

"I'm afraid even scientists occasionally make mistakes, General. But in the end the date is of no significance."

"On the contrary, dates are always significant. Treason itself is mostly a question of dates, as the saying has it. First you claim Major

Esterhazy only came to your attention in April. Now we have established it was at least March. But there is evidence in your file on Esterhazy indicating it was even earlier."

He passes the captain a newspaper cutting. The captain dutifully comes round from behind the table and hands it to me. It is an announcement of the death of the marquis de Nettancourt, Esterhazy's father-in-law, dated 6 January 1896.

"I've never seen this before."

Pellieux affects astonishment. "Well then, where did it come from?"

"I presume it must have been added to the file after I left."

"But you would agree at first glance that this suggests you were taking an interest in Esterhazy two months before the arrival of the *petit bleu?*"

"At first glance, yes. I think that may be the reason why someone put it there."

Pellieux makes a note. "Go back to the *petit bleu*. Describe its arrival."

"Major Henry brought it in as part of a delivery late one afternoon."

"In what form was this delivery?"

"The material always arrived in small, cone-shaped brown paper sacks. This particular cone was bulkier than usual, because Henry had missed a meeting with our agent due to his mother's illness."

"Did you examine the contents with him?"

"No, as I mentioned earlier, he had a train to catch. I put it straight in my safe and gave it to Captain Lauth the following morning."

"Is it possible that someone could have interfered with the cone between your being handed it by Henry and you giving it to Lauth?"

"No, it was locked up."

"But *you* could have interfered with it. In fact *you* could have added to it the fragments of the *petit bleu*."

I feel my face turning red. "That is an outrageous accusation."

"Your outrage is irrelevant. Answer the question."

"Very well, the answer is yes. Yes, I could, theoretically, have added the *petit bleu* to the consignment. But I did not."

"Is this the *petit bleu?*" Pellieux holds it up. "Do you recognise it?"

The light in the chamber is dim. I have to lean forward and half rise from my seat to make it out. It looks more worn than I remember it: I assume it must have been handled many times over the past year. "Yes. That looks like it."

"Do you realise that under a microscope it is possible to see that the original address has been scratched out and that of Major Esterhazy written over it? And also that chemical analysis has revealed that the ink on the back of the telegram card is different to that on the front? One is iron gall ink while the other contains an ingredient found in the trees of Campeche."

I jerk my head back slightly in surprise. "Then it's been tampered with."

"Indeed it has. It is a forgery."

"No, General—it has been tampered with since I left Paris. When I was still in the section I swear that was a genuine document—I must have held it in my hands a hundred times. May I examine it more closely? Perhaps it is slightly different . . ."

"No, you have already identified it. I don't want it damaged any further. The *petit bleu* is a fake. And I suggest that the individual most likely to have perpetrated the forgery is you."

"With respect, General, that is a preposterous allegation."

"Is it? Then why did you ask Captain Lauth for his assistance in making the *petit bleu* look more genuine?"

"I did not."

"You did. You ordered him to have it franked by the postal authorities, so that it would look as if it had actually been delivered—deny it if you dare!"

The lies and accusations are flying at me so fast I am finding it difficult to keep track. I grip the armrests of my chair and reply as calmly as I can, "I asked Lauth if he could photograph the *petit bleu* in such a way that it would appear to be a whole document rather than one that had been torn up—exactly the technique he used earlier with the *bordereau*. And my motive was the same: to have a version that could be circulated within the ministry without compromising our source. Lauth pointed out, correctly, that the address side had not been franked, therefore anyone looking at it would deduce that it must have been intercepted before it was posted. That was when

I mused on the possibility of getting it franked. But it was no more than that and the idea was dropped."

"Captain Lauth gives a different version."

"Perhaps he does. But why would I go to such lengths to falsely implicate a man I had never even met?"

"That is for you to tell us."

"The notion is absurd. I had no need to forge any evidence. The *bordereau* alone is proof of Esterhazy's guilt—and no one can suggest I altered that!"

"Ah yes, the *bordereau*," says Pellieux, sorting through his papers. "Thank you for bringing that up. Did you, either directly or indirectly, pass a facsimile of the *bordereau* to *Le Matin* in November last year?"

"No, General."

"Did you, directly or indirectly, pass details of the so-called secret dossier to *L'Éclair* that same September?"

"I did not."

"Have you passed information, directly or indirectly, to Senator Scheurer-Kestner?"

The question is inevitable; so is my answer. "Yes, I have, indirectly."

"And the intermediary was your lawyer, Maître Leblois?"

"Yes."

"And you knew when you gave this information to Leblois that it would be passed to the senator?"

"I wanted the facts placed in the hands of a responsible person who could raise the matter confidentially with the government. I never intended the details to reach the press."

"Never mind what you intended, Colonel. The fact is, you went behind the backs of your superior officers."

"Only when it became clear that I had no alternative—that my superiors would not fully investigate this whole affair."

"You showed Maître Leblois various letters sent to you by General Gonse?"

"Yes."

"Just as last year you showed Maître Leblois the secret dossier, the existence of which he then leaked to *L'Éclair*?"

"No."

"But there is a witness who saw you showing the secret file to Leblois."

"I showed him one file only—it was not secret. It related to carrier pigeons, of all things. Major Henry witnessed that."

"*Colonel* Henry," Pellieux corrects me. "He has just been promoted. And I am not interested in pigeons but in the secret dossier about Dreyfus. You showed it to your lawyer last September, who then revealed it either to the Dreyfus family or to *L'Éclair* in order to embarrass the army. That is your modus operandi."

"I deny that absolutely."

"Who is Blanche?"

Once again the sudden switch in his angle of attack catches me off balance. I say slowly, "The only Blanche I know is Mademoiselle Blanche de Comminges, the sister of the comte de Comminges."

"She is a friend of yours?"

"Yes."

"An intimate friend?"

"I have known her a long time, if that is what you mean. She has a musical salon attended by a number of officers."

"She sent you this telegram in Tunisia: *We have proof that the bleu was forged by Georges. Blanche.* What are we to make of that?"

"I received a telegram with that wording. But I am sure it was not from her."

"Why?"

"Because she knows nothing of the secret details of the Dreyfus case nor of my involvement in it."

"Even though she has gone around Paris quite openly, I understand, for several years now, telling people of her conviction that Dreyfus is innocent?"

"She has her opinion. That has nothing to do with me."

"This salon of hers—does it include many Jews?"

"A few perhaps—among the musicians."

Pellieux makes another note, as if I have just conceded something highly significant. He searches through his file. "Here is another coded telegram sent to you in Tunisia: *Stop the Demigod. Everything is discovered. Extremely serious matter. Speranza.* Who is Speranza?"

"I have no idea."

"And yet this person wrote to you a year ago, shortly after you left the Statistical Section."

"No."

"Yes, they did. I have the letter here." Pellieux gives it to the captain, who once again walks round to hand it to me:

I am leaving the house. Our friends are dismayed. Your unfortunate departure has upset everything. Hasten your return, hurry! As the holiday time is very favourable for the cause, we are counting on you for the 20th. She is ready but cannot and will not act until she has talked to you. Once the Demigod has spoken, we will act.

Speranza

Pellieux stares at me. "What do you say to that?"

"I don't know what to say. I've never seen it before."

"No, you wouldn't have done. It was intercepted by the Statistical Section last December and a decision was taken not to forward it to you, due to the highly suspicious nature of the language. But still your position remains that none of it means anything to you?"

"Yes."

"Then what do you make of this, which *was* allowed to be delivered to you after you left Paris but before you went to Tunisia?"

Most honourable sir,

I would never have believed it had I not seen it with my own eyes. As of today, the masterpiece is finished: we are to call it Cagliostro Robert Houdin. The comtesse speaks of you all the time and tells me every day that the Demigod asks when it will be possible to see the Good God.

Her devoted servant who kisses your hand.

J

The copy has been written out by Lauth and is stamped "Secret," with a serial number appended by Gribelin. I remember reading the original when I was stuck in some godforsaken garrison town last winter: in my drab quarters it was like opening a bouquet from the boulevard Saint-Germain. I say, "It's from an agent of mine, Germain Ducasse. He's reporting on the closing-down of an operation I was running against the German Embassy. When he writes 'the masterpiece is finished' he means that the apartment we were renting has been cleared out successfully. 'Robert Houdin' is the cover name of a police agent, Jean-Alfred Desvernine, who was working for me on the investigation of Esterhazy."

"Ah," says Pellieux, as if he has caught me out. "So 'J' is a man?"

"Yes."

"And yet he 'kisses your hand'?"

I think how amused Ducasse would be if he could see the general's expression of disgusted disbelief.

Pellieux says, "Don't smirk, Colonel!"

"I'm sorry, General. He is an affected young fellow, I admit, and quite silly in some respects. But he did his work well, and is perfectly trustworthy. It's merely a joke."

"And 'Cagliostro'?"

"Another joke."

"Pardon me: I'm a simple family man, Colonel. I don't understand these 'jokes.'"

"Cagliostro was an Italian occultist—Strauss wrote an operetta about him, *Cagliostro in Vienna*—and a man less likely to be susceptible to the occult than Desvernine you could not hope to find. Therein lies the irony. It's all very harmless, General, I assure you. But obviously suspicious minds in the Statistical Section have used it to build a case against me. I do hope that at some point your inquiry will investigate these other forgeries which are obviously designed to blacken my name."

"On the contrary, I think you have blackened your own name, Colonel, by associating in the first place with this circle of neurotic homosexuals and table-turners! So I take it the 'comtesse' referred to must be Mademoiselle Blanche de Comminges?"

"Yes. She is not actually a comtesse but she can sometimes behave like one."

"And the 'Demigod' and the 'Good God'?"

"They are nicknames invented by Mademoiselle de Comminges. A mutual friend of ours, Captain Lallemand, is the Demigod; I'm afraid to say that I am the Good God."

Pellieux regards me contemptuously: to my other sins can now be added blasphemy. "And why is Captain Lallemand the Demigod?"

"Because of his fondness for Wagner."

"And is he also part of a Jewish circle?"

"Wagner? I very much doubt it."

It is a mistake, of course. One should never attempt wit in these circumstances. I know it the moment the words leave my lips. The major and the captain and even the secretary smile. But Pellieux's face sets rigid. "There is nothing in the least amusing about the situation you are in, Colonel. These letters and telegrams are highly incriminating." He flicks back to the beginning of his file. "Now, let us go over the discrepancies in your testimony once again. Why did you falsely claim to have taken possession of the *petit bleu* at the end of April last year when in fact it was pieced together at the beginning of March . . . ?"

The interrogation continues throughout the day—the same questions, again and again, designed to catch me in a lie. I am familiar with the technique; Pellieux is remorseless in deploying it. At the end of the afternoon session he consults an antique silver pocket watch and says, "We will resume tomorrow morning. In the meantime, Colonel, you are not to communicate with anyone, or to leave, for so much as a minute, the supervision of the officers appointed by this inquiry."

I stand and salute.

Outside it is dusk. In the waiting room Mercier-Milon pulls back the edge of the curtain and peers down at the crowd of reporters in the place Vendôme. He says, "We should try to leave by a different route." We go downstairs to the cellar and cross a deserted kitchen to a rear door that opens on to a yard. It has started raining. In the gloom the piles of rubbish seem to move and rustle like living things, and as we pick our way past them I see the wet brown backs of rats slithering among the rotted food. Mercier-Milon finds a gate in the wall that leads to the garden at the back of the Ministry of Justice. We pass across a muddy lawn and out on to the rue Cambon. A couple of journalists, posted as pickets, see us emerge through the wall next to a streetlamp and we have to sprint two hundred metres to the taxi rank in the rue Saint-Honoré, where we seize the only cab. We pull away just as our pursuers catch up with us.

The jolt of the horse throws us back in our seats, damp and breathless, and Mercier-Milon laughs. "My God, Georges, we're certainly not young men anymore!" He pulls out a large white cotton handkerchief and mops his face and grins at me. For a moment he seems to forget that I am in his custody. He opens the window and shouts up to the driver, "Hôtel Terminus!" then slams it shut.

He spends most of the short journey with his arms folded, staring out at the street. It is only as we pull into the rue Saint-Lazare that he suddenly says, without turning round, "You know, it's funny, General Pellieux asked me yesterday why I'd testified in Dreyfus's defence."

"What did you tell him?"

"I said one could only speak as one found—that he was always a good soldier and loyal as far as I was concerned."

"And what did he say to that?"

"He said he'd tried to keep an open mind on the subject himself. But last week when he was asked to lead this inquiry he was shown evidence at the ministry by General Gonse that absolutely proved beyond question that Dreyfus was a traitor. And from that moment on he's had no doubt that your allegations about Esterhazy are false—the only question now as far as he's concerned is whether you've been duped by a syndicate of Jews or paid by them." He turns to look at me at last. "I thought you ought to know."

At that moment the taxi pulls up, and even before the door is opened we are surrounded by reporters. Mercier-Milon clambers out and descends into the melee, using his elbows to clear a path. I follow, and once I reach the lobby the concierge puts his arms across the entrance to prevent anyone following us in. On the marble floor, beneath the lurid diamanté chandeliers, Périer is already waiting to rush me straight upstairs. I turn to thank Mercier-Milon for his warning, but he has already gone.

I am not allowed to eat downstairs in public. I don't protest: I have no appetite in any case. Dinner is brought up to our room and I push a piece of veal around my plate with my fork until I give up in disgust. Just after nine, a bellboy delivers a letter that has been left for me at reception. On the envelope I recognise Louis's writing. I'd like to read what he has to say. I suspect he wants to warn me of something before tomorrow's hearing. But I don't want to give Pellieux any excuse to bring fresh disciplinary charges against me. So I burn it, unopened, in the grate in front of Périer.

That night I lie awake listening to Périer snoring in the other bed and try to calculate the weakness of my position. It seems to me precarious whichever way I look at it. I have been delivered to my enemies trussed hand and foot by the tiny threads of a hundred lies and innuendos carefully spun out over the past year. Most people will be only too happy to believe I work for a Jewish syndicate. And as long as the army is allowed to investigate its own misdeeds I see no hope of escape. Henry and Gonse can simply invent whatever "absolute proof" they require and then show it privately to the likes of Pellieux, safe in the knowledge that such loyal staff officers will always do what is expected of them.

Outside in the rue Saint-Lazare even at midnight there is a greater profusion of motorcars than I have ever heard before. The sound of pneumatic tyres on wet asphalt is new to me, like a continual tearing of paper, and eventually it lulls me to sleep.

The next morning when he comes to pick me up, Mercier-Milon has reverted to his former brusque silence. His only comment is to tell me to bring my suitcase: I will not be returning to the hotel.

In the place Vendôme, in the room set aside for the inquiry, Pellieux and the others are in exactly the same positions as when I left them, as if they have spent the night under dust sheets, and the general resumes where he left off as though there had been no interruption. "Tell us once again, if you would, the circumstances in which you came into possession of the *petit bleu* . . ."

This goes on for another hour or so, and then he says, without any change of tone, "Madame Monnier—how much of your work have you disclosed to her?"

My throat tightens immediately. "Madame Monnier?"

"Yes, the wife of Monsieur Philippe Monnier of the Foreign Ministry. What have you told her?"

I say in a strained voice, "General—please—I insist—she has nothing to do with this."

"That is not for you to determine." He turns to the secretary. "Colonel Picquart's documents, please." And while the secretary opens his dispatch box, Pellieux switches his attention back to me. "You will probably not be aware of the fact, Colonel, because you were at sea, but an official search was carried out of your apartment on Tuesday, following an allegation by Major Esterhazy that you were keeping official papers there."

For a moment I can only gape at him. "No, I most certainly was not aware of it, General. And if I had been I would have protested strongly. Who authorised this raid?"

"I did, at the request of Colonel Henry. Major Esterhazy claims to have received information from a woman whose name he does not know but who swears that she is an acquaintance of yours. This woman, whom he has only seen heavily veiled, says that you have been keeping secret documents relating to his case at your private address."

It is such an absurd idea, Pauline and Esterhazy together, that I find myself emitting a gasp of laughter. But then the secretary places several bundles of letters in front of Pellieux and I recognise them as my private correspondence: old letters from my mother and my dead brother; correspondence from my family and friends; business letters and love letters; invitations and telegrams kept for their sentimental value. "This is an outrage!"

"Come now, Colonel—why such sensitivity? I don't believe we have taken any action against you that you haven't taken against Major Esterhazy. Now," he says, picking up a collection of Pauline's letters tied with a blue silk ribbon, "it's apparent from the nature of her letters to you that you have an intimate relationship with Madame Monnier—one that I assume her husband is not aware of?"

My face is burning now. "I absolutely refuse to answer that question."

"On what grounds?"

"On the grounds that my relationship with Madame Monnier has no conceivable relevance to this inquiry."

"Surely it does if you disclosed secret information to her, or if she is the so-called veiled lady in contact with Major Esterhazy? And most certainly it does if you have left yourself open to blackmail as a result of it."

"But none of those things is true!" Now I know what Louis was trying to warn me about in his letter the previous evening. "Tell me, General, am I at any point going to be asked about the central facts of this business?"

"There is no need to be impertinent, Colonel."

"For example, about the fact that Esterhazy plainly wrote the *bordereau*—that even the government's main expert concedes his handwriting is a perfect match?"

"That is outside the scope of this inquiry."

"Or the use of falsified material in the dossier used to convict Dreyfus?"

"The Dreyfus case is res judicata."

"Or the conspiracy within the General Staff to keep me in North Africa—or even to send me to my death—to prevent my exposing what had happened?"

"That is outside the scope of this inquiry."

"Then if you will forgive me, General, I believe your inquiry to be a sham and that your conclusions were written before I even started to give my evidence, and I hereby withdraw my cooperation from this process."

And with that I stand, salute, turn on my heel and stride out of the room. I expect to hear Pellieux bellowing at me to stay where I am. But he says nothing, whether because he is too surprised to react or because he feels he has made his point and is happy to see the back of me I do not know and nor, at that moment, do I care. I retrieve my suitcase from the empty waiting room and descend the stairs. I pass a few officers, who give me sidelong looks. None tries to stop me. I go out through the cathedral-like door and into the place Vendôme. My exit is so unexpected that most of the journalists don't notice me hurrying past them and I am almost at the corner before I hear them shouting—"There he goes!"—and then the sound of their feet running over the cobbles after me. I put my head down and increase my pace, ignoring their questions. A couple scramble to get ahead of me and try to block my path, but I push them aside. On the rue de Rivoli I spot a taxi and flag it down. The reporters fan out along the street searching for cabs to follow me; one athletic fellow even tries to keep up with me on foot. But the driver cracks his whip, and when I look back he has given up the chase.

The rue Yvon-Villarceau runs north to south between the rue Copernic and the rue Boissière. Directly opposite my apartment building, at the northern end, the foundations are being sunk for a new block. As we pass the entrance I scan the street for reporters and police, but all I can see are workmen. I tell the driver to pull up round the corner, then pay the fare and walk back.

The double doors are glazed and barred. I cup my hands and peer through the dusty glass into the empty vestibule. At my feet, mud and rubble have turned the cobblestones into a country lane; the smell of freshly dug earth seasons the cold rain. I feel like a visitor returning after a long interval to the scene of an earlier life. I open the door and am halfway to the stairs when I hear the familiar faint click of a latch. But whereas before the concierge would always scuttle from her lair to engage me in conversation, now she keeps her distance, watching me through a crack in her doorway. I pretend not to notice and mount the steps, carrying my suitcase up to the fourth floor. On the landing there is no sign of forced entry: she must have given the authorities her key.

The moment I open the door I am shocked by how thoroughly the place has been searched. The carpet has been rolled back. All my books have been removed from their shelves, shaken out and replaced in haphazard order; bookmarks litter the floor. The chest in which I keep my old letters has been forced and emptied; the drawers of the escritoire also forced; even my sheet music has been taken out of the piano stool and sifted for clues; the piano lid has been removed and propped against the wall. I switch on the desk lamp and pick up a photograph of my mother that has fallen to the floor; the glass is cracked. Suddenly I visualise Henry standing in this very spot—*Colonel* Henry, as I must now learn to call him—licking his clumsy butcher's fingers as he turns the pages of my correspondence, reading aloud some intimate endearment for the amusement of the men from the Sûreté.

The image is intolerable.

A faint sound comes from the other room—a creak, a breath, a groan. Slowly I draw my revolver. I take a couple of steps across the bare boards and cautiously push open the door. Curled up on the bed, looking up at me through eyes bruised and swollen by crying, still wearing her coat, her hair dishevelled, her face white, as if she has fainted or suffered an accident, is Pauline.

"They told Philippe," she says.

She has been here all night. She read in the papers that I'd been brought back to Paris so she came round at midnight assuming I'd be here. She stayed, waiting. She didn't know where else to go.

I kneel beside the bed, holding her hand. "What exactly has happened?"

"Philippe has thrown me out. He won't let me see the girls."

I squeeze her fingers, momentarily speechless. "Have you slept?"

"No."

"At least take off your coat, my darling."

I stand and pick my way through the damage in the drawing room. In the kitchen I heat a saucepan on the gas ring and make her a drink of cognac, hot water and honey, all the while struggling to comprehend what is happening. Their methods stagger me—the ruthlessness, the speed. When I take the glass through to her, she has undressed to her shift and got into bed and is lying half raised on the pillows with the sheet drawn tight around her neck. She looks at me warily.

"Here. Drink this."

"God, it's disgusting. What is it?"

"Cognac. The army cure for everything. Drink it."

I sit at the bottom of the bed and smoke a cigarette and wait until she is suffiently revived to start telling me what happened. On Friday afternoon she went out to tea with a friend: everything normal. When she returned home, Philippe was back from the office early. There was no sign of the girls. "He looked strange, mad . . . At that moment I guessed what had happened. I was almost sick with worry." She asked him calmly where they were. He said he had sent them away. "He said that I was not morally fit to be the mother of his children—that he wouldn't tell me where they were, not unless I told him the truth about my affair with you. I had no choice. I'm sorry."

"Are they safe?"

She nods, cupping the glass between her hands for warmth. "They're with his sister. But he won't let me see them." She starts to cry. "He says he won't let me have custody of them after the divorce."

"Well, that's nonsense. Don't worry. He can't do that. He'll calm down. He's just shocked and angry to have found out you've been having an affair."

"Oh, he knew about *that*," she says bitterly. "He's always suspected. He said he could tolerate it so long as no one else knew. It was being called in and told about it by his superiors—that's what he can't abide."

"And who told the Foreign Ministry, did he say?"

"The army."

"Unbelievable!"

"He said the army are convinced I'm this 'veiled lady' the papers keep talking about. He said it will destroy his career to be married to a woman mixed up in it all. He says the girls . . ." She starts to cry again.

"My God, what a mess!" I put my head in my hands. "I am so very sorry to have dragged you into this."

For a while neither of us says anything, and then, as ever, when faced with emotional turmoil, I try to take refuge in practicalities. "The first thing we need to do is find you a decent lawyer. I'm sure Louis will take it on, or at least he'll know someone good who can. You'll need a lawyer to deal with the army on your behalf, and to try to keep your name out of the papers. And to handle the divorce— Philippe *will* divorce you, you're sure of that?"

"Oh yes—if it's a question of his career, I have no doubt."

Even this I try to put in a good light. "Well then at least it will be in his interests to keep it quiet. And perhaps you can use that to negotiate custody of the children . . ." My voice trails off. I don't know what else to say, except to repeat: "I am so very sorry . . ."

She reaches out her arms to me. And so we cling to each other on my narrow bed, like survivors of a shipwreck, and that is when I vow to myself that I will have revenge.

19

A few days later, just before midnight, a note is pushed under my door. By the time I step outside to check the landing, whoever has brought it has gone. The message reads: 11, *rue de Grenelle*—*if you are sure*.

I hold it to the fire and watch as it catches light, then drop it in the grate. Later I take the poker and crush the cinders to powder. If my maid is an informant, as I strongly suspect, it really would be too rich a joke if she were to take my torn-up litter to the Statistical Section for them to piece it back together. I have tried to convince Louis of the need for these precautions. "Use intermediaries wherever possible," I tell him. "Pay a stranger to deliver your messages. Trust nothing to the postal services. Avoid regular patterns of behaviour. Plant false trails if you can—go and see people whose views might be considered suspect, purely in order to confuse your watchers. Take indirect routes. Switch taxis. Remember their resources are extensive but not inexhaustible: we can run them pretty ragged if we try . . ."

When I go to bed, I am careful to keep my gun nearby.

The concierge brings me the morning's newspapers; she leaves them outside the door. I wait until she's gone before I fetch them in, and then I read them in bed, wearing my dressing gown. I have nothing else to do. As usual, the Dreyfus affair is the dominant story. It unfolds each day like a serial, peopled by an exotic cast of characters I scarcely recognise, including me (*the forty-three-year-old high-flying bachelor spymaster who has betrayed his former chiefs*). Among the latest plot twists are the letters Esterhazy sent to his then mistress, Madame de Boulancy, thirteen years ago, which have ended up in *Le Figaro* (*If this evening I were told that I am to be killed tomorrow like an Uhlan captain while running my sword through the French, I would certainly be perfectly happy. I wouldn't harm a little dog, but I would have a hundred thousand Frenchmen killed with pleasure*). Esterhazy has denounced these as Jewish forgeries and demanded, through his lawyer, a full court-martial to clear his name—a request to which the army has agreed. Émile Zola has written another of his passionate evocations of Dreyfus's plight: *a being cut off from everyone else, isolated not only by the ocean but by eleven guards who surround him night and day like a human wall . . .* Meanwhile, in the Chamber of Deputies there has been a full-scale debate on the affair, opened by the Prime Minister, who took shelter behind the ramparts of res judicata: "Let me be clear at the outset. There is no Dreyfus case! [*Applause*] There is not and cannot be a Dreyfus case! [*Prolonged applause*]" And for the avoidance of any doubt on the matter, General Billot, summoned to the tribune from the Ministry of War, has restated the government's position even more strongly: "Dreyfus has been rightly judged and unanimously condemned. On my soul and conscience, as a soldier and the head of the army, I hold that verdict truly delivered and Dreyfus guilty."

I lay aside the papers. Really, it is beyond hypocrisy; it is beyond even lying: it has become a psychosis.

My uniform hangs in my wardrobe, like the sloughed-off skin of some former life. I have not been formally discharged from the army. Technically I am on indefinite leave pending the verdict of Pellieux's inquiry and the minister's response. But I prefer to dress in civilian clothes in order not to draw attention to myself. Just before noon I put on a good stout overcoat and a bowler hat, take my umbrella from the stand and go out into the day.

Outwardly, I hope, I wear my usual mask of detachment, even irony, for there has never been a situation, however dire, even this one, that did not strike me as containing at least some element of the human comedy. But then I think of Pauline, of how when I discovered her on my bed she could only keep repeating the same phrase, over and over: "He won't let me see the girls . . ." She has given a deposition to Pellieux and has fled the press and gone to stay with her brother, a naval officer, and her sister-in-law near Toulon. Louis has agreed to handle her legal affairs. He has advised us not to have any contact until the divorce is finalised. We said goodbye in a rainstorm in the Bois de Bolougne, watched by an agent of the Sûreté. And it is for what they have done to her, more even than what they have done to Dreyfus, that I cannot forgive the General Staff. For the first time in my life I carry hatred inside me. It is an almost physical thing, like a concealed knife. Sometimes, when I am alone, I like to take it out and run my thumb along its cold, sharp blade.

My watcher is there as usual, on the opposite side of the street, leaning against the wooden fence surrounding the building site, smoking a cigarette; no doubt he will have a partner somewhere. This particular fellow I have registered before—scrawny, red-bearded, in a thick brown jacket and flat cap. He has given up even pretending to be anything other than a police agent. He flicks away his cigarette and slouches after me, about twenty paces behind, his hands in his pockets. Like a company commander in a bad mood I decide this sluggard could do with a thorough workout, and I quicken my speed until I am almost running—across the avenue Montaigne and along to the place de la Concorde and over the river to the boulevard Saint-Germain. I glance back. I am sweating despite the December cold, but I am not suffering half as much as my tail is, to judge by the look of him: his face is now as red as his hair.

What I need is a guardian of the peace, and I know exactly where to find one: close to the police commissary of Saint-Thomas-d'Aquin, patrolling on the corner of the boulevard Raspail. "Monsieur!" I call to him, drawing closer. "I am a colonel in the French army and this man is following me. I request that you arrest him and take us both to your commanding officer so that I can lay a formal complaint."

He moves with gratifying alacrity. "You mean this gentleman, Colonel?" He takes the elbow of the breathless agent.

The red-bearded man gasps, "Let . . . go of me, you . . . idiot!"

Seeing what is happening, the second Sûreté agent, this one dressed as a travelling salesman with a cardboard briefcase, breaks cover to cross the street and argue on behalf of his partner. He too is perspiring and frustrated and also makes an insulting remark about the general intelligence of uniformed policemen, at which the guardian of the peace loses his temper and within a minute they are both in custody.

Ten minutes later I am able to leave my name and address with the duty sergeant in the commissary and slip away unescorted.

The rue de Grenelle is only just round the corner. Number 11 is an imposing ancient property. I check along the street to make sure I am unobserved and then ring the bell. Almost at once the front door opens and a maid lets me in. Behind her, Louis waits anxiously in the hallway. He glances past my shoulder. "Are you being followed?"

"Not anymore." I give the maid my umbrella and hat. From behind a closed door comes a drone of male voices.

Louis helps me off with my coat. "Are you really sure you want to do this?"

"Where are they? Through there?"

I open the door myself. Six middle-aged men in morning coats standing around a blazing fire cease talking and turn to look at me: I am reminded of a group portrait by Fantin-Latour—*Homage to Delacroix*, perhaps. Louis says, "Gentlemen, this is Colonel Picquart."

There is a moment of silence and then one of the men—bald-headed and with a heavy drooping moustache, whom I recognise as Georges Clemenceau, the left-wing politician and editor of the radical newspaper *L'Aurore*—starts a round of clapping in which everyone joins. As Louis ushers me into the room, another man, dapper and attractive, calls out cheerfully, "Bravo Picquart! *Vive* Picquart!" and I recognise him too, from the surveillance photographs that used to cross my desk, as Mathieu Dreyfus. Indeed, as I go round shaking their hands, I find I know all these men by sight or by reputation: the publisher Georges Charpentier, whose house this is; the heavily bearded senator for the Seine, Arthur Ranc, the oldest man in the room; Joseph Reinach, a left-wing Jewish member of the Chamber of Deputies; and of course the pudgy figure in pince-nez to whom I am introduced last, Émile Zola.

———

A fine lunch is served in the dining room, but I spend too much time talking to eat very much. I tell my fellow guests that I need to say my piece and leave; that every minute we spend together increases the chances that our meeting will be discovered. "Monsieur Charpentier may believe his servants are above acting as informants for the Sûreté, but regrettably experience has taught me otherwise."

"It has certainly taught me," adds Mathieu Dreyfus.

I bow to him. "My apologies for that."

Opposite my place hangs a large portrait of Charpentier's wife and children by Renoir, and from time to time as I recount my story my gaze wanders up to it and I experience that strange feeling of disconnection that can sometimes afflict me when I talk to a group of people. I tell them that they ought to take a look at a certain Colonel Armand du Paty de Clam, who was the officer who first interrogated Dreyfus and whose lurid imagination has shaped so much of the affair. I describe the methods of interrogation he used, which amounted almost to torture. And then there was my predecessor, Colonel Sandherr, a sick man who became convinced, wrongly, that the spy must be on the General Staff. I say that the greatest public misconception is that what was handed over to the Germans was of crucial military importance, whereas really it was the merest trivia. Yet the treatment of Dreyfus—the secret trial, the degradation, the imprisonment on Devil's Island—has been so extreme the world has somehow become convinced that the very existence of France must have been at stake. "People say to one another, 'There has to be more to it than meets the eye,' when the truth is there is less. And the longer this scandal goes on, the more colossal and absurd becomes the discrepancy in size between the original crime and the monumental efforts to cover up the judicial error."

At the far end of the table I see Zola taking notes. I pause for a sip of wine. One of the children in the Renoir is sitting on a large dog. The pattern of the dog's fur echoes the colouring of Madame Charpentier's dress, and thus what seems a natural pose is actually artfully contrived.

I go on. Without revealing classified information, I tell them how I discovered the real traitor, Esterhazy, more than twenty months ago, and how Boisdeffre and especially Billot were initially supportive of my inquiry, but then how completely they changed their view when they realised it would mean reopening the Dreyfus case. I recount my exile to Tunisia, the General Staff's attempt to send me on a suicide mission, and the way they are using the forgeries and false testimony presented to General Pellieux's inquiry to frame me just as they framed Dreyfus. "We have arrived at the ludicrous position, gentlemen, of the army being so determined to keep an innocent man imprisoned that they are actively helping the guilty man to evade punishment, and are perfectly willing to put me out of the way too—for good, if necessary."

Zola says, "It's fantastical! The most astonishing story there has ever been."

Ranc says, "It makes one ashamed to be French."

Clemenceau, who is also taking notes, says, without looking up, "So who are the senior members of the military hierarchy most culpable, Colonel Picquart, in your opinion?"

"Among the senior ranks I would pick out the five generals: Mercier, Boisdeffre, Gonse, Billot and now Pellieux, who is running a cover-up disguised as an inquiry."

Mathieu Dreyfus interjects, "And what do you think will happen to you now, Colonel?"

I light a cigarette. "I would imagine," I say, twirling the match and extinguishing it with as much nonchalance as I can summon, "that after Esterhazy is formally cleared of all charges, they will discharge me from the army and put me in prison."

There is a muttering of disbelief around the table. Clemenceau says, "But surely even the General Staff wouldn't be that stupid?"

"I fear they've trapped themselves in a position where their logic doesn't leave them much alternative. If Esterhazy is innocent—as they are determined to find him, in order to avoid reopening the Dreyfus case—then it follows that the campaign against him is a wicked conspiracy; and as I am the one ultimately responsible for that campaign, I must be punished."

Reinach says, "So what is it you would like us to do, Colonel?"

"That is not really for me to say. I've told you as much as I can, without disclosing national secrets. I can't write an article or publish a book myself—I'm still subject to army discipline. What I do believe is that somehow this affair must be taken out of the jurisdiction of the military and elevated to a higher plane—the details need to be assembled into a coherent narrative, so that everything can be seen for the first time in its proper proportions." I nod to the Renoir and then glance at Zola. "Reality must be transformed into a work of art, if you will."

"It already is a work of art, Colonel," he replies. "All that is required is an angle of attack."

Before the hour is up, I stub out my cigarette and rise to my feet. "Excuse me, gentlemen, but I should be the first to leave. It would be better if everyone departed at intervals, perhaps of ten minutes? Please don't get up." I turn to Charpentier: "Is there a back way out of the house?"

"Yes," he says, "there's a garden gate. You can get down to it through the kitchen. I'll take you myself."

"I'll fetch your things," says Louis.

I make my way round the dining room shaking the hand of each man in turn. Mathieu covers mine with both of his. "My family and I cannot adequately express our gratitude to you, Colonel."

There is something proprietorial about his warmth which makes me feel awkward, even chilly.

"You have no reason to thank me," I reply. "I was simply obeying my conscience."

The street outside is clear and I take advantage of the fact that I have temporarily shaken off my police tail to walk quickly along the boulevard Saint-Germain to the de Comminges house. I give my card to the footman and am shown into the library while he goes upstairs to announce me. A minute later the door is flung open and Blanche rushes in and flings her arms around me.

"Darling Georges!" she cries. "Do you realise you're now the most famous person I know? We're all in the drawing room having tea. Come along right now—I want to show you off!"

She tries to pull me after her, but I resist. "Is Aimery in?"

"Yes, and he'll be thrilled to see you. Come upstairs. I insist." She tugs at my hand again. "We want to hear everything!"

"Blanche," I say gently, detaching her hand from my arm, "we need to talk in private, and I think perhaps Aimery should join us. Would you mind getting him?"

For the first time she sees that I am serious. She gives a nervous laugh. "Oh, Georges," she says, "this is too ominous!" But she goes and fetches her brother.

Aimery saunters in, as young-looking as ever, wearing a well-cut grey suit and carrying two cups of tea. "Hello, Georges. I suppose if you won't come to the samovar, the tea will have to come to you."

And so the three of us sit by the fire, and while Aimery sips his tea and Blanche smokes one of her brightly coloured Turkish cigarettes, I describe how her name has been used on a fake telegram, almost certainly dreamed up by du Paty, sent to me in Tunisia. Her eyes gleam. She seems to think it a great adventure. Aimery, though, scents the danger at once.

"Why would du Paty use Blanche's name?"

"Because she knows Germain Ducasse, and Ducasse worked for me on an intelligence operation against Esterhazy. And so it looks as though we're all part of this imaginary 'Jewish syndicate' that is working to free Dreyfus."

"It's utterly ridiculous," says Blanche through a mouthful of smoke. "No one will believe it for an instant."

Aimery asks, "Why use Blanche's name? I also know Ducasse. Why not use mine?" He sounds genuinely puzzled. He glances at me, and then at his sister. Neither of us can quite bring ourselves to meet his gaze. A few awkward seconds pass. Aimery is no fool. "Ah," he says quietly, nodding slowly, "I see."

"Oh, for heaven's sake," exclaims Blanche irritably, "you're worse than Father! What does it matter?"

Aimery, who is suddenly very tense and silent, folds his arms and stares hard at the carpet, leaving it to me to explain: "I'm afraid it does matter, Blanche, because you're bound to be questioned about the telegrams, and then it's certain to reach the newspapers, and there will be a scandal."

"Let there be—"

Aimery interrupts her furiously: "Just be quiet, Blanche—for once! It doesn't only concern you. It drags the whole family into the mess! Think of your mother. And don't forget I'm a serving officer!" He turns to me. "We'll need to talk to our lawyers."

"Of course."

"In the meantime, I think it would be better if you didn't come to this house or make any attempt to contact my sister."

Blanche appeals to him: "Aimery . . ."

I stand to leave. "I understand."

"I'm sorry, Georges," says Aimery. "That's just the way it has to be."

Christmas and the New Year pass, the former spent with the Gasts in Ville-d'Avray, the latter with Anna and Jules in the rue Cassette; Pauline stays in the south. I sell my Erard piano to a dealer for five thousand francs and send her the money.

Esterhazy's court-martial is fixed for Monday, 10 January 1898. I am summoned to appear as a witness; so is Louis. But on the Friday before the hearing, his father finally succumbs to his long illness and dies in Strasbourg; Louis is excused to go home to his family.

"I don't know what I should do," he says.

"My dear friend," I reply, "there is no doubt about it. Go and be with your family."

"But the trial . . . You'll be alone . . ."

"Frankly, it will make no difference to the outcome whether you are there or not. Go."

On Monday, in the predawn darkness, I rise early, don the pale blue tunic of the 4th Tunisian Rifles, pin on the ribbon of the Legion of Honour, and, trailed by a pair of plainclothes police agents, make the familiar journey across Paris to the military court building in the rue Cherche-Midi.

The day is hostile from the start: cold, grey, spitting rain. In the street between the prison and the courthouse a dozen gendarmes stand dripping in their caps and capes, but there are no crowds for them to control. I walk over the slippery cobbled forecourt into the same bleak ex-nunnery in which Dreyfus was tried more than three years ago. A captain of the Republican Guard shows me into a holding room for witnesses. I am the first to arrive. It is a small whitewashed chamber with a single barred window set above head height, a flagstone floor and hard wooden chairs ranged around the sides. A coal-burner in the corner barely suffices to take the edge off the chill. Above it is a picture of Christ with a glowing index finger raised in benediction.

A few minutes later the door opens and Lauth sticks his blond head around the corner. I see from his uniform he has been promoted to major. He takes one look at me and hastily withdraws. Five minutes later he comes back in with Gribelin and they go over to the corner furthest away from me. They don't look once in my direction. *Why are they here?* I wonder. Then two more of my former officers show up. The same procedure: straight past me and into the corner huddle. Du Paty marches through the door as if he expects a band to strike up a tune at his entrance, whereas Gonse sidles in, smoking his inevitable cigarette. All keep their backs to me except for Henry, who enters loudly, banging the door, and nods as he passes.

"You have a good colour, Colonel," he says cheerfully. "It must be all that African sunshine!"

"And yours must be all that cognac."

He roars with laughter and goes to sit with the others.

Gradually the room fills up with witnesses. My old friend Major Curé of the 74th Infantry Regiment carefully ignores me. I recognise the Vice President of the Senate, Auguste Scheurer-Kestner, who offers me his hand and murmurs quietly, "Well done." Mathieu Dreyfus enters with a slim, quiet, dark-haired young woman on his arm, dressed entirely in widow's black. She seems so young I assume she must be his daughter, but then he introduces her: "This is Madame Lucie Dreyfus, Alfred's wife. Lucie, this is Colonel Picquart." She gives me a faint smile of recognition but doesn't say anything, and nor do I. I feel uncomfortable, remembering those intimate, passionate letters of hers—*Live for me, I entreat you* . . . On the other side of the room du Paty eyes her keenly through his monocle and whispers something to Lauth: there was a story that he made a pass at her when he went to search her apartment after Dreyfus was arrested; I can believe it.

And so we sit, the military on one side of the room and I with the civilians, listening to the sounds of the proceedings getting under way above us: the thump of feet climbing the stairs, the cry of "Present arms!" as the judges arrive, and then a long interval of silence during which we wait for news. Eventually the clerk of the court appears and announces that the civil suits brought by the Dreyfus family have been rejected, and that therefore there will be no reconsideration of the original court-martial verdict, which stands. Also, the judges have voted by a majority that all the evidence given by military personnel will be heard in secret. Thus we have lost the battle before it even starts. With a practised stoicism, Lucie rises, expressionless, embraces Mathieu and leaves.

Another hour passes, during which presumably Esterhazy is being questioned, and then the clerk returns and calls, "Monsieur Mathieu Dreyfus!" As the original complainant against Esterhazy to the Minister of War, he has the privilege of going first. He does not return. Forty-five minutes later Scheurer-Kestner is called. He does not return either. In this way the room gradually empties of its various handwriting experts and officers until at last, in the middle of the afternoon, Gonse and the men of the Statistical Section are all summoned en bloc. They file out, every one of them avoiding eye contact, except for Gonse, who at the last minute pauses on the threshold to look back at me. I cannot fathom his expression. Is it hatred, pity, bafflement, regret, or all of these? Or is it that he just wants to carry one last image of me in his mind before I disappear for ever? He stares for several seconds, and then he turns on his heel and the door closes, leaving me alone.

For several hours I wait, occasionally standing to pace the room to try to keep myself warm. More than ever, I wish Louis were with me.

If I had any doubts of it before, I have none now: this is not Ester-hazy's court-martial; it is mine.

By the time the clerk comes to fetch me, it is dark. Upstairs the court has been cleared of all civilians apart from the various lawyers. There are no outsiders. The atmosphere, in contrast to the freezing waiting room, is warm from the closely packed male bodies, almost clubbable; there is a drifting fug of tobacco smoke. Gonse, Henry, Lauth and the other officers of the Statistical Section watch me as I approach the judges' bench. Behind General Luxer, who is the president of the court, sits Pellieux, of all people; and there to my left is Esterhazy, lounging back more or less as I remember him on the only other occasion I saw him, with his feet stretched out and his arms hanging loosely at his sides, as relaxed as if he were still in the nightclub in Rouen. I have time only for a sidelong glance, but I am struck again by the singularity of his appearance. The bald, oddly delicate round head cranes up to look at me; a glittering eye, like a falcon's, focuses on me for an instant and then flickers away. He appears bored.

Luxer says, "State your name."

"Marie-Georges Picquart."

"Place of birth?"

"Strasbourg."

"Age?"

"Forty-three."

"When did the defendant first come to your attention?"

"About nine months after I was appointed chief of the secret intelligence section of the General Staff . . ."

In all, I testify for perhaps four hours—an hour or so in the darkness of that late January afternoon and three hours the following morning. Pointless to relate it all: it is Pellieux redux. Indeed, Pellieux himself, in defiance of all the rules of procedure, seems to be in control of the court-martial. He leans forward to whisper advice to the president of the judges. He asks me hectoring questions. And whenever I try to bring up the names of Mercier, Boisdeffre and Billot, he interrupts me and orders me to be silent: "These distinguished officers have no relevance whatever to the case of Major Esterhazy!" His methods are so heavy-handed that halfway through the Tuesday morning session one of the judges asks the president of the court to intervene: "I see that Colonel Picquart is the true defendant here. I request that he be permitted to present all the explanations necessary to his defence."

Pellieux scowls and briefly falls silent, but Esterhazy's slippery young advocate, Maurice Tézenas, quickly takes over the attack: "Colonel Picquart, you have sought from the beginning to substitute my client for Dreyfus."

"That is not true."

"You forged the *petit bleu*."

"No."

"You conspired with your attorney, Maître Leblois, to blacken my client's name."

"No."

"You showed him the secret file relating to the conviction of Dreyfus as part of a plot to undermine public confidence in the original verdict."

"I did not."

"Come now, Colonel—several witnesses yesterday testified to this very court that they saw you do it!"

"That is impossible. What witnesses?"

"Colonel Henry, Major Lauth and Monsieur Gribelin."

I glance across the room to where they sit, impassive. "Well, they are mistaken."

Tézenas says, "I request that these officers step forward and confront this witness."

"Gentlemen, if you please." Luxer beckons to them to approach the bench. Esterhazy watches with an air of utter indifference, as if he is attending a particularly tedious play, the ending of which he already knows. Luxer says, "Colonel Henry, is there any doubt in your mind that you saw Colonel Picquart show documents from the so-called secret dossier to Maître Leblois?"

"No, General. I went into his office late one afternoon about a departmental matter and he had the file on his desk. I recognised it at once because it has the initial letter 'D' on it, which I wrote there myself. The colonel had it open and was showing a particular document, containing the words 'that lowlife D,' to his friend Monsieur Leblois. I saw it all, as plain as I see you now, General."

I look at him in amazement: how is it possible to lie so brazenly? He stares back at me, entirely unfazed.

You order me to shoot a man and I'll shoot him . . .

Luxer continues: "And so your testimony, Colonel Henry, is that you then went away and immediately described what you had seen to Major Lauth and Monsieur Gribelin?"

"I did. I was profoundly shocked by the whole thing."

"And the two of you both still swear this conversation took place?"

Lauth says fervently, "Yes, General."

"Absolutely, General," confirms Gribelin. He darts a glance at me. "I might add that I, too, saw Colonel Picquart show the file to his friend."

They have come to hate me, I realise, far more than they ever hated Dreyfus. I maintain my composure. "May I ask, Monsieur President, if Maître Leblois could come and give his opinion of this?"

Tézenas says, "I'm afraid, Monsieur President, that Maître Leblois is in Strasbourg."

"No," I say. "He returned late last night, accompanying the body of his father. He is waiting downstairs."

Tézenas shrugs. "Is he? My apologies: I did not know."

Louis is fetched. For a man in mourning, he is remarkably collected. Questioned about the meeting and the dossier, he confirms that there was no such meeting, no such file, "except for some nonsense about pigeons." He turns to the bench. "Could the court ask Colonel Henry when this incident is alleged to have occurred?"

Luxer gestures to Henry, who says, "Yes, it was in September '96."

"Well that is quite impossible," replies Louis, "because my father first fell ill in '96 and I was in Strasbourg the entire period from August to November of that year. I am quite sure of this—indeed I can prove it, because it was a condition of my visa that I had to report daily to the German authorities throughout my stay."

Luxer says, "Is it possible that you have made a mistake about the dates, Colonel Henry?"

Henry makes a pantomime of thinking this over, weighing his head from side to side. "Yes, I suppose it's possible. It could have been sooner than that. Or perhaps it could have been later."

"Or it could have been never at all," I say, "because I didn't take possession of the secret file until August, as Monsieur Gribelin can attest: it was he who retrieved it for me from Henry's desk. And in October, General Gonse over there"—I point to him—"took the file away from me again. So this entire incident simply could not have happened."

For the first time Henry stumbles, looks flustered. "Well, I'm not sure . . . I can only repeat what I saw . . ."

Pellieux comes to his rescue. "If I might make an observation, Monsieur President, at more than a year's distance it is quite difficult to give a precise date . . ."

Luxer agrees. The session moves on. At lunchtime I am allowed to stand down.

Esterhazy's lawyer takes five hours to make his closing speech. The hearing continues until eight o'clock at night. At one point during his advocate's monologue Esterhazy seems to nod off, the bald cranium tilting back. When at last the judges rise to consider their verdict, he is led away past me, and gives me a stiff salute containing more than a hint of mockery. Mathieu Dreyfus, who has returned for the verdict and is sitting next to me, mutters, "What a rogue!" I get up with Louis to stretch my legs. I assume we will have several hours to wait. But less than five minutes later comes the cry of "Present arms!" and the doors reopen. The judges troop back in and the clerk reads out the verdict. "In the name of the people of France . . . the council declares unanimously . . . the accused is innocent . . . he leaves the court without a stain upon his honour . . ."

The rest of his words are lost in the volley of applause that cannonades around the stone walls. My brother officers stamp their feet. They clap. They cheer: *"Vive l'armée!" "Vive la France!"* and even "Death to the Jews!" The outcome was predetermined. I should not be shocked. And yet there are limits to how well the imagination can prepare one for disaster. As Mathieu and I make our way out of the courtroom, pursued by jeers and insults—"Death to the syndicate!" "Death to Picquart!"—I feel as if I have tumbled deep into some mineshaft from which it will be impossible to clamber back. All is darkness—indeed, Dreyfus is actually worse off than he was six months ago, for he has now been doubly condemned. It is impossible to imagine the army holding a third hearing.

Outside, beyond the murkily lit courtyard, a crowd of more than a thousand has gathered, despite the cold. They are clapping rhythmically and chanting their hero's name: "Es-ter-hazy! Es-ter-hazy!" All I want to do is get away. I walk towards the gate, but Louis and Mathieu restrain me. Louis says, "You mustn't go out there yet, Georges. Your picture has been in the papers. You'll be lynched."

At that moment Esterhazy comes out of the court building, escorted by his lawyer, Henry and du Paty and followed by an applauding retinue of black-uniformed soldiers. Esterhazy's face is transfigured, almost luminous with triumph. He wears a cape which he sweeps up onto his shoulder in a gesture of imperial magnificence, then steps out into the street. A terrific cheer goes up. Hands stretch out to pat his back. Someone shouts, "Hats off to the martyr of the Jews!"

Mathieu touches me on the arm. "Now we should go." He takes off his overcoat and helps me put it on over my distinctive tunic. With my head down and with him on one side of me and Louis on the other, I push my way out into the rue Cherche-Midi and turn in the opposite direction to Esterhazy, moving quickly along the wet pavement towards the distant traffic.

The next day is the funeral of Louis's father, Georges-Louis Leblois. A Lutheran pastor, a believer in scientific progress, a radical thinker who denied the divinity of Christ, the old man wished to be cremated. However, no such facilities exist in Strasbourg, therefore the ceremony has to take place in Paris at the new crematorium of Père-Lachaise. The silence of the immense cemetery, with its shaded alleys, and the grey city in the plain below reaching towards the blue

hills on the horizon make a profound impression on me. The mourn-
ers come up to me to commiserate on the previous day's verdict,
shaking my hand and speaking in low tones, so that it almost feels as
if I am the one who has died and I am attending my own obsequies.

While this is going on, I discover later, General Billot is signing
my arrest warrant, and when I return to my apartment I find a notification that I will be taken into custody the next day.

They come for me just before dawn. I am already dressed in civilian clothes, my suitcase packed. An elderly colonel, accompanied
by a private soldier, knocks on my door and shows me a copy of the
warrant from General Billot: *Colonel Picquart has been investigated for
a serious breach of professional duties. He has committed grave errors in
his service, contrary to army discipline. Therefore I have decided that he
is to be held under arrest in the fortress of Mont-Valérien, until further
orders.*

The colonel says, "Sorry to call so early, but we thought we'd try
to avoid these ghastly newspaper people. May I take your service
revolver, please?"

The manager of the building, Monsieur Reigneau, who lives several doors along the street, comes to see what all the noise is about.
I pass him with my escort on the stairs. Afterwards he reveals to *Le
Figaro* my parting words: "You see what is happening to me. But I am
quite calm. You will have read in the papers all that they say about
me. Continue to believe that I am an honest man."

Drawn up outside is a large military carriage harnessed to two
white horses. There has been a hard frost overnight. It is still dark.
A red lamp from the building works opposite gleams faintly on the
frozen puddles. The private takes my suitcase and clambers up next
to the driver while the colonel politely opens the door and allows
me to go first into the carriage. Nobody is in the street to witness my
disgrace, apart from Reigneau. We turn left into the rue Copernic
and head towards the place Victor Hugo. There are a few early risers
queuing to buy newspapers on the corner of the roundabout, and
even more further along at the kiosk on the place de l'Étoile. As we
pass I catch a glimpse of a huge banner headline, "J'Accuse . . . !"
and I say to the colonel, "If a condemned man is allowed a final
request, do you think we might stop for a newspaper?"

"A *newspaper?*" The colonel looks at me as if I am mad. "Well, I suppose so, if you must."

He calls up to the driver to pull over. I get out and walk back towards the vendor. The private soldier trails behind me at a discreet distance; ahead the sky is just beginning to lighten above the avenue du Bois de Boulogne, silhouetting the bare tops of the trees. The paper everyone is queuing to buy is Clemenceau's *L'Aurore*, and the headline, spread across the top of all six columns, is:

J'Accuse . . . !

LETTER TO THE PRESIDENT OF THE REPUBLIC
BY ÉMILE ZOLA

I join the queue to buy a copy and walk slowly back towards the carriage. There is just enough light from the streetlamps for me to make it out. The piece takes up the entire front page, thousands of words of polemic, cast in the form of a letter to President Fauré (*Knowing your integrity, I am convinced that you are unaware of the truth . . .*). I skim it with increasing astonishment.

Can you believe that for the last year General Billot, Generals Gonse and Boisdeffre have known that Dreyfus is innocent, and they have kept this terrible knowledge to themselves? And these people sleep at night, and have wives and children they love!

Colonel Picquart carried out his duty as an honest man. He kept insisting to his superiors in the name of justice. He even begged them, telling them how impolitic it was to temporise in the face of the terrible storm that was brewing and that would break when the truth became known. But no! The crime had been committed and the General Staff could no longer admit to it. And so Colonel Picquart was sent away on official duty. He got sent further and further away until he landed in Tunisia, where they tried eventually to reward his courage with an assignment that would certainly have seen him massacred.

I come to a halt in the middle of the pavement.

And the astounding outcome of this appalling situation was that the one decent man involved, Colonel Picquart, who alone had done his duty, was to become the victim, the one who got ridiculed and punished. O justice, what horrible despair grips our hearts? It was even claimed that he himself was the forger, that he had fabricated the letter-telegram in order to destroy Esterhazy. Yes! We have before us the ignoble spectacle of men who are sunken in debts and crimes being hailed as innocent, whereas the honour of a man whose life is spotless is being vilely attacked. A society that sinks to that level has fallen into decay.

Behind me the soldier says, "We really ought to be going, Colonel, if you don't mind."
"Yes, of course. Just let me finish this."
I flick through to the end.

I accuse Colonel du Paty de Clam of being the diabolical creator of this miscarriage of justice . . .
   I accuse General Mercier of complicity, at least by mental weakness, in one of the greatest inequities of the century.
   I accuse General Billot of having held in his hands absolute proof of Dreyfus's innocence and concealing it, thereby making himself guilty of crimes against mankind and justice . . .
   I accuse General Boisdeffre and General Gonse of complicity in the same crime . . .
   I accuse General Pellieux of conducting a fraudulent inquiry . . .
   I accuse the three handwriting experts . . .
   I accuse the Ministry of War . . .
   I accuse the first court-martial of violating the law by convicting the accused on the basis of evidence that was kept secret, and I accuse the second court-martial of knowingly acquitting a guilty man in obedience to orders . . .

In making these accusations I am aware that I am making myself liable to a punishable offence of libel . . .

Let them dare to bring me before a court of law and investigate in the full light of day!

I am waiting.

With my deepest respect,
Monsieur President,
Émile Zola

I fold up the paper and clamber back into the carriage.

The elderly colonel says, "Anything interesting?" Without waiting for my reply he adds: "I didn't think so. There never is." He thumps the roof of the carriage. "Drive on!"

20

Mont-Valérien is a huge square-fronted fortress on the western edge of the city, part of the ring of defensive garrisons around Paris. I am escorted up a winding staircase to the third floor of a wing reserved for officers. I am the only prisoner. Day or night there is little to hear in winter except the wind moaning around the battlements. My door is kept locked at all times; a sentry guards the foot of the stairs. I have a small sitting room, a bedroom and a lavatory. The barred windows offer panoramic views across the Seine and the Bois de Boulogne to the Eiffel Tower, eight kilometres to the east.

If my enemies on the General Staff imagine that this represents some kind of hardship for me, they are mistaken. I have a bed and a chair, pen and paper, and plenty of books—Goethe, Heine, Ibsen. Proust kindly sends me his collected writings, *Les Plaisirs et les Jours*; my sister a new French–Russian dictionary. What more does a man want? I am imprisoned and I am liberated. The solitary burden of secrecy that I have carried all these months has been lifted.

Two days after my arrival the government is obliged to accept the challenge that Zola has thrown down to it, and lodges a charge against him of criminal libel. This will have to be heard not in secret, in some poky chamber controlled by the army, but in public in the Court of Assize inside the Palace of Justice. The case is pushed to the top of the waiting list so that the trial can start as soon as possible. The fortress commander refuses to allow visits from anyone who is not a serving officer, but even he can't prevent me from seeing my lawyer. Louis brings me the subpoena. I am summoned to give evidence on Friday, 11 February.

I study it. "What will happen if Zola is found guilty?"

We are sitting in the visitors' room: bars on the windows, two plain wooden chairs and a wooden table; a guard stands outside the door and pretends not to listen.

Louis says, "He'll go to prison for a year."

"It was a brave thing he did."

"It was a damned brave thing," agrees Louis. "I only wish he'd tempered his bravery with a little prudence. But he got carried away and couldn't resist putting in this sentence at the end about the Esterhazy court-martial—'I accuse them of knowingly acquitting a guilty man in obedience to orders'—and it's for that the government are going after him."

"Not for his accusations against Boisdeffre and the others?"

"No, all that they ignore. Their intention is to restrict the trial to this one tiny issue on which they can be certain of winning. It also means that anything to do with Dreyfus will be ruled inadmissible unless it relates strictly to the Esterhazy court-martial."

"So we'll lose again?"

"There are occasions when losing is a victory, so long as there is a fight."

In the Ministry of War they are clearly nervous about what I might say. A few days before the trial an old comrade of mine, Colonel Bailloud, comes out to Mont-Valérien to "try to talk some sense" into me. He waits until we are in the yard, where I am allowed to take exercise for two hours each day, before delivering his message.

"I am empowered to tell you," he says pompously, "on the highest authority, that if you show some discretion, your career will not suffer."

"If I keep my mouth shut, you mean?"

"'Discretion' was the word that was used."

My first response is to laugh. "This is from Gonse, I take it?"

"I prefer not to say."

"Well, you can tell him from me that I haven't forgotten I'm still a soldier and that I'll do my best to reconcile my duty of confidentiality with my obligations as a witness. Is that sufficient? Now clear off back to Paris, there's a good fellow, and let me walk in peace."

On the appointed day I am taken by military carriage to the Palace of Justice on the Île de la Cité, wearing my uniform as a Tunisian rifleman. I have given my word that I won't attempt to leave the precincts of the palace and will return to Mont-Valérien with my gaolers at the end of the day's session. As a quid pro quo I am allowed to walk into the building freely, without an escort. In the boulevard du Palais there is an anti-Semitic demonstration. "Death to the Jews!" "Death to the traitors!" "Yids to the water!" My face is recognised, perhaps from some of the vile caricatures that have appeared in *La Libre Parole* and similar rags, and a few ruffians break away from the rest and try to pursue me into the courtyard and up the steps of the palace, but they are stopped by the gendarmes. I can understand why Mathieu Dreyfus has announced he will not be attending the court.

The high vaulted hall of the palace, ablaze on this dull February day with electric light, is crowded and noisy like the concourse of some fantastical railway station: clerks and court messengers hurrying with legal documents, lawyers in their black robes gossiping and consulting with their clients, anxious plaintiffs and defendants, witnesses, gendarmes, reporters, army officers, poor people seeking shelter from the winter cold, ladies and gentlemen of high fashion who have managed to acquire a ticket to the Zola sensation—the whole of society throngs the Salle des Pas-Perdus and the endless Galerie des Prisonniers. Bells ring. Shouts and footsteps echo on the marble. I pass more or less unnoticed apart from the occasional nudge and stare. I find my way to the witness room and give my name to the usher. Half an hour later I am called.

First impressions of the Assize Court: size and grandeur, space, heavy wooden panelling and gleaming brass fixtures, the density of the crowd, the buzz of their conversation, the silence that falls as I walk up the aisle, my boots clicking on the parquet floor, through the little wooden gate in the railing that separates the judge and jury from the spectators, towards the semicircular bar of the witness stand in the well of the court.

"Will the witness state his name?"

"Marie-Georges Picquart."

"Place of residence?"

"Mont-Valérien."

That draws a laugh, and I have a moment to take my bearings: to

one side of me the box of twelve jurors, all of them ordinary trades-
men; high on his bench the big round-faced judge, Delegorgue, in
his scarlet robes; beneath him a dozen lawyers in their priestlike
black vestments, including the Advocate General, Van Cassel, leading for the government; seated at a table Zola, who gives me an
encouraging nod, as does his co-defendant, Perrenx, manager of
L'Aurore; alongside them their counsel—Fernand Labori for Zola,
Albert Clemenceau for Perrenx, and Georges Clemenceau, who has
somehow gained permission to sit with his brother, even though he
is not a lawyer; and behind me, like the congregation in a church,
the spectators, including a solid block of dark-uniformed officers,
among them Gonse, Pellieux, Henry, Lauth and Gribelin.

Labori rises. He is a young giant, tall and broad, blond-haired and
-bearded—a piratical figure: "the Viking," as he is known, famous for
his combative style. He says, "Will Colonel Picquart tell us what he
knows of the Esterhazy case, of the investigation that he made, and
of the circumstances that accompanied or followed his departure
from the Ministry of War?"

He sits.

I grip the wooden rail of the witness stand to stop my hands shaking and take a breath. "In the spring of 1896, the fragments of a
letter-telegram fell into my hands . . ."

I speak uninterruptedly for more than an hour, pausing occasionally
to take sips of water. I draw on my training as a lecturer at the war
school. I try to imagine I am teaching a particularly complicated lesson in topography. I don't use notes. Also I am determined to keep
my composure—to be polite, precise, unemotional—not to betray
any secrets, nor to indulge in personal attacks. I confine myself to
the overwhelming case against Esterhazy: the evidence of the *petit
bleu,* his immoral character, his need for money, his suspicious interest in artillery matters, the fact that his handwriting matches that
of the *bordereau.* I describe how I took my suspicions to my superiors
and ended up being sent to North Africa, and the machinations that
have been launched against me since. The packed courtroom listens
to me in complete silence. I can feel my words striking home. The

faces of the General Staff officers, when I happen to turn and catch them, look grimmer by the minute.

At the end, Labori questions me. "Does the witness think that these machinations were the work of Major Esterhazy alone, or does he think that Major Esterhazy had accomplices?"

I take my time replying. "I believe that he had accomplices."

"Accomplices inside the Ministry of War?"

"There certainly must have been one accomplice who was familiar with what was going on in the Ministry of War."

"Which in your opinion was the more damaging evidence against Major Esterhazy—the *bordereau* or the *petit bleu*?"

"The *bordereau*."

"Did you say as much to General Gonse?"

"I did."

"Then how could General Gonse instruct you to separate the Dreyfus case from the Esterhazy case?"

"I can only tell you what he said."

"But if Major Esterhazy is the author of the *bordereau*, the charge against Dreyfus falls?"

"Yes—that is why to me it never made sense to separate them."

The judge intervenes. "Do you remember sending for Maître Leblois to call on you at your office?"

"Yes."

"Do you remember the date?"

"He came in the spring of '96. I wanted his advice on the issue of carrier pigeons."

"Monsieur Gribelin," says the judge, "will you step forward? This is not your recollection, I believe?"

I half turn to watch Gribelin rise from his place among the General Staff. He comes to join me at the front of the court. He doesn't look in my direction.

"No, Monsieur President. One evening in October '96 I went into Colonel Picquart's office to get leave of absence. He was sitting at his desk with the carrier pigeon file to his right and the secret file to his left."

The judge looks at me. I say politely, "Monsieur Gribelin is mistaken. Either his memory fails him or he has confused the files."

Gribelin's body stiffens. "Believe what I say: I saw it."

I smile at him, determined to keep control of my temper. "But I say that you did not see it."

The judge interjects: "Colonel Picquart, did you once ask Monsieur Gribelin to stamp a letter?"

"To stamp a letter?"

"To stamp a letter, not with the date of its arrival, but with an earlier date?"

"No."

Gribelin says sarcastically, "Colonel, let me refresh your memory. You returned to your office one afternoon at two o'clock. You sent for me, and as you were taking off your overcoat, you said: 'Gribelin, could you get the post office to stamp a letter?'"

"I have no such recollection."

The judge says, "But surely you made the same request of Major Lauth?"

"Never." I shake my head. "Never, never."

"Major Lauth, would you come forward, please?"

Lauth rises from his place next to Henry and comes to join us. Staring straight ahead, as if on parade, he says, "Colonel Picquart asked me to remove all traces of tearing from the *petit bleu*. He said, 'Do you think we could get this stamped by the post office?' He also said that I should testify that I recognised the handwriting on the *petit bleu* as being that of a certain foreign gentleman. But I said to him, 'I never saw this handwriting before.'"

I look at the pair of them: clearly years of running spies has made facile liars of them both. I grit my teeth. "But this was a document torn into sixty pieces," I say, "fastened together by adhesive strips on the side where the address was written. How could a stamp have been put on that? It would have looked ridiculous."

Neither answers.

Labori is on his feet again. He hitches up his robes and says to Lauth, "You write in your deposition that Colonel Picquart could very easily have added the *petit bleu* to the cone of unprocessed intelligence material waiting in his safe—in other words, that it is a fabrication."

"That is true. He could."

"But you don't have any proof?"

"Nevertheless, I believe he did it."

"Colonel Picquart?"

"Major Lauth may believe it, but that doesn't make it true."

The judge says, "Let us go back to the incident with the secret file. Colonel Henry, would you approach the witness?"

Now Henry heaves himself to his feet and comes forward. Close up, I can see he is in an agitated state, flushed and sweating. All three of them seem to be under great strain. It is one thing to repeat their lies in a small and secret military court; it is quite another to do it here. They can never have expected this. He says, "It was in October, I think. I've never been able to fix the date precisely. All I know is that there was an open file in the room. The colonel was sitting down, and at his left sat Monsieur Leblois, and before them on the desk were several files, among them the secret file, which I had labelled with blue pencil. The envelope was open, and the document in question—the one with the words 'that lowlife D'—was outside it."

The judge says, "Colonel Picquart, what have you to say?"

"I repeat that I never had the file on my desk in the presence of Maître Leblois, either open or closed. In any case, it would have been impossible for this incident to have occurred as Colonel Henry describes it, because Maître Leblois can prove that he didn't return to Paris until November the seventh."

Henry blusters, "Well I say it was October. I've always said October, and I can't say anything else."

I ask the judge, "May I question Colonel Henry?" He gestures for me to go ahead, and I say to Henry, "Tell me, did you enter my office by the door opposite the desk, or by the little side door?"

After a slight hesitation he says, "By the main door."

"And about how far into the office did you come?"

"Not far. I can't say exactly whether it was just half a pace or a full one."

"But whichever it was, you must have been on the other side of my desk—that is, on the side opposite to where I was sitting. So how could you have seen the document?"

"I saw the document perfectly."

"But the writing on that document is very murky even if it's directly beneath your eyes. How could you possibly have made it out at such a distance?"

"Listen, Colonel," he replies, still trying to bluff his way out of it, "I know that document better than anyone and I would certainly recognise it at a distance of ten paces. There's no question about it. Let me say it bluntly once and for all. You want the light? You shall have it!" He points at me and turns to the jury. *"Colonel Picquart is lying!"*

He delivers the line in exactly the same theatrical tone and with the same gesture of accusation that he used at the Dreyfus court-martial: *The traitor is that man!* There is a gasp in the courtroom and in that instant I forget my vow to keep my cool. Henry has just called me a liar. I turn on him and raise my hand to silence him. "You do not have the right to say that! I shall demand satisfaction for that remark!"

There is noise all around me now—some applause, some jeers, as the realisation spreads that I have just challenged Henry to a duel. Henry looks at me in surprise. The judge gavels for order but I am barely listening. I can control myself no longer. All the frustrations of the past year and a half burst forth. "Gentlemen of the jury, you have seen here men like Colonel Henry, Major Lauth, and the keeper of the archives, Gribelin, make the most foul accusations against me. You've just heard Colonel Henry call me a liar. You've heard Major Lauth, without a shred of proof, suggest I invented the *petit bleu*. Well, gentlemen, do you want to know why this is happening? All the architects of the Dreyfus affair . . ."

"Colonel!" warns the judge.

". . . that is, Colonel Henry and Monsieur Gribelin, aided by Colonel du Paty de Clam, at the direction of General Gonse, are covering up the mistakes that were made under my predecessor, Colonel Sandherr. He was a sick man, already suffering from the paralysis that killed him, and they have gone on covering up for him ever since—perhaps out of some misplaced sense of loyalty, perhaps for the sake of the department: I don't know. And shall I tell you what my crime really was, in their eyes? It was to believe that there was a better way of defending our honour than blind obedience. And because of that, for months now, insults have been heaped upon me by newspapers that are paid for spreading slander and lies."

Zola cries out, "That's right!" The judge is gavelling me to stop. I press on.

"For months I have been in the most horrible situation that any officer can occupy—assailed in my honour, and unable to defend myself. And tomorrow perhaps I shall be thrown out of this army that I love, and to which I have given twenty-five years of my life. Well then—so be it! I still believe it was my duty to seek truth and justice. I believe that is the best way for any soldier to serve the army, and I also believe it was my duty as an honest man." I turn back to the judge and add quietly, "That is all I want to say."

Behind me there is some applause and a lot of jeering. A lone voice calls out, *"Vive Picquart!"*

That night, to avoid the mob, I have to be smuggled out of a side door on to the quai des Orfèvres. The sky above the palace is the colour of blood, flecked with drifting sparks, and when we turn the corner we can see that on the embankment on the other side of the Seine a crowd of several hundred are burning books—Zola's books, I discover afterwards, together with any journals they can lay their hands on that are sympathetic to Dreyfus. There is something pagan about the way the figures seem to dance around the flames above the darkness of the river. The gendarmes have to force a way through for our carriage. The horses shy; the driver has to fight to bring them under control. We cross the river and have barely travelled a hundred metres along the boulevard de Sébastapol when we hear the cascading sound of plate glass shattering and a mob comes running down the centre of the street. A man yells, "Down with the Jews!" Moments later we pass a shop with its windows smashed and paint daubed across a storefront sign that reads *Levy & Dreyfus.*

The next day when I return to the Palace of Justice, I am taken not to the Assize Court but to a different part of the building, and questioned by a magistrate, Paul Bertulus, about the forged messages I received in Tunisia. He is a big, handsome, charming man in his middle forties, appointed to the task by General Billot. He has an upturned moustache and a red carnation in his buttonhole and looks as if he would be more at home watching the racing at Longchamps than sitting here. I know him by reputation to be a conservative, a royalist and a friend of Henry's, which presumably is why he was given the task. Therefore I have the very lowest expectations of his diligence as an investigator. Instead, to my surprise, the more I describe what befell me in North Africa, the more obviously disturbed he becomes.

"So let me be clear, Colonel. You are quite certain that Mademoiselle Blanche de Comminges did not send you these telegrams?"

"Without doubt her name has only been dragged into this affair by Colonel du Paty."

"And why would he do that?"

I glance at the stenographer who is recording my evidence. "I would be willing to tell you that, Monsieur Bertulus, but only in confidence."

"That is not a regular procedure, Colonel."

"This is not a regular matter."

The magistrate thinks about it. "Very well," he says eventually. "However, you must understand that I may have to act on what you tell me, whether you want me to or not."

I have an instinct that I can trust him and so I agree, and after the stenographer has left the room I tell him the story of du Paty's liaison with Blanche, replete with the detail of the stolen letter allegedly returned by a woman wearing a veil. "That is why I say du Paty must be behind it in some way or other. His imagination is lurid but restricted. I am sure that he is the one who gave Esterhazy this device from romantic fiction about a 'veiled lady' who is somehow known to me."

"It's barely credible."

"I agree. But you can see how devastating it would be to Mademoiselle de Comminges's position in society if the full details ever became known."

"So you are suggesting Colonel du Paty is a direct link between Major Esterhazy's allegations and an officially sanctioned conspiracy against you involving forged messages?"

"I am."

"Is forgery a method commonly employed by the intelligence department?"

I have to suppress a smile at his naïvety. "There's an officer who works for the Sûreté—Jean-Alfred Desvernine. He once brought a forger to see me with the pseudonym of Lemercier-Picard. I suggest you have a word with Desvernine. He might be able to help."

Bertulus makes a note of the name and then calls the stenographer back into the room.

That afternoon, while I am still being deposed, there is a quick knock at the door and Louis puts his head into the room. He is sweating, out of breath. "Forgive my intrusion," he says to Bertulus, "but Colonel Picquart is needed urgently in court."

"I am afraid he is in the process of giving evidence to me."

"I appreciate that, and Maître Labori sends his apologies, but he really does need to call the colonel as a rebuttal witness."

"Well, if he must, he must."

As we hurry along the corridor Louis says, "General Pellieux is on the witness stand and trying to destroy your evidence. He is claiming that Esterhazy couldn't possibly have written the bordereau because he didn't have access to that level of intelligence."

"But that's nonsense," I say. "I dealt with all this yesterday. And anyway, what has it to do with Pellieux? Why isn't Gonse handling that part of their case, or Henry?"

"Haven't you noticed? They now have Pellieux doing everything. He's the only decent spokesman they've got, and he isn't tainted like the others." When we reach the doors of the courtroom he turns. "You do realise what this means, Georges, don't you?"

"What?"

"They're on the run. For the first time they're actually scared they're going to lose."

Inside the court, Pellieux is at the witness stand and clearly just reaching his peroration, addressing the jury directly as if he were an advocate. Louis and I stand at the back to listen. "Gentlemen," he cries, striking his breast, "I have a soldier's soul, and it revolts against the infamies heaped upon us! I say that it is criminal to try to take away from the army its confidence in its chiefs. What do you imagine will become of this army on the day of danger—nearer, perhaps, than you think? What do you imagine will be the conduct of the poor soldiers led by chiefs of whom they have heard such things said? It is to butchery that they would lead your sons, gentlemen of the jury! But Monsieur Zola will have won a new battle, he will write a new *Débâcle*,* he will spread the French language throughout the universe and throughout a Europe *from whose map France will have been wiped!*"

The section of the court occupied by army officers erupts in cheers. Pellieux holds up a finger to silence them. "One word more, gentlemen. We should have been glad if Dreyfus had been acquitted three years ago. It would have proved there was no traitor in the French army. But what the recent court-martial was not willing to accept was that an innocent man should be put in Dreyfus's place, whether Dreyfus was guilty or not."

He stands down to renewed acclamation from the General Staff. I move forward towards the well of the court, past Gonse and Henry, who are both on their feet applauding. Pellieux struts back to his seat like a prizefighter who has just won a bout, and I stand aside to let him pass. His eyes are shining. He doesn't even notice me until he draws level with me, and then he says out of the corner of his mouth as he goes by, "All yours."

In the event, much to Labori's irritation, the judge rules that it is too late in the day for me to be called and that my testimony will

---

* Zola's novel about the Franco-Prussian War of 1870.

have to wait until the next session. I return to Mont-Valérien and pass a sleepless night, listening to the wind and staring long into the small hours at the light on top of the Eiffel Tower, glowing like a red planet in the heavens above Paris.

The next morning, once I am standing at the front of the court, Labori says, "Yesterday General de Pellieux declared that Major Esterhazy couldn't have obtained the documents listed in the *bordereau*. What do you say in answer to that?"

I begin cautiously: "Some things I shall say perhaps will contradict what General de Pellieux has said, but I believe it my duty to state what I think. The central point is that the documents listed in the *bordereau* are much less important than people have been led to believe."

Once again I am careful to speak forensically. I point out that five sets of data were supposedly handed over with the *bordereau*. Yet four of them were not actual documents at all but simply "notes," which required no inside knowledge of the General Staff: notes on the hydraulic brake of the 120 millimetre cannon, on covering troops, on changes to artillery formations, and on the invasion of Madagascar. "Well, why only notes? Surely anyone who had anything serious to offer and not simply what he had picked up in conversation or seen in passing would have said, 'I send you a *copy* of such and such a document.' Now, there *was* a copy handed over: the fifth document— the firing manual—and surely it's not a coincidence that we know Major Esterhazy was able to get access to that, and indeed arranged to have it transcribed. But here again the author speaks of having it for only a limited amount of time, whereas an officer on the General Staff, such as Dreyfus, would have had unlimited access."

There is a large ornate clock to my right. I can hear it ticking in the silence of the court whenever I pause between my points, such is the intensity with which my audience is concentrating. And from time to time, out of the corner of my eye, I can see the doubts beginning to creep across the faces not just of the jurors but even of some of the General Staff officers. Pellieux, less confident now, keeps rising to interrupt me, venturing further and further out onto thin ice, until he makes a significant mistake. I am in the process of pointing out that the concluding phrase of the *bordereau*—"I am leaving on manoeuvres"—also indicates that its author was not working in the Ministry of War, because the General Staff's manoeuvres are in the autumn and the *bordereau* was supposedly written in April, when Pellieux comes forward again.

"But the *bordereau* wasn't written in April."

Before I can answer, Labori is on him in a flash. "Yes it was—or at least so it has always been said by the ministry."

"Not at all," insists Pellieux, although there is a tremor of uncertainty in his voice. "I appeal to General Gonse."

Gonse comes forward and says, "General Pellieux is correct: the *bordereau* must have been written around the month of August, since it contains a reference to a note on the invasion of Madagascar."

Now Labori pounces on Gonse. "So when exactly was the note on Madagascar drawn up by the General Staff?"

"In August."

"Wait." Labori searches through his bundle of documents and pulls out a sheet of paper. "But in the original indictment of Captain Dreyfus, which was read out at his trial, it is alleged that he copied the Madagascar note in February, when he was in the relevant department. I quote: 'Captain Dreyfus could easily have procured it then.' How do you reconcile those two dates?"

Gonse's mouth flaps open in dismay. He looks at Pellieux. "Well, the note was written in August. I don't actually know if there was a note in February . . ."

"Ah, now, gentlemen!" mocks Labori. "You see how important it is to be exact?"

It is such a trivial discrepancy, and yet one can feel the change of mood inside the courtroom like a drop in barometric pressure. Some people start to laugh, and Pellieux's face turns rigid and flushes with anger. He is a vain man, a proud man, and he has been made to look a fool. Worse, the whole of the government's case seems suddenly fragile. It has never been tested properly by an advocate of Labori's quality: under pressure it is starting to appear as fragile as matchwood.

Pellieux requests a brief recess. He stalks back to his seat. Quickly the officers of the General Staff, including Gonse and Henry, form a huddle around him. I can see his finger jabbing. Labori sees it too.

He frowns at me, spreads his hands and mouths, "What is this?" But all I can offer is a shrug: I have no idea what they are discussing.

Five minutes later, Pellieux marches back to the front of the court and indicates that he wishes to say something.

"Gentlemen of the jury, I have an observation to make concerning what has just taken place. Until now, we on our side have kept strictly within the bounds of legality. We have said nothing of the Dreyfus case, and I don't wish to speak of it now. But the defence has just read publicly a passage from the indictment which was supposed to stay behind closed doors. Well, as Colonel Henry says: they want the light; they shall have it! In November of '96 there came into the Ministry of War *absolute proof* of the guilt of Dreyfus. This proof I have seen. It is a document, the origin of which cannot be contested, and it contains roughly these words: 'A deputy is going to ask questions about the Dreyfus case. Never admit the relations that we had with that Jew.' Gentlemen, I make this declaration on my honour, and I appeal to General Boisdeffre to support my testimony."

There is a collective intake of breath around the court which then subsides into an exhalation of muttering as people turn to their neighbours to discuss what this means. Again Labori, baffled, stares across at me. It takes me a few seconds to work out that Pellieux must be referring to the letter supposedly retrieved from the German Embassy—the one that turned up so conveniently just before I was removed from Paris, and that Billot read out but wouldn't show me. I nod vigorously to Labori and make a grabbing gesture with my hands. Pellieux has made another blunder. He must seize this moment before it is lost.

Already Gonse, recognising the danger, is on his feet and hurrying forward. He calls out anxiously to the judge, "I ask for the floor." But Labori is too quick for him.

"Excuse me, but I have the floor, General. A matter of exceptional gravity has just arisen. After such a statement, there can be no restriction of the debate. I point out to General Pellieux that no document can have any scientific value as proof until it has been discussed openly. Let General Pellieux explain himself without reserve and let the document be produced."

The judge asks, "General Gonse, what do you have to say?"

Gonse's voice is a high croak. He sounds as if he is being strangled. "I confirm the testimony of General Pellieux. He has taken the initiative, and he has done well. I would have done the same in his place." He rubs his hands nervously up and down the sides of his trousers. He looks utterly wretched. "The army doesn't fear the light. To save its honour, it doesn't fear at all to tell the truth. But prudence is a necessity, and I do not believe that proofs of this character, though they are indeed real and absolute, can be brought here and made public."

Pellieux says bluntly, "I ask that General Boisdeffre be sent for to confirm my words," and ignoring both the judge and the hapless Gonse he calls out to his aide-de-camp, standing in the aisle: "Major Delcassé, take a carriage and go for General de Boisdeffre at once."

During the recess, Labori comes over to where I am standing. He whispers, "What kind of document is he talking about?"

"I can't tell you—not in any detail. It would breach my oath of secrecy."

"You have to give me *something*, Colonel—the Chief of the General Staff is about to walk in."

I glance over to where Pellieux, Gonse and Henry are sitting, too absorbed in their own conversation to pay any attention to me. "I can tell you it's a pretty desperate tactic. I don't think Gonse and Henry are very happy at the situation they've been put in."

"What line of questioning do you suggest I take with Boisdeffre?"

"Ask him to read the document out in full. Ask whether they will allow it to be forensically examined. Ask him why they only seem to have discovered the 'absolute proof' of Dreyfus's guilt two years after they sent him to Devil's Island!"

Boisdeffre's arrival outside the courtroom is announced by a round of applause and cheering from the corridor. The door bangs open. Several orderly officers hurry in ahead of him and then the great man himself begins his slow progress from the rear of the chamber towards the bar of the court. It is the first time I have seen him for fifteen months. Tall and dignified, walking stiffly, buttoned up tightly in his black uniform, which contrasts sharply with the whiteness of his hair and moustache, he seems to have aged a great deal.

The judge says, "General, thank you for coming. An incident has occurred that we did not expect. Let me read to you the stenographic record of the testimony given by General Pellieux."

After he has finished, Boisdeffre nods gravely. "I shall be brief. I confirm General Pellieux's deposition in all points as exact and authentic. I have not a word more to say, not having the right." He turns to the jury. "And now, gentlemen, permit me, in conclusion, to say one thing to you. You are the jury; you are the nation. If the nation has no confidence in the commanders of its army, in those who are responsible for the national defence, they are ready to leave this heavy task to others; you have only to speak. I will not say a word more. Monsieur President, I ask your permission to withdraw."

The judge says, "You may withdraw, General. Bring in the next witness."

Boisdeffre turns and walks towards the exit to loud applause from all around the court. As he passes me, his gaze flickers for an instant across my face and a muscle twitches slightly in his cheek. Behind him, Labori is calling: "Pardon me, General, I have some questions to put to you."

The judge tells him to be quiet. "You do not have the floor, Maître Labori. The incident is closed."

His mission accomplished, Boisdeffre continues his steady tread away from the witness stand. Several of the General Staff officers rise to follow him, buttoning their capes.

Labori is still trying to summon him back. "Pardon me, General Boisdeffre—"

"You do not have the floor." The judge hammers his gavel. "Bring in Major Esterhazy."

"But I have some questions to put to *this* witness . . ."

"It was an incident outside the scope of the trial. You do not have the floor."

"I demand the floor!"

It is too late. From the back of the courtroom comes the sound of a door closing—courteously, not slammed—and Boisdeffre's intervention is over.

After the drama of the last few minutes, the arrival of Esterhazy is an anticlimax. Labori and the Clemenceau brothers can be heard debating in loud whispers whether they should walk out of the trial in protest at Boisdeffre's extraordinary intervention. The jury—that collection of drapers, merchants and market gardeners—still look stunned at having been threatened by the Chief of the General Staff in person that if they find against the army, the entire High Command will take it as a vote of no confidence and will resign. As for me, I sit shifting in my seat in an agony of conscience as to what I should do next.

Esterhazy—trembling, his unnaturally large and protruding eyes darting constantly this way and that—begins by making an appeal to the jury. "I do not know whether you realise the abominable situation in which I am placed. A wretch, Monsieur Mathieu Dreyfus, without the shadow of a proof, has dared to accuse me of being the author of the crime for which his brother is being punished. Today, in contempt of all rights, in contempt of all the rules of justice, I am summoned before you, not as a witness, but as an accused. I protest with all my might against this treatment . . ."

I cannot bear to listen to him. Ostentatiously I stand and walk out of the court.

Esterhazy shouts after me, "During the last eighteen months there has been woven against me the most frightful conspiracy ever woven against any man! During that time I've suffered more than any one of my contemporaries has suffered in the whole of his life . . . !"

I close the door on him and search the corridors for Louis until I find him on a bench in the vestibule de Harlay staring at the floor.

He looks up, grim-faced. "You realise we have just witnessed a *coup d'état*? What else is one to call it when the General Staff is allowed to produce a piece of evidence the defence isn't allowed to see, and then threatens to desert en masse unless a civilian court accepts it? The tactics they used on Dreyfus they are now trying to use on the entire country!"

"I agree. That's why I want to be recalled to the witness stand."

"Are you sure?"

"Will you tell Labori?"

"Be careful, Georges—I'm speaking as your lawyer now. You break your oath of confidentiality and they will put you away for ten years."

As we walk back to the court, I say, "There's something else I'd like you to do for me, if you would. There is an officer of the Sûreté, Jean-Alfred Desvernine. Would you try to contact him discreetly, and say I need to meet him in the strictest confidence? Tell him to keep an eye on the papers, and the day after I'm released I'll be in the usual place at seven in the evening."

"The usual place . . ." Louis makes a note without passing comment.

Back in court, the judge says, "Colonel Picquart, what is it you wish to add?"

As I walk towards the stand, I glance across at Henry, sitting crammed in his seat between Gonse and Pellieux. His chest is so vast his arms folded across it appear stubby, like clipped wings.

I stroke the polished wood of the handrail, smoothing the grain. "I wish to say something about the document that General Pellieux has mentioned as absolute proof of Dreyfus's guilt. If he hadn't brought it up, I would never have spoken of it, but now I feel I must." The clock ticks, a trapdoor seems to open at my feet and I step over the edge at last. "It is a forgery."

The rest is quickly told. When the howling and the shouting have died down, Pellieux steps forward to make a violent attack upon my character: "Everything in this case is strange, but the strangest thing of all is the attitude of a man who still wears the French uniform and yet who comes to this bar to accuse three generals of having committed a forgery . . ."

On the day the verdict is announced, I am taken by carriage from Mont-Valérien for the final time. The streets around the Palace of Justice are crammed with roughs carrying heavy sticks, and when the jury retires to consider its verdict our group of "Dreyfusards," as we are starting to be called, stands together in the centre of the court, for mutual protection as much as anything else: me, Zola, Perrenx, the Clemenceau brothers, Louis and Labori, Madame Zola and Labori's strikingly beautiful young Australian wife, Marguerite, who has brought along her two little boys by her previous marriage. "This way we'll all be together," she tells me in her strongly accented French. Through the high windows we can hear the noise of the mob outside.

Clemenceau says, "If we win, we will not leave this building alive."

After forty minutes the jury returns. The foreman, a brawny-looking merchant, stands. "On my honour and my conscience the declaration of the jury is: as concerns Perrenx, guilty, by a majority vote; as concerns Zola, guilty, by a majority vote."

There is uproar. The officers are cheering. Everyone is on their feet. The ladies of fashion at the back of the court clamber onto their seats to get a better view.

"Cannibals," says Zola.

The judge tells Perrenx, manager of *L'Aurore*, that he is sentenced to four months in prison and a fine of three thousand francs. Zola is given the maximum penalty of a year in gaol and a fine of five thousand. The sentences are suspended pending appeal.

As we leave, I pass Henry standing with a group of General Staff officers. He is in the middle of telling a joke. I say to him coldly, "My witnesses will be calling on yours in the next few days to make arrangements for our duel; be ready to respond," and I am pleased to see that this has the effect, at least briefly, of knocking the smile off his porcine face.

Three days later, on Saturday, 26 February, the commandant of Mont-Valérien calls me to his office and leaves me standing at attention while he informs me that I have been found guilty of "grave misconduct" by a panel of senior officers and that I am dismissed from the army forthwith. I will not receive the full pension of a retired colonel but only that of a major: thirty francs per week. He is further authorised to tell me that if I make any comments in public again regarding my period of service on the General Staff, the army will take "the severest possible action" against me.

"Do you have anything to say?"

"No, Colonel."

"Dismissed!"

At dusk, carrying my suitcase, I am escorted to the gate and left on the cobbled forecourt to make my own way home. I have known no other life except the army since I was eighteen years old. But all that is behind me now, and it is as plain Monsieur Picquart that I walk down the hill to the railway station to catch the train back into Paris.

21

The next evening I occupy the familiar corner table in the café of the gare Saint-Lazare. It is a Sunday, a quiet time, a lonely place. I am one of only a handful of customers. I have taken precautions getting here—diving into churches, leaving by side doors, doubling back on myself, dodging down alleys—with the result that I am fairly sure no one has followed me. I read my paper, smoke a cigarette and manage to make my beer last until a quarter to eight, by which time it is obvious Desvernine is not coming. I am disappointed but not surprised: given the change in my circumstances since we last met, one can hardly blame him.

I walk outside to catch an omnibus home. The lower deck is crowded. I climb up to the top, where the chill through the open sides is enough to deter my fellow passengers. I sit about halfway down the central bench, my chin on my chest and my hands in my pockets, looking out at the darkened upper storeys of the shops. I have not been there a minute when I am joined by a man in a heavy overcoat and muffler. He leaves a space between us.

He says, "Good evening, Colonel."

I turn in surprise. "Monsieur Desvernine."

He continues to stare straight ahead. "You were followed from your apartment."

"I thought I'd lost them."

"You lost two of them. The third is sitting downstairs. Fortunately, he works for me. I don't think there's a fourth, but even so, I suggest we keep our conversation brief."

"Yes, of course. It was good of you to come at all."

"What is it you want?"

"I need to speak to Lemercier-Picard."

"Why?"

"There's been a lot of forgery in the Dreyfus case: I suspect he may have had a hand at least in some of it."

"Oh." Desvernine sounds pained. "Oh, that won't be easy. Can you be more specific?"

"Yes, I'm thinking in particular of the document mentioned in the Zola trial the other day, the so-called absolute proof that General Boisdeffre vouched for. If it's what I think it is, it consists of about five or six lines of writing. That's a lot for an amateur to forge, and there's plenty of original material to compare it with. So I suspect they must have brought in a professional."

" 'They' being who in particular, Colonel—if you don't mind my asking?"

"The Statistical Section. Colonel Henry."

"Henry? He's acting chief!" Now he looks at me. "I'm sure I can get access to money, if that's what your man wants."

"It will be what he wants: I can tell you that now—and a lot of it. When do you need to see him?"

"As soon as possible."

Desvernine huddles down in his coat, thinking it over. I can't see his face. Eventually he says, "Leave it with me, Colonel." He stands. "I'll get off here."

"I'm not a colonel anymore, Monsieur Desvernine. There is no need to call me that. And you aren't obliged to help me. It's a risk for you."

"You forget how much time I spent investigating Esterhazy, Colonel—I know that bastard inside out. It sickens me to see him walking free. I'll help you, if only because of him."

For my duel against Henry I need two witnesses to make the arrangements and ensure fair play. I travel out to Ville-d'Avray to ask Edmond Gast to be one of them. We sit on his terrace after lunch with a blanket across our knees, smoking cigars. He says, "Well, if you're dead set on it, then of course I should be honoured. But I beg you to reconsider."

"I've issued the challenge in public, Ed. I can't possibly withdraw. Besides, I don't want to."

"What weapons will you choose?"

"Swords."

"Come on, Georges—you haven't fenced for years!"

"Neither has he, by the look of him. In any case, I have a cool head and a little physical agility."

"But surely you're a better shot than you are a swordsman? And with pistols there's a healthy convention of deliberately missing."

"Yes, except that if we use pistols and he wins the draw and chooses to go first, he may not try to miss. It would certainly solve all their problems if he put a bullet through my heart. No, that's too much of a risk."

"And who will be your other witness?"

"I wondered if you'd ask your friend Senator Ranc."

"Why Ranc?"

I puff on my cigar before I reply. "When I was in Tunisia, I made a study of the marquis de Morès. He killed a Jewish officer in a duel by using a heavier sword than was allowed by regulations—pierced him through his armpit and severed his spinal cord. I think it would be good life insurance for me to have a senator on hand. It might deter Henry from trying any similar tricks."

Edmond looks at me in alarm. "Georges, I'm sorry, but really this is madness. Never mind yourself—you owe it to the cause of freeing Dreyfus not to put yourself in harm's way."

"He called me a liar in open court. My honour demands a duel."

"Is it *your* honour you're trying to avenge, or Pauline's?"

I do not reply.

The following evening, on my behalf, Edmond and Ranc call at Henry's apartment in the avenue Duquesne, directly opposite the École Militaire, to issue the formal challenge. Afterwards Edmond says, "He was plainly at home—we could see his boots in the passage, and I could hear his little boy crying 'Papa,' and then a man's voice trying to hush the lad. But he sent his wife out to talk to us. She took the letter and said he would respond to it tomorrow. I get the feeling he's anxious to avoid a fight."

Wednesday passes without any reply from Henry. At about eight o'clock in the evening there is a knock at the door and I get up to answer it, assuming it will be his witnesses bringing me his answer, but instead standing on the landing is Desvernine. He comes in briefly without taking off his hat or coat.

"Everything is fixed," he says. "Our man is staying at a lodging house, the hôtel de la Manche, in the rue de Sèvres. He's using one of his aliases—Koberty Dutrieux. Do you have a weapon, Colonel?"

I open my jacket to show him my shoulder holster. Since my service revolver was taken from me, I have bought myself a British gun, a Webley.

"Good," he says. "Then we should go."

"Now?"

"He doesn't stay long in one place."

"And we won't be followed?"

"No, I swapped shifts and made sure I'm in charge of your surveillance this evening. As far as the Sûreté are concerned, Colonel, you will be tucked up in your apartment all night."

We take a taxi across the river and I pay off the driver just south of the École Militaire. The remainder of the journey we complete on foot. The section of the rue de Sèvres in which the hotel stands is narrow and poorly lit; the Manche is easy to miss. It occupies a narrow, tumbledown house, hemmed in between a butcher's shop and a bar: the sort of place where commercial travellers might lay their heads for a night and assignations can no doubt be paid for by the hour. Desvernine goes in first; I follow. The concierge is not at his desk. Through a curtain of beads I can see people eating supper in the little dining room. There is no elevator. The narrow stairs creak with every tread. We come out onto the third floor and Desvernine knocks at a bedroom door. No answer. He tries the handle: locked. He puts his finger to his lips and we stand listening. A muffled conversation comes from the room next door.

Desvernine fishes in his pocket and produces a set of lock-picking tools, identical to the one he lent me. He kneels and goes to work. I unbutton my coat and jacket and feel the reassuring pressure of the Webley against my breast. After a minute the lock clicks. Desvernine stands, calmly folds away his tools and returns them to his pocket. He looks at me as he quietly opens the door. The room is dark. He feels for the light switch and turns it on.

My first instinct is that it is a large ebony doll—a tailor's mannequin perhaps, made of black plaster, folded into a sitting position and propped up just beneath the window. Without turning round or saying anything, Desvernine holds up his left hand, warning me not to move; in the other he has a gun. He crosses the floor to the window in three or four strides, looks down at the object and whispers, "Close the door."

Once I am in the room, I can just about tell it is Lemercier-Picard, or whatever his name was. His face is purplish-black and has fallen forward onto his chest. His eyes are open, his tongue protrudes, there is dried mucus all down the front of his shirt. Buried deep in the folds of his neck is a thin cord which runs up behind him, tight as a harp string, and is tied to the window casement. Now that I am closer I can see that his feet and the lower part of his legs, which are bare and bruised, are in contact with the floor but his hips are suspended just above it. His arms hang at his sides, fists tightly balled.

Desvernine reaches out his hand to the swollen neck and feels for a pulse, then squats on his haunches and quickly frisks the corpse.

I say, "When did you last speak to him?"

"This morning. He was standing at this very window, as alive as you are now."

"Was he depressed? Suicidal?"

"No, just frightened."

"How long has he been dead?"

"He's cold, but no stiffness yet—two hours; perhaps three."

He straightens and goes over to the bed. A suitcase lies open. He turns it upside down and shakes out the contents, then sifts through the pathetic little heap of belongings, extracting pens, nibs, pencils, bottles of ink. A tweed jacket hangs on the back of a chair. He tugs

AN OFFICER AND A SPY

a note case from the inside pocket and flips through it, then checks the side pockets: coins in one, the room key in the other.

I watch him. "No note?"

"No paper of any sort. Curious for a forger, wouldn't you say?" He puts everything back in the suitcase. Then he lifts the mattress and pats underneath it, opens the drawer of the nightstand, looks in the shabby cupboard, rolls back the square of matting. Finally he stands defeated with his hands on his hips. "It's all been gone through thoroughly. They haven't left a scrap. You should go now, Colonel. The last thing you need is to be caught in a room with a corpse—especially this one."

"What about you?"

"I'll lock the door and leave everything as we found it. Maybe wait around outside for an hour or two, see who shows up." He gazes at the corpse. "This'll be booked straight through as a suicide—just you wait—and you won't find a policeman or a crook in Paris who'll say anything different, the poor bastard." He passes his hand tenderly across the contorted face and closes the staring eyes.

The next day two colonels turn up at my apartment: Parès and Boissonnet, both noted sportsmen and old drinking companions of Henry's. They inform me grandly that Colonel Henry refuses to fight me on the grounds that I, as a cashiered officer, am a "disreputable person," with no honour to lose: therefore there can have been no insult.

Parès gives me a look of cold contempt. "He suggests, *Monsieur* Picquart, that you seek satisfaction from Major Esterhazy instead. He understands that Major Esterhazy is anxious to challenge you to a duel."

"No doubt he is. But you may inform Colonel Henry—and Major Esterhazy too—that I have no intention of stepping down into the gutter to fight a traitor and embezzler. Colonel Henry accused me in public of being a liar, at a time when I was still a serving officer. That is when I issued the challenge, and in those circumstances he is bound by honour to give me satisfaction. If he refuses to do so, the world will note the fact and draw the obvious conclusion: that he is both a slanderer and a coward. Good day, gentlemen."

After I close the door on them I realise I am trembling, whether from nerves or fury I cannot tell.

Later that night Edmond comes round with the news that Henry has decided to accept my challenge after all. The duel will take place the day after tomorrow, at ten-thirty in the morning, at the indoor riding school of the École Militaire. The weapons will be swords. Edmond says, "Henry will automatically have an army surgeon in attendance. We need to nominate a doctor of our own to accompany us. Is there anyone you would prefer?"

"No."

"Then I'll find someone. Now pack a bag."

"Why?"

"Because I have my carriage outside and you're coming home to practise fencing with me. I don't want to be a witness to your being killed."

I debate whether or not to tell him about Lemercier-Picard and decide against it: he is anxious enough as it is.

Friday is passed in Edmond's barn, where he puts me through my paces for hour after hour, relearning the basic principles of compound attack and circular parry, riposte and remise. The next morning, we leave Ville-d'Avray soon after nine to drive back into Paris. Jeanne kisses me fervently all over my face as if she doesn't expect to see me again. "Goodbye, dearest Georges! I shall never forget you. Farewell!"

"My dear Jeanne, this is not good for my morale . . ."

An hour later we turn into the avenue de Lowendal to find a crowd of several hundred waiting outside the entrance to the riding school, many of them cadets from the École Militaire—the sort of young men I used to teach but who now jeer me as I emerge from the carriage in my civilian clothes. A line of troopers guards the door. Edmond knocks, a bolt is drawn and we are admitted into that familiar grey-lit chilly space, with its stink of horse shit, ammonia and straw. Trapped birds beat their wings against the skylights. A trestle table has been set up in the middle of the vast manège against which Arthur Ranc rests his bulky frame. He comes over to me with his hand outstretched. He may be nearer seventy than sixty but his beard is full and black and the eyes behind his pince-nez are bright with interest. "I've fought plenty of duels in my time, my dear fellow," he says, "and the thing to remember is that two hours from now you'll be sitting down to lunch with the keenest appetite you'll ever enjoy in your life. It's worth the fight just for the pleasure of the meal!"

I am introduced to the adjudicator, a retired sergeant major of the Republican Guard, and to my doctor, a hospital surgeon. We wait for fifteen minutes, our conversation becoming increasingly strained, until a burst of cheering from the street signals the arrival of Henry. He enters followed by the two colonels, ignores us and strides directly to the table, pulling off his gloves. Then he removes his cap and sets it down and begins unbuttoning his tunic, as if preparing for a medical procedure he is anxious to get over with as quickly as possible. I take off my own jacket and waistcoat and hand them to Edmond. The adjudicator chalks a thick line in the centre of the stone floor, paces off a position to either side of it and marks each with a cross, then summons us over to him. "Gentlemen," he says, "if you please, unbutton your shirts," and we expose our chests briefly to prove we are wearing no protection; Henry's is pink and hairless, like the belly of a pig. Throughout this procedure he looks at his hands, the floor, the rafters—anywhere except at me.

Our weapons are weighed and measured. The sergeant major explains, "Gentlemen, if one of you is wounded, or a wound is perceived by one of your witnesses, the combat will be stopped unless the wounded man indicates he wishes to continue fighting. After the wound has been inspected, if the injured man desires, the fight may resume." He gives us our swords. "Prepare yourselves."

I flex my knees and make a few practice thrusts and parries, then turn to face Henry, who stands about six paces away, and now at last he looks at me, and I see the hatred in his eyes. I know at once he will try to kill me if he can.

"En garde," says the sergeant major, and we take up our positions. He checks his watch and raises his cane, then brings it down. "Allez!"

Henry rushes at me immediately, flashing his sword with such speed and force that mine is almost knocked from my hand. I have no choice but to retreat under the flail of blows, parrying as best I can by instinct rather than method. My feet become entangled, I stumble slightly, and Henry slashes at my neck. Both Ranc and Edmond cry out in protest at such an illegal stroke. I sway backwards and feel the wall behind my shoulders. Already Henry must have driven me twenty paces from my marker and I have to duck and twist away from him, darting to the side and taking up a fresh defensive posture, yet still he comes on.

I hear Ranc complain to the adjudicator, "But this is ridiculous, monsieur!" and the adjudicator calls out, "Colonel Henry, the purpose is to settle a dispute between gentlemen!" but I can see in Henry's eyes that he hears nothing except the pumping of his own blood. He lunges at me once again and this time I feel his blade on the tendon of my neck, which is as close as I have come to death since the day I was born. Ranc calls out, "Stop!" just as the tip of my sword catches Henry on the forearm. He glances down at it and lowers his weapon, and I do the same as the witnesses and doctors hurry across to us. The sergeant major consults his watch. "The first engagement lasted two minutes."

My surgeon stands me directly beneath a skylight and turns my head to inspect my neck. He says, "You're fine: he must have missed you by a hair."

Henry, though, is bleeding from his forearm—not a serious cut, merely a graze, but enough for the adjudicator to say to him, "Colonel, you may refuse to continue."

Henry shakes his head. "We'll carry on."

While he is rolling back his sleeve and wiping the blood away Edmond says to me quietly, "This fellow is a homicidal lunatic. I've never seen such a display."

"If he tries it again," adds Ranc, "I shall have the thing stopped."

"No," I say, "don't do that. Let's fight it to the end."

The adjudicator calls, "Gentlemen, to your places!"

"*Allez!*"

Henry tries to start the reengagement where he left it, with the same aggression as before, driving me back towards the wall. But the lower part of his arm is braided with blood. His grip is slippery. The slashing strokes no longer carry the old conviction—they are slowing, weakening. He needs to finish me quickly or he will lose. He throws everything into one last lunge at my heart. I parry the blow, turn his blade, thrust, and catch the edge of his elbow. He bellows in pain and drops his sword. His seconds shout, "Stop!"

"No!" he shouts, wincing and clutching his elbow. "I can continue!" He stoops and retrieves his sword with his left hand and attempts to fit the hilt into his right, but his bloodied fingers won't close on it. He tries repeatedly, but each time he attempts to raise it, the sword drops to the floor. I watch him without pity. "Give me a minute," he mutters, and turns his back to me to hide his weakness.

Eventually the two colonels and his doctor persuade him to go over to the table to allow the wound to be examined. Five minutes later Colonel Parès approaches where I am waiting with Edmond and Ranc and announces, "The cubital nerve is damaged. The fingers will be unable to grip for several days. Colonel Henry must withdraw." He salutes and walks away.

I put on my waistcoat and my jacket and glance across to where Henry sits slumped on a chair, staring at the floor. Colonel Parès stands behind him and guides his arms into the sleeves of his tunic, then Colonel Boissonnet kneels at his feet and fastens his buttons.

"Look at him," says Ranc contemptuously, "like a great big baby. He's completely finished."

"Yes," I say. "I believe he is."

We do not observe the usual custom following a duel and shake hands. Instead, as word filters out into the avenue de Lowendal that their hero has been wounded, I am hurried away through a rear exit to avoid the hostile crowd. According to the front pages the next day, Henry leaves to the cheers of his supporters, his arm in a sling, and is driven in an open landau around the corner to his apartment, where General Boisdeffre waits in person to offer him the best wishes of the army. I go out to lunch with Edmond and Ranc, and discover that the old senator is indeed correct: I have seldom had a better appetite nor more enjoyed a meal.

This buoyant mood persists, and for the next three months I wake each morning with a curious sense of optimism. On the face of it, my situation could hardly be worse. I have nothing to do, no career to go to, an inadequate income, and little capital to draw on. I still cannot see Pauline while her divorce is pending in case we are observed by the press or the police. Blanche has gone away: it was only after much string-pulling by her brother and various sub-terfuges (including the pretence that she was a fifty-five-year-old spinster with a heart condition) that she managed to avoid being called as a witness at the Zola trial. I am hissed at in public and libelled in various newspapers, which are tipped off by Henry that I have been seen meeting Colonel von Schwartzkoppen in Karlsruhe. Louis is removed as deputy mayor of the seventh arrondissement and sanctioned by the Order of Advocates for "improper conduct." Reinach and other prominent supporters of Dreyfus lose their seats in the national elections. And while Lemercier-Picard's death cre-ates a great sensation, it is officially declared a suicide and the case is closed.

Everywhere the forces of darkness are in control.

But I am not entirely ostracised. Parisian society is divided, and for each door that is now slammed in my face, another opens. On Sundays I begin regularly to go for lunch at the home of Madame Geneviève Straus, the widow of Bizet, on the rue de Miromesnil, along with such new comrades-in-arms as Zola, Clemenceau, Labori, Proust and Anatole France. On Wednesday evenings it is often din-ner for twenty in the salon of Monsieur France's mistress, Madame Léontine Arman de Caillavet, "Our Lady of the Revision," in the avenue Hoche—Léontine is an extravagant grande dame with carmine-rouged cheeks and orange-dyed hair on which sits a rimless hat of stuffed pink bullfinches. And on Thursdays I might walk a few streets west, towards the porte Dauphine, for the musical soirées of Madame Aline Ménard-Dorian, in whose scarlet reception rooms decorated with peacock feathers and Japanese prints I turn the pages for Cortot and Casals and the three ravishing young sisters of the trio Chaigneau.

"Ah! You are always so cheerful, my dear Georges," these grand hostesses say to me. They flutter their fans and their eyelashes at me in the candlelight, and touch my arm consolingly—for a gaolbird is always a trophy for a smart table—and call across to their fellow guests to take note of my serenity. "You are a wonder, Picquart!" their husbands exclaim. "Either that or you are mad. I am sure I should not retain my good humour in the face of so much trouble."

I smile. "Well, one must always wear the mask of comedy for society . . ."

And yet the truth is I am not wearing a mask: I do feel quite confident about the future. I am sure in my bones that sooner or later, although by what means I cannot foresee, this great edifice the army has constructed—this mouldering defensive fortress of worm-eaten timber—will collapse all around them. The lies are too extensive and ramshackle to withstand the pressures of time and scrutiny. Poor Dreyfus, now entering his fourth year on Devil's Island, may not live to see it, and nor for that matter may I. But vindication will come, I am convinced.

And I am proved right, even sooner than I expected. That summer, two events occur that change everything.

First, in May, I receive a note from Labori summoning me urgently to his apartment in the rue de Bourgogne, just around the corner from the Ministry of War. I arrive within the hour to find a nervous young man of twenty-one, obviously up from the provinces, waiting in the drawing room. Labori introduces him as Christian Esterhazy.

"Ah," I say, shaking his hand somewhat warily, "now that is an infamous name."

"You mean my cousin?" he responds. "Yes, he has made it so, and a blacker rogue never drew breath!"

His tone is so vehement I am taken aback. Labori says, "You need to sit down, Picquart, and listen to what Monsieur Esterhazy has to tell us. You won't be disappointed."

Marguerite brings in tea and leaves us to it.

"My father died eighteen months ago," says Christian, "at our home in Bordeaux, very unexpectedly. The week after he passed over, I received a letter of condolence from a man I'd never met before: my father's cousin, Major Walsin Esterhazy, expressing his sympathy and asking if he could be of any practical assistance in terms of financial advice."

I exchange glances with Labori; Christian notices. "Well, Monsieur Picquart, I can see that you know what must be coming! But please bear in mind that I had no experience in these matters and my mother is a most unworldly and religious person—two of my sisters are nuns, in fact. To tell the tale briefly, I wrote back to my chivalrous relative and explained that I had an inheritance of five thousand francs, and my mother would receive one hundred and seventy thousand through the sale of property, and that we would welcome advice in making sure it was safely invested. The major replied, offering to intercede with his intimate friend Edmond de Rothschild, and naturally we thought, 'What could be safer than that?'"

He sips his tea, gathering his thoughts before continuing. "For some months all went well, and we would receive regular letters from the major enclosing cheques which he said were the dividends from the money the Rothschilds had invested on our behalf. And then last November he wrote to me asking me to come to Paris urgently. He said he was in trouble and needed my help. Naturally I came at once. I found him in a terrible state of anxiety. He said he was about to be denounced in public as a traitor, but that I was not to believe any of the stories. It was all a plot by the Jews, to put him in Dreyfus's place, and that he could prove this because he was being helped by officers from the Ministry of War. He said it had become too dangerous for him to meet his principal contact, and therefore he asked if I would meet him on his behalf and relay messages between them."

"And who was this contact?" I ask.

"His name was Colonel du Paty de Clam."

"You met du Paty?"

"Yes, often. Usually at night, in public places—parks, bridges, lavatories."

"Lavatories?"

"Oh yes, although the colonel would take care to be disguised, in dark glasses or a false beard."

"And what sort of messages did you relay between du Paty and your cousin?"

"All sorts. Warnings of what might be about to appear in the newspapers. Advice on how to respond. I remember there was once an envelope containing a secret document from the ministry. Some messages concerned you."

"Me?"

"Yes, for example there were two telegrams. They've stayed in my mind because they were very odd."

"Can you remember what they said?"

"I remember one was signed 'Blanche'—that was written by du Paty. The other—a foreign name . . ."

"Speranza?"

"Speranza—that's it! Mademoiselle Pays—she wrote that one out, on the colonel's instructions, and took it to the post office in the rue Lafayette."

"Did they give a reason why they were doing this?"

"To compromise you."

"And you helped because you believed your cousin was innocent?"

"Absolutely—at least I did then."

"And now?"

Christian takes his time replying. He finishes his tea and replaces the cup and saucer on the table—slow and deliberate gestures that do not quite conceal the fact that he is quivering with emotion. "A few weeks ago, after my cousin stopped paying my mother her monthly money, I checked with the Rothschilds. There is no bank account. There never was. She is ruined. I believe that if a man could betray his own family in such a fashion, he could betray his country without any conscience. That is why I have come to you. He must be stopped."

It is obvious what should be done with the information, once it has been verified: it must be passed to Bertulus, the dapper magistrate with the red carnation in his buttonhole, whose slow investigation into the forged telegrams is still proceeding. Because I am the one who laid the original complaint, it is agreed that I should write to him, alerting him to the crucial new witness. Christian agrees to testify, then changes his mind when his cousin discovers he has been to see Labori, and then changes it back again when it is pointed out that he can be subpoenaed in any case.

Esterhazy, obviously aware now that disaster is closing in on him, renews his demands that I should fight him in a duel. He lets it be known in the press that he is prowling the streets near to my apartment in the hopes of meeting me, carrying a heavy cane made of cherry wood and painted bright red with which he proposes to stove in my brains. He claims to be an expert in the art of *savate*, or kickboxing. Finally he sends me a letter and releases it to the newspapers:

> In consequence of your refusal to fight, dictated solely by your fear of a serious meeting, I vainly looked for you for several days as you know, and you fled like the coward that you are. Tell me what day and where you will finally dare to find yourself face-to-face with me in order to receive the castigation which I have promised you. As for me I shall, for three days in succession, from tomorrow evening at 7 p.m., walk in the rues de Lisbonne and Naples.

I do not reply to him personally, as I have no desire to enter into direct correspondence with such a creature; instead I issue a statement of my own to the press:

> I am surprised that M. Esterhazy has not met me if he is looking for me, as I go about quite openly. As for the threats contained in his letter, I am resolved if I fall into an ambush fully to use the right possessed by every citizen for his legitimate defence. But I shall not forget that it is my duty to respect Esterhazy's life. The man belongs to the justice of the country, and I should be to blame if I took it upon myself to punish him.

Several weeks pass and I cease to keep my eyes open for him. But then one Sunday afternoon at the beginning of July, on the day before I am due to hand Christian's evidence to Bertulus, I am walking along the avenue Bugeaud after lunch when I hear footsteps running up behind me. I turn to see Esterhazy's red cane descending on my head. I duck away and put up an arm to shield my face so that the blow falls only on my shoulder. Esterhazy's face is livid and contorted, his eyes bulging like organ stops. He is shouting insults—"Villain! Coward! Traitor!"—so close that I can smell the absinthe on his breath. Fortunately I have a cane of my own. My first strike at his head knocks his bowler hat into the gutter. My second is a jab to his stomach that sends him sprawling after it. He rolls on his side, then drags himself up onto his hands and knees and crouches, winded, on the cobbles. Then, supporting himself with his ridiculous cherry-red cane, he starts to struggle to his feet. Several passersby have stopped to watch what is going on. I grab him in a headlock and shout for someone to fetch the police. But the *promeneurs,* not surprisingly, have better things to do on a beautiful Sunday afternoon, and at once everyone moves on, leaving me holding the traitor. He is strong and wiry, twisting back and forth, and I realise that either I will have to do him serious damage to quieten him down or else let him go. I release him, and step back warily.

"Villain!" he repeats. "Coward! Traitor!" He staggers about trying to pick up his hat. He is very drunk.

"You are going to prison," I tell him, "if not for treason, then for forgery and embezzlement. Now don't come near me again, or next time I'll deal with you more severely."

My shoulder is stinging badly. I am relieved to walk away. He doesn't try to follow, but I can hear him shouting after me—"Villain! Coward! Traitor! *Jew!*"—until I am out of sight.

The second event that summer is much more significant and takes place four days later.

It is early in the evening, Thursday, 7 July, and as usual at that time of the week I am at Aline Ménard-Dorian's neo-Gothic mansion: to be exact, I am standing in the garden prior to going into the concert, sipping champagne, talking to Zola, whose appeal against his conviction is being heard in a courtroom in Versailles. A new government has just been formed and we are discussing what effect this is likely to have on his case when Clemenceau, with Labori at his heels, suddenly erupts onto the patio carrying an evening newspaper.

"Have you heard what's just happened?"

"No."

"My friends, it is a sensation! That little prig Cavaignac* has just made his first speech in the chamber as Minister of War, and claims to have proved once and for all that Dreyfus is a traitor!"

"How has he done that?"

Clemenceau thrusts the paper into my hands. "By reading out verbatim three intercepted messages from the secret intelligence files."

"It cannot be possible . . . !"

It cannot be possible—and yet here it is, in black and white: the new Minister of War, Godefroy Cavaignac, who replaced Billot barely a week ago, claims to have ended the Dreyfus affair with a political *coup de théâtre*. "I'm going to show to the Chamber three documents. Here is the first letter. It was received in March 1894, when it came into the intelligence department of the Ministry of War . . ." Omitting only the names of the sender and the addressee, he goes through them one by one: the infamous message from the secret file (*I am enclosing twelve master plans of Nice which that lowlife D gave me for you*), a second letter which I do not recognise (*D has brought me many very interesting matters*), and the "absolute proof" that turned the course of Zola's trial:

> *I have read that a deputy is going to ask questions about Dreyfus. If someone asks in Rome for new explanations, I will say that I have never had any dealings with this Jew. If someone asks you, say the same, for no one must ever know what happened to him.*

---

* Godefroy Cavaignac (1853–1905), fervent Catholic, appointed Minister of War 28 June 1898.

I hand the paper on to Zola. "He really declaimed all of this rubbish out loud? He must be crazy."

"You wouldn't have thought so if you'd been in the Chamber," replies Clemenceau. "The entire place rose in acclamation. They think he's settled the Dreyfus issue once and for all. They even passed a motion ordering the government to print thirty-six thousand copies of the evidence and post them in every commune in France!"

Labori says, "It's a disaster for us, unless we can counter it."

Zola asks, "Can we counter it?"

All three look at me.

That evening, after the concert, which includes the two great Wagner piano sonatas, I make my excuses to Aline and instead of staying for dinner, and with the music still playing in my head, I go to find Pauline. I know that she is lodging with an elderly cousin, a spinster, who has an apartment not far away, close to the Bois de Boulogne. At first, the cousin refuses to fetch her to the door: "Have you not done her enough harm already, monsieur? Is it not time to let her be?"

"Please, madame, I need to see her."

"It is very late."

"It's not yet ten, still light—"

"Good night, monsieur."

She closes the door on me. I ring the bell again. I hear whispered voices. There is a long pause and this time when the door opens Pauline is standing in her cousin's place. She is dressed very soberly in a white blouse and dark skirt, her hair pulled back, no makeup. She might almost be a member of a religious order; I wonder if she is still going to confession. She says, "I thought we had agreed not to meet until things were settled."

"There may not be time to wait."

She purses her lips, nods. "I'll get my hat." As she goes into her bedroom, I see on the table in the little sitting room a typewriter: typically practical, she has taken the money I gave her and invested part of it in learning a new skill—the first time she has ever had an income of her own.

Outside, when we are round the corner and safely out of sight of the apartment, Pauline takes my arm and we walk into the Bois. It is a still, clear summer evening, the temperature so perfectly poised that there seems to be no climate, no barrier between the mind and nature. There are simply the stars, and the dry scent of the grass and the trees, and the occasional faint splash from the lake, where two lovers drift in a boat in the moonlight. Their voices carry louder than they realise in the motionless air. But we have only to walk a few hundred paces, strike out from the sandy paths and enter the trees, and they, and the city, cease to exist.

We find a secluded place beneath an immense old cedar. I take off my tailcoat and spread it on the ground for us, loosen my white tie, sit down beside her and put my arm around her.

"You'll ruin your coat," she says. "You'll have to get it cleaned."

"It doesn't matter. I won't need it for a while."

"Are you going away?"

"You could put it that way."

I explain to her then what I intend to do. I made my mind up listening to the concert; listening to the Wagner, in fact, which always has a heady effect on me.

"I am going to challenge the government's version of events in public."

I have no illusions about what will happen to me as a result—I can hardly complain that I haven't been given fair warning. "I suppose I should regard my month in Mont-Valérien as a kind of trial run." I put a brave face on it, for her sake. Inwardly I am less confident. What is the worst I can expect? Once the prison doors close on me, I will be in some physical jeopardy—that has to be taken into account. Incarceration will not be pleasant, and may be prolonged for weeks and months, possibly even a year or more, although I do not mention that to Pauline: it will be in the government's interests to try to spin out legal proceedings as long as they can, if only in the hope that Dreyfus may die in the interim.

When I've finished explaining, she says, "You sound as though you have made up your mind already."

"If I pull back now, I may never get a better chance. I'd be obliged to spend the rest of my life with the knowledge that when the moment came, I couldn't rise to it. It would destroy me—I'd never be able to look at a painting or read a novel or listen to music again without a creeping sense of shame. I'm just so very sorry to have mixed you up in all of this."

"Don't keep apologising. I'm not a child. I mixed myself up in it when I fell in love with you."

"And how is it, being alone?"

"I've discovered I can survive. It's oddly exhilarating."

We lie quietly, our hands interlaced, looking up through the branches to the stars. I seem to feel the turning of the earth beneath us. It will just be starting to get dark in the tropics of South America. I think of Dreyfus and try to picture what he is doing, whether they still manacle him to his bed at night. Our destinies are now entirely intertwined. I depend upon his survival as much as he depends on mine—if he endures, then so will I; if I walk free, then he will too.

I remain there with Pauline for a long time, savouring these final hours together, until the stars begin to fade into the dawn, then I pick up my coat and drape it over her shoulders, and arm in arm we walk back together into the sleeping city.

22

The next day, with the help of Labori, I draft an open letter to the government. At his suggestion I send it not to the devout and unbending Minister of War, our toy Brutus, but to the anticlerical new prime minister, Henri Brisson:

Monsieur Prime Minister,

Until the present moment I have not been in a position to express myself freely on the subject of the secret documents which, it is alleged, establish the guilt of Dreyfus. Since the Minister of War has, from the tribune of the Chamber of Deputies, quoted three of those documents, I deem it a duty to inform you that I am in a position to establish before any competent tribunal that the two documents bearing the date 1894 cannot be made to apply to Dreyfus, and that the document dated 1896 shows every evidence of being a forgery. It would seem obvious therefore that the good faith of the Minister of War has been imposed upon, and that the same is true of all those who have believed in the relevance of the first two documents and in the authenticity of the last.

> *Kindly accept, Monsieur Prime Minister,*
> *my sincere regards,*
> *G. Picquart*

The letter reaches the Prime Minister on Monday. On Tuesday, the government files a criminal charge against me, based on the Pellieux investigation, accusing me of illegally revealing "writings and documents of importance for national defence and security." An investigating judge is appointed. That same afternoon—although I am not there to witness it, but only read about it the next morning in the papers—my apartment is raided, watched by a crowd of several hundred onlookers jeering "Traitor!" On Wednesday, I am summoned to meet the government-appointed judge, Albert Fabre, in his chambers on the third floor of the Palace of Justice. In his outer office two detectives are waiting and I am arrested, as is poor Louis Leblois.

"I warned you to think carefully before getting involved," I say to him. "I have ruined too many lives."

"Dear Georges, think nothing of it! It will be interesting to observe the justice system from the other side for a change."

Judge Fabre, who to his credit at least seems slightly embarrassed by the whole procedure, tells me I am to be held in La Santé prison during his investigation, whereas Louis will remain free on bail. Outside in the courtyard, as I am being put into the Black Maria in full view of several dozen reporters, I have the presence of mind to remember to give Louis my cane. Then I am taken away. On arrival at the prison I have to fill in a registration form. In the space for "religion" I write "nothing."

La Santé, it turns out, is no Mont-Valérien: there is no separate bedroom and WC here, no view to the Eiffel Tower. I am locked in a tiny cell, four metres by two and a half, with a small barred window that looks down onto an exercise yard. There is a bed and a chamber pot: that is all. It is the height of summer, thirty-five degrees Celsius, occasionally relieved by thunderstorms. The air is baking hot and stale with the smell of a thousand male bodies—our food, our bodily waste, our sweat—not unlike a barracks. I am fed in my cell, and locked up twenty-three hours a day to prevent me communicating with the other prisoners. I can hear them, though, especially at night, when the lights are turned off and there is nothing to do except lie and listen. Their shouts are like the cries of animals in the jungle, inhuman and mysterious and alarming. Often I hear such howls and screams, such inarticulate beggings for mercy, that I assume the next morning my warders will tell me of some horrendous crime that has been committed overnight. But daylight comes and the place goes on as before.

Thus does the army try to break me.

There is some variety in my routine. A couple of times a week I am taken out of La Santé, guarded by two detectives, and returned by Black Maria to the Palace of Justice, where Judge Fabre takes me very slowly through the evidence I have already recounted many times before.

When did Major Esterhazy first come to your attention?

When Fabre has finished for the day, I am often allowed to meet Labori in a nearby office. The great Viking of the Paris bar is officially my attorney now, and through him I am able to keep in touch with the progress of our various battles. The news is mixed. Zola, having lost his appeal, has fled into exile in London. But the magistrate Bertulus has arrested Esterhazy and Four-Fingered Marguerite on charges of forgery. We lodge a formal request with the Public Prosecutor that he should also arrest du Paty for the same offence. But the Prosecutor rules that this is "beyond the scope of M. Bertulus's investigation."

Tell me again the circumstances in which you came into possession of the petit bleu . . .

About a month after my arrest, Fabre, as investigating judge, enters that stage of proceedings, so beloved by the frustrated dramatists of the French legal system, of staging confrontations between witnesses. The ritual is always the same. First I am asked, for the twentieth time, about a particular incident—the reconstruction of the *petit bleu,* the showing of the pigeon file to Louis, the leaks to the newspapers. Then the judge presses an electric bell and one of my enemies is admitted to recount his version of the same event. Finally I am invited to respond. Throughout these performances the judge scrutinises us carefully, as if he can send out X-rays into our souls and see who is lying. In this way I am brought face-to-face again with Gonse, Lauth, Gribelin, Valdant, Junck, and even the concierge Capiaux. I must say that for men who are at liberty and supposedly triumphant, they look pale and even haggard, especially Gonse, who seems to have developed a nervous tic below his left eye.

The greatest shock, however, is Henry. He enters without looking at me and retells in a monotone his story about seeing Louis and me with the secret file. His voice has lost its old strength and I notice he has shed so much weight that when he starts to sweat he can insert his entire hand between his neck and the collar of his tunic. He has just finished his account when there is a knock at the door and Fabre's clerk enters to say that there is a telephone call for the judge in the outer office. "It is urgent: the Minister of Justice."

Fabre says, "If you will excuse me for a moment, gentlemen."

Henry looks at him anxiously as he leaves. The door closes and we are alone together. Immediately I am suspicious that this is a trap, and glance around to see where a listener might be concealed. But I can see no obvious hiding place, and after a minute or two, curiosity gets the better of me.

I say, "So, Colonel, how is your hand?"

"What, this?" He looks at it and flexes it, as if checking it works. "This is fine." He turns and stares at me. The weight that has fallen from his cheeks and jowls seems to have stripped away the padding of his defences and left him lined with age; his dark hair is flecked with grey. "And you?"

"I am well enough."

"Do you sleep?"

The question surprises me. "Yes. Do you?"

He coughs to clear his throat. "Not so well, Colonel—monsieur, I should say. I'm not sleeping much. I'm sick and tired of this whole damned business, I don't mind telling you."

"We can agree on that much at least!"

"Is prison bad?"

"Let's say it smells even worse than our old offices."

"Ha!" He leans in closer to me, and confides, "To be honest, I've asked to be relieved of my duties in intelligence. I'd like to get back to a healthier life with my regiment."

"Yes, I can see that. And your wife, and your little boy—how are they?"

He opens his mouth to reply, but then stops and gulps, and to my amazement his eyes suddenly fill with tears and he has to look away, just as Fabre comes back into the room.

"So, gentlemen," he says, "the secret file . . ."

———

It is after lights-out, about two weeks later. I am lying on my thin prison mattress, no longer able to read, waiting for the cacophony of the night to begin, when there is a sound of bolts being drawn back and keys turned. A strong light is shone in my face.

"Prisoner, follow me."

La Santé is built according to the latest scientific principles on a hub-and-spoke design—the prisoners' cells form the spokes, the governor and his staff occupy the hub. I follow the warder all the way down the long corridor towards the administrative block at the centre. He unlocks a door then conducts me around a curving passage to a small windowless visitors' room with a steel grille set in the wall. He stays outside but leaves the door open.

From behind the grille a voice says, "Picquart?"

The light is dim. It's hard for me to make him out at first. "Labori? What's going on?"

"Henry has been arrested."

"My God. For what?"

"The government has just put out a statement. Listen: 'Today in the office of the Minister of War, Colonel Henry admitted that he was the author of the document of 1896 in which Dreyfus was named. The Minister of War immediately ordered his arrest and he was taken to the fortress of Mont-Valérien.'" He pauses for my reaction. "Picquart? Did you hear that?"

It takes me a moment to absorb it. "What made him confess?"

"Nobody knows yet. This only happened a few hours ago. All we have is the statement."

"And what about the others? Boisdeffre, Gonse—do we know anything about them?"

"No, but all of them are finished. They staked everything on that letter." Labori leans in very close to the grille. Through the thick mesh I can see his blue eyes bright with excitement. "Henry would never have forged it purely on his own initiative, would he?"

"It's unimaginable. If they didn't directly order it, then at the very least they must have known what he was up to."

"Exactly! You do realise now we'll be able to call him as a witness? Just let me get him on the stand! What a prospect! I'll make him sing about that and everything else he knows—all the way back to the original court-martial."

"I would love to know what made him admit it after all this time."

"No doubt we'll discover in the morning. Anyway, there it is—wonderful news for you to sleep on. I'll come back again tomorrow. Good night, Picquart."

"Thank you. Good night."

I am taken back to my cell.

The animal noises are particularly loud that night, but it isn't those that keep me awake—it is the thought of Henry in Mont-Valérien.

The next day is the worst I have ever spent in prison. For once I cannot even concentrate to read. I prowl up and down my tiny cell in frustration, my mind constructing and discarding scenarios of what might have happened, what is happening and what could happen next.

The hours crawl past. The evening meal is served. The daylight begins to retreat. At around nine o'clock the warder unlocks my door again and tells me to follow him. How long that walk is! And the curious thing is, right at the very end of it, when I am in the visiting room, and Labori turns his face to the grille, I know exactly what he is going to say, even before I have registered his expression.

He says, "Henry's dead."

I stare at him, allowing the fact to settle. "How did it happen?"

"They found him this afternoon in his cell at Mont-Valérien with his throat cut. Naturally they're saying he killed himself. Strange how that seems to keep happening." He says anxiously, "Are you all right, Picquart?"

I have to turn away from him. I am not sure why I am weeping—out of tiredness, perhaps, or strain; or perhaps it is for Henry, whom I never could bring myself to hate entirely, despite everything, understanding him too well for that.

I think of Henry often. I have little else to do.

I sit in my cell and ponder the details of his death as they emerge over the weeks that follow. If I can solve this mystery, I reason, then perhaps I can solve everything. But I can only rely on what is reported in the papers and the scraps of gossip that Labori picks up on the legal circuit, and in the end I have to admit that probably I will never know the full truth.

I do know that Henry was forced to admit that the "absolute proof" document was a forgery during a terrible meeting in the Minister of War's office on 30 August. He could not do otherwise: the evidence was irrefutable. It seems that in response to my accusation of forgery, Cavaignac, the new Minister of War, supremely confident of his own correctness in all matters, ordered that the entire Dreyfus file be checked for authenticity by one of his officers. It took a long while—the file had by now swollen to three hundred and sixty items—and it was while this process was going on that I met Henry for the last time in Fabre's chambers. I understand now why he seemed so broken: he must have guessed what was coming. Cavaignac's aide did something that apparently no one else in the General Staff had thought to do in almost two years: he held the "absolute proof" under a strong electric lamp. Immediately he noticed that the heading of the letter, My *dear friend*, and the signature, *Alexandrine*, were written on squared paper, the lines of which were bluish-grey, whereas the body of the letter—*I have read that a deputy is going to ask questions about Dreyfus . . .*—was on paper whose lines were mauve. It was obvious that a genuine letter that had been pieced together earlier—in fact in June 1894—had been disassembled and then put back together with a forged central section.

Summoned to explain himself, in the presence of Boisdeffre and Gonse, Henry at first tried to bluster, according to the transcript of his interrogation by Cavaignac released by the government:

HENRY: *I put the pieces together as I received them.*
CAVAIGNAC: *I remind you that nothing is graver for you than the absence of an explanation. Tell me what you did.*
HENRY: *What do you want me to say?*
CAVAIGNAC: *To give me an explanation why one of the documents is lined in pale violet, the other in blue-grey.*
HENRY: *I cannot.*

CAVAIGNAC: *The fact is certain. Reflect on the consequences of my question.*

HENRY: *What do you wish me to say?*

CAVAIGNAC: *What you have done.*

HENRY: *I have not forged papers.*

CAVAIGNAC: *Come, come! You have put the fragments of one into the other.*

HENRY: *[After a moment of hesitation] Well, yes, because the two things fitted admirably, I was led to this.*

Is the transcript accurate? Labori thinks not, but I have little doubt. Just because the government lies about some things, it doesn't mean they lie about everything. I can hear Henry's voice rising off the page better than any playwright could imitate it—bombastic, sulky, wheedling, cunning, stupid.

CAVAIGNAC: *What gave you the idea?*

HENRY: *My chiefs were very uneasy. I wished to pacify them. I wished to restore tranquillity to men's minds. I said to myself, "Let us add a phrase. Suppose we had a war in our present situation."*

CAVAIGNAC: *You were the only one to do this?*

HENRY: *Yes, Gribelin knew nothing about it.*

CAVAIGNAC: *No one knew it? No one in the world?*

HENRY: *I did it in the interest of my country. I was wrong.*

CAVAIGNAC: *And the envelopes?*

HENRY: *I swear I did not make the envelopes. How could I have done so?*

CAVAIGNAC: *So this is what happened? You received in 1896 an envelope with a letter inside, an insignificant letter. You suppressed the letter and fabricated another.*

HENRY: *Yes.*

In the darkness of my cell I play out this scene again and again. I see Cavaignac behind his desk—the overambitious young minister: the fanatic with the temerity to believe he could end the affair once and for all and who now finds himself tripped up by his own hubris. I see Gonse's hand trembling as he smokes and watches the interrogation. I see Boisdeffre by the window staring into the middle distance, as immutably aloof as one of the stone lions that no doubt guard the gate of his family château. And I see Henry occasionally looking round at his chiefs in mute appeal as the questions rain down on him: *Help me!* But of course they say nothing.

And then I picture Henry's expression when Cavaignac—not a soldier but a civilian Minister of War—orders him to be arrested on the spot and taken to Mont-Valérien, where he is locked up in the same rooms that I occupied in the winter. The next day, after a sleepless night, he writes to Gonse (*I have the honour of requesting you to agree to come and see me here: I absolutely must speak to you*) and to his wife (*My adored Berthe, I see that except for you everyone is going to abandon me and yet you know in whose interest I acted*).

I visualise him stretched out on his bed at noon, drinking a bottle of rum—which was the last time he was seen alive—and again six hours later, when a lieutenant and an orderly enter the room and find him still lying on the same bed saturated in blood, his body already cold and stiff, his throat slit twice with a razor, which (an odd detail, this) is clenched in his left hand even though he is right-handed.

But between these two scenes, between noon and six—between Henry alive and Henry dead—my imagination fails me. Labori believes he was murdered, like Lemercier-Picard, to keep him quiet, and that his killing was staged to look like a suicide. He cites medical friends of his who state that it is physically impossible for a person to sever their carotid artery on both sides. But I am not convinced that murder would have been necessary, not with Henry. He would have known what was expected of him after Boisdeffre and Gonse both failed to raise their voices in his defence.

You order me to shoot a man and I'll shoot him.

That afternoon, at the same time as Henry's lifeblood is flowing out of him, Boisdeffre is writing to the Minister of War:

Minister,

I have just received proof that my trust in Colonel Henry, head of the intelligence service, was not justified. That trust, which was total, led me to be deceived and to declare authentic a document that was not, and to present it to you as such.

In these circumstances, I have the honour of asking you to relieve me of my duties.

Boisdeffre

He retires at once to Normandy.

Three days later Cavaignac also resigns, albeit defiantly (*I remain convinced of the guilt of Dreyfus and as resolute as ever to fight against a revision of the trial*); Pellieux submits his resignation; Gonse is transferred out of the Ministry of War and goes back to his regiment on half pay.

I assume, like most people, that it is all over: that if Henry could have arranged the forging of one document, it will be accepted that he could have done it many times, and that the case against Dreyfus has collapsed.

But the days pass, Dreyfus stays on Devil's Island and I remain in La Santé. And gradually it becomes apparent that even now the army will not acknowledge its mistake. I am refused parole. Instead I receive a notification that I will stand trial with Louis in three weeks' time in an ordinary criminal court for illegally transmitting secret documents.

On the eve of the hearing Labori visits me in prison. Normally he is ebullient, even aggressive; today he looks worried. "I have some bad news, I'm afraid. The army are bringing fresh charges against you."

"What now?"

"Forgery."

"They're accusing *me* of forgery?"

"Yes, of the *petit bleu*."

I can only laugh. "You have to credit them with a sense of humour."

But Labori refuses to join in. "They will argue that a military investigation into forgery takes precedence over a civil proceeding. It's a tactic to get you into army custody. My guess is the judge will agree."

"Well," I shrug, "I suppose one prison is much like another."

"That's precisely where you're wrong, my friend. The regime at Cherche-Midi is much harsher than here. And I don't like the thought of you in the clutches of the army—who can tell what accidents might befall you?"

The next day when I am taken into the criminal court of the Seine I ask the judge if I can make a statement. The courtroom is small and jammed with journalists—not just French, but international: I can even see the bald dome and massive side-whiskers of the most famous foreign correspondent in the world, Monsieur de Blowitz of the London *Times*. It is to the reporters that I address my remarks.

"This evening," I say, "I may well be taken to Cherche-Midi, so this is probably the last time that I can speak in public before the secret investigation. I want it to be known that if Lemercier-Picard's shoelaces or Henry's razor are ever found in my cell, it will be murder, for never would a man such as I, even for one instant, contemplate suicide. I shall face this accusation, my head held high, and with the same serenity that I have always shown before my accusers."

To my surprise there is loud applause from the reporters, and I am escorted out of the chamber to shouts of "*Vive Picquart!*" "*Vive la verité!*" "*Vive la justice!*"

Labori's prediction is correct: the army wins the right to deal with me first, and the following day I am taken to Cherche-Midi—to be locked, I am told with relish, in the very same cell in which poor Dreyfus used to bash his head against the wall exactly four years before.

I am kept in solitary confinement, forbidden most visitors and let out for only an hour a day into a tiny yard, six paces square, surrounded by high walls. I crisscross it, back and forth, from corner to corner, and circle the edge, like a mouse trapped in the bottom of a well.

The accusation is that I scratched off the original addressee of the telegram-card and wrote in Esterhazy's name myself. The offence carries a sentence of five years. The questioning goes on for weeks.

Tell us the circumstances in which you came into possession of the petit bleu . . .

Fortunately, I haven't forgotten that I asked Lauth to make photographic copies of the *petit bleu* soon after it was pieced together: eventually these are fetched and show clearly that the address had not been tampered with at that time; only subsequently was it altered as part of the conspiracy to frame me. Still I am kept in Cherche-Midi. Pauline writes, asking to visit me; I tell her not to— it might get into the papers, and besides, I don't want her to see me in this condition; I find it easier to endure it alone. Occasionally the boredom is alleviated by trips to court. In November I lay out the whole of my evidence yet again, this time to the twelve senior judges of the Criminal Chamber, who are beginning the civil process of considering whether the verdict against Dreyfus is safe.

My continued detention without trial becomes notorious. Clemenceau, who is allowed to visit me, proposes in *L'Aurore* "the nomination of Picquart to the post of Grand Prisoner of State, vacant since the Man in the Iron Mask." At night, after they have turned out my light and I can no longer read, I can hear demonstrations both for and against me in the rue Cherche-Midi. The prison has to be protected by seven hundred troops; the hooves of the cavalry clatter down the cobbled streets. I receive thousands of letters of support, including one from the old Empress Eugénie. So embarrassing does this become to the government that Labori is told by officials of the Ministry of Justice that he should ask the civil courts to intervene and release me. I refuse to permit him to do so: I am more useful as a hostage. Every day that I am locked up, the more desperate and vindictive the army looks.

Months pass, and then on the afternoon of Saturday, 3 June 1899, Labori comes to see me. Outside the sun is shining strongly, penetrating even the grime and bars of the tiny window; I can hear a bird singing. He puts a large and inky palm to the metal grille and says, "Picquart, I want to shake your hand."

"Why?"

"Must you always be so damned contrary?" He rattles the steel mesh with his long, thick fingers. "Come: for once, just do as I ask." I place my palm to his and he says quietly, "Congratulations, Georges."

"On what?"

"The Supreme Court of Appeal has ordered the army to bring Dreyfus back for a retrial."

I have waited for this news for so long, and yet when it comes I feel nothing. All I can say is, "What reasons did they give?"

"They cite two, both drawn from your evidence: first, that the 'lowlife D' letter *doesn't* actually refer to Dreyfus and shouldn't have been shown to the judges without informing the defence, and second, that—how do they put it? Oh yes, here's the line: 'facts unknown to the original court-martial tend to show that the *bordereau* could not have been written by Dreyfus.'"

"What language you lawyers talk!" I savour the legalese on my tongue as if it were a delicacy: "'Facts unknown to the original court-martial tend to show . . .' And the army can't appeal against this?"

"No. It's done. A warship is on its way to pick up Dreyfus now and bring him back for a new court-martial. And this time it won't be in secret—this time the whole world will be watching."

23

I am released from gaol the following Friday, on the same day that Dreyfus is disembarked from Devil's Island and begins the long voyage back to France aboard the warship *Sfax*. In light of the Supreme Court ruling, all charges against me are dropped. Edmond is waiting for me with his latest toy, a motorcar, parked outside the prison gates to drive me back to Ville-d'Avray. I refuse to speak to the journalists who surround me on the pavement.

The abrupt change in my fortunes disorientates me. The colours and noises of Paris in the early summer, the sheer *aliveness* of it, the smiling faces of my friends, the lunches and dinners and receptions that have been organised in my honour—all this after the solitary gloom and stale stink of my cell is overwhelming. It is only when I am with other people that I realise how much I have been affected. I find making conversation with more than one person bewildering; my voice is reedy in my ears; I am breathless. When Edmond takes me up to my room, I am unable to climb the stairs without pausing on every third or fourth step and clinging on to the handrail: the muscles that control my knees and ankles have atrophied. In the mirror I look pale and fat. Shaving, I discover white hairs in my moustache.

Edmond and Jeanne invite Pauline to stay and tactfully give her the room next to mine. She holds my hand under the table during dinner and afterwards, when the household is asleep, she comes into my bed. The softness of her body is both familiar and strange, like the memory of something once lived and lost. She is finally divorced; Philippe has been posted abroad at his request; she has her own apartment; the girls are living with her.

We lie in the candlelight, facing each other.

I stroke the hair from her face. There are lines around her eyes and mouth that weren't there before. I have known her since she was a girl, I realise. We have grown old together. I am suddenly overwhelmed by tenderness towards her. "So you're a free woman?"

"I am."

"Would you like me to ask you to marry me?"

A pause.

"Not particularly."

"Why not?"

"Because, my darling, if that is how you choose to pose the question, I don't think there's much point, do you?"

"I'm sorry. I'm not much used to any sort of conversation, let alone this kind. Let me try again. Will you marry me?"

"No."

"Seriously, you're refusing me?"

She takes her time answering. "You're not the marrying sort, Georges. And now I'm divorced I realise that neither am I." She kisses my hand. "You see? You've taught me how to be alone. Thank you."

I am not sure how to respond.

"If that's what you want . . . ?"

"Oh yes, I'm perfectly content as we are."

And so I am denied a thing I never really wanted. Yet why is it I feel obscurely robbed? We lie in silence, and then she says, "What are you going to do now?"

"Get fit again, I hope. Look at pictures. Listen to music."

"And afterwards?"

"I'd like to force the army to take me back."

"Despite the way they've behaved?"

"It's either that or I let them get away with it. And why should I?"

"So people must be made to pay?"

"Absolutely. If Dreyfus is set free, it follows that the whole of the army leadership is rotten. There will be some arrests, I shouldn't wonder. This is only the beginning of a war which may go on for some time. Why? You think I'm wrong?"

"No, but I think perhaps you are in danger of becoming an obsessive."

"If I weren't an obsessive, Dreyfus would still be on Devil's Island."

She looks at me. Her expression is impossible to interpret. "Would you mind blowing out the candle, darling? I'm suddenly very tired."

We both lie awake in the darkness. I pretend to fall asleep. After a few minutes she gets out of bed. I hear her slip on her peignoir. The door opens and I see her for a moment silhouetted in the faint glow from the landing, and then she vanishes in the darkness. Like me, she has got used to sleeping alone.

Dreyfus is landed in the middle of the night in a running sea on the coast of Brittany. He cannot be brought back to Paris for his retrial; it is considered too dangerous. Instead he is taken under cover of darkness to the Breton town of Rennes, where the government announces that his new court-martial will be held, a safe three hundred kilometres to the west of Paris. The opening day of the hearings is fixed for Monday, 7 August.

Edmond insists on coming with me to Rennes, in case I need protection, even though I assure him there's no need: "The government has already told me I'll be provided with a bodyguard."

"All the more reason to have someone around who you can trust."

I don't argue. There is an ugly, violent atmosphere. The President has been attacked at the races by an anti-Semitic aristocrat wielding a cane. Zola and Dreyfus have been burned in effigy. The *Libre Parole* is offering discounted fares to its readers to encourage them to travel to Rennes and break a few Dreyfusard heads. When Edmond and I leave for the railway station at Versailles early on Saturday morning, we are both carrying guns and I feel as though I am on a mission into enemy territory.

At Versailles, we are met by a four-man bodyguard: two police inspectors and two gendarmes. The train, which originated in Paris, pulls in soon after nine, packed from end to end with journalists and spectators heading for the trial. The police have reserved us the rear compartment in the first-class section and insist on sitting between me and the door. I feel as though I am back in custody. People come to gawp at me through the glass partition. It is stiflingly hot. There is a flash as someone tries to take a photograph. I stiffen. Edmond puts his hand on mine. "Easy, Georges," he says quietly.

The journey drags interminably. It is late in the afternoon by the time we pull into Rennes, a town of seventy thousand but without any suburbs as far as I can see. One minute the view is woodland and water meadows and a barge being pulled along a wide river by a horse, and then suddenly it is factory chimneys and stately houses of grey and yellow stone with blue slate roofs, trembling in the haze of heat. The two inspectors jump out ahead of us to check the platform, then Edmond and I clamber down, followed by the gendarmes. We are marched quickly through the station towards a pair of waiting cars. I am vaguely aware of a flurry of recognition in the crowded ticket hall, cries of *"Vive Picquart!"* met by a few countering jeers, and then we are into the cars and driving up a wide, tree-lined avenue filled with hotels and cafés.

We have barely travelled three hundred metres when one of the inspectors, sitting next to the driver, turns round in his seat and says, "That is where the trial will be held."

I know that the venue has been transferred to a school gymnasium in order to accommodate the press and public, and for some reason I have pictured a drab municipal lycée. But this is a fine building, a symbol of provincial pride, almost like a chateau: four storeys of high windows, pink brick and pale stone, capped by a tall roof. Gendarmes guard the perimeter; workmen unload a cart full of timber.

We turn a corner.

"And that," adds the inspector a moment later, "is the military prison where Dreyfus is being held."

It lies just across the street from the side entrance to the school. The driver slows and I glimpse a large gate set into a high, spiked wall, with the barred windows of a fortress just visible behind it; in the road, mounted cavalry and foot soldiers face a small crowd of onlookers. As a connoisseur of prisons, I would say it looks grim; Dreyfus has been in there a month.

Edmond says, "Odd to think he's so close to us, poor fellow. I wonder what sort of shape he's in."

That's what everyone wants to know. That is what has drawn three hundred journalists from across the globe to this sleepy corner of France; has led to the engagement of special telegraph operators to handle what are anticipated to be some two-thirds of a million words of copy per day; has obliged the authorities to equip the Bourse de Commerce with a hundred and fifty desks for reporters; has lured cinematographers to set up their tripods outside the military gaol in the hope of recording a few seconds of jerky images of the prisoner crossing the yard. That is why Queen Victoria has sent the Lord Chief Justice of England to observe the opening of the trial.

Until now, only four outsiders have been permitted to see him since his return to France: Lucie and Mathieu and his two lawyers, the faithful Edgar Demange, attorney at the first court-martial, and Labori, who has been brought in by Mathieu to sharpen the attack on the army. I have not spoken to them. All I know of the prisoner's condition is what I read in the press:

> On Dreyfus's arrival at Rennes, the Préfet sent word to Mme Dreyfus that she could see him that morning. Accordingly at 8:30, her father, mother and brother walked with her to the prison. She alone was admitted to his cell on the first storey, and she remained till 10:15. A captain of the gendarmerie was present, but discreetly kept at a distance. She is said to have found him less altered than she expected, but she seemed much dejected on leaving the prison.

Edmond has rented rooms in a quiet residential street, the rue de Fougères, in a pretty, white-shuttered, wisteria-covered house owned by Madame Aubry, a widow. A tiny front garden is separated from the road by a low wall. A gendarme is on guard outside. The house stands on a hill only a kilometre from the courtroom. Because of the summer heat, the hearings are scheduled to begin at seven and finish at lunchtime; our intention is to walk there early each morning.

On Monday, I get up at five. The sun hasn't risen but it is light enough for me to shave. I dress carefully in a black frock coat with the ribbon of the Legion of Honour in my buttonhole; the bulge of the Webley in my shoulder holster is barely visible. I pick up my cane and a high silk hat, knock on Edmond's door, and together we set off down the hill towards the river, trailed by two policemen.

The houses we pass are solid, prosperous bourgeois villas, their shutters tightly closed; nobody is awake up here. Down at the bottom of the hill, along the brick embankments of the river, laundry-women in lace caps are already on the steps tipping out baskets of dirty washing, while three men wearing harnesses strain to drag a barge piled with scaffolding and ladders. They turn to watch us as we pass—two gentlemen in top hats followed by two gendarmes—but without curiosity, as if such a sight is commonplace at this hour of the morning.

The sun is up by now; it's already hot; the river an opaque algae-green. We cross a bridge and turn towards the lycée, to be greeted by a double line of mounted gendarmes drawn up across the empty street. Our papers are checked and we are directed to where a small crowd queues to pass through a narrow door. We go up a few stone steps, through another doorway, past a cordon of infantry with fixed bayonets, and abruptly we are in the courtroom.

It is twenty metres long, perhaps, by fifteen wide, and two storeys high, filled with clear Breton daylight that pours in on both sides through a double tier of windows. The airy space is thronged with several hundred people. At the far end is a stage with a table and seven crimson-backed chairs; on the wall behind them a white plaster Christ nailed to a black wooden cross; below them, facing each other across the well of the court, the desks and chairs of the prosecution and defence; on both sides, running the length of the hall, the jammed narrow tables and benches of the press, whose numbers dominate the room; and at the back, behind another line of infantry, the public. The central section is reserved for the witnesses, and here we all are again—Boisdeffre, Gonse, Billot, Pellieux, Lauth, Gribelin. We carefully avoid one another's gaze.

"Excuse me," rasps a quiet voice at my back that raises the hairs on my neck. I stand aside and Mercier edges past me, without giving me a look. He walks up the aisle and takes a seat between Gonse and Billot, and immediately the generals begin a whispered conclave. Boisdeffre looks shattered, vacant—he is said to have become a recluse; Billot strokes his moustache and seems bemused; Gonse nods, obsequious; Pellieux has his back half turned. It is Mercier, now on the retired list, gesturing with his fist, who is suddenly the dominant figure again; he has assumed the leadership of the army's cause. In this affair there must be a guilty party, he has declared to the press. And that guilty party is either Dreyfus or me. Since it is not me, it is Dreyfus. Dreyfus is a traitor. I will prove it. His leathery masklike face briefly turns in my direction; the gun-slit eyes are momentarily trained on mine.

It is almost seven. I take a seat just behind Mathieu Dreyfus, who turns and shakes my hand. Lucie nods to me, her face as pale as a midday moon, and manages a brief, strained smile. The lawyers enter clad in their black robes and their strange conical black hats, the giant figure of Labori gesturing with elaborate courtesy for the older Demange to go ahead of him. Then a cry from the back of the court—"Present arms!"—a crash of fifty boots stamping to attention, and the judges file in, led by the diminutive Colonel Jouaust. He wears a bushy white moustache even larger than Billot's, so huge the top of his face seems to peer over it. He mounts the stage and takes the central chair. His voice is dry and hard: "Bring in the accused."

The sergeant usher marches to a door near the front of the court, his tread very loud in the sudden silence. He opens the door and two men step through. One is the escorting officer and the other is Dreyfus. The courtroom gasps, I among them, for he is an old man—a little old man, with a stiff-limbed walk and a baggy tunic his frame is too shrunken to fill. His trousers flap around his ankles. He moves jerkily into the middle of the courtroom, pauses at the couple of steps that lead to the platform where his lawyers sit, as if to summon his strength, then mounts them with difficulty, salutes the judges with a white-gloved hand and takes off his cap to reveal a skull almost entirely bald, except for a fringe of silver hair at the back which hangs over his collar. He is told to sit while the registrar reads out the orders constituting the court, then Jouaust says, "Accused—stand."

He struggles back to his feet.

"What is your name?"

In the silent courtroom the response is barely audible: "Alfred Dreyfus."

"Age?"

"Thirty-nine." That draws another shocked gasp.

"Place of birth?"

"Mulhouse."

"Rank?"

"Captain, breveted to the General Staff." Everyone is leaning forward, straining to hear. It is difficult to understand him: he seems to have forgotten how to formulate his words; there is a whistling sound through the gaps in his teeth.

After various bits of legal procedure, Jouaust says, "You are accused of the crime of high treason, of having delivered to an agent of a foreign power the documents that are specified in the memorandum called the *bordereau*. The law gives you the right to speak in your defence. Here is the *bordereau*."

He nods to a court official, who hands it to the prisoner. Dreyfus studies it. He is trembling, appears close to breaking down. Finally, in that curious voice of his—flat even when charged with emotion—he says: "I am innocent. I swear it, Colonel, as I affirmed in 1894." His stops; his struggle to maintain his composure is agony to watch. "I can bear everything, Colonel, but once more, for the honour of my name and my children, I am innocent."

For the rest of the morning, Jouaust takes Dreyfus through the contents of the *bordereau*, item by item. His questions are harsh and accusatory; Dreyfus answers them in a dry and technical manner, as if he were an expert witness in somebody else's trial: no, he knew nothing of the hydraulic brake of the 120 millimetre cannon; yes, he could have acquired information about covering troops, but he had never asked for it; the same was true of the plans for invading Madagascar—he could have asked but he didn't; no, the colonel is mistaken—he wasn't in the Third Department when changes were made to artillery formations; no, the officer who claimed to have lent him a copy of the firing manual was also mistaken—he had never had it in his possession; no, he had never said that France would be better off under German rule, certainly not.

The double tier of windows heats the courtroom like a greenhouse. Everyone is sweating apart from Dreyfus, perhaps because he is accustomed to the tropics. The only time he shows real emotion again is when Jouaust brings up the old canard that he confessed on the day of his degradation to Captain Lebrun-Renault.

"I did not confess."

"But there were other witnesses."

"I do not remember any."

"Well then, what conversation did you have with him?"

"It was not a conversation, Colonel. It was a monologue. I was about to be led before a huge crowd that was quivering with patriotic anguish, and I said to Captain Lebrun-Renault that I wished to cry out my innocence in the face of everybody. I wanted to say that I was not the guilty man. There was no confession."

At eleven, the session ends. Jouaust announces that the next four days of hearings will be held behind closed doors, so that the judges can be shown the secret files. The public and press will be barred, and so will I. It will be at least a week before I am called to give evidence.

Dreyfus is escorted back the way he came without once looking in my direction, and the rest of us file out into the brilliant August heat, the journalists all running away down the street towards the special telegraph operators in their haste to be first with their description of the Prisoner of Devil's Island.

Edmond, with characteristic attention to the finer things in life, has found a restaurant close to where we are staying—"a hidden gem, Georges, it might almost be Alsace"—Les Trois Marches in the rue d'Antrain, a rustic inn on the edge of open country. We walk to it for lunch, labouring up the hill in the broiling sun, trailed by my bodyguards. The auberge is a farmhouse, run by a couple named Jarlet, with a garden, orchard, stables, barn and pigsty. We sit out on benches under a tree drinking cider, buzzed by wasps, discussing the events of the morning. Edmond, who has never seen Dreyfus before, is remarking on his curious ability to repel sympathy—"Why is it that whenever he proclaims 'I am innocent,' even though one knows for certain that he is, the words somehow lack conviction?"—when I notice a group of gendarmes standing talking across the street.

Jarlet is laying out a plate of *pâté de campagne*. I point the gendarmes out to him. "Two of those gentlemen are with us, but who are the others?"

"They are standing guard outside the house of General de Saint-Germain, monsieur. He commands the army in this area."

"Does he really require police protection?"

"No, monsieur, the guards are not for him. They are for the man who is staying in his house—General Mercier."

"Did you hear that, Edmond? Mercier is living across the road."

Edmond shouts with laughter. "That's wonderful! We must establish a permanent bridgehead in the vicinity of the enemy." He turns to the patron. "Jarlet, from now on, I'll pay to reserve a table for ten, for every lunch and dinner, for as long as the trial lasts. Is that all right with you?"

It is indeed all right with M. Jarlet, and from that time on begins the "Conspiracy of Les Trois Marches," as the right-wing papers call it, with all the leading Dreyfusards gathering here to eat the Jarlets' good plain bourgeois fare each day at noon and seven—regulars include the Clemenceau brothers, the socialists Jean Jaurès and René Viviani, the journalists Lacroix and Séverine, the "intellectuals" Octave Mirabeau, Gabriel Monod and Victor Basch. Quite why Mercier needs a bodyguard to protect him from such roughs as these is not at all clear—does he imagine that Professor Monod is going to attack him with a rolled-up copy of the *Revue Historique*? On Wednesday I ask for my own police protection to be withdrawn. Not only do I view them as unnecessary, I suspect they pass on information about me to the authorities.

All week people come and go to Les Trois Marches. Mathieu Dreyfus puts in an appearance, but never Lucie, who is staying with a widow in the town, while Labori, who has lodgings close to us, walks up the hill most evenings with Marguerite after he has finished consultations with his client in the military prison.

"How is he bearing up?" I ask one night.

"Amazingly well, all things considered. My God, but he's a strange one, isn't he? I've seen him almost every day for a month, yet I don't believe I know him any better now than I did in the first ten minutes. Everything is at a distance with him. I suppose that's how he has survived."

"And how are the secret sessions going? What does the court make of the intelligence files?"

"Ah, how the military adore all that stuff! Hundreds and hundreds of pages of it—love letters and buggers' billets-doux and gossip and rumours and forgeries and false trails that lead nowhere. It's like the Sibylline Books: you can put the leaves together however you like and read whatever you want into them. Yet I doubt if more than twenty lines apply directly to Dreyfus."

We are standing smoking cigarettes a little way apart from the others. It is dusk. There is laughter behind us. Jaurès's voice, which was created by nature for talking to an audience of ten thousand rather than a table of ten, booms out over the garden.

Labori says suddenly, "I see we are being watched."

Across the road, in one of the upper windows, Mercier is plainly visible, gazing down at us.

"He has just had his old comrades round to dinner," I say. "Boisdeffre, Gonse, Pellieux, Billot—they are in and out of there constantly."

"I hear he's planning to run for the Senate. This trial is a great platform for him. If it weren't for his political ambitions, their side would lack direction."

"If it weren't for his political ambitions," I reply, "the whole thing might never have happened. He thought Dreyfus could be his ticket to the presidency."

"He still does."

Mercier is scheduled to give his evidence on Saturday—the first day that the press and public will be allowed back into the courtroom since the opening session. His appearance is only slightly less eagerly awaited than that of Dreyfus himself. He arrives in court wearing the full undress uniform of a general—red tunic, black trousers, with a kepi of crimson and gold. On his breast glints the medal of a Grand Officer of the Legion of Honour. When he is called, he rises from his place among the military witnesses and walks to the front of the court carrying a black leather document case. He stands no more than two paces from where Dreyfus is sitting, but doesn't once glance in his direction.

"My deposition," he says, in his quiet, hoarse voice, "will have to be a trifle long."

Jouaust says unctuously, "Usher, fetch a chair for the general."

Mercier speaks for three hours, producing document after document from his black leather case—among them the "lowlife D" letter, which he continues to insist refers to Dreyfus, and even the fabricated Guénée reports about a spy in the intelligence department, although he leaves out the name of the source, Val Carlos. He passes them up to Jouaust, who hands them along the line of judges. After a while, Labori leans back in his chair and cranes his head to look at me, as if to say, "What is this idiot doing?" I am careful to maintain a neutral expression, but I think he is right: by introducing the evidence of the secret dossier into open court, Mercier is exposing a dangerous flank for Labori to attack in cross-examination.

On and on drones Mercier, like some paranoid, illiterate editorial in *La Libre Parole* seeing Jewish conspiracies everywhere. He alleges that thirty-five million francs have been raised to free Dreyfus in England and Germany. He quotes as if it is fact what Dreyfus is supposed to have said about the occupation of Alsace-Lorraine, and has always denied: "For us Jews it is not the same thing; where we are, our God is." He drags up the old myth of the "confession" before the degradation. He spins the most fantastical explanation as to why he showed the secret dossier to the judges at the court-martial, claiming that because of the Dreyfus controversy the country was "within two finger-breadths of war" with Germany—so much so that he had ordered General Boisdeffre to be ready to dispatch the telegrams that would trigger a full mobilisation while he, Mercier, sat with President Casimir-Perier in the Élysée Palace until half past midnight waiting to see if the German emperor would back down.

Casimir-Perier, who is sitting with the witnesses, actually rises to challenge this lie, and when Jouaust won't permit him to intervene, he shakes his head at such nonsense, which causes a sensation in the court.

Mercier takes no notice. It is the old paranoia about Germany, the lingering stench of defeatism after 1870. He presses on. "Now," he says, "at that moment, should we have desired war? Should I, as Minister of War, have desired for my country a war undertaken in these conditions? I did not hesitate to say 'no.' On the other hand, was I to leave the court-martial in ignorance of the charges against Dreyfus? These documents"—he pats the case on the stand in front of him—"then formed what was called the secret dossier, and I regarded it as imperative that the judges should see them. Could I not have relied on the comparative secrecy of a trial behind closed doors? No, I have no confidence in closed doors! Sooner or later the press manages to get hold of all it wants and publishes it, despite the threats of the government. In these circumstances, I placed the secret documents in a sealed envelope and sent them to the president of the court-martial."

Dreyfus is sitting straight up in his chair now, looking at Mercier with intense astonishment, and something else, something beyond amazement—for the first time: burning anger.

Mercier does not see it because he is carefully not looking at him. "Let me add one last word," he says. "I have not reached my age without having had the sad experience of learning that all that is human is liable to error. But if I am weak-minded, as Monsieur Zola has alleged, I am at least an honest man and the son of an honest man. And if the slightest doubt had ever crossed my mind, I should be the first to declare it"—and now finally he turns in his chair to look at Dreyfus—"and to say, before you all, to Captain Dreyfus, 'I have blundered in good faith.'"

The cheap theatrical touch is too much for the prisoner to bear. Suddenly, and incredibly, without the least trace of stiffness in his legs, Dreyfus springs to his feet, clenches his fist and swings round at

Mercier as if to strike him, roaring in a terrible voice, half cry and half sob: *"That is what you should say!"*

The whole court draws in its breath. The officials are too stunned to move. Only Mercier seems unaffected. He ignores the figure looming over him. "I would say to Captain Dreyfus," he repeats patiently, "'I have been honestly mistaken. I acknowledge it in good faith and will do all in my power to repair a terrible mistake.'"

Dreyfus is still on his feet, staring down at him, his arm raised. *"It is your duty!"*

There is a round of applause, mostly from the journalists; I join in.

Mercier smiles slightly, as if confronted by overemotional children, shakes his head, waits for the demonstration to die down. "No, it is not so. My conviction since 1894 has not undergone the slightest change. In fact it has actually been strengthened, not only by a thorough study of the secret dossier but by the pathetic case that has been made for Dreyfus's innocence by his supporters, despite all the frantic efforts and the millions spent on his behalf. There. I have done."

With that, Mercier closes his leather case, stands, bows to the judges, collects his kepi from the shelf in front of him, tucks the documents under his arm, and turns to walk out of the court, to a loud accompaniment of jeers. As he passes the press benches, one of the reporters—it is Georges Bourdon of *Le Figaro*—hisses at him, "Assassin!"

Mercier stops and points at him. "This fellow just called me an assassin!"

The army prosecutor rises. "Monsieur President, I demand that man be arrested for contempt."

Jouaust calls to the sergeant-at-arms, "Take him into custody!"

As soldiers close in on Bourdon, Labori rises. "Monsieur President, excuse me, but I would like to question the witness."

"Of course, Maître Labori," replies Jouaust, coolly checking his watch, "but it is already after twelve, and tomorrow is Sunday. You will have your chance at six-thirty on Monday morning. Until then the court is adjourned."

24

Mercier's testimony is held to have been a disaster—a grave disappointment to his own side, as he failed to provide the promised "proof" that Dreyfus was guilty, and an opportunity for ours, in that Labori—generally considered to be the most aggressive cross-examiner at the Paris bar—will now have the chance to challenge him on the witness stand about the secret file. All he needs is sufficient ammunition, and on Sunday morning I walk to his lodgings to help him prepare. I have no qualms about breaking the last vestiges of my oath of confidentiality: if Mercier can talk about matters of national security, so can I.

"The point about Mercier," I say, when Labori and I are ensconced in his makeshift study, "is that the Dreyfus affair would never have happened without him. He was the one who ordered the spy hunt to be confined to the General Staff—the original and fundamental error. He was the one who ordered that Dreyfus should be held in solitary confinement for weeks in order to break him. And he was the one who ordered the compilation of the secret dossier."

"I'll challenge him on those three points." Labori is making rapid notes. "But we're not saying that he knew all along that Dreyfus was innocent?"

"Not at the very beginning. But when Dreyfus refused to confess, and they realised that the only thing they had against him was the handwriting of the *bordereau*—that was when they started to panic, in my view, and to fabricate the evidence."

"And you think Mercier knew of this?"

"Definitely."

"How?"

"Because at the beginning of November, the Foreign Ministry broke an Italian cipher telegram that showed that Panizzardi had never even heard of Dreyfus."

Labori, still writing, raises his eyebrows. "And this was shown to Mercier?"

"Yes. The decrypt was handed to him personally."

Labori stops writing and sits back in his chair, tapping his pencil against his notebook. "So he must have been aware more than a month before the court-martial that the 'lowlife D' letter couldn't refer to Dreyfus?" I nod. "Yet he went ahead anyway and showed it to the judges, along with a commentary pointing out its importance in proving Dreyfus's guilt?"

"And he was still maintaining the same position yesterday. The man is quite shameless."

"So what did the Statistical Section do with the Italian telegram? Presumably they simply ignored it?"

"No, worse: they destroyed the original War Ministry copy and substituted a false version which implied the opposite—that Panizzardi knew all about Dreyfus."

"And Mercier is ultimately responsible for this?"

"That is my belief, after months of thinking about it. There are plenty of others with dirty hands—Sandherr, Gonse, Henry—but Mercier was the driving force. He was the one who should have halted the proceedings against Dreyfus the moment he saw that telegram. But he knew it would do him terrible damage politically, whereas if he brought off a successful prosecution he might just ride it all the way to the Élysée. It was a stupid delusion, but then he's fundamentally a dim man."

Labori resumes writing. "And what about this other document from the secret file he quoted yesterday—the report by the Sûreté officer, Guénée—can I tackle him on that?"

"It was falsified, without a doubt. Guénée claimed to have been told by the Spanish military attaché, the marquis de Val Carlos, that the Germans had a spy in the intelligence section. Henry swore Val Carlos told him the same story three months later and he used it against Dreyfus at the original court-martial. But look at the language: it's all wrong. I raised it with Guénée soon after I discovered it. I never saw a man look so shifty."

"Should we summon Val Carlos as a witness? Ask him to confirm if he ever said it?"

"You could try, although I'm sure he'd plead diplomatic immunity. Why don't you call Guénée?"

"Guénée died five weeks ago."

I look at him in surprise. "Died of what?"

"Of 'cerebral congestion,' according to the medical certificate, whatever that may be." Labori shakes his large head. "Sandherr, Henry, Lemercier-Picard and Guénée—that secret file turned out to be a blood pact."

I rise at five on Monday morning, shave and dress carefully. My gun lies on the nightstand beside my bed. I pick it up, weigh it in my hand, ponder it, then put it away in the chest of drawers.

A gentle knock at my door; Edmond's voice: "Georges, are you ready?"

As well as lunch and dinner, Edmond and I have also taken to having breakfast at Les Trois Marches. We eat omelettes and baguettes in the small parlour. Across the road, the shutters of Mercier's house remain tightly shut. A gendarme wanders up and down outside it, yawning.

At a quarter to six, we begin to descend the hill. The sky is filled with rain clouds for the first time; their greyness matches the stone buildings of the quiet town; the air is cooler, glassy. Shortly before we reach the canal there comes from behind us a shout of "Good morning, gentlemen!" and I turn and see Labori hurrying to catch us up. He is wearing a dark suit and a straw boater and swinging a large black briefcase.

"We shall have some amusement today, I think."

He seems in an excellent mood, like a sportsman eager to get into the arena. He joins us and walks between us, I to his right and Edmond to his left, along the wide dirt path beside the canal. He asks me some last-minute detail about Mercier—"Was Boisdeffre present in the room when the Minister ordered Sandherr to disperse the secret file?"—and I am on the point of replying when I hear a noise at our backs. I suspect an eavesdropper and half turn.

Someone is there all right—a big, youngish fellow, red hair, black jacket, white cap—with a revolver pointing from his hand. There is a tremendous bang that sends the ducks scattering across the water, crying in alarm. Labori says in mystification, "Oh, oh, oh . . ." and drops to one knee, as if winded. I put out my hand as he topples forward on his face, his briefcase still in his hand.

My first instinct is to kneel and try to support him. He sounds more puzzled than in pain: "Oh, oh . . ." There is a hole in his jacket almost in the dead centre of his back. I look round to see the assassin about a hundred metres away, running away along the side of the canal. A different instinct—a soldier's instinct—kicks in.

I say to Edmond, "Stay here."

I set off in pursuit of the gunman. After a few seconds I am aware of Edmond running behind me. He shouts, "Georges, be careful!"

I yell over my shoulder, "Go back to Labori!" and lengthen my stride, pumping my arms.

Edmond runs for a little longer then gives up the chase. I put my head down, forcing myself to go faster. I am gaining on my quarry. Exactly what I will do if I get my hands on him, given that he presumably has five bullets left and I am unarmed, I am not sure: I will deal with that situation when it arises. In the meantime, there are bargemen up ahead and I shout out to them to grab the assassin. They look to see what is happening, drop their ropes and block his path.

I am close now—twenty metres perhaps—close enough to see him point his gun at them and hear him scream, "Get out of my way! I've just killed Dreyfus!"

Whether it's the gun or the boast, it does the trick. They stand aside and he runs on, and when I race past them, I have to hurdle a foot that is stuck out to trip me over.

Abruptly the houses and the factories fall away and we are into open Breton country. Beyond the canal to my right I can see the railway line and a train steaming into the station; to my left are fields with cows and distant woodland. The gunman suddenly leaves the towpath, darts off to the left and heads towards the trees. A year ago

I would have caught him. But all those months in prison have done for me. I am out of breath, have cramp, my heart feels strange. I leap a ditch and land badly, and by the time I reach the edge of the wood he has had plenty of time to conceal himself. I find a stout stick and crash around in the undergrowth for half an hour, slashing at the ferns, startling pheasants, conscious all the while that I might be in his sights, until at last the silence of the trees defeats me and I make my way, limping, back to the canal.

I have to walk back more than three kilometres and so I miss the immediate aftermath of the shooting. Edmond describes it all for me later: how, when he returned to Labori, the great advocate had somehow managed to drag his body on top of his briefcase in order to deter various individuals who had recognised him and were trying to steal his notes; how Marguerite Labori had rushed to the scene wearing a black and white summer dress, and had cradled her husband in her lap, trying to keep him cool with the aid of a small Japanese fan; how he had lain on his side with his arm around her, talking calmly, but scarcely shedding blood—an ominous sign as it often suggests the bleeding is internal; how a shutter had been fetched and four soldiers had heaved Labori onto it and carried the giant with difficulty back to his lodgings; how the doctor had examined him and announced that the bullet was lodged between the fifth and sixth ribs, millimetres from his spine, and the situation was grave—the patient was unable to move his leg; how Labori's fellow advocate, Demange, had hurried over from the courtroom along with his assistants to find out what was happening; how Labori had grasped his colleague's hand and said, "Old chap, I'm going to die perhaps, but Dreyfus is safe"; and how everyone had remarked on the way that Dreyfus in court had received the news of his lawyer's shooting without the slightest change in his facial expression.

By the time I get back, which must be nearly an hour after the attack, the scene of the assault is oddly deserted, as if nothing has happened. At Labori's lodgings his landlady tells me he has been taken to the house of Victor Basch, a Dreyfusard professor at the local university, who lives in the rue d'Antrain, the same street as

Les Trois Marches. I walk up the hill to find a group of journalists in the road outside and a pair of gendarmes guarding the door. Inside, Labori has been laid out, unconscious by now, on a mattress in a downstairs room, and Marguerite is beside him, holding his hand. His face is deathly white. The doctor has summoned a surgeon, who has not yet arrived; his own interim opinion is that it is too dangerous to operate and that the bullet is best left where it is: the next twenty-four hours will be crucial in showing the extent of the damage.

There is a police inspector in the front parlour, questioning Edmond. I give him my description of the attacker, the chase and the location of the wood into which he ran. "Cesson Forest," says the inspector. "I'll have it searched," and he goes out into the hall to speak to one of his men.

While he is out of the room, Edmond says, "Are you all right?"

"Disgusted at my physical fitness; otherwise fine." I pound the arm of my chair in frustration. "If only I had been carrying my gun—I'd have brought him down easily."

"Was it Labori he was after, or you?"

I hadn't thought of that. "Oh, Labori—I'm sure of it. They must have been desperate to stop him cross-examining Mercier. We'll need to find a replacement for him when the trial resumes."

Edmond looks stricken. "My God, didn't you hear? Jouaust would only agree to an adjournment of forty-five minutes. Demange has had to go back to examine Mercier."

"But Demange isn't prepared! He doesn't know the questions to ask!"

It is a disaster. I hurry out of the house, past the journalists, down the slope towards the lycée. It is starting to rain. Huge, warm drops explode on the street stones, filling the air with a fragrance of moist dust. Several of the reporters set off after me. They trot alongside asking questions and somehow managing to write down my answers.

"So the assassin is still at large?"

"As far as I know."

"Do you think he'll be caught?"

"He could be—whether he will be is another question."

"Do you think the army is behind it?"

"I hope not."

"You don't rule it out?"

"Let me put it this way: I think it curious that in a town filled with five thousand police and soldiers, an assassin is able to gun down Dreyfus's advocate and melt away without apparent difficulty."

That is what they want to hear. At the entrance to the lycée they peel away and run off in the direction of the Bourse de Commerce to telegraph their stories.

Inside, Mercier is on the stand and I realise within a minute of taking my seat that Demange is making heavy work of questioning him. Demange is a decent, civilised man of nearly sixty with blood-hound eyes, who has faithfully represented his client for almost half a decade. But he isn't prepared for this session, and even if he were, he lacks Labori's forensic menace. He is, to put it bluntly, a windbag. His habit is to preface every question with a speech, giving Mercier plenty of time to think of his answer. Mercier brushes him aside with ease. Asked about the falsified Panizzardi telegram in the Ministry of War archive, he denies all knowledge of it; asked why he didn't place the telegram in the secret dossier and show it to the judges, he says it is because the Foreign Ministry wouldn't have liked it. After a few more minutes of this he is allowed to step down. As he walks back up the aisle, his glance flickers in my direction. He stops and bends down to speak to me, holds out his hand. He knows the entire courtroom is watching us. He says, with great solicitation, loud enough for half the audience to hear, "Monsieur Picquart, this is the most appalling news. How is Maître Labori's condition?"

"The bullet is still inside him, General. We will know better tomorrow."

"It is a profoundly shocking incident. Will you be sure to give Madame Labori my best wishes for her husband's recovery?"

"Certainly, General."

His strange sea-green eyes hold mine, and for a fractional instant I glimpse the shadow, like a fin in the water, of his dull malevolence, and then he nods and moves away.

———

The following day is the Feast of the Assumption, a public holiday, and the court does not sit. Labori survives the night. His fever diminishes. There are hopes of a recovery. On Wednesday, Demange rises in court and pleads for an adjournment of two weeks, until either Labori is well enough to resume work or a new advocate can be fully briefed: Albert Clemenceau has agreed to take on the case. Jouaust turns the request down flat: the circumstances are unfortunate but the defence will have to get by as best it can.

The first part of the morning's session is devoted to the details of Dreyfus's confinement on Devil's Island, and as the terrible harshness of the regime is described, even the prosecution witnesses—even Boisdeffre, even Gonse—have the decency to look embarrassed at the catalogue of torments inflicted in the name of justice. But when, at the end, Jouaust asks the accused if he has any comment to make, Dreyfus merely responds stiffly, "I am here to defend my honour and that of my children. I shall say nothing of the tortures I have been made to undergo." He prefers the army's hatred to its pity. What seems to be coldness, I realise, is partly a determination not to be a victim; I respect him for it.

On Thursday, I am called to give evidence.

I walk to the front of the court, and climb the two steps to the raised platform, conscious of the silence that has fallen behind me in the crowded court. I feel no nervousness, just a desire to get it done. Before me is a railing with a shelf, on which witnesses can place their notes or military caps; beyond that the stage and the row of judges—two colonels, three majors and two captains—and to my left, sitting barely two metres away, Dreyfus. How curious it is to stand there close enough to shake his hand, and yet not to be able to speak to him! I try to forget his presence as I stare firmly ahead and swear to tell the complete truth.

Jouaust begins, "Did you know the accused before the events for which he is charged?"

"Yes, Colonel."

"How did you know him?"

"I was a professor at the École Supérieure de Guerre when Dreyfus was a pupil."

"Your relations went no further than that?"

"Correct."

"You were not his mentor, or his ally?"

"No, Colonel."

"You were not in his service, nor he in yours?"

"No, Colonel."

Jouaust makes a note.

Only now do I risk a brief sidelong glance at Dreyfus. He has been so long at the centre of my existence, has changed my destiny so utterly, has grown so large in my imagination, that I suppose it would be impossible for the man to be the equal of all he represents. Even so, it is strange to contemplate this quiet stranger who, if I had to guess, I would say was a retired minor official from the Colonial Service, blinking at me through his pince-nez as if we have just happened to find ourselves in the same railway compartment on a very long journey.

I am recalled to the present by Jouaust's dry voice saying, "Describe the events as you know them . . ." and I look away.

My evidence takes up the whole of the day's session, and most of the next. There is no point in my describing it again—*petit bleu*, Esterhazy, *bordereau* . . . I deliver it, once more, as if it were a lecture, which in a sense it is. I am the founder of the school of Dreyfus studies: its leading scholar, its star professor—there is nothing I can be asked about my specialist field that I do not know: every letter and telegram, every personality, every forgery, every lie. Occasionally, officers of the General Staff rise like sweaty students to challenge me on specific points; I flatten them with ease. From time to time as I speak, I scan the furrowed faces of the judges in the same way that I used once to survey those of my pupils, and wonder how much of this is sinking in.

When at last Jouaust tells me to stand down and I turn and walk back to my seat, it seems to me—I may be mistaken—that Dreyfus gives me the briefest of nods and a half-smile of thanks.

Labori's recovery continues, and in the middle of the following week, with the bullet still lodged in the muscles of his shoulder, he returns to court. He enters accompanied by Marguerite to loud applause. He acknowledges his reception with a wave and walks to his place, where he has been provided with a large and comfortable armchair. The only obvious sign of his injury, apart from his damp and chalky pallor, is the stiffness of his left arm, which he can hardly move. Dreyfus stands as he passes and warmly shakes his good hand.

Privately, I am not convinced that he is as fit to return to his duties as he insists he is. Gunshot injuries are something I know about. They take longer to get over than one imagines. Labori should have had an operation to have the bullet removed, in my opinion— but that would have taken him out of the trial altogether. He is in a lot of pain and isn't sleeping. And there is also a mental trauma he is refusing to acknowledge. I can see it when he goes out into the street—the way he slightly recoils every time a stranger approaches with his hand extended, or flinches when he hears hurrying footsteps behind him. Professionally it expresses itself in a certain irritability and shortness of temper, particularly with the president of the court, whom Labori delights in goading:

JOUAUST: *I urge you to speak with moderation.*
LABORI: *I have not said a single immoderate word.*
JOUAUST: *But your tone is not moderate.*
LABORI: *I'm not in control of my tone.*
JOUAUST: *Well, you should be—every man is in control of his own person.*
LABORI: *I'm in control of my person, just not of my tone.*
JOUAUST: *I shall withdraw your permission to speak.*
LABORI: *Go ahead and withdraw it.*
JOUAUST: *Sit down!*
LABORI: *I will sit down—but not on your orders!*

One day, at a legal strategy meeting I attend together with Mathieu Dreyfus, Demange says in his slightly pompous manner, "We must never forget our central objective, my dear Labori, which is not, with all due respect, to flay the army for its errors but to ensure our client walks free. As this is an army hearing, in which the out-come will be decided by military officers, we need to be diplomatic."

"Ah yes," retorts, Labori, "'diplomatic'! This would be the same diplomacy, I take it, that led to your client spending four years on Devil's Island?"

Demange, red-faced with fury, gathers together his papers and leaves the room.

Wearily, Mathieu gets up to go after him. At the door he says, "I understand your frustration, Labori, but Edgar has stood by my fam-ily loyally for five years. He has earned the right to set the direction of our strategy."

On this issue, I agree with Labori. I know the army. It does not react to diplomacy. It responds to force. But even for me, Labori goes too far when he decides to telegraph—without consulting Demange—the Emperor of Germany and the King of Italy, asking them to allow von Schwartzkoppen and Panizzardi (both of whom have withdrawn to their native countries) to come to Rennes to give evidence. The Chancellor of Germany, Count von Bülow, replies as if to a madman:

> His Majesty the Emperor and King, our most gracious master, considers it naturally and totally impossible to accede in any man-ner to Maître Labori's strange suggestion.

The bitterness between Labori and Demange afterwards worsens to such an extent that Labori, white with pain, announces he will not deliver a closing speech: "I cannot be a party to a strategy in which I do not believe. If that old fool thinks he can win by being polite to these murdering bastards, let him try it alone."

As the end of the trial draws near, the Préfecture of Police in Rennes, Dureault, approaches me in the crowded courtyard of the lycée dur-ing an adjournment, when everyone is outside stretching their legs. He beckons me to one side and says in a low voice: "We have good intelligence, Monsieur Picquart, that the nationalists are planning to arrive in force at the time of the verdict, and that if Dreyfus is acquitted there is liable to be serious violence. In the circumstances, I fear we cannot guarantee your safety, and I would urge you to leave the town before then. I hope you understand."

"Thank you, Monsieur Dureault. I appreciate your candour."

"One further piece of advice, if I may. I suggest you catch the night train in order to avoid being seen."

He moves away. I lean against the wall in the sunshine and smoke a cigarette. I shall not be sorry to go. I have been here nearly a month. So has everyone. There are Gonse and Boisdeffre promenading up and down, arm in arm, as if clinging to each other for support. There are Mercier and Billot, sitting on a wall, swinging their legs like schoolboys. There is Madame Henry, the nation's widow, veiled from head to foot in black, floating across the courtyard like the Angel of Death, on the arm of Major Lauth, whose relationship with her is said to be intimate. There is the stubby, hairy figure of Bertillon, with his suitcase full of diagrams, still insisting that Dreyfus forged his own handwriting in order to produce the *bordereau*. There is Gribelin, who has found a shadow to stand in. Not everyone is here, of course. There are some ghostly absences—Sandherr, Henry, Lemercier-Picard, Guénée—and a few that are not so ghostly: du Paty, who has avoided giving evidence by insisting he is too ill; Scheurer-Kestner, who really is ill, and said to be about to die from cancer; and Esterhazy, who has gone to earth in the English village of Harpenden. But otherwise here we all are, like the inmates of an asylum, or the passengers on some legal *Flying Dutchman*, doomed to circle one another, and the world, for ever.

A bell rings, summoning us back into court.

Edmond and I have a farewell supper at Les Trois Marches on the evening of Thursday, 7 September. Labori and Marguerite are there, but Mathieu and Demange don't come. We drink a final toast to victory, raising our glasses in the direction of Mercier's house, and then we take a taxi to the deserted railway station and board the evening train to Paris. No one sees us leave. The town sinks away into the dark behind us.

The verdict is due on Saturday afternoon, and Aline Ménard-

Dorian decides it offers the most wonderful opportunity for a luncheon party. She arranges with her friend the Under-Secretary of State for Posts and Telegraphs to have a telephone line left open from her drawing room to the Bourse de Commerce in Rennes—we will thus have the result almost as soon as it is announced—and invites all her usual salon, plus a few others, to a buffet at one o'clock in the rue de la Faisanderie.

I don't feel much like going, but her invitation is so insistent—"it would be utterly wonderful to have you with us, my dearest Georges, to share in your moment of glory"—that I feel it would be churlish to refuse; besides, I have nothing else to do.

Back from exile, Zola attends, along with Georges and Albert Clemenceau, Jean Jaurès, and de Blowitz of the London *Times;* there must be fifty or sixty of us, including Blanche de Comminges with a young man named d'Espic de Ginestet, whom she introduces as her fiancé. A liveried footman crouches by the telephone in the corner, checking occasionally with the operator to ensure the line is still working. At three-fifteen, after we have finished eating— or not eating, in my case—he signals to our host, Paul Ménard, Aline's husband, an industrialist of radical sympathies, and hands him the instrument. Ménard listens gravely for a moment and then announces, "The judges have retired to consider their verdict." He returns the telephone to the white-gloved hand of the footman.

I go out onto the terrace to be alone, but several other guests follow me. De Blowitz, whose spherical body and bulbous ruddy features give him the look of a character out of Dickens—Bumble, perhaps, or Pickwick—asks me if I can remember how long the judges spent deliberating at the first court-martial.

"Half an hour."

"And would you say, monsieur, that the longer they take, the more likely the outcome is to be favourable to the accused, or the reverse?"

"I really couldn't answer that. Excuse me."

The minutes that follow are a torture. A neighbouring church chimes the half-hour, and then four o'clock. We patrol the patch of lawn. Zola says, "They are obviously weighing the evidence thoroughly, and if they do that then surely they must come down on our side. It is a good sign."

"No," says Georges Clemenceau, "men are being induced to change their minds and that cannot be good for Dreyfus."

I go back into the drawing room and stand at the window. Outside in the street a crowd has gathered. Someone shouts up to ask if there is any news. I shake my head. At a quarter to five, the footman signals to Ménard, who goes over to the telephone.

Ménard listens and then announces, "The judges are returning to the courtroom."

So their deliberations lasted for an hour and a half. Is that long or short? Good or bad? I am not sure what to make of it.

Five minutes pass. Ten minutes. Someone makes a joke to alleviate the tension, and people laugh. Suddenly Ménard holds up his hand for silence. Something is happening at the other end of the line. He frowns. Slowly, crushingly, his arm descends. "Guilty," he says quietly, "by five votes to two. Sentence reduced to ten years' imprisonment."

Just over a week later, at the end of the afternoon, Mathieu Dreyfus comes to see me. I am surprised to find him on my doorstep. He has never been to my apartment before. For the first time he looks grey and crumpled; even the flower in his buttonhole is faded. He perches on the edge of my small sofa, nervously turning his bowler hat around and around between his hands. He nods to my escritoire, which is strewn with papers, the desk lamp lit. "I see I am disturbing you at your work. Forgive me."

"It's nothing—I thought I might try to write some sort of memoir while it's all still fresh in my mind. Not for publication, though—at least not in my lifetime. Can I get you a drink?"

"No. Thank you. I won't stay long. I'm catching the evening train to Rennes."

"Ah. How is he?"

"Frankly, Picquart, I fear he's preparing himself for death."

"Oh, come, come, Dreyfus!" I say, sitting down opposite him. "If your brother could survive four years on Devil's Island, he can with-stand a few more months in prison! And I'm sure it won't be much longer than that. The government will have to let him go in time for the Universal Exhibition, otherwise there'll be a boycott. They can't possibly allow him to die in gaol."

"He's asked to see the children for the first time since his arrest. Can you imagine the effect that will have on them—to see their father in such a state? He wouldn't subject them to that ordeal unless it was to say goodbye."

"Are you sure his health is so poor? Has he been examined by a doctor?"

"The government has sent a specialist to Rennes. He says Alfred is suffering from malnutrition and malarial fever, and possible tuber-culosis of the spinal marrow. His opinion is that he won't last long in captivity." He looks at me miserably. "For that reason—I've come to tell you—I'm sorry to say it—we've decided to accept the offer of a pardon."

A pause. I wish I could keep the coldness out of my voice. "I see. There is an offer on the table, then?"

"The Prime Minister is worried about the country becoming per-manently divided."

"I'm sure he is."

"I know this is a blow to you, Picquart. I can see that it places you in an awkward position . . ."

"Yes, well how could it not?" I burst out. "To accept a pardon is an admission of guilt!"

"Technically, yes. But Jaurès has drafted a statement for Alfred to issue the moment he emerges from prison." He pulls a creased sheet of paper from his inside pocket and hands it over.

The government of the Republic grants me my freedom. It means nothing to me without my honour. Beginning today, I shall persist in working towards an overturning of the frightful judicial error whose victim I continue to be . . .

There is more, but I have read enough. I give it back. "Well, these are very noble words," I say bitterly. "Naturally they would be—one can always rely on Jaurès for noble words. But the reality is the army has won. And the very least they'll insist on in return is an amnesty for those who organised the conspiracy against your brother." *And against me,* I want to add. "It will make it impossible for me to pursue my legal claim against the General Staff."

"In the short term, perhaps. But in the long run, with a different political climate, I have no doubt we can win a full exoneration in the courts."

"I wish I shared your faith in our legal system."

Mathieu stuffs the statement back in his pocket and stands. There is defiance in the way he plants his legs apart. "I'm sorry you feel as you do, Picquart. I understand that for the sake of your cause you'd prefer to have my brother die a martyr, if that is what it takes. But his family wants him back alive. He isn't reconciled to this decision himself, to be honest with you. I think it would make a difference if I could tell him he had your agreement."

"My agreement? Why should that matter to him?"

"Nevertheless, I believe it does. What message may I give him from you?"

He stands there, implacable.

"What do the others say?"

"Zola, Clemenceau and Labori are opposed. Reinach, Lazare, Basch and the rest say yes, with varying degrees of enthusiasm."

"Tell him I am opposed as well."

Mathieu nods curtly, as if he expected nothing else, and turns to leave.

"But tell him that I understand."

Dreyfus is released on Wednesday, 20 September 1899, although the news is not made public for another day, to enable him to travel without being accosted by members of the public. I learn about his freedom from the newspapers like everyone else. Wearing a dark blue suit and a soft black hat for disguise, he is driven away by automobile from the prison in Rennes at dusk by officers of the Sûreté and taken to join Mathieu at the railway station in Nantes, where the brothers catch the southbound sleeper. At a family house in Provence he is reunited with his wife and children. Afterwards he moves to Switzerland. He doesn't return to Paris. He fears assassination.

As for me, I scratch a living and, with Labori's help, pursue various newspapers for libel. In December I refuse to accept the government's offer of a general amnesty for all those involved in the affair, even though I am told I will be restored to the army and given a command. Why should I put on the same uniform as Mercier, du Paty, Gonse, Lauth and that gang of criminals?

In January, Mercier is elected as senator for the lower Loire on a nationalist platform.

From Dreyfus I hear nothing. And then, more than a year after his release, one bleak day in the winter of 1900, I go downstairs to collect my mail and find a letter, postmarked Paris. The address is in handwriting familiar to me only from secret files and courtroom evidence.

> My Colonel,
> I have the honour to request that you set a day and a time when you will allow me to express to you in person my gratitude.
>
> > Respectfully,
> > A. Dreyfus

It comes from an address in the rue de Châteaudun.

I carry it back upstairs. Pauline has stayed overnight, as she does quite often now the girls are getting older. Madame Romazzotti is how she prefers to style herself these days, having reverted to her maiden name: people assume she is a widow. I tease her that it makes her sound like a spiritualist on the boulevard Saint-Germain.

She calls from the bedroom, "Anything interesting?"

I read the note again.

"No," I call back, "nothing."

Later that morning I take one of my visiting cards and write on the back: Sir, I will let you know the day when I can see you. G. Picquart.

And then I do nothing about it. He is not the kind of man who finds it easy to say thank you; very well; I am not the sort who finds it easy to be thanked; therefore let us spare ourselves the bathos of the encounter. Later, I am accused in the newspapers of flatly refusing to meet Dreyfus. One anonymous friend of the family—it turns out to be the Zionist pamphleteer Bernard Lazare—tells *L'Echo de Paris*, a right-wing newspaper:

> We do not understand Picquart, or his attitude . . . you probably do not know, nor do many others, that Picquart is energetically anti-Semitic.

How am I to answer this? Perhaps by observing that if the true measure of a man's character, as Aristotle says, is his actions, then mine have hardly been those of an energetic anti-Semite. Still, there is nothing like an accusation of anti-Semitism to get all one's old prejudices flowing, and I write bitterly to a friend: "I knew that one day I would be attacked by the Jews, and notably by the Dreyfuses . . ."

Thus our beautiful cause descends into tantrums, disappointment, reproaches and acrimony.

On the parade ground of the École Militaire, the companies of cadets wheel and stamp on the packed brown dirt. I stand behind the railings of the place de Fontenoy, as I often do, and watch as they are put through their paces. So much of my life is contained here in this spot. This is where I was taught as a young officer, and where I did my teaching. This is where I witnessed Dreyfus's degradation. Over there in the riding school is where I fought my duel with Henry.

"Companies—*attention!*"

"Companies—*present arms!*"

The young men march past, eyes right, in perfect step, and the worst of it is they do not even see me. Or if they do, they see me without registering me—just another middle-aged civilian in a black suit and bowler hat watching wistfully from the other side.

And yet, in the end, we win—not in a flash of glory, as we had always hoped; not at the climax of some great trial, with the condemned man, vindicated at last, carried shoulder-high to freedom.

We win quietly, behind closed doors, when tempers have cooled, in committee rooms and archives, as all the facts are sieved and sieved again, by careful jurists.

First, Jaurès, the leader of the socialists, makes a forensic speech in the Chamber of Deputies, lasting a day and a half, setting out the entire affair with such clarity that the new Minister of War, General André, agrees to look again at all the evidence—that is in 1903. Then the result of the André inquiry prompts the Criminal Chamber to take up the case itself, and conclude that it should be reviewed by the Supreme Court of Appeal—that occupies 1904. Then a year is lost in political turmoil over the separation of Church and State—farewell 1905. But finally, the Supreme Court of Appeal quashes the Rennes verdict and exonerates Dreyfus entirely—that happens on 12 July 1906.

On the thirteenth, a motion is laid before the Chamber of Deputies to restore Dreyfus to the army with the rank of major, and to award him the highest available distinction, the cross of the Legion of Honour; that passes by a margin of 432 to 32, and when Mercier tries to speak against it in the Senate, he is howled down. On the same day, a second motion is debated, restoring me to the army with the rank I might have hoped to achieve if I had not been dishonourably discharged in 1898; this resolution passes by an even larger margin, of 449 to 26. To my astonishment I find myself walking back onto the parade ground of the École Militaire for Dreyfus's medal ceremony in the uniform of a brigadier general.

On 25 October, my friend Georges Clemenceau becomes prime minister; I am in Vienna at the time. That evening, dressed in white tie and tails, with Pauline on my arm, I take my seat at the Vienna State Opera to watch Gustav Mahler conduct *Tristan und Isolde*. I have been looking forward to this performance for weeks. But just before the house lights dim, I notice an official from the French Embassy hovering in the aisle, and then a telegram begins to be passed along the row, from gloved to jewelled hand. Eventually it reaches Pauline, who gives it to me.

Please be informed that I have today named you Minister of War. Return to Paris immediately. Clemenceau

Epilogue

THURSDAY, 29 NOVEMBER 1906

25

M ajor Dreyfus to see the Minister of War . . ."
I hear him announce himself to my orderly at the foot of
the marble staircase in that familiar voice with its trace of German.
I listen to the click of his boots as he mounts the steps, and then
slowly he emerges into view—the cap, the epaulettes, the gold buttons, the braid, the sword, the stripe on his trousers: all exactly as it
was before the degradation, but with the addition of the red ribbon
of the Legion of Honour on his artilleryman's black tunic.

He comes to a halt on the landing and salutes. "General Picquart."

"Major Dreyfus." I smile and extend my hand. "I have been waiting for you. Please come through."

The ministerial office is unchanged since the days of Mercier and
Billot, still panelled in duck-egg blue, although Pauline, who acts
as chatelaine, likes to arrange fresh flowers each day on the table
between the large windows overlooking the garden. The trees this
afternoon are bare; the lights of the ministry burn bright in the late
November gloom.

"Sit down, Major," I say. "Make yourself comfortable. Have you
been in here before?"

"No, Minister." He lowers himself onto the gilt chair and sits
very formally, stiff-backed.

I take the seat opposite him. He has thickened out, looks good,
almost sleek in his expensively cut uniform. The pale blue eyes
behind the familiar pince-nez are wary. "So then," I say, putting my
fingertips together, and contemplating him long and hard, "what is
it you want to discuss?"

"It concerns my rank," he says. "The promotion I have received, from captain to major, takes no account of the years I spent wrongly imprisoned on Devil's Island. Whereas your promotion—if you'll forgive me for pointing it out—from colonel to brigadier general, treats your eight years out of the army as though they were spent in active service. I believe this is unfair—prejudiced, in fact."

"I see." I feel my smile hardening. "And what do you want me to do about it?"

"Rectify it. Promote me to the rank I should have achieved."

"Which would be what, in your opinion?"

"Lieutenant colonel."

I pause. "But that would require special legislation, Major. The government would have to go back to the Chamber of Deputies and introduce a new motion."

"It should be done. It is the right thing."

"No. It is impossible."

"Might I ask why?"

"Because," I say in exasperation, "it is politically impossible. The motion passed in July, when feelings were overwhelmingly in your favour because it was the day after your exoneration. This is now November—the mood is already quite different. Also, I have a difficult enough task as it is—as I'm sure you will appreciate—coming back into this building as Minister of War and trying to work with so many officers who were for so long our bitter enemies. I must swallow my anger every day and put past battles behind me. How can I now turn round to them and tear open the whole controversy yet again?"

"Because it is the right thing to do."

"I'm sorry, Dreyfus. It simply cannot be."

We sit in silence. Suddenly there is more than just a strip of carpet between us: there is a chasm, and I would number those few seconds as among the most excruciating of my life. Eventually I can bear it no longer and get to my feet. "If that is all . . . ?"

At once, Dreyfus also stands. "Yes, that is all."

I show him towards the door. It seems an appalling note on which to end.

"It is a matter of some regret to me, Major," I say carefully, "that we have not met alone in private until now."

"No. Not since the morning of my arrest, when you took me to your office before conducting me to meet Colonel du Paty."

I feel my face colouring. "Yes, I apologise for my part in that lugubrious charade."

"Ah well. You made up for it, I think!" Dreyfus looks around the office and nods in appreciation. "It is a great thing to have done all that, and at the end of it to have been appointed to the Cabinet of the French Republic."

"And yet, you know, the strange truth is I would never have attained it without you."

"No, my General," says Dreyfus, "you attained it because you did your duty."

Acknowledgements

A novel such as this is heavily dependent on the work of others, and I would like to express my thanks to all whose books have opened up this subject for me. The first general history I read was *The Affair: The Case of Alfred Dreyfus* by Jean-Denis Bredin: still the preeminent account for the general reader. *The Man on Devil's Island: Alfred Dreyfus and the Affair That Divided France* was also immensely useful, and I thank its author, Dr. Ruth Harris of New College, Oxford, for the additional information and advice she gave me. I have also benefited from *Dreyfus: A Family Affair, 1789–1945* by Michael Burns, *Why the Dreyfus Affair Matters* by Louis Begley, *France and the Dreyfus Affair* by Douglas Johnson, *The Dreyfus Affair* by Piers Paul Read and the monumental *Histoire de l'affaire Dreyfus* by Joseph Reinach, which remains indispensable even though it was published in 1908. *Zola: A Life* by Frederick Brown and George Painter's two-volume life of Proust were also useful.

Among more specialist books, I owe an immense debt to *The Dreyfus Affair: A Chronological History* by George R. Whyte, which has rarely left my side for a year. Another extremely valuable source was *Georges Picquart: dreyfusard, proscrit, ministre: La justice par l'exactitude* by Christian Vigouroux, the first biography of Picquart to be published for more than a century, which contains family letters and information drawn from police files. I have been fortunate in being able to benefit from the very latest scholarship on the affair contained in *Le Dossier Secret de l'affaire Dreyfus* by Pierre Gervais, Pauline Peretz and Pierre Stutin. The associated website, www.affairedreyfus.com, which went online while I was writing, contains a wealth of information, including links to photographs and transcripts of all the documents in the secret file, recently released by the French Ministry of Defence.

For primary research I read the transcripts of the Zola libel trial, the Rennes court-martial, and the various inquiries and hearings of 1898, 1904, 1905 and 1906; all can now be found online. Most major French newspapers of the period are freely available at the website of the Bibliothèque nationale de France, www.gallica.bnf.fr. I also found invaluable the digital archive of the London *Times*, which I accessed through the London Library.

I have quoted extensively from Dreyfus's own writings, published variously in *Five Years of My Life*, *The Dreyfus Case* (written with his son, Pierre) and *Carnets, 1899–1907*. Other useful contemporary sources are *My Secret Diary of the Dreyfus Case* by Maurice Paléologue and *L'Affaire Dreyfus: L'Iniquité, la Réparation* by Louis Leblois. Finally, *The Tragedy of Dreyfus* by G. W. Steevens, an eyewitness account of the proceedings at Rennes, contrary to its title, is a comic delight—the affair as written by Jerome K. Jerome—and I have used his version of Bertillon's insane testimony almost verbatim.

The idea of retelling the story of the Dreyfus case first came up during lunch in Paris with Roman Polanski at the beginning of 2012: I shall always be grateful to him for his generosity and encouragement. I should also like to thank my English-language editors, Jocasta Hamilton of Hutchinson in London and Sonny Mehta of Knopf in New York, for their wise advice and suggestions; thanks too to my literary agent, Michael Carlisle. For many years, my German translator, Wolfgang Müller, has worked on my manuscripts whilst they were still being written, and as usual he has made many suggestions and corrected many mistakes. My French editor, Ivan Nabokov, has also been a great source of support.

Finally, there is one other name to mention. Over the course of twenty-five years of married life—a total achieved just as this book was completed—my wife, Gill Hornby, has been obliged to share our house with successive waves of Nazis, codebreakers, KGB men, hedge fund managers, ghostwriters and assorted ancient Romans;

this time it was officers of the French General Staff. I thank her for her love, tolerance and shrewd literary judgement over a quarter of a century.

All the errors that remain, factual and stylistic, along with the various sleights of hand in narrative and characterisation invariably required to turn fact into fiction, remain my sole responsibility.

A NOTE ABOUT THE AUTHOR

Robert Harris is the author of eight best-selling novels: *Father-land*, *Enigma*, *Archangel*, *Pompeii*, *Imperium*, *The Ghost Writer*, *Conspirata* and *The Fear Index*. Several of his books have been adapted to film, most recently *The Ghost Writer*, which was directed by Roman Polanski. Harris's work has been translated into thirty-seven languages. He lives in the village of Kintbury, England, with his wife, Gill Hornby.

A NOTE ON THE TYPE

The text of this book has been set in Goudy Old Style, one of the more than one hundred typefaces designed by Frederic William Goudy (1865–1947). Produced in 1914, its smooth, even color combined with its generous curves and ample cut marks it as one of Goudy's finest achievements.

Typeset by Scribe,
Philadelphia, Pennsylvania

Printed and bound by Berryville Graphics,
Berryville, Virginia

Designed by Betty Lew

Mon cher [...]

[...] vous envoie [...] que vous [...]

Dès que [...] êtes parti
j'ai étudié la question
après et j'ai vu que certaines
questions de domicile etc sont
toutes subordonnées à cette
principale dont voilà la
diction.

[...] et [...] seulement
toujours à [...]
Je suis au lit avec
mon [...], de sorte
que je ne puis aller
à l'Opéra dans la loge
ce soir. Je ne puis
d'écrire de nouvelles
de reste je n'en connais
pas. J'espère que tu
t'amuses que tu es
[...] et que tu
[...] de bonnes
nouvelles de Berlin.
Mille et mille
[...]